PROPHECY OF AXAIN

THIS IS JUST THE BEGINNING

STEVEN ATWOOD

ISBN 13: 9781949788037

Published by Dragons & Lasers Press

Carrollton, GA 30116

RAVENWARD

PROPHECY OF AXAIN, PREQUEL

CHAPTER 1

Thea the Loyal

THE MOMENTS LEADING UP TO A BATTLE WERE USUALLY WORSE than the battle itself. Thea's plate mail armor glistened in the early morning sun. Laying behind a short rock wall, she held up an eyeglass, studying Nightfall Meadows.

"Well?" Kade Ravenward asked. "What do you see, *ma'am* knight?" He crossed his arms.

Thea focused on some activity near the clearing's edge. "I see a farmhouse with a dock on the Fadyhl Waters. It seems to be just on the edge where a boat can safely cross over from Etrana."

The strong, blond-haired man scratched his chin. "We can't have that; they could trade with the Vulwin Elves without paying taxes," Kade said.

"Shut up, you greedy goblin," the youthful man with long brown hair said as he approached them from behind. "Focus, people; we only get one shot at this."

Thea unsuccessfully tried to hide the smirk making its way onto her face. "Sire, it seems like the reports were right. The Feral Orcs are raiding the farm for food."

Kade brushed his shoulder-length blond hair away from his eyes. "Galin, do we need her? She's stating the obvious here. Besides, we don't know what they're doing. If they are a raiding party under the Darkstriders, this is far more than merely hunting for food. They could be establishing a beachhead for a major attack."

Thea rolled her eyes. "With all due respect, my lord, that's not possible. Where's their siege equipment? Why aren't they building bigger docks to handle larger ships to bring more troops on shore? No, my lord, they aren't establishing a beachhead."

Galin grinned as Kade's face grew redder. "Kade, relax. She's right, and you know it. True, they may want to establish a beachhead, but they are a long way from doing that," Galin said. The king put his hand on Thea's shoulder. "Ready?"

Her stomach twisted. This was her first battle. After years of training, would Thea cower in the face of a real opponent? She'd heard about knights who were viewed as the most honorable, but fled at the first sight of battle. Would she be that way? Would she run away as they all expected her to? "I won't let you down, sire."

"I know you won't." Galin motioned Kade's pyromancer to come forward. "Beldroth, I need you to give us some cover, or at least a diversion while we cross the field. The orcs knew what they were doing when they burnt down everything within six hundred yards of their camp."

"The farmhouse, you mean?" Beldroth asked.

"Yeah, I think that's where their camp is. Feral Orcs will flee once their leader is dead."

The sensual woman with flowing, long brown hair

smiled. "With pleasure, my lord." Beldroth reached under her red cloak and pulled out a pouch of cedar chips. "I can only maintain the barrage for at most twenty seconds." She sat down behind the rock wall with the farmhouse in full view. Beldroth pulled out her spell book and began to prepare for the assault.

Thea the Loyal pierced the ground with her sword. Kneeling behind it, she placed both hands on its hilt and closed her eyes. A circle with a blindfolded man carrying an ax in one hand and an olive branch in the other entered her mind. Thea prayed to the God of Justice. "Lord Ramir, grant us the strength and courage to carry out your judgment upon these creatures. Amen."

"Ready, Thea?" Galin asked. After she nodded, he turned to Beldroth. "Light them up."

Beldroth held the cedar chips in her hands a few inches above her lap. "Den nrad nier." Her dark eyes turned red. White smoke rose from the cedar.

Thea stood up, waving at her men to follow her. One by one, each lightly armored man rose with sword and shield in hand.

"Den nrad nier; Den nrad nier."

Thea gasped as a cloud formed above the tiny farmhouse. Not a white or even a black cloud, but a cloud that glowed like the embers in a fire. At first it was small, and then it grew and grew. Thea waved her knights forward. She was slow at first, increasing her pace with every step. In front of her, the Feral Orcs were scattering in fear as the menacing shadow expanded over them.

"Ramir is definitely with us today," Thea said to herself.

She raised her hand, giving the signal to stop.

It started with a single ember falling like a meteorite from the cloud. It slammed into the ground right by the farmhouse door. The two orcs hiding behind the woodpile exploded into flames. Then came another, and another. As soon as one ember crashed to the ground, two more appeared.

The foul stench of burning flesh began to overtake her, forcing her to taste breakfast for a second time.

Beldroth's blood-curdling scream could be heard across the field. As soon as the first sound left her throat, the rain of fire stopped and the cloud vanished.

Thea blinked. "Sire, are we attacked from behind?"

"No, but we lost our cover," Galin said. He turned towards his men. "Follow—"

"Follow me!" Kade shouted as he charged into the disorientated Feral Orcs.

"That bastard," Galin muttered. "Come on, Thea, before he takes all the glory."

With nothing left to fear from the sky, the orcs regrouped, forming a line. Most carried two weapons in their powerful, over-sized arms. Some used axes while others used short swords, and the rest used some combination of the two. There was only one exception; the one who carried a great ax and was twice the size of the others.

Thea raised her sword, pointing at the orc line. "Charge!"

Two hundred yards.

The largest of the Feral Orcs yelled something. He charged towards Thea with his clan close behind him.

Yes, that one must be the leader. If we kill him, it's over, Thea thought.

One hundred twenty-five yards.

Thea was nearly at a sprint, roaring as she passed Kade.

"Damn you."

Seventy-five yards.

The orc leader raised the great ax above its head. After giving a thunderous roar, the orc line sprinted towards Thea.

Fifty yards.

As the greenish monsters came closer, her body wanted

to flee. She needed to prove herself. This was it. If she turned now, that bastard Kade would be right. Thea gritted her teeth. A fierce cry bellowed from her lungs. "Follow me!" With her shield raised and her sword overhead, Thea charged directly at the huge orc.

With its great ax raised in the air, the massive creature barreled towards Thea.

Great axes are powerful, but slow and clumsy. Pulling her shield in tightly into her body, she raced towards it.

Ten yards.

An orc cut in front of their leader. It leaped into the air and spun like a top, with two axes hacking anything in its path.

Judging where it would land, she stopped quickly.

The creature missed its marked, burying one of the axes into the ground.

Her eyes met the orc's as she slammed her shield into its face. With a full adrenalin rush, she dropped her sword like a curtain. Thea's broadsword severed the Feral Orc's head from its body, splattering its green blood across her face. More . . . she wanted more. Greedy, wicked eyes bored into the leader's inhuman soul.

The large creature took a step back, flailing the great ax in Thea's direction.

"Thea, he's mine!" Kade shouted as he hacked another orc, making his way to her.

She didn't hear him. More . . . she wanted to spill more orc blood. Who cared about orders or status? She'd tasted glory for the first time. It was orgasmic; no, it was better than that. Thea rammed her shield into the orc's chest, forcing it to take a step back.

Kade pushed Thea aside as he charged into the huge orc, knocking her down.

The great ax slammed into Kade's shield, throwing him

back into the melee. It grinned at Thea as it raised the mighty weapon into the air.

I am going to die! Rolling over on her back, she braced behind her shield.

The massive weapon split Thea's shield in half. As it reared up for another attack, she swung her sword at its legs.

The leader quickly sidestepped and kicked Thea in the face in one fluid motion.

"Thea!" Galin charged towards her, slicing orcs as he went.

The king! How could she be rescued by the king? Nothing would be worse that. Thea tossed away what was left of her shield. The broadsword her adopted father gave her now lay across her hands like a shield, protecting her body.

The leader raised the great ax again, sending it towards Thea's chest with all its might.

She was nearly blinded by the glint off the great ax. The broadsword's flat side was braced to take the full force of the weapon. Was this it? Was her first battle going to be her last? As the ax crashed into her sword, the blade snapped like a dried twig.

Thea dropped the broken blade. While holding onto the hilt, she did a half-roll to the left. With the orc leaning over her, a small area just below the ribs was exposed. Her iron grasp on the hilt with a partial blade could not be broken. She held onto it as if her life depended on it, because it did. With every ounce of strength, she thrust the partial blade's jagged end into the leader's torso.

Screaming in agony and surprise, the huge orc fell on top of Thea, pinning her to the ground.

Thea struggled to push the behemoth off her body.

"Thea, watch out!" Galin screamed as he charged toward her with his sword raised.

What is he talking about? I already killed the leader. She quickly looked around for her new foe and saw another orc charging at her with two axes. What could she do? Her sword was broken and she was pinned to the ground. Sweat poured down her face, stinging her eyes. "Can someone help get this thing off of me?" Her bloodshot eyes opened wide as the orc leaped towards her.

In mid-air, Galin slammed his shield into the orc's side. The cracking of its ribs was deafening. Before the creature hit the ground, Galin's sword pierced its heart. He knelt down next to Thea. "You all right?"

Thea smiled. "Just a little squished by this fat thing. Some help please, sire?"

As he pushed the hulking creature off her, Thea saw the king's army rush past them. "What's going on?"

Galin extended his hand to help her up. "After you killed the leader, the rest of them fled back to their boats. Thank you, Thea. You did the kingdom a great service today."

Thea blushed. "No, sire, I owe you my life. I swear to you that your family will be on the throne as long as I live, even after you're gone."

"You don't have to do that," Galin said.

Kade chuckled as he joined Galin. "Especially since he has no children. He has no heir to the throne."

Galin smiled. "Fair enough. What's our status?"

"We overran them. Every orc still here is dead. Some escaped on the boats, not a lot, but enough to warn their tribe to stay away from my kingdom."

"*My* kingdom, you mean."

"Of course, *sire*."

Thea rolled her eyes at the squabbling brothers. Whoever would have thought that twelve seconds would have made such trouble between fraternal twin brothers? She wiped her sword on the dead orc and returned it to its sheath. "I can manage the cleanup here, sire."

Galin nodded. "Very well." His gazed lingered over towards Kade. "I guess you missed another chance at the throne."

Kade stared at his brother walking away from the battlefield. "True, but it won't be long," he muttered.

Thea frowned.

CHAPTER 2

Spoils of War

As THE ARMY ENTERED THROUGH THE GATES OF STAERDALE Castle, Thea broke away from the formation. Being the only female knight, she was granted some minimal privileges, such as changing in her own quarters rather than in front of her fellow knights. Merchants holding up chickens and other bobbles rushed up to her as she trotted down the street. That ride never seemed to get old. It was still the same as when her father would bring her to meet with the king, Galin's father, Galin III of Ravenward. People seemed to beg more now than she remembered, but she was only a child then. What child paid attention to the poor? Certainly not her. Her horse stopped in front of a modest house with a thatched roof.

"Great job today, Dena," Thea said as she hopped off the horse. Dena's large, dark-brown eyes complemented her brown mane with white stripes along her back. Thea loved

Dena, her only true, loyal friend. "Be back in a minute." She tied Dena off to the hitching post outside the door.

Thea entered her quiet home. It was a simple two-room house, where the smaller room had an unkempt bed next to the window. The larger room had an oversized fireplace with a single rocking chair in the middle of the room. Along the far wall were shelves so crude that any artisan would have hung himself if he had made them. Thea was strong-willed and believed she could do anything. Over in the corner was an armor stand made by her father. She walked up to it, tossing the plate mail armor pieces onto the dirt floor.

Thea frowned. She spent so little time at home that it became unkempt and disheveled. In the castle or in front of her fellow knights, no one was more organized or neater than she. So much so, in fact, that they occasionally accused her of being the 'knight's nanny.' The first time she heard it, Thea broke the surprised knight's nose.

Things will be different now. No longer was she the only knight not to see battle. No longer was she going to be the object of every joke in the Great Hall. She'd proved herself.

She rubbed her lower back, which was sore from the long ride from Nightfall Meadows. The battle with the Feral Orcs was over, but the war against the Darkstriders continued. Even though they won the battle, the toughest fight today was not on the field, but in the king's court. Today was her first battle, but this would not be her first time in court, which can be far more dangerous than two armies of orcs. She paused at her door. Court would be different this time because now she was a participant rather than an observer. She already had a title, wasn't that enough? No, *real* knights are landowners, as well as great fighters. What was her leverage? She killed the Feral Orc leader, which was the turning point in the battle and the Galin knew it. After taking a deep breath, she headed for the castle.

. . .

Thea strode the halls of Staerdale Castle as if she owned them. As she approached the Great Hall's two large solid oak doors, she took a deep breath. No more wishing, wanting, or telling others what she *would* do; it was time to do it. The resolve on her face masked her anxiety as she passed through the doorway into the Great Hall.

A faint fragrance of rose petals invaded her senses. They may have been thrown about the marble flagstone floor only to mask the lack of plumbing in the castle, but they did far more than that for Thea. With each step, the aroma bolstered her confidence. The hall was twice as long as it was wide. Instinctively, Thea glanced at the catwalk nearly eight feet off the ground all along its the walls, just below the windows overlooking the castle gate. The red tapestries with gold fringe had a dark-blue triangle on the top half. Below the triangle, a colorful embroidery depicted the Ravenward family history. Everything from great battles to the most famous kings the royal family had ever produced. In front of the tapestries, in between large support pillars, was a single line of chairs and benches.

Thea's breath grew shorter as her stomach twisted into knots. There he was, the one who seemed to hate her the most, Duke Kade of Ravenward, standing right next to Beldroth. Thea loved Galin like a brother. The king's father took Thea in when her noble parents were murdered by a band of orcs. After their death, her family's lands were dispersed and divided among the neighboring lords, leaving her with nothing. She stepped up onto the dais along with several other knights, Duke Kade, and a few old men who continued to serve as advisers to the king. She gazed over at the two empty thrones along the wall at the far end of the dais. "When are they supposed to arrive, my lord?" she asked Kade.

"Soon; my brother is late already," Kade replied. He pulled out a small parchment from his flowing green robes.

"What's that?" Thea asked.

"My province's list of expenses for the war effort. My dear, war is very expensive, and I'm tired of paying my brother's bills."

"You mean the king's bills."

Kade pointed at the door to the left of the larger throne. "The king has to realize that time wasted can be more costly than war. In order to pay his bills, I have to nearly starve my people. Don't think he's an angel because he saved you today. Oh no, you'll be paying that debt the rest of your life at a far greater cost."

Thea wanted to hit Kade. How could someone, especially the king's own brother, hate him so much? How could anyone lie like that and get away with it? Her eyes narrowed. "You're just jealous of him."

Kade laughed. "Of what? His wife's ugly, and they don't have any children."

"Your twin brother is the king, and you're not. That's why you're—"

"Enough!" Galin bellowed as he and Queen Nina passed through the door behind the thrones. "Thea, you know better than to challenge my brother."

She lowered her eyes. "Sire, I apologize." Thea looked towards Kade. "My lord, please forgive me."

Kade threw his hand up in front of Thea's face while he turned towards Galin. "Galin, what were the spoils from the battle today?"

Galin helped the seventeen-year-old queen with fiery red hair to her throne. She sat down slowly, keeping one hand on her belly. "Kade, must you always talk about money?" Nina asked.

"It's all right, Nina," Galin said as he assumed his position on the throne. "The Feral Orcs brought gold and—what did you call the other items, Beldroth?"

Beldroth's long blond hair was let down, contrasting with her black robes. "Material spell components. The ones found were not for neutral or light magic; they could only be used for dark magic."

"Darkstriders then?" Kade asked.

A young girl carrying a tray came out the same door the king and queen had used earlier. "Tea, sire?"

"Please," Galin said as he took a cup from her. "Thank you, Sally."

"Do we have to be interrupted now? This is important, Galin," Kade said.

After Sally had given Nina her cup, she assumed the place of the Queen's handmaiden behind the throne.

Thea elbowed Kade. "My lord, the king was speaking."

"It's all right, Thea. My finance minister tells me the gold and magic components are worth nearly 250,000 crowns," Galin said.

Kade passed Galin the small parchment he'd kept under his robes. "That's great news, Galin. Ithsein province has been the greatest contributor to the kingdom of Axain. We've supplied weapons, food, and men to confront our enemies..."

Thea rolled her eyes. Was it just her, or could Kade flip his attitude like a copper coin? The king wouldn't fall for this, would he? Kade, along with his pyromancer, Beldroth, was an expert on manipulating the royal court. Sometimes, she wished he would just shut up.

"...I provided you a list of the people's needs to compensate them for their sacrifice. Galin, my people are going without basic needs to protect the kingdom." Kade glanced over at Beldroth with pleading eyes.

"Sire," Beldroth began, "its worse than my lord is saying. If we don't cut our taxes, the people could revolt. That would endanger the *entire* kingdom."

"Let me see," Galin said as his eyes lowered onto the parchment. "You're asking for lands from Axain, gold for armor, weapons, castle construction, the building of a wall, and livestock imported from the Vulwin Elves." Galin straightened up. "You want tax exemption for the use of Port Eldham? Is there nothing here for the people? Seriously, Kade, this list seems more like a royal slush fund rather than taking care of the people's needs."

"Galin, I—"

Galin raised his hand, silencing Kade. "Thea, what do you think?" he asked as he handed her the parchment.

Thea's fingers trembled as she took the paper from the king. This was her chance, but she didn't want to make things worse with the king's brother, either. Her stomach danced and twisted. Should she say what she really thought or what the king wanted to hear? What did the king want to hear? Thea's eyes darted from Galin to Kade and back again. Arguing is one thing; accusing Duke Kade of trying to swindle the king out of much-needed resources was quite another. No, she was a knight sworn to be honorable. "Sire, I think *all* the spoils should be reinvested into the kingdom's security."

"What about my people? Will you be there if they rebel?" Kade demanded.

Thea turned towards Kade. "Are your taxes that high because of the king's demands or yours?"

Kade's mouth opened, but nothing came out. "He—I—the king's, of course."

Beldroth's eyes glistened and her face darkened. "Careful, young one," she whispered.

Galin tried to hide his snicker by sipping his tea. "I think the young knight has it right. What do you think, my dear?"

Nina handed her cup to Sally. "I know she does." She smiled at Thea. "You did all the women in the kingdom proud today."

Galin shook his head. "No, she was not a female knight. Today, she *is* a knight." He stood up, addressing everyone in the room. "For those of you who don't know, Thea was instrumental in winning the battle today. She slew the Feral Orc leader, which was the turning point of the day." His eyes veered towards Kade. "One of us tried to do everything possible to take all the glory for himself, regardless of the outcome or who it would hurt..."

Where's he going with this? Thea thought.

"...True nobility derives from the burning desire to help and serve others, not lining one's purse."

Kade's face reddened. "Galin, what are you—"

Galin smiled. "Thea, you did a great service to our kingdom today. I want to repay my debt by giving you your family's land back and 150,000 crowns to make it productive again."

"What?" Kade demanded. "Those are *my* lands!"

"They're *Thea's* family's lands, not yours."

"I won't do it."

Beldroth gave a sharp elbow to Kade's ribs. "He didn't mean that, sire."

Galin's calm face twisted in anger. "To pay for the 150,000 crowns, I will levy a new tax on all goods entering Axain destined to be traded with the Vulwin Elves, in addition to the port tax."

"That will break me, Galin. You can't do that! I'll have to raise taxes again!" Kade said.

"You're not king yet, Kade, which means I can."

"You haven't had a son after how many years of trying? I'm the heir to the throne, Galin. You know that. My loyalty is to our father, and when I promised to keep our family on the throne, I meant it. Did you?"

Thea moved in front of Kade, blocking him from the king.

"We're done here." Galin helped Nina up from her throne. With Nina and Sally in tow, Galin headed for the door behind the thrones.

"Sire, thank you so much," Thea said.

"You deserve it."

Thea watched the door close behind them.

CHAPTER 3

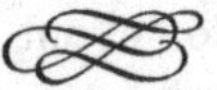

Big News

THEA BARELY NOTICED THE SLIGHT BREEZE ON HER FACE AS SHE rode Dena over the cobblestone road. Marlie's Bakery filled the air with the fragrance of freshly baked sweetbread, causing her stomach to rumble. One day, her manor would be like this . . . someday. Now that Galin had given her land and a lot of money to get started, she was truly on equal grounds with the other knights. What kind of bakers or merchants should she have in the square just outside of her manor? Maybe then she'd find someone to love. Children . . . yes, she wanted children. But, who had the time? She certainly didn't. Always on Galin's short leash, Thea had to be ready to leave for months at a time. Despite all that, she wanted a child.

Clop. Clop. Clop.

Thea strained her eyes as she turned the corner, putting the setting sun directly in front of her. She squinted to keep the sun's attack at bay. There it was, the clanging of a black-smith hammer on raw steel over an anvil. Could he repair her sword? If so, he was a better blacksmith than Thea thought. She knew Brock Feran from his failed attempt to become a knight. Unlike Thea, Brock was not born with noble blood. No, he was a commoner through and through. The only thing not common about Brock was his skill with a bastard sword.

Clop. Clop. Clop.

Smoke from his forge pierced her nostrils. With the sun recoiling behind the mountain, Brock's Blacksmith Shop came into focus. Like its owner, it was simple; a wooden building with a thatched roof. The completely enclosed portion was Brock's home. A long wooden roof extended from the right side of the house parallel to the main street. Street side, there were three support columns made from oak. Attached to the farthest column from the house was a weapons rack filled with daggers and short swords. An athletic man with a well-developed upper body stood over the anvil in the center of the room. The forge, facing towards the anvil, shared the chimney with the house in the center of the wall.

Bang. Bang. Bang.

As Thea got closer, her nose began to itch from the smoke. She dismounted Dena, tying her off to the hitching post next to the small weapons display. Carrying what was left of her sword, she stepped inside the open-air shop. She couldn't take her eyes off him. Brock's arms had grown enormously in just a few years. Thea licked her lips.

Brock tossed the ball peen hammer down on a small table and placed the steel he had been working on back into the forge. He looked up at the rack hung between two columns and grabbed a brown towel that was hanging on a long nail. Brock paused, as if in thought, and kept his back to her.

Was he ignoring her? *Is he still mad after all these years?* "Brock, I need some help."

"What?" Brock asked with his back still turned toward Thea. "What do you want now?"

Yup, he was still bitter. *How long can one man hold a grudge?* "My sword broke when we fought the orcs at Nightfall Meadows."

Reluctantly, Brock faced Thea. "Let me see." He took the broken sword from her. "There's only about eight inches of the blade left. I can make a dagger out of it if you want. Fix it? No way. I could make you a new blade and attach your hilt to it."

Thea smiled. "Good, I need it in a couple days."

"Days? I'm not one of your subordinate knights anymore. I don't take orders from you. I'll get to it when I can. Remember, you're not the only knight at Staerdale Castle." He tossed the busted sword onto the small table, hitting the hammer. "Check back with me in a few weeks."

Her face reddened. *How could he talk to her like that?* She may be a woman, but she was also a knight and of noble blood, unlike *him*. Brock was the best—and the only—blacksmith at the market. "Brock, are you mad at me? I haven't been down here for months."

Brock sighed. "I'm sorry, Thea. It's just that the anniversary is coming up again. All I can think about is everything I've lost because of *him*."

Thea leaned against a column. "Do you actually keep track of the day you were removed from the knighthood? Seriously, Brock—"

He picked up Thea's sword and brought it over to the workbench on the other side of the anvil. "Yes, I do. Seeing you here today only makes it worse. I was a good knight and beat nearly all of them. Until—"

"Until you fought Kade," she finished.

"I whooped him, and he knew it. It was because of him that I'm no longer a knight; no one else. Now look at me, I'm just a glorified whetstone." Brock popped the pummel from her sword. "The king gave me permission to become a knight after the work my father did for him. If Kade didn't rouse the other knights against me because I was the son of a blacksmith, I wouldn't be here right now."

Thea rolled her eyes. "Here we go again. Brock, you aren't a noble and your family line decides that, not the king."

Brock slammed down the small hammer. "How can you side with him? That *same* king made an exception for a woman to be a knight. Why not a commoner?"

"You're better off here," she said under her breath.

"What did you say?"

"You—you've got no idea what the life of a knight is like. It's nothing like we thought it would be, not at all. We fought for honor, right?"

Brock nodded. "Yeah."

"There's none after you become a knight. Until today, I wasn't treated like a knight at all. I had no real title, money, or land. Every time I entered a conversation, I had to be better than everyone else just to keep their respect." She felt her blood race towards her face.

"Was that because of them or you?"

"I—please, just fix my sword." Thea abruptly turned and started towards Dena.

"Thea, wait a second." Brock laid his tools down and sighed. "You're right; *both* of us shouldn't have been knights. When the king gave me the choice, I chose to leave."

Thea stopped short. "You did what?"

"The king said it was up to me, but it would be best for the kingdom if I left. He gave me this shop and enough crowns to get started. My father was here before he died of the fever that winter. I learned about being a blacksmith all my life, except for the brief time I was a knight. So yes, I chose the honorable thing by putting the people ahead of myself. That's something Kade would never do."

Did he leave by his choice? She didn't know that, nor did anyone else. When Kade told the trainees that Brock was thrown out, he gave the impression that he was dragged out, fighting the whole time. "I'm sorry, Brock."

"It's not been all bad. The truth is, I wouldn't have met Sally if I was still a knight." Brock smiled as he resumed removing the hilt from Thea's sword.

"Sally who?"

"Sally Healy, she's the queen's handmaiden. I love her."

"Does she know it?" Thea asked.

Brock started to pry the guard off the sword's tang. "I haven't told her, if that's what you mean. I'm loyal to the king's family, and his son who sits on the throne now. They were both good men."

Thea nodded. "After the king saved my life, I pledged myself to his family, not just him. When can I have my sword?"

He smiled at her. "Give me a week; some of the other knights can wait a little longer."

"Thanks, Brock." Thea grinned as she climbed on top of Dena. "I'm heading home. Maybe we can go to the tavern sometime—with Sally, of course."

"Why not tonight?"

"The queen has some big announcement tomorrow. I have to dress up for it and act like a lady."

Brock grinned. "Good luck with that."

~

After the next sunrise, Thea fell out of bed. The small room was barely big enough for the bed, but she still managed to fall onto the floor. The single item hanging on the wall was a small cracked mirror. She was still wearing the torn red tunic from last night. Reaching for a hairbrush, Thea raked through her hair, tearing out every knot. Why did it matter, anyway? She was a knight, not a lady. Bags drooped from her eyes, a strong reminder that she *shouldn't* have stopped at the tavern last night on her way home. Sure, Thea had every reason to celebrate, but was it a celebration or an escape?

She tossed her rancid tunic onto the floor. Thea couldn't afford to have her own private bath, until yesterday. Add that to the list of things she'd buy for her manor house. Land, title, and crowns all came with a heavy price; her constant involvement in the king's court. She would prefer to ride out and see her new land and begin to spend her newly found wealth, but the king's court demanded her attention. Queen Nina was making an announcement today—unusual, but not unheard of.

Thea walked into the main room, looking for the wash-bowl. She smiled as her eyes zeroed in on the small piece of cracked pottery sitting on the counter underneath the southern window. Cupping the warm water in her hands, she washed her hangover away. Dabbing her face with the small brown towel next to the bowl, she decided. Today was the day. Once her court obligations were fulfilled, she *would* see her new lands and the peasants who would serve her. After she was completely dried off, Thea put on fresh tunic. After throwing on her cape, she mounted Dena and headed towards the castle.

. . .

Duties at the king's court were the worst part of being a knight. No glory, no honor, just a bunch of sniveling old men fighting over table scraps.

As the double doors opened, the Great Hall was displayed in all its grandeur. Lords, ladies, knights, and members of the Ravenward clan bustled around the dais. Who did she want to mingle with first? On the queen's side of the hall stood Kade and Beldroth; she'd rather have a tooth pulled than talk to them. Lyonus, the treasury adviser, was obviously engaged with Coala, the high priestess; no point even trying that one. Her eyes were drawn back to her old spot in the corner, where the other *real* knights gathered. It was near Kade, but she could stand his vileness for a few hours. Besides, he never even seemed to notice her anyway. Thea spied the only knight younger than herself and smiled.

"Sir Robert," Thea said as she made her way towards him. Kade looked over and turned back to Beldroth in disgust when he saw Thea. Ignoring Kade, she reached out and took Robert's hand.

The handsome young man smiled. "Good to see you, too. Why'd you leave the tavern so early last night?"

Thea shook her head. "My body this morning told me I stayed out way too late. If I'd stayed longer, I'd never have gotten out of bed."

He grinned. "You're right." Robert looked toward the throne. "What's keeping them? The king's never this late."

"No idea." Thea's father told her many times that the best way to defeat your enemies in the king's court was to listen more than to speak. Maybe the queen was rehearsing her speech or planning how to deal with the sharks that would certainly try to take advantage of whatever she announced today. No one fit that category more than Kade. Her eyes shifted towards him, standing next to his servant, Beldroth.

Robert stared at Thea. "It's been nice talking to you when you were paying attention. I've got to go."

"I'll see you soon," Thea said.

Kade leaned into Beldroth and lowered his voice. "What could be so important that they had to call us back to the castle?"

Thea strained her ears to eavesdrop on their conversation.

Beldroth's lips curled. "Maybe to give you the throne, my lord." Her lifeless, nearly black eyes twinkled. "Does it matter?"

"I guess not. I'm just tired of waiting for my turn."

She took his hand and caressed it. "Patience; you need to learn patience."

"That's easy for you to say," he retorted.

"You only have to wait because you *choose* to," Beldroth said.

Thea swallowed hard. What did she mean by that? Obviously, Kade wanted to be king. The only way he could ever be king was if—if Galin died. No, even Kade wouldn't murder his family. What kind of monster would even think of it? Women have enormous persuasion over men. Thea had the necessary looks and knew how to use that ability, but chose not to. Was Beldroth as honorable? She was leading Kade on, but why?

Kade lowered his eyes. "I won't kill my own brother," he whispered.

"If you want to be king, you will," Beldroth replied. "And I will be your queen."

"Enough of that talk," Kade snapped.

Thea grimaced. Wasn't that treason? *Who am I to accuse the king's brother? A mere lowly knight who openly dislikes him.*

Silence fell over the small crowd as the ornate door

behind the thrones opened. Galin led Nina out into the Great Hall. All heads followed the queen as Galin sat her down.

Galin's failed attempt to hide a smile was obvious to everyone. He sat down on the throne, lowering his head to regain his composure. "Lords, ladies, and knights, thank you for coming so quickly. Your queen has some news that affects the whole kingdom."

Thea's eyes darted towards Kade. His face twisted as if he'd discovered her grand announcement.

Grinning, Queen Nina stood up. "The court knows that the king and I have no children, despite trying since I was sixteen years old..."

"I was right," Kade muttered to himself.

"Quiet," Beldroth said.

"...I began to believe that I was barren..."

Kade rolled his eyes.

Thea focused her attention on Kade, rather than on Nina. How desperate was he to get the throne? How far would he go?

"...The goddess Odella blessed me last night when I found out that I was carrying Galin's child." Nina's grin broke free. "I'm pregnant. We're having a baby."

Cheers and clapping drowned out what Beldroth whispered to Kade. But Kade's face gave away his *true* feeling about the news.

Galin stood beside his loving wife. "As you can imagine, we have a lot of things to do."

"Sire," Coala began, "what if it's a girl? Who will be your heir then?"

Kade's ears perked up.

"She would, of course. If a woman can be a valiant knight, why can't a queen rule?" Galin asked. "We're only in our twenties. I think we'll be having more children." Smiling,

Galin and Nina left the Great Hall, disappearing behind the thrones.

"I—I can't believe it," Kade said. "I'm forever cursed to be a servant for my brother's family."

Thea attempted to filter out the other conversations in the room to listen closer.

Beldroth licked her lips. "All is not lost, my lord." She placed his hand around her lower back. "Maybe I can take your mind off things."

Vomit crawled up Thea's throat, only to be pushed right back down. She was obviously more than a servant.

Kade's eyes lit up. "What do you mean? Are you finally going to say yes?"

"We'll talk about solving your problem and satisfying me away from here," Beldroth said.

Thea watched Beldroth lead Kade out of the Great Hall like a pony. His problem? What problem? It couldn't be—yes, that's it. It had to be. They were going to kill the king's family. *Should I tell him now? No, I can't. I need evidence before I accuse the king's brother of anything.* What kind of evidence can you get before a crime is committed? The *plan*. She needed to hear the plan. Thea hurried after Kade and Beldroth.

CHAPTER 4

Secrets

THEA RODE DENA DOWN THE COBBLESTONE STREET. Merchants, beggars, and the smell of freshly baked bread surrounded her with each step, but she was focused. Her self-appointed mission was clear; she had to protect the king. Thea's eyes never left her target, Kade, only a hundred yards in front of her.

Beldroth, riding next to him, kept moving her head as if they were talking. Kade raised one hand above his horse as if responding to a question or something.

Was it happening now? Thea asked herself. For a moment, she inhaled the pleasant aroma emanating from the nearby bakery. Her stomach growled, reminding her that she hadn't eaten all day.

Kade and Beldroth stopped in front of the Drow Inn and Tavern. He tied both horses to the hitching post just outside the door.

Thea smiled as she recognized the disappointment on Kade's face as they went inside. "I guess they're only talking tonight," she said to herself.

Thea tied Dena off on a different hitching post, away from Kade's and Beldroth's horses. Surely, Kade would recognize Dena. She opened the worn saddlebag and pulled out an old, dark-green hooded cloak. She hadn't worn that cloak for at least a year. The cloak was dirty, torn, and it stunk. Kade would simply turn away in disgust and disregard her just as fast. Breathing through her mouth, she threw the cloak over her shoulders and pulled the hood down.

"Here we go," Thea muttered. She opened the door and stepped inside.

Unlike Thea's usual watering hole, the Rusted Feathers, the Drow Inn and Tavern was quiet, with only a few patrons sampling the brew. True, it was in a shady part of town, but it was still within the castle walls. It couldn't be that bad, could it? Candles mounted on the walls beat back the darkness of the night. Twelve chairs surrounded a long oak bar, but only three were occupied. Small tables with four chairs each were sprinkled throughout the rest of the tavern. Her eyes scanned the room, looking for Kade. Her stomach twisted when she saw them.

Am I paranoid? Thea thought. *I could get into real trouble for spying on the king's brother. Do I think he wants the throne? Yes, no question. But is he willing to kill his own family for it?*

"Can I help you?" asked a young woman wearing an apron and holding her nose.

"I'm hungry, what do you have to eat?" Thea asked in a gruff voice.

The woman frowned. "I'm sorry, but we don't serve beggars here. You have to leave."

Thea reached into her pocket and pulled out a crown. "I can pay for it."

"We have a chicken dinner and pale ale."

"That'll be fine."

"Please find a seat and I will bring you your ale," the young woman said as she scurried away.

She thinks I either stole it or killed someone for it, Thea thought. Kade and Beldroth were sitting at a table along the wall, near the corner. Thea went to the corner table, close to the couple. She was close enough to hear them and dirty enough to be ignored. Why would the king's brother be threatened by a commoner anyway? To most people, it didn't matter who was on the throne.

Kade sipped his ale. "Why do you always tease me like that?"

Beldroth grinned. "Because it pleases me, and you have something to look forward to."

"Sure," Kade replied. "If you weren't a critical part of my army, you'd already have serviced me, or you'd be dead."

Beldroth reached across the table, caressing Kade's trembling hand. "What are you going to do?"

"Griping about not being on the throne is one thing, but usurping the throne is something else. I can't do that to my brother."

"You owe it to the people. You're so honorable, caring, and kind to all your people; not just the nobles, unlike your brother," Beldroth said.

Kade smiled. "You always know how to cheer me up." He took another sip. "He is firstborn, which makes him king. There's nothing I can do about it."

"By twelve seconds," Beldroth reminded him. "You're twins, remember that. You're both firstborn children to your father, he just came out first."

"What am I supposed to do?" Kade asked.

"You need to..."

Thea jolted back as a large mug of ale was placed in front

of her. "Your dinner will be out in a minute," the young woman said.

"Thank you," Thea replied.

"...I'll never do that," Kade said.

What did I miss? Thea thought. Was that the proof she needed? Lost by some wine wench.

"Kade, you have to. Please, for the sake of your people, you need to take the throne now," Beldroth said. "If you don't, you'll be serving his snot of a child until you die."

Kade shook his head. "That would require me to kill my brother's family. I won't do it."

Thea's eyes zeroed in on Beldroth's left hand. A ring with a strange marking on the face began to glow as Beldroth pressed her hands against Kade's wrist.

"Yes you will . . . you have to," Beldroth said soothingly.

"I—I—" Kade shook his head. "No, I won't. There has to be another way to get what my people need."

Beldroth frowned. "I see. What if your way doesn't work? Should your people suffer because of your . . . fearfulness?"

Thea blinked. How can that pyromancer talk to the king's brother like that? Why does he let her do it? She'd seen Kade behead men and women for *far* less.

Kade's face reddened. "How dare you talk to me like that!" He slammed his fist on the table, nearly knocking over his ale. "You have no right!"

"My apologies," Beldroth said as her fingers traced the face of her ring. A soft glow radiated from its face, capturing Kade's eyes. "Please forgive me."

"Of course, I'm sorry, too."

Beldroth pulled her hands back as the ring's glow vanished. "My teacher told me that sometimes, we need to look into the darkness to find the light."

"What does that mean?" Kade asked.

"Who else wants Galin off the throne besides you? There

may be other ways for you to take your rightful place on the throne."

"Allies? That's treason." Kade stood up, glaring down at Beldroth. "I have everything under control. Good night." He stormed out of the tavern.

"You'll come to my friends soon," Beldroth said softly. She dropped a few crowns on the table as she stood up. A smile worked its way onto her face. Beldroth tossed a crown on Thea's table. "That's so you can take a bath, *Thea*."

Thea nearly choked on her ale. "What?"

"I hope you got what you needed." Grinning, Beldroth strolled out of the tavern.

She knew; she knew the whole time. Why didn't she say anything before? Was Beldroth going to tell the king's brother that she was spying on him? Thea took another sip of ale. No, not likely. "So much for my disguise," Thea mumbled. She dropped two crowns on the table. What would she tell the king? Should she? Tell him what? That Kade's pyromancer wants him to take the throne, but he refused. Shaking her head, she stood up and headed for the door. *I swear that King Galin and his child will remain on the throne for as long as I live,* Thea thought.

~

Beating the morning sun, Thea rode Dena to the knights' stables, just outside of the training grounds near the northern castle wall. She got off her horse. The sun yawned as it crept over the castle walls. There was no tavern stop last night; well, not for fun anyway, and she felt good.

Staerdale Castle had been her home ever since her parents died. The previous king was close friends with Thea's father, who was desperately trying to have a son. A band of Feral Orcs raided the market in Nightfall Meadows, killing everyone, including her parents. The king took Thea in, raising her as his own. She showed skill in the art of war, so the king broke with tradition and made her a knight. Galin and Thea practically grew up as brother and sister, but she never forgot her true place.

Thea walked out onto the training grounds' practice field, where Galin was already waiting. "I wanted to get some sparring done before my council meeting this morning," he said. The twenty-three-year-old man's blue eyes twinkled in the morning sun. "Up for a match?"

It felt like they were kids again. She half-expected to see Galin's father cheering them both on from the edge of the circle. "Of course, sire, if you don't mind losing again." She walked over to one of three weapons racks along the edge of the practice field. Every weapon had its edge ground off for sparring. Thea looked over the assortment of swords, axes, hammers, daggers, and spears. "Which weapons?"

Galin smiled. "Let's keep it simple; grab a sword." He grasped the hilt of a training sword and moved to the center of the field.

"Should we put armor on before we start?" Thea asked.

"You think you'll lose that badly?"

"I was just thinking of you, sire." Thea flicked a long sword from the weapons rack into her other hand. Should she tell him anything? This would be her best chance. No one else around and he was in a great mood.

Galin began to sidestep around Thea. "Ready?"

Thea nodded. "Your move, sire." Her eyes watched his every muscle, looking for that small twitch, telegraphing his attack.

His front foot started to move towards her.

With her sword already in the attack position, Thea sidestepped.

Galin lunged forward, thrusting his sword at her midsection.

Thea batted his attack away. She hit his butt with the flat side of her sword as she stepped by him. "You can do better than that, sire."

He moved forward another step and whirled around. Galin raised his sword. His shoulders jerked downwards.

She stepped forward, raising her sword into a blocking position.

In a single motion he pulled his foot back, changing the trajectory of his sword. Instead of slashing straight down, it slammed into Thea's side, just below her sword.

Even a dull bastard sword delivers a crippling blow. She felt the air rush out of her lungs. Thea dropped to the ground, gasping for air. "You got me."

Galin extended his hand. "I didn't think you'd fall for that feint."

Thea smiled. "I did. What can I say?"

"Again?" Galin asked.

"No, I'm good. Thank you, sire." She walked over and placed her training sword back into the weapons rack. "Obviously I need to practice more before I can take you on again."

Galin rolled his eyes. "Thea, stop it." He returned his weapon to its proper place in the weapons rack. "Is everything all right?"

"What do you mean?"

"Nina tells everyone that we're having a baby and my adopted sister runs off without saying a word. Are you mad at us?"

Thea winced. "No, not at all. I—I'm worried about you." She said it. There was no turning back now.

"About what?" Galin asked. "I'm in a castle surrounded by knights and stone walls. What are you afraid of?"

"Sire, I overheard Kade and his pyromancer in the Great Hall talking about how he deserves the throne over you."

"Kade? Please, he has many faults, but he'll never go that far. It's been that way even before father brought you into the family. As he got older, Kade always seemed to keep the welfare of the people in mind."

"Is that why your father gave him the entire Ithsein province? Because he's caring?" Thea asked.

Galin laughed. "Hardly; he gave it to him because Kade wouldn't shut up about how he deserved to rule over me."

"Has he said anything recently to you, sire?"

"Nope, nothing. I'm sure he was just blowing off steam, especially after hearing that Nina is pregnant. That ensures he will never be on the throne." Galin started walking towards the knights' stables. "That mage, however, might not be as honorable as Kade."

Thea stopped him. "What if she is the one plotting something?"

"If she is, my brother will take care of it. I trust him."

"Sire—"

Galin waved her off. "Sorry, I have to get to my council meeting." He trotted off towards the castle entrance.

She watched him disappear around the corner. "I'll make sure you and your family are safe, even from your brother." She climbed on top of Dena and rode towards her modest house.

CHAPTER 5

Port Eldham

A FULL GROWING SEASON HAD PAST, AND THEA HAD GIVEN UP her suspicions long ago. With her family's land restored, she began building a manor suitable for a knight in good standing. After collecting her first round of taxes, Thea understood how the nobles could think so highly of themselves and completely disregard the people. The temptation was so strong. It took immense effort, but she did not give in. Soon, she became known as an honorable lord, just like her father.

The wind lifted Thea's hair off her shoulders as Dena trotted towards the sea. She glanced over at her companion. "Brock, ready for some good food?"

Brock patted Lyonus' head as he pulled ahead of Dena. "I'll beat you there."

"Like hell you will!" Thea said. She cracked the reins and Dena took off, pulling away from Lyonus.

"Show off," Brock muttered.

The salt air brought a smile to Thea's face. Port Eldham was a great walled keep surrounded by villages filled with merchants and artisans. She pulled Dena's reins back, stopping the horse.

After a few moments, Brock stopped Lyonus next to her. "You didn't have to wait for me."

She laughed. "Really? I'm escorting you, remember? Let's go."

Brock smiled. "I can't wait to see Sally." Brock followed Thea towards the port.

Like all great keeps in the realm, the entrance was elaborately decorated and fortified to withstand the best siege equipment of the day. Thea and Brock passed underneath the raised portcullis. Her stomach grumbled as the aroma of freshly cooked fish invaded her nostrils. As they continued down the cobblestone street merchants approached them, holding up their wares. Thea waved them off. What was once flattering became annoying at best.

"I think that's it," Brock said, pointing straight ahead at the raised deck near the dock.

Thea squinted. "This is my first Winter Festival with the king. Brock, are you sure?"

Brock nodded. "Aye, facing towards us you have some knights standing guard behind the head table, and the banquet is on the raised deck."

"Okay, follow me." Thea turned Dena towards the hitching post near the raised deck. She got down from her horse and tied her off. "Ready, Brock?"

"Aye."

The raised deck was completely roped off, except for the small entrance near the edge of the water. As Thea stepped up onto the deck, she was ambushed by the sweet smell of roasted lamb. Facing the water was the head table, filled with dignitaries, minus the king and queen. In between the head table and the water were rows of tables and chairs. "Where do we sit?" Thea asked.

"I don't know," replied Brock. "Sally never told me."

A young man waving his hands grabbed Thea's attention. "That's Robert. Want to sit with him?" Without waiting for a reply, Thea cut through the crowd towards him, right in front of the head table.

"Thea, good to see you," the young knight said. He pulled out a chair. "Please, sit with me."

"Thank you, Robert." She looked over at Brock. "Do you know Brock?"

"Of course, he's the best blacksmith in the kingdom," Robert replied.

"I'm not the best, but thank you," Brock said.

Thea sat down as Robert pushed her chair in. She looked up at the head table to see Kade and Beldroth sitting directly above her. "Great, I managed to avoid him for nearly nine months and you get me to sit right under him. Thanks a lot, Robert."

Brock waved to Sally, who sat right next to Beldroth. "I think these are great seats, Thea."

"I can see why you would." Thea waved over the wine wench. "How's that going, anyway?"

"Well—"

"Excuse me, lords and lady," the young girl said as she handed Thea and Brock a glass of red wine.

"Well," Brock began, "things are going great. I love her, Thea. I really do. But she spends so much time with the queen."

"She's the queen's handmaiden. That's expected."

"I know, but I don't like it. Soon, every minute she is not with the queen, she'll be with me."

Thea blinked. "Are you sure?"

Brock nodded. "Aye, I'm proposing to her after the feast today. I already have her father's blessing."

She smiled. "I'm happy for you."

"Anyone ask you yet?" Robert asked.

"No, I haven't even been courted," Thea replied.

"She's married to that sword of hers," Brock said.

Kade stood up. "My lords, ladies, and knights, the king and queen will be here any moment. Please be ready to show them the utmost respect, as tradition dictates."

Brock snickered. "That must have really hurt him to say that."

It must have, Thea thought. Nine months and the sky never fell, nor did Kade murder his brother's family. She was wrong about him. Besides the typical family feuding, they seemed to be happy with each other. Since the hostilities with the Feral Orcs had died down, Thea spent most of her time at the manor, away from Staerdale Castle and the king's court.

It started at the head table. They turned their heads towards the back entrance of the deck, through the line of both the human and elven knights. The lords, ladies, and knights sitting at the tables became silent like a wave running across the ocean. The only sound coming from the deck was a small bird nesting underneath.

Wearing a flamboyant robe, Galin, with the queen at his side, walked towards the head table. He pulled the chair out for his overly pregnant wife.

Thea could see how uncomfortable Nina was. Galin, her adopted brother, smiled at her. After all, it was at his insistence that she would attend the festival.

Once Galin sat down, a tall and deeply tanned elf with long blond hair and green eyes made his way to the head table. Unusually muscular, for an elf. He had a golden dove tattooed on his neck, small but noticeable.

Galin stood back up, standing proudly next to the newcomer. "Thank you all for coming this fine day. Every year at this time, King Faeler," Galin said, pointing at the elf, "and I renegotiate our trade agreements, just as we have always done for the last one hundred years."

Faeler stepped forward. "King Galin the Fourth, my people extend our deepest gratitude for your aid in the war against the Darkstriders. My Dark Elf brothers take advantage of lesser creatures for their own selfish ends. The Vulwin Elves appreciate everything you have done. In the past few months, there has been no Darkstrider activity in our territory, and we owe that all to you." Faeler extended his hand. "Take my hand as a long-lasting ally."

Galin took his hand and shook it vigorously. "King Faeler, as long as a Ravenward sits on this throne, you have an ally."

Is that better for them or us? Thea thought. Allies are always good, but sometimes one side fares better than the other. She'd fought alongside the Vulwin Elves, but they never spoke to human knights before. She always thought they were more than just a little snobbish. As Faeler sat down, he glanced over at Beldroth, and a strange expression came over him. It was not in admiration of her beauty, rather unconscious fear. What did he sense that she didn't? No matter what he thought, Faeler was obviously not entirely sure either. It was almost as if he recognized something . . . or was she at it again?

Galin clasped his hands together. "Now that the war with the Darkstriders is over and their Feral Orc minions are driven back into their caves where they belong, it is time for us to rebuild." He lowered his head as if trying to choose the right words. "War is expensive, and we've all paid a heavy price. In war, trade routes, villages, farmland, and trading posts all get burnt to the ground. The economic means for our two kingdoms to survive has been disrupted. We have to rebuild."

Thea saw Kade's blank stare at his brother. *Does he know where this is going?*

"As a temporary measure, we have to raise taxes until the coffers are replenished. The port tariffs will increase to ten percent of the products' value which, of course, is mirrored at King Faeler's port on the other side."

"That'll bankrupt us," Kade muttered.

Ignoring his brother, Galin continued, "Additionally, I am instituting a fifteen percent tariff for all products entering Axain."

Kade abruptly stood up. "The Axain kingdom or the province?"

"I'm sorry, Kade. I meant the province," Galin replied.

With his mouth hanging open, Kade slowly slid back down into his seat.

Thea rubbed her chin. Her manor was just inside the Axain province so that tax wouldn't affect her, but it would destroy Kade. If he wanted to trade with the Vulwin Elves, he would have to pay a forty-five percent tax before his goods were even purchased.

"How long will this temporary tax be in place?" a noble asked.

"A few years, I think. You've got to remember, we are paying for ten years of war," Galin replied.

"Sire," Kade said as he stood up again. "You can't tax goods coming into Axain. Ithsein is largely made up of artisan, who support the rest of my people through their taxes. Once they hear about this new tax, they'll leave Ithsein and move to Axain to avoid it. That will destroy the province our father gave me. You can't do that!"

"I'm sorry, Kade, it's done. Now sit back down," Galin said.

"Do you even care about your people, brother? How many people will starve because of your deal with *them*?"

"I said that's enough. Now, sit down."

Ignoring his brother, Kade turned toward Faeler. "King Faeler, I bid you farewell." With his face reddened, Kade bolted off the raised deck, with Beldroth in tow.

"King Faeler, please forgive my brother," Galin said as he sat down at the table.

Following Galin's lead, Faeler took his place at the head table. "It's all right, Galin. We all have family problems that we have to *deal* with."

Thea rolled her eyes. *I guess Kade hasn't changed*, she thought. He always wanted to show up his brother, but this time it was different. It actually seemed like he cared for his people. Was that for the audience or had he really changed? She refocused on Nina. Her face was contorting while grasping her lower back. Was she having the baby? Thea pointed towards the queen. "Sire."

Galin's eyes widened as his wife's face twisted in pain. "Nina? The baby?"

Nina nodded.

"I—King Faeler..."

"Just go, have your heir," Faeler said after taking a sip of wine.

"Thea!" Galin cried. "Escort us back to Staerdale Castle, now."

"Yes, your majesty." Thea and Brock raced to their horses as the knights led Galin, Nina, and Sally towards the royal coach. After the royal family was inside, Thea took charge of the king's escort. "I want two as rear guards and two flank guards, fifty yards out on all sides. Bottom line, we're going fast, and we're not going to wait for you, so keep up."

Brock laughed. "I feel like I'm a knight again."

Thea cracked her reins on Dena's back. "Follow me." She charged down the road, leading the royal coach to home.

~

"She's been in there for hours," Galin grumbled while he tapped his fingers on the arm of his throne in the Great Hall.

"I'm sure everything is all right, sire," Thea said. *Did I sound convincing?* She was just as unsure as Galin. How would she know, anyway? To make matters worse, once Kade got word that Nina was *really* in labor, he and Beldroth both showed up at the Great Hall to welcome the new child into the world. Being stuck with those three in a small room was the worst kind of purgatory. Brock was the only ray of hope in the room. Too bad he preferred Sally over her.

Galin walked over to Kade and extended his hand to him. "Kade, I'm glad you came."

Beldroth's thin lips twisted like a vine. "We almost didn't get the message."

Ignoring Beldroth, Kade took his brother's hand. "Of course I came."

"You care a lot about your people, don't you?"

Kade nodded. "Don't you?"

Galin returned to his throne. "Of course I do. What was that supposed to mean? I'm the king, you need to start respecting that."

Thea rolled her eyes. "Sires, do we need to do this now?"

Brock grabbed Thea's tunic. "Better stay out of this," he whispered.

"I respect the throne, not the *thing* that's in it. Our father said that a true king looks after his people before his own desires. If you hurt the people, no matter why *you* think it's justified, you're no longer a good king. Those are father's words, not mine. Your rules have no place in *my* province," Kade said.

Galin looked away from Kade. "Brother, what have I done to hurt you so badly? Would you rather split the kingdom of Axain in two? My son—"

"What if it's a girl?"

" . . . Or daughter, will rule over the entire kingdom, not just a slice."

Kade frowned. "You'd go against our traditions? You'd prefer that your daughter take the throne rather than your own brother?"

Galin nodded. "Some traditions are foolish. Thea proves that. Besides, father disobeyed them and the sky never fell, did it?"

"What do you want from me?" Kade demanded.

"I—"

Crack! The door behind the thrones slammed into the wall. The queen's slender, blond-haired handmaiden rushed into the Great Hall. Everything stopped. All eyes zoomed in on little Sally Healy. "Sire, forgive me," she said as she knelt before Galin.

"Get up and tell me," Galin said. "Is Nina all right?"

"Yes, sire, she has your *son* in her arms as we speak. My lady has requested your presence."

A son, Thea thought, *more like an indisputable heir.*

Galin glared at Kade. "You love your people, brother, but it's time you loved your family. When we present him to the kingdom, I'm going to declare you as his senior adviser..."

"See, my lord, already his son has you under his boot," Beldroth muttered.

Thea glared at her.

"...when he comes of age, you will train him to be a great knight and to always remember the people first, like yourself..."

Beldroth's ring began to glow, just like in the Drow Inn and Tavern. Was Thea the only one who saw it?

Galin continued. "...If my son takes your best qualities and mine, he will be a great king that would make our father proud."

"Sire, the queen's waiting for you," Sally said.

"I won't train someone to be my master, not any more than you would," Kade said.

Thea stared at the ring. It was glowing even brighter. Was Beldroth doing something to Kade?

"You have to. Obey your king, Kade," Galin said.

Beldroth leaned into Kade's ear. "If you'd listened to me you wouldn't have this problem. For the sake of your people, you need to take action now."

Thea grabbed Beldroth's arm, pulling her away from Kade. "What did you just say?"

"Give my best to Nina, *brother*. When you're ready to act like a real king, I'll support you. Like father said, the people don't exist to serve you; you exist to serve the people." Kade pushed Thea off Beldroth. "Come on, let's go."

Thea watched Kade and Beldroth storm out of the Great Hall. What did Beldroth say? She looked over to see Galin with his face in his hands. "Sire, the queen," Thea said.

"He's lost it."

"Sire?"

"Kade, he's lost it. Our father never said any of that." Galin rushed out of the Great Hall to see his new son.

If their father never said that, Thea thought, *then who did?*

CHAPTER 6

Darkstriders

THE WOODEN FLOOR CREAKED AS KADE PACED AROUND THE small inn room. "I can't believe he said that to me."

Sitting on the corner of the bed, Beldroth's licked her lips. "Galin said it to you because he thinks you're weak, nothing more. Why else would he declare that you're his son's servant before he's even an hour old?" She rubbed the ring's face and it began to glow.

Kade's eyes were tempted by Beldroth's provocative figure. His heart beat faster. Was he in love? Why did he wait so long to have his pyromancer? He shook his head. "I'm not sure what to do." He sat down next to her, hoping to see her true feelings for him.

She lifted his head until her eyes met his. Her ring was glowing a bright orange color, unseen by Kade. "You have to kill them. The whole family. Before it's too late." She pulled him in closer and kissed his cheek.

For a second, he stopped breathing. He opened his mouth, inviting her tongue to explore its depths.

She pulled back. "Well?"

His heart thumped faster. Parts of his body showed its excitement towards her. "I—I think you're right. It's time to take what is rightfully mine." Kade pulled her in close, passionately kissing her. His hands went up underneath her cloak.

Losing herself, she forced him down on the bed.

He sat up and pulled off her cloak, tossing it to the floor.

She pushed him back down again. The passionate beast straddled his waist like a horse as she tore off her shirt.

This was like a dream come true. After years of waiting, Kade was finally going to have his pyromancer. He pulled himself up, nuzzling against her chest.

She ripped the shirt off his muscular body, throwing him back down. Beldroth threw herself on top of him, kissing his ear.

Kade felt his manhood trying to burst through his trousers. Her smile told him everything he needed to know. She wanted him as badly as he wanted her.

Her lips moved along his neck. Her hands slid down his chest. "Close your eyes," she said.

Kade slammed his eyes shut. Feeling his belt being ripped from pants, his breaths got shorter and his heart raced. *Here it comes*, he thought.

"Keep your eyes closed, my love."

He felt the wetness of her kiss on his chest. Her hand wandered. Her warm body mounted him like a rodeo rider. *I have to see*, he thought. *I want to look into her eyes as we make love together.*

Kade's eyes opened in gleeful pleasure, only for a moment. Pointed ears with blue skin and long, flowing black hair replaced the beautiful Beldroth he had always known.

She was a Dark Elf! He shut his eyes again, trying to imagine the woman he saw on top of him just a moment before, instead of that *creature*. What had he done? Jumping out of bed, Kade pushed her off him. "You're a Dark Elf!"

The sensual blue creature only smiled. "We have all the necessary human parts, just like any elf." Beldroth slid her pants back on. "You weren't supposed to see me like this. My people have the ability to make ourselves look like any other sentient creature. But, it takes enormous concentration, and passion destroys it."

"I should turn you in," Kade said.

"What would they do to you? Sleeping with a member of the Darkstriders and having her at your side for years." She tossed Kade's clothes at him. "Galin would think hanging is too humane."

Kade swallowed. "Now, I'm a traitor *and* a servant. How could this get any worse?"

"My lord—"

"I'm not your lord. Stop calling me that."

"Kade, we want you to get the throne. It's better for you and us. Think of your people. Do it for them," Beldroth said.

Kade buttoned his shirt. "If I do it, what's in it for you? I can't believe that you're doing this out the goodness of your heart."

Beldroth's thin lips twitched. "You're right. We just want to be left alone, and no interference when we have disputes with our Vulwin Elf brothers. They started the war by exiling us. Humans need to stay out of *elven* affairs."

"What do I get out of it? I could very well get the throne without your help."

"Negotiating?"

"Always."

Beldroth smiled. "I don't have the authority, but there's

someone here who does. I'll get word to him and we'll see him tonight. Okay?"

"Sure," Kade replied. "How do you propose we take down my brother?"

"I thought you'd never ask."

~

Kade and Beldroth rode down the dark cobblestone road towards the best tavern in Staerdale Castle, the Rusted Feathers. Whenever they were at the castle, the couple always came by to sample their newest brew. Kade saw an old man ejected out the door by an overweight bouncer. "Looks like he had too much." His eyes bounced from one shadow to the next. During the hundreds of times he'd made this trek, there was never anyone there, but this time he had to be sure.

"Stop that," Beldroth said. "You look paranoid."

Paranoid? No, paranoid is only when you *think* someone will be looking for you. "I'm not paranoid." Kade lowered his voice. "Why are we meeting here? This place is always full of commoners, knights, and nobles."

Her thin lips twitched. "Where else can you talk about the ills of the kingdom and fit right in?"

Kade laughed. "You're right. If they charged everyone who wanted to take over the kingdom after a few beers with treason, we'd have no one left to rule over." He pulled back on the reins, stopping his horse next to the hitching post near the corner of the tavern. "No precautions then?"

"I didn't say that," Beldroth said as she tied off her horse. "Don't worry, I've got it all under control. Follow me."

Kade smiled. "I think you're enjoying this too much."

Cigar smoke hit Kade smack in the face as he stepped through the door. Music . . . how he loved the music! Kade didn't care for the fiddle, but the fiddling here was different. It added a certain playfulness to the Rusted Feathers' already pleasant atmosphere. He grinned. "At the bar?"

Beldroth shook her head. "No, are you out of your mind?" She motioned over towards the only Vulwin Elf in the Rusted Feathers, the bartender. "Fi saved us a booth." She trudged through the wall of patrons in line for another ale.

Instead of following Beldroth through the crowd, Kade veered away from the bar on the left wall. The main floor was sprinkled with small tables with four simple chairs around them. But tonight, there was not one table with only four patrons. "Excuse me," Kade said as he pushed his way through the sea of people. *Where did she go?* Kade thought. He should have listened.

Thump. Thump. Thump.

Kade's breath shortened as his eyes bounced from woman to woman, trying to find his escort. Why was he so scared? On the eve of achieving his lifelong goal, he was behaving like a—*commoner*, not a king. Continuing in the general direction, Kade finally broke free from the mass of people. *There she is*, he thought.

Beldroth was standing on the far end of the rectangular-shaped bar, on the opposite end from the door. It was the farthest booth to the left, right next to the stairs going up to the second floor. The only one that may hear them was the bouncer who had played toss-the-drunk earlier. Would he care? Doubtful. What about the next booth? The one that shared a high-backed bench. One lone girl sat in the booth. Surely, she would hear them. He moved in close to Beldroth. "What about *her*?"

She pulled out a small pouch and set it on the table. "She won't see anything; neither will anyone else."

Kade slid into the booth next to Beldroth. "Good."

"May I get you a drink, sir?" the beer wench asked.

After a nod from Beldroth, Kade said, "Please, a pale ale for each of us. Thank you."

"Just be a moment." The young girl scurried off.

"What will that do?" Kade asked.

"You'll see. But we need to wait until we get our drinks." Her right hand slithered along the table and grasped Kade's left hand.

Beldroth's eyes softened when she looked at him and he knew it. Kade pulled his hand away. "Did they have to travel far? I'm surprised they could meet so quickly." Kade shrugged. "I'll be amazed if they can even get into the castle."

Beldroth grinned. "You're in for a real surprise."

The brown-haired beer wench plopped two large mugs and a pitcher down on the table. She looked directly at Beldroth. "Ma'am, Fi said he'll put tonight's tab on your account. Is that okay?"

"Yes, but we'd like some privacy. If we want another drink, we'll get it ourselves," Beldroth said.

"Thank you, ma'am, enjoy." After a quick curtsy, the beer wench moved on to the next table.

Kade poured the ale up to the rim in both mugs. He slid one over to Beldroth. "Do you burn the bag or something?"

Ignoring him, Beldroth's eyes focused on the small bag. "Med rolva efolto terolta."

Kade couldn't take his eyes off the bag. It glowed. It glowed a bright green. His head pulsed with pain. Kade gasped; he couldn't make out his hands. Were his eyes failing? Was she betraying him?

"Med rolva efolto terolta."

He clasped his eyes shut as hard as he could. "I can't see," Kade muttered. Throbbing pain morphed into a dull ache. The veins on his face visibly pulsated. He could almost hear his heartbeat. "Beldroth, you have to stop this."

"Med rolva efolto terolta." She closed her eyes in a prayer

to Methos, thanking him for his dark powers. "It's over, Kade. Open your eyes."

The pain had gone. His heart settled down. Slowly, Kade opened one eye, staring at Beldroth. There she was in her true form, a beautiful Dark Elf. "Won't they see you?" Kade asked as he opened both eyes.

Beldroth shook her head. "Anyone within five feet from the bag is protected by the illusion. As a side effect, you can see the true forms of *all* the Dark Elves in the room."

"All?" Kade turned towards the line of patrons waiting to get another ale. His mouth opened, but no words came out. There were Dark Elves in line and sitting at the tables. He looked over at the bouncer. No wonder Beldroth wasn't worried about being discovered *here*. "So many. Do you have people in the castle itself?"

"Of course; we'd be stupid not to." Beldroth sipped her ale. "Here they come."

Kade saw two Dark Elves approach their booth. "Can they see us?"

"Nope, I just told them where we were sitting," Beldroth replied. "Once they get within five feet, they'll see us."

The pair of Dark Elves appeared to be nearly opposites. The one on the left was tall and built like a heavy infantry soldier, where the other elf was not. They slid onto the bench, opposite Kade and Beldroth.

"Are you sure he can be trusted?" asked the taller and bald elf.

Beldroth smiled. "He has no choice, now." She pointed at the larger elf. "This is Ryul. He's the commander of one of our Feral Orc Regiments." Pointing at the smaller one, she said, "This is Tanyl. He is the one I told you about. Tanyl is the only Dark Elf here that has the authority to negotiate on behalf of the Darkstriders."

Kade extended his hand to Tanyl. "Pleasure to meet you."

Tanyl's pointed ears twitched. "We already know each other and frankly, I don't like you."

"I—"

"But I'm here on behalf of the Darkstriders, not myself." His dark-blue skin glistened in the candlelight. "You understand the plan? No questions?"

Beldroth opened her mouth to speak.

Tanyl glared at her. "I was talking to Kade."

Kade's hand shook as he saw the utter fear in Beldroth's eyes. "No, questions. But, I do want to know what I get out of all this."

"Besides the throne?"

"Yes."

"How can we help you?" Tanyl sneered.

"Gold, and lots of it. Also, I want free and open trade routes with the Etranan continent," Kade said.

"You'd have to talk to your Vulwin allies for that, but when we control that port, your wish will be granted." Tanyl looked over at Beldroth. "Is that why I was summoned? For gold and trade routes?"

Beldroth bowed her head. "No, my lord. He wasn't going to do it unless he talked to you."

They need me more than I need them, Kade thought. "That's not all, Tanyl. After I solidify my power in the kingdom, I want an ally to annex Leonga to the north."

"Why stop there?" Tanyl asked. "Once you control the Gnome and Dwarf kingdoms, you'd have the whole continent."

Kade leaned across the table. "Who said I'd stop?"

Ryul grinned. "He sounds like a Dark Elf."

"Anything else?" Tanyl asked.

"I want Beldroth to be my queen," Kade replied.

Tanyl raised an eyebrow at Beldroth. "Did he even ask you?"

"No, my lord, he didn't."

"Kade, I like your ambition. Curious, how you can know someone for over two years and never realize the true darkness in his heart," Tanyl said. "I was given reports concerning your grumblings about the throne for years, but this goes way beyond every one of them."

Ryul's head whipped around as the sound of a shattering mug came from the booth behind him. "She can hear us."

Tanyl rolled his eyes. "The commoner in the next booth? Unlikely; she probably just had too much to drink."

"Maybe you're right." Ryul faced Kade and Beldroth. "Our armies can help you with your ambitions, but we need the king's permission to do so."

"I wasn't talking about now. I don't even have the throne yet." Kade sipped his ale. "Tanyl, can you give me assurances that the Darkstriders will be my ally under my terms?"

Tanyl rubbed his chin. "Wait, you haven't heard my terms yet."

"Your terms?"

"Surely, you didn't think this would be one-sided did you?"

"I suppose not."

"Good." Tanyl leaned into the bench's high back. "Your alliance with the Darkstriders will be public—"

Kade's mouth dropped open. "I can't do that."

"Don't worry, we'll give you all the evidence you need to prove it was the Vulwin Elves. Also, my people will walk freely among yours. If we are to guarantee trade routes, we need to learn to work together, wouldn't you agree?"

"I—"

"Good. My last condition is that you have a Dark Elf as your High Consular. This one is non-negotiable," Tanyl said.

"What if we fail?" Kade asked.

Beldroth's warm hands embraced his. "We'll take you in. You're a true friend to the Darkstriders."

Tanyl scowled at Beldroth. "Only because you have proven yourself to be a great commander of troops. If you fail, I'll give you an army."

Kade nodded. "That sounds good."

"Do we have a deal?" Tanyl extended his hand towards Kade.

"We do," Kade said as he took Tanyl's hand in friendship. "I—"

Ryul stood up as the girl in the next booth bolted out of the Rusted Feathers. "I told you she heard us!"

"Leave her," Tanyl ordered. "You'll cause more problems if you go after her."

"He's right," Kade said. "If we're going to do this, we have to do it quickly."

Tanyl nodded as he stood up. "I'll have everything ready in four days."

After Tanyl and Ryul left the Rusted Feathers, Beldroth placed her hands over the small bag. There was a quick flash, and then it was gone.

Kade saw the Dark Elf he grew to admire instantly turn into the woman he loved. Every Dark Elf in the bar looked *human*. "Beldroth, let's go to my keep. We've got a lot of items to work out."

"Of course—your majesty." Beldroth followed Kade out of the Rusted Feathers.

CHAPTER 7

The Secret is Out

THEA TOOK ANOTHER LOOK AROUND HER OLD SMALL HOUSE inside the Staerdale Castle Walls. It was nearly empty. Her modest furniture was already given away to some of Brock's friends. All that was left were a few sacks filled with nearly ten years of memories. *Poor Dena*, Thea thought as she strained bringing a heavy sack outside and tossing it into the cart. Her heroic, honorable horse was reduced to pulling a cart. Maybe she cared more than the silly horse did? Moving into the manor was the right and proper thing to do. In fact, she had wanted to do this all her life. But wanting to do something and actually doing it are two entirely separate things. She'd lived here ever since her parents had died. You can't govern your lands from a distance though, and she knew it. Thea sighed and headed back inside.

"Thea, wait!" Brock yelled.

Thea smiled at Brock and Sally as they raced towards her. "I appreciate you coming to see me off."

Sally shook her head. "I'm sorry, but that's not why we came."

"Thea," Brock began, "We need to talk inside."

"Sure." Thea led the other two inside her empty house and closed the door behind them. For the first time, Brock actually looked *scared*. Sally's eyes were puffy and her cheeks were red like she had been crying all night. "What's wrong? Are you two all right?"

Brock grasped Sally's hand. "We're fine. In fact, she said yes."

Thea smiled. "Congratulations. When is the wedding?"

Brock shook his head. "That's not why we're here." He glanced at Sally. "You'd better tell her."

Tell me what? Thea thought. As long as she had known Brock, he'd never behaved like this. She'd seen him upset, sure, but never scared like this. "Well?"

"They were everywhere," Sally said. "I was at the Rusted Feathers in one of the booths along the back wall."

"Who was with you?"

"No one, I was alone." Sally's eyes widened. "Lord Kade and his pyromancer sat in the booth behind me. I thought nothing of it. Frankly, I can't stand either one of them, and the last thing I wanted to do was to talk to them."

"Did they see you?" Thea asked.

"No, I don't think so." Sally glanced over at Brock. "Are you sure? She'll think I'm crazy."

Brock put his arm around his fiancée. "Magic is involved, Sally, and Thea has seen what it can do. She won't think that."

Thea smiled at Sally. "You know I won't. Please tell me what you saw."

Sally swallowed hard. "Okay. I was there to meet Heather. You know, the baker's daughter?"

"I know her," Thea replied.

"We were going to discuss the wedding. I got there a little early to start writing down some ideas for the reception. Thea, I didn't even have an ale that night." Sally's lips began to tremble. "From the booth where Lord Kade and Beldroth sat, I heard strange words. Couldn't understand them, but I *felt* them. My head hurt and I couldn't see, only for a second. When it passed, I saw some people I thought I knew transform before my eyes. Their skin turned blue and their ears were pointed, like an elf."

Thea blinked. "Dark-blue skin? You're describing a Dark Elf. You can't be right, Sally. We'd know if they were here."

Sally grabbed Thea's wrist. "Nearly half the people in the tavern were Dark Elves. As soon as this happened, I pulled my cloak over my face. Even Lord Kade was surprised—"

"How do you know?

"I heard him. Beldroth told him that she cast a spell to prevent people outside the bubble—I don't know what else to call it—from hearing their conversation. She also said that anyone within it can see through the Dark Elf illusions." Sally recoiled to Brock's side. "That's when *they* came in..."

Was Sally crazy? Thea had seen magic hundreds of times, but nothing on this scale. How could Dark Elves walk freely among the people without anyone even knowing? If what Sally was saying was true, Thea probably drank and played Knucklebones with the *enemy*. That can't be true. Infiltration on such levels could only mean—

"...Two elves walked straight towards Lord Kade's and Bedroth's booth, right behind me. One was significantly larger than the other. There was something familiar about the smaller one. I can't place him; it was just a feeling." Sally tore her eyes away from Thea. "I—I—what happens if they find out I know who they are? Brock, what will happen to us? Our families?"

Brock gave Sally a hug. "What happens to us if what they said comes to pass? The children we're going to have; what will happen to them if we do nothing?"

"Sally, please tell me. You're both beginning to scare me," Thea interrupted.

Sally nodded. "They were discussing terms, negotiating the spoils after—" Her eyes welled up and the dam holding back her tears burst.

"After what? Come on, Sally." Thea advanced on Sally. "What is it?"

Brock pushed Thea away from Sally. "Take it easy."

"Brock, tell me."

"They're going to kill them," Brock said.

"Who, the king?"

Brock shook his head. "No, his *whole* family, including their baby. They were deciding how to rule Axain after Kade usurps the king. Dark Elves will rule side by side with Kade, breaking our alliance with the Vulwin Elves permanently."

"You do realize you're talking about the Darkstriders?" Thea asked.

"And Kade's in league with them," Brock replied.

"I see. Give me a minute." Thea began to pace around the small room. This was no accusation of jealousy or sibling rivalry, it was treason. How do you tell the king that his own brother is plotting with the Darkstriders to kill his entire family? Thea thought. If she brought it up, wouldn't the king liken it to her earlier accusations? Probably. "Sally, did they say when they were going to attempt it?"

"No. I ran out before they left." Sally looked away. "I was scared."

"Did they see you leave?"

"Probably, I can't be sure," Sally replied.

If she was going to overthrow the king and her plans were discovered, what would she do? If you abandoned them, you're more likely to hang for plotting against the king. If you're a prominent member of the court and depart suddenly, you would lose everything. No, the only option that made any sense was to accelerate the plan. With so many Dark Elves among people, a coup would not be that hard to pull off. Thea glared at Sally. "Sally, this is very important. Did they say *how* they were going to do it?"

"I'm sorry, but if they did, it must have been after I left." Sally clung to Brock. "Please do something, Thea."

Thea nodded. "I'm going to tell the king."

ould I believe me? Thea thought as the quick, rhythmic pounding of her feet onto the Staerdale Castle's floor grew louder with each step. Sure, Galin had been surrounded by magic all of his life and would easily believe that magic could conceal the Dark Elves. But, Kade, a traitor? A tiny bead of sweat rolled down her cheek. *Yes, he has to believe me,* she thought.

Outside the decorative double doors stood two well-muscled knights. The larger one held his hand up, blocking Thea's path. "Sorry, Thea, the king needs his privacy tonight."

The doors were normally only closed when the king was meeting with the war council. Was the council convened? Did it matter? If the war council was convened, this was the perfect time to tell him. Surely, the others would help Galin see reason. She swallowed. "I have to see the king."

"Sorry, you know the rules. The king can't be disturbed when the door is closed."

"Is the war council convened?"

"I'm not sure."

Thea frowned. "Jason, who's with the king?"

The smaller one pushed Thea aside, knocking her to the ground. "None of your damn business. Now get lost."

"That was uncalled for, Kevin," Jason said as he pushed the smaller man into the wall. "Thea, you can't go in. I'm sorry."

She took his hand and pulled herself up. "Jason, the king's life is in danger. I have to see him."

"No," Kevin said.

Jason glared at his partner. "Is it serious?"

"I wouldn't be here if it weren't. He'll thank you for letting me pass. Trust me," Thea said.

Jason nodded. "Okay."

"What? You can't do that!" Kevin said.

"The king's life is more important than some stupid regulation." Jason opened the double doors. "Make it fast."

Thea smiled. "I will." She grinned at the defeated Kevin as she strolled through the door.

Her eyes focused on the long table in the center of the Great Hall. Galin sat at the head of the table surrounded by his four top advisers. *Here we go,* she thought. Thea's pace quickened. Her eyes never left Galin.

Galin looked up. "Thea, what are you doing here?"

"Sire, forgive this intrusion, but I have reason to believe you're in danger. I need to speak with you," Thea said.

"In danger?"

Thea nodded.

"Gentlemen, that will be all for now. Please give us some privacy."

After the advisers had left the room, Thea sat down next to the king. "Sire, there's a plot to overthrow you and kill your whole family."

"How do you know?"

"Sally—"

"Nina's handmaiden?"

"Yes. She told me about a meeting she overheard in the

Rusted Feathers." Thea swallowed. "Sire, there were Dark Elves *in* the Rusted Feathers."

"Not possible."

"In the booth behind her, she heard a spell being cast. Then, she saw many people in the tavern transform into Dark Elves."

"Transform?"

"They only appeared human because of an illusion. The spell allowed anyone in the bubble to see through it."

Galin frowned. "How is it we didn't know they could do this before? Beldroth has been with Kade for years, surely she'd have noticed something."

Thea lowered her gaze.

"What?"

"She's one of them. Sally saw her without her illusion. No question, she's a Dark Elf."

"Does Kade know? Is my brother in danger too?"

Thea shook her head. "Sally also saw your brother with them."

"Them?"

"There were two other Dark Elves and one of them claimed to be a commander for a Feral Orc Regiment. I—"

"No, Kade would never betray us like that. I know he's been jealous about the throne for years, but this? He'd never go that far." Galin's face twisted and his gaze hardened. "You've been telling me that Kade was going to kill me for some time now."

"I—I suppose I have," Thea said.

"You were wrong all those times because nothing ever happened. Why should I believe you now?"

"Sire?"

"Every time the accusation was worse than the one before, isn't that right?" Galin asked.

"I—"

"Why do you hate my brother?"

"I don't, sire. He hates you," Thea replied. "You have to believe me. You're like a brother to me."

"And you're like a sister to me, but the question still stands. What's their plan? You said Sally was there," Galin said.

"She didn't hear that. It was more like a negotiation."

"Negotiation?"

"Yes, Kade was negotiating terms for the Darkstriders to help him take the throne."

Galin laughed. "That actually sounds like Kade."

"I think—"

"But, that's it. Thea, I don't believe your story. You've come to me many times about the same matter and he never tried to kill me once. Wish me to die in battle? Sure, but murder my family? He's too duty-driven for that. Kade learned that lesson better than I did."

"Sire, can you just take precautions?" Thea asked.

"I should have both you and Sally flogged for accusing Kade of treason."

"Sire—"

Galin stood up. "Ever since I gave you your family's land back, you've been on a vendetta against my brother. Get out."

Thea's heart sank as Galin turned his back towards her. This is what she got for trying to save his life? She knew it would be difficult, but this? She never expected to be thrown out. "Yes, sire." She curtsied and headed for the door.

"Tell those two idiot guards to get in here on your way out."

Thea exited the double doors as Jason and Kevin hurried inside. *I'm sorry*, she thought.

CHAPTER 8

Queen Nina

THEA PATTED DENA'S NECK AS SHE RODE HER DOWN THE cobblestone street. Why didn't Galin listen to her? He had no problem believing in magic, but not his brother's betrayal. Thea's grip tightened on the reins. This was going to be a bad day.

"Thea, hold up!" shouted a voice behind her.

Thea spun around in the saddle. "Robert, what do you want?"

The handsome young knight smiled as he approached. "More like, what did you do to piss off the king so badly?"

"Told the truth," Thea replied as she nudged Dena to move on. "What do you want? I just want to be alone."

"Talking does help," Robert said. "Besides, just because the king won't believe you doesn't mean I won't." He smiled. "Besides, who am I going to drink with if you leave the castle?"

Thea grinned. "It's only three in the afternoon."

"Yup, and we're both off duty. Sounds like a date to me. Unless you're too busy."

"Sure. You're buying the first round."

"As long as you buy the rest," Robert replied. "You're the one that's rich, remember. Rusted Feathers then?"

"No, not this time."

"Why not?"

"I—I'll tell you when we get to the *other* tavern," Thea said.

"We're not going to the Drow Inn and Tavern, are we? That place is a dive."

Thea nodded. "Yeah, and it's private. I'll tell you what I said to the king when we get there."

"Okay." Robert followed Thea to the Drow Inn and Tavern.

Thea's nose wrinkled as the vile odor of vomit ambushed her as she entered the tavern.

"What's that?" Robert asked, holding his nose.

"The usual end result of a whiskey-slamming contest. The loser always heaves on the floor," the old man said as he finished wiping up the vomit. "Can I get you two a drink?"

Thea look around at the empty tavern. The solid oak bar on the left wall only had two patrons sitting on its stools. "Is that—?"

"Who?" Robert said, following Thea as she moved closer to the couple.

"Brock? Sally? What are you doing here?" Thea asked.

Brock turned around with his mug in hand. "Sally wanted to relax, but not at—what's he doing here?"

"Who? Robert?" Thea replied.

"I don't think he's one of them," Sally whispered to Brock.

"If you're going to whisper, Sally, you need to be quieter. Besides, I'm here to help Thea. The king threw her out today. He was pretty upset," Robert said.

"May we join you?" Thea asked.

"Sally?" Brock asked.

"It's okay. We're friends, after all," Sally replied.

The old man appeared with two mugs of ale. "Here you go," he said as he slid the mugs across the bar to Thea and Robert.

"Thank you," Robert replied.

Thea and Robert sat side by side next to Brock. "The king—he didn't believe me," Thea said.

"Which part?" Brock asked.

"Hold on," Robert interrupted. "I thought you were going to tell me, Thea. If I'm going to help, you have to tell me what's going on."

"You're right," Thea said. "Last night Sally overheard some Dark Elves negotiate with Kade to help him overthrow the king."

Robert's face froze as if every muscle was unable to move.

"Sally didn't hear the actual plan, but it's clear that Kade intends to kill the king."

"I see," Robert said.

Thea's eyes focused on every muscle in his face, looking for that sparkle in his eye, but it was gone. "Robert, we can't let that happen."

Robert stared down into his ale. "No, that's not right."

"What?" Brock asked. "Sally was there. She heard them."

"Thea, do we know how they'll attack the king? Do we even have a guess?"

Sally took a sip of her ale. "Kade and Beldroth were meeting two Dark Elves. I didn't see them, but one introduced the other as a commander of a Feral Orc regiment."

"Anything else?" Robert asked.

"Well, I'm not sure."

"Go on, Sally," Thea said.

"I was so scared." Sally looked around. "That's why I

insisted on coming here, even though the ale is awful. I—I heard them say the Dark Elves need to be open allies with Kade and they would ensure we thought the Vulwin Elves were responsible. I don't know how."

"You didn't tell me that before." Thea took a swig of her ale. Was she being played by a scared girl looking for attention? No, she'd known Sally far too long to believe that. Why the self-doubt? For the first time, she was doubting Sally. Why? What's different? She just went to the king to tell him about the plot, and now she doubts it? Thea ran her fingers through her hair. Rubbing her eyes, she saw a faint glow. So faint that normally she would've missed it. "Robert, what's wrong with your ring? It's glowing?"

"My ring?" Robert covered up the decorative ring with his family's coat of arms on its face and laughed. "Maybe the ale here is worse than I thought."

She struggled to focus on that ring. As the glow faded into the shadows, so did her doubts about Sally's story. What just happened? Thea concentrated on Sally. "Did they say what evidence?"

"No," Sally replied.

Robert rubbed his chin. "If they did this, they would have to kill the king's entire family, not just him."

Thea nodded. "Especially, the new baby."

"Right. But, the only real way to get past the king's knights is to—" Robert's eyes widened.

"To draw them out," Thea finished. "That can be done only one way."

"Aye, they have to attack, and there is only one place besides Port Eldham where they can cross the sea from Etrana: Nightfall Meadows."

"They wouldn't even think of attacking Staerdale Castle itself, the siege would take too long. The outlying garrisons would attack them from behind and Kade would be found out," Thea said. "It would have to be Nightfall Meadows."

"Kade can only appear to be the legitimate ruler if the king dies on the battlefield," Brock said. "What about the king's family?"

Thea shrugged. "The queen will be kept in the background and his son is too young to rule. Kade could deal with them at any time. The farther away from the king's death, the less suspicious it would seem. Who's to say otherwise if Kade tells the kingdom two years from now that they died from a fever?"

Robert grinned. "That's a brilliant plan."

Brock took another swig. "How do we stop it?"

"Simple, we keep the king away from the battle," Thea said.

"How?" Robert asked.

Brock looked over at his fiancée. "When you want a man to do something to protect himself and he refuses, tell his wife. She'll *make* him take precautions."

Thea jumped from her stool. "I'm going to tell the queen." She tossed a few crowns on the bar and rushed out the door.

S*he must believe me,* Thea thought as she plowed down the corridor towards the Queen's antechamber. She swore to keep the Ravenward family safe, and she wasn't going to let them down. Why should the queen believe her? She practically grew up with the king and he didn't. What would cause a wife to take seriously a tale that her husband had discarded?

A guard was posted outside the large, ornate oak door. He smiled as she approached.

"Thea, how are you?"

Thea returned a false smile. "Good. I have important news for the queen; it's urgent."

"Sure." He moved off to the side while opening the great door for Thea.

"Thank you," Thea said as she moved past him.

As she stepped into the doorway, fresh roses invaded her senses. Oak floorboards creaked under her feet with each step. In the center of the floor was a small rug with the Ravenward coat of arms. A small breeze hit the left side of her face. Thea saw a bird's nest in the corner of the stone window. This had to be the most peaceful room in Staerdale Castle.

"Thea, what are you doing here?" Nina asked.

"Sorry, my lady," Thea said as she curtsied. "I—There's a plot by the king's brother to stop your son from getting the throne."

Nina leaned back into her overstuffed pillow chair in the center of the room. "Galin told me about your ideas."

Thea swallowed and gave a quick glance at the two ladies sitting on either side of the queen. "My lady, that means he wants to kill the king, you, and your son."

Nina rolled her eyes. "Do you know how many plots I've been warned about over the years?"

"What does it hurt to listen?" asked the younger noblewoman on Nina's left. "Besides, if it's not real, it could be a good story."

"Clara, I don't know."

"Nina," said the other noblewoman, "she's trying to do her duty. What harm is there in letting her speak? This one may actually be true."

Nina motioned a handmaiden to bring her some tea. "Thea, these two noblewomen who came to your defense are Clara Gilford and Bonnie Lyons. They're both married to dukes in the kingdom. Let's hear how I'm in danger this time."

Thea sighed. "Kade and Beldroth had a meeting at the Rusted Feathers with some Darkstriders."

"Darkstriders?"

"Yes, Beldroth cast a spell to protect the meeting from being overheard."

Nina's eyes grew more intense. "Yes, magic could do that."

"Also, if you were inside the bubble you could see through the Dark Elf illusions. Apparently, the Dark Elves have an innate ability to conceal themselves as any other sentient creature."

Nina blinked. "How's this possible? Surely, the Vulwin Elves would have told us."

"My lady, I honestly can't answer that. I only know what the witness told me."

"Okay, continue." Nina took a sip of her tea.

"After the veil was lifted, there were several Dark Elves among the patrons, and Beldroth was one of them. The witness couldn't believe it—"

"They could be among us _here_." Nina set her tea down.

Thea nodded. "Yes, my lady. I believe so."

"Go on."

"Two Dark Elves sat down with them. My witness overheard them negotiating the spoils after Kade takes the throne. One claimed to be a Feral Orc regiment commander and the other said he spoke for the Darkstriders."

"Some kind of ambassador?" Nina asked.

Thea nodded. "That would be a good guess, my lady, but there's no way to be sure."

Nina took another sip of tea.

"After they discussed that they would kill your family, my witness got scared and ran out."

"How are they going to do it?"

"My lady—"

"You never said what their plan was to kill my family. What's their plan?"

"Um—I—I . . ."

Nina frowned. "Everyone get out. I need to speak to this knight alone."

Thea stayed silent until the door slammed shut. "My lady—"

"Now I know why Galin didn't believe you."

"But—"

"Where's your evidence? You accuse the king's brother of treason and have *nothing*? If he didn't think of you like a sister, you'd already be swinging from the gallows."

"My lady—"

"What do you want me to do? Since we've been married, even before Galin's father died, we've received hundreds of death threats and warnings. None of them has *ever* happened. I—"

Thea shook her head. "I swore to protect your family and I am performing that duty now. What harm would it do to take some precautions? Yes, I know that my previous warnings of Kade's plots didn't turn out to be true. But, this one is different."

"Why?"

"Because someone both you and I trust witnessed it."

"Who?"

"Sally."

Nina blinked. "My Sally?"

Thea nodded.

"Why didn't she tell me?"

"She's afraid of being sent to the gallows, my lady."

Putting her tea down on the small table near the window, Nina walked over to the bird's nest. "Do you know why I haven't had this removed?"

What? Where did that come from? Thea frowned. "My lady—"

"Do you?"

"No."

"Their singing reminds me that all the world is not dark like the hearts of men." Nina sat back down in her fluffy chair. "I'm sure my husband is doing the right thing, but there is no harm in taking some *discreet* precautions."

"I—"

Nina held up her hand, silencing Thea. "If that plot comes to pass, that means the king will already be dead. The next most important thing would be to get my son out of the castle."

"How?"

"Both the king's and queen's antechambers have a means to get outside the castle walls, and the king doesn't know where and how the door works in here. It was done that way intentionally."

"Why?"

"In case of a coup, the heir must be saved to one day take back the throne from the usurper. Those were the words of Galin's father. Only myself and my handmaidens know how to access this tunnel," Nina said.

"My lady, before we talk about our defeat, let's stop it from happening in the first place."

Nina nodded. "We have to keep Galin safe from himself." Her eyes narrowed. "What if you're wrong?"

"Nothing, and everyone is safe. I will retire my duties as a knight and take my post managing my new lands."

"Thank you, Thea. You may go."

Thea curtsied. "Thank you for listening, my lady." She turned and headed towards the door. *How does she save the king from himself?*

CHAPTER 9

Attack!

THEA LEANED OVER THE BATTLEMENT ABOVE STAERDALE Castle's main gate. Her fingers swirled the tiny loose stones on top of the wall. Ever since the queen took her seriously, Thea was duty bound to stay and guard the castle. Most of the knights didn't believe her story. Why should they? If the situation were reversed, would she?

"Thea, are you still here?" a male voice said.

She turned and saw Brock carrying two steaming mugs with a sword dangling from his side. "Brock, why are you wearing a sword?"

"Sally convinced the queen to add me to her personal security guards while I am not at the blacksmith shop." He handed her a cup of coffee.

Thea grinned. "You mean she tricked the queen to spend more time with you."

Brock nodded. "Aye. Sally has been at the castle every

night for the past week, ever since you told the queen about Kade's plot."

"I hope I did the right thing," Thea said, turning back towards the world beyond the walls. "Haven't seen anything yet, and I'm beginning to wonder if I will."

"Sally overheard the king and queen fighting about Kade."

"On whether or not he's a traitor?"

"No, on what to do about it. Seems like there have been some reports backing up the warning you gave the king."

"What reports? Why haven't they told me?"

Brock shook his head. "No idea. Heck, I'm not even sure it's real."

"It doesn't matter anyway." Thea took a sip of her coffee. "I—"

"Look," Brock said, pointing far off in the distance.

"What?" Thea strained her eyes to see the faint flickering light. "Nightmare Falls?"

Brock nodded. "Could be."

If it were during the day, they would have never seen the fire far off in the distance, but they might be able to see the enemy soldiers. No screams; why no screams? Every time a village is attacked, there is always screaming. True, Nightfall Meadows is ten miles away, but surely screaming, fleeing peasants would run towards the castle. Unless—unless they were taken quickly. She glanced over at the warning bell hanging from the battlement to her left. Should she ring it now? What if she was wrong?

"Thea," Brock said, interrupting her thoughts. "We've got to tell someone."

"Not yet. We don't know if it's an out-of-control fire or an attack."

A bead of sweat rolled down Brock's cheek. "What do we do now?"

"Keep watching." Her eyes scanned every shadow, anticipating the worst. The darkness beyond the castle torches hid the truth from her eyes. Thea closed her eyes in a vain attempt to hear *something*. No sound or movement; there was nothing at all. "Brock, just in case, go below and let the sergeant-of-the-guard know what we saw and come right back up here."

"Got it." Brock rushed down the stone steps.

If Kade was attacking, the army might not come down to Staerdale Castle itself. At least, not at first. How would she attack the castle? Perhaps seize Port Eldham, Nightfall Meadows, and surround the castle outside of arrow and ballista range. Siege the castle for the next few months, starving them out. Yes, that's how she'd do it; but Kade was never that patient.

"A rider is coming from the north!" a guard on the northern wall called out.

Thea twisted her head left. Her eyes pierced the dark shroud at the end of the torchlight. A knight, one of Galin's knights, was slumped over on his horse as it galloped towards the gate. Her eyes widened as the arrow in his back glistened in the torchlight. "Open the gate!"

She rushed down the stone steps and bolted towards the gate. Thea motioned Brock to join her and he ran.

"Thea, what is it?" Brock said.

"Daniel, Sir Daniel."

The massive gate partially opened and closed immediately after the knight rode through.

Thea grabbed the reins, stopping the horse. "Daniel, can you hear me?"

Brock's massive arms pulled the wounded knight from his horse, laying him down next to a small pile of hay. "He's hurt bad."

"I know."

Daniel's blue eyes cracked open. "Where—where am I?"

"Your horse brought you back to Staerdale Castle," Brock said.

"I'm not going to make it, am I?"

Thea shook her head. "Sure you will. I—"

"You're a terrible liar. I'll see you in the next life." Daniel closed his eyes as if willing for a faster death.

"No, Daniel you have to tell us first. What happened?" Thea demanded.

"Vulwin Elves were leading the Feral Orcs in the attack."

"They're our allies!" Brock said.

"That's why they took us by surprise," Daniel said. "Thea, they're heading toward Port Eldham."

"Our only chance is—" Thea jumped up. "Brock, tell the sergeant-of-the-guard to tend to Daniel."

"Then what?"

"Go to Sally and protect the baby."

"Why? If they're going to siege the castle, we've got a lot of time."

"No, Kade's not that patient." Thea glared at Brock. "Now do what you're told, *blacksmith*."

Brock bolted inside the castle.

Time to tell the king, Thea thought. She sprinted towards the castle entrance.

I have to protect the king. Thea stormed down the corridor towards the Great Hall. Murmurs from the servants in the corridors couldn't pull her eyes away from the elaborate doors. Thea's eyes narrowed and her pace increased as she got closer to the Great Hall. As she approached, the two guards opened the double doors.

"Sire," Thea said as she stepped into the Great Hall.

"Thea, what's going on?" Galin asked.

Brock stood behind the Queen, next to Sally.

"Brock, I told you to guard the prince," Thea said.

Galin turned around. "Do what she says, both of you."

"Yes, sire," Brock said as he and Sally rushed out the door behind the thrones.

"Well?" Galin asked.

"Nightfall Meadows has been attacked by what appears to be Vulwin Elves. They're heading for Port Eldham," Thea said.

"Faeler wouldn't betray us. He made peace with us over a century ago."

Thea swallowed. "I believe it is the Dark Elves pretending to be Vulwin Elves. Sire, do you remember what I told you about their ability to look like any humanoid life?"

"I do. That would make more sense. But—we can't be sure, either."

"Sire!" Robert yelled as he ran into the Great Hall.

"What is it, Robert?"

"We sent some scouts to confirm Daniel's report about the Darkstriders movements."

Galin cocked one eye. "And?"

"They're almost to Port Eldham now. If they take it—"

Galin collapsed into his throne. "We may never get them out. I've got to stop them."

Nina reached over, grabbing Galin's hand. "Send your most trusted knights to lead the fight, but I don't want you to go."

His eyes dropped down as he gazed through Nina's eyes into her soul. "I have to."

"What about our son? It seems that Thea was right, at least in part. What if we haven't seen their whole army yet?" Nina asked.

"Any word on Kade?"

"No, sire," Thea said. "But, Queen Nina is right. If you are killed in battle, Kade will assume the throne until your son is old enough—"

"He would kill both Nina and my son," Galin finished.

Robert stepped forward. "Sire, for the sake of the kingdom, please stay here."

"Would Kade be patient enough to siege the castle? Would he? Would I?" Galin closed his eyes as if playing out different scenarios in his mind.

"Sire?" Robert asked.

Galin's eyes snapped open. "Robert, send for my war council and ready the knights. Once you're done, join Thea on the walls with some archers and pikemen."

"I'm not going?" Thea asked.

"No, I want you to command the defense of Staerdale Castle. If these are Dark Elves disguised as Vulwin Elves, they have to finish this before word gets back to King Faeler—"

"Which means they're attacking tonight," Thea finished.

"Yes, but they need the port first to prevent reinforcements from coming to our aid. Hopefully, my brother is not with them."

"Sire, I'll see to the castle's defenses," Thea said.

Galin gripped Nina's hand. "We'll be here."

"Yes, sire." Thea curtsied and bolted out the door.

~

Sweat rolled down Thea's back underneath her breastplate. Her fingers tapped on the battlement above the gate like a drum. After everything was ready to defend the castle against Kade's forces, she sat on the wall and waited. Staerdale Castle had the widest moat and its walls had never been breached in over one hundred fifty years. The odds were definitely on her side.

Port Eldham was too far to see how the battle was going, not that it would do much good anyway. All Thea could do was wait. She swallowed some water from her water skin.

"Didn't your shift end over an hour ago?" Robert said, walking up behind her.

"I am in charge, you know," Thea replied.

Robert leaned on the battlement. "I know, but you still have to rest."

"I can rest when it's over."

"The battle at Port Eldham could take days. You're better off getting some sleep now so you can fight harder when they actually attack."

Mental fog rolled in as she yawned. "I guess—" Thea caught something in the corner of her eye. A glow, a very faint glow on Robert's hand. "Why is your ring glowing?"

"What?" Robert snatched up his hand, gazing at his family's signet ring. "What are you talking about?"

Thea blinked as her exhaustion receded. "I guess it was nothing."

"Okay, no problem. Since this is *my* shift, I'll be checking the watchtowers."

"Sure." Thea's eyes continued scanning the horizon, vainly attempting to pierce the darkness. The sweat rolling down her back chilled her spine. The battlement became cold to the touch. Her breath became steam as it escaped from her mouth. "Robert—"

"I—I know," Robert replied as he ran to her side. "It's started."

Thea turned her head back towards the group of infantrymen beneath her on the ground. "Get down!"

High above the castle, twenty red lights appeared. Just for a second, they hung in space like a picture on the wall, and then they fell. Each fiery object picked up speed as it raced towards the ground. Each light split in two, making twenty into forty. Forty became eighty. Eighty become one hundred sixty fiery projectiles.

Thea pulled Robert close against the battlement. "It's Beldroth."

"I know."

When the first projectile hit the ground it broke apart, sending fiery shrapnel into the flesh of anyone within a few yards and set ablaze the hay on the ground. Then came the next one, followed by the succession of fiery deaths to those not under cover within the castle walls.

Thea clasped her hands over her ears, trying to keep the screams of people being burnt alive out of her mind.

Robert held onto Thea tightly. "We just need to hang on until they get closer."

Thea nodded. She looked up, only to see another wave being rained down upon them. "I hope we last that long." She peeked over the battlement.

A Vulwin Elf soldier broke through the veil of darkness, followed by another, and another.

"I guess we don't have long to wait," Thea said. "It's them."

"What?" Robert looked over the battlement. "Vulwin Elves, it's true!"

"Dark Elves can look like any other humanoid, remember that."

"But that takes concentration. How can you fight and still keep your form?"

Thea blinked. "How do you know that?"

Robert shrugged. "Everything about magic takes concentration, and the mage usually can't do anything else. I've been around Beldroth a lot too, you know."

The deafening sound of another fiery wave of projectiles detonating on the ground caused Thea to cower against the battlement. After a moment, she stood up. "Kade's forces are attacking now!" Thea shouted. "Get to your posts!"

Brock ran up to the wall just below Thea. "How many?"

Thea looked back at the enemy line forming in front of

the castle. "Can't tell yet." She turned back towards Brock. "Tell the king, and then get to Sally and protect that baby at all costs. If Kade gets in, we have to save the prince."

Robert grabbed Thea's shoulder. "He won't."

"I hope you're right," Thea said as she watched Brock run into the castle. "Archers on the walls!"

Robert ran past Thea towards the watchtower. He directed the archers to their positions as they raced up the stairs.

Thea concentrated on the advancing threat. Her stomach tightened as a battering ram emerged from behind the line of Vulwin Elves. Is that how they planned to get inside the castle walls? Breaching castle walls was always a costly attack, but why start with that? Why not start with a trebuchet or a catapult to wear down the defenses? Something didn't seem right. Maybe—

"They're in position," Robert said.

"I don't suppose we have a pyromancer or a war mage here?"

"Sorry, they went to Port Eldham with the—"

Thea blinked. "It was a diversion. The whole attack."

"This isn't," Robert said, pointing at the line of Vulwin Elves. "Why did they stop?"

Why did they stop? Thea thought. The knights and infantryman stood to one side as if waiting for something. "Ready the archers!"

As Robert waved a red flag, the archers on the wall notched an arrow and steadfast, waiting for the command.

Hooded, gray-cloaked figures emerged without swords or bows or visible weapons of any kind. Thea's eyes focused on their hands. They were moving their hands like Beldroth did at— "Aim for the mages!" Thea yelled. "Loose the arrows before they finish casting their spell."

The archers loosed their arrows across the field. As they

plunged to the earth, several elven knights, infantryman, and mages fell to the ground in agony.

Elven screams brought a smile to Thea's face. But, it was short-lived. The mages were still casting their spell. "Again!"

Another mass of arrows flew across the sky, taking down even more elves, but the mages didn't stop.

"I don't like this," Robert said.

A chill ran down Thea's spine. Her armor became cold to the touch. A loud crackling sound came from down below. A small patch of ice appeared in the moat and spread like a virus. "They're freezing the moat!"

"Aye."

"Watch for the siege ladders. They're going to try to breach the walls!" Thea yelled.

The mages moved forward, still moving their hands as if casting another spell. Elven knights and infantrymen moved slowly, keeping pace with the mages.

They needed to concentrate on those trying to climb over the walls, but the elves had no ladders. "They're not going over the walls or using the battering ram on the gate," Thea said. "They're—loose another volley! Kill the mages, quickly! Loose at will!"

Robert grabbed Thea's shoulder. "Even Beldroth can't do that."

"Maybe she was always on the other side."

Another mass of arrows flew across the sky. A woman wearing a red hooded robe ran out in front of the formation.

"That's Beldroth," Thea said. "She's casting something."

The arrows plunged towards the earth.

Beldroth moved her hands left and right.

The arrows accelerated towards their targets.

In a seemingly triumphant moment, Beldroth raised both of her hands towards the sky.

Thea's mouth dropped as the arrows incinerated in mid-air; not one hit the ground.

"Save the arrows," Robert muttered.

A familiar chill came over Thea. She looked up. Her heart sank as she saw more fiery projectiles appear above them. "Take cover!" Thea and Robert dove behind the wall and hugged the battlement for protection.

Screams rang in Thea's ears as the fiery projectiles crashed into the ground. She got up on one knee to look over the battlement. The mages were casting something, but this time the elven knights and infantrymen were charging.

The wall shook.

Thea was knocked down but quickly got back up. More screams made her turn towards the gate. Rubble was in the courtyard. The screeching of bending metal reached her ears. "They've breached the gate."

The distorted heavy iron gate crashed to the ground, crushing a vendor's cart.

Robert nodded. "Here they come."

The mass of Vulwin Elves flowed through the breach like a river, killing everything in their path.

"We have to get to the king," Thea said.

"After you."

Thea drew her sword and jumped down on the elf infantryman below her. He crashed to the ground, unable to raise his weapon. She slammed her sword into his back, taking his life. She should have run, but didn't. Something was happening to the elf. His skin turned into a dark blue and his ears grew more defined. "He's a Dark Elf."

"Doesn't matter," Robert said. "Let's go."

The two hundred yards from the castle walls to the castle entrance seemed more like two hundred miles.

"Follow me," Thea said.

Three elves charged at Thea. She parried away one,

slashed another's stomach, spilling out his insides, and pierced another's heart, all in one fluid motion. They took a few more steps towards the castle. Robert and Thea fought back-to-back, slashing, thrusting, and spilling elven blood on the ground.

Thea no longer felt anything except her drive to get to the king. Nothing else mattered. It was almost like her mind turned off and her body took over. Five, six, seven, eight, and more elves fell by her hand.

"Look over by the castle portcullis!" Robert said.

Humans from within the castle were pushing back against the onslaught, calling the survivors to join them.

"They won't hold for long," Thea replied.

"Come on." Robert pushed his way through the fighting crowd.

As they moved towards the tiny bubble of hope, Thea slashed more elves with nearly every step. "Almost there." Thea's world came crashing down as Robert's scream pierced her eardrums. Her sword followed her head towards Robert's assailant. With all her strength, she thrust her sword into the elf's eye, piercing the back of his skull. After he had hit the ground, Thea put her boot on his throat as she yanked her sword from his skull. "Robert!" She knelt down to pull him out of danger.

"Watch out!" Robert yelled as he flung a throwing knife right past Thea's head and into the elf charging at her.

"I'll get you out of here."

"No, get to the king. Save the kingdom!" Robert struggled to get up. "Hurry, before they kill you, too."

Thea saw the young knight charge into a crowd of elves, diverting them away from her and the castle gate. She bolted past the last few elves and the human perimeter. The clanging of swords and axes resumed with more human screams than elf. Instead of staying to fight, she ran down the corridor. Was she doing the right thing? She turned. The war cries charging at her weren't human. *They broke through,* she thought. If she went straight to the king, they'd find him that much easier. She had to lose them in the castle's maze of corridors first. Thea sprinted down the corridor to the right, just past the kitchen.

CHAPTER 10

Usurper

"Sire, look out!" a Vulwin Elf yelled as he thrust his sword into a knight's gullet.

Kade crashed down onto the stone floor just inside the castle, quickly popping back up to face his next adversary. Clanging of swords and axes rang through his ears. Screams from Galin's falling knights brought a half-smile to his face. Sure, he knew all of them, was even friends with some, but the throne was far more important. "Thank you."

Beldroth helped Kade to his feet. "The perimeter outside the castle is secured and we have a good foothold inside."

I'm really going to be king, Kade thought. "How about the tunnel exits beyond the walls?"

Her human form melted into her natural Dark Elf self. Beldroth pulled from her red robes a crystal sphere with swirling clouds in the center. She closed her eyes and held the crystal ball in her hands. "Sama an ninag to nikin. Sama an ninag to nikin."

Clouds within the crystal ball began to swirl faster and faster.

I hate it when she does that, Kade thought.

"Sama an ninag to nikin."

They swirled faster and faster.

"Sama an ninag to nikin!"

Kade covered his eyes as a bright-white light flashed from within the crystal. He swallowed as her malevolent eyes slowly opened. Her hands were empty, as if the crystal ball was used up in the spell. "Well?"

"I've cast a Clairvoyant Eye near the exits you showed us. They haven't come through yet, but I'll know if they do," Beldroth said.

"Why haven't you done this for me before?"

The corners of her mouth curled. "I have to be in my natural form to cast this spell."

"Can you find Galin with that?"

Beldroth shook her head. "No, I can only cast that spell once per day. Besides, I don't have another crystal ball."

The Vulwin Elf who commanded Kade's forces moved down the corridor towards him. "Are we safe to change?"

Beldroth nodded. "Yes, Ryul."

Ryul's skin turned a dark blue. His flowing brown hair disappeared underneath his scalp. "What about the humans? Will—"

"They'll know who their real allies are soon enough," Kade said. "We have to find the king before he escapes."

"I'll take some men and find them," Ryul said.

"Stick to the outer rooms, along the perimeter. I'll keep to the inner chambers. If you find him, send word *before* you kill him."

"Aye." Ryul grabbed twelve Dark Elf knights, motioning them to follow.

"Where to?" Beldroth asked.

Kade smiled. "Let's start with the Great Hall."

Kade wore his blood-soaked chest plate like a badge of honor. With Beldroth on his right and ten Dark Elf Knights in tow, Kade marched down the long corridor towards the Great Hall. He couldn't see the doors yet, only a few more turns to go.

"Traitor!" Three soldiers charged at Kade.

He sidestepped the lead soldier's lunge. Kade slammed the hilt of his bastard sword into the soldier's head. As the unconscious man fell, Kade effectively swung his sword at his opponent and his head rolled back towards his companions.

The soldier on the left wildly swung his sword at Kade.

Kade slammed himself against the wall, avoiding the blow.

Realizing his mistake, the soldier stepped back.

Seeing the fear in his enemy's eyes, Kade charged him.

The soldier raised his sword in defense.

Kade easily knocked it away. The soldier's eyes opened wide as Kade slammed his sword into the man chest.

Beldroth murmured a few words. Her hands were flexed, with her fingers pointed at the soldier on the right. Fire appeared in front of her palms. Faster than an arrow, it flew across the corridor, right through the soldier's chest. Upon impact, he exploded into flames. The dead man fell to the floor.

"Almost there," Kade said as he led them around the corner.

A few minutes and fourteen soldiers later, they were at the last corner before the Great Hall. "I think Galin's in there.

There are too many soldiers guarding it to mean anything else."

Beldroth nodded. "He's bound to have a lot inside as well."

"Aye," Kade replied. "We need to surprise him. But as soon as we attack the guards at the door, we lose that advantage."

"I agree. As soon as they hear a fight outside the door, they'll just get the king out."

Kade peeked around the corner. "I see six guards outside the Great Hall. We can't take them down fast enough."

Beldroth stood up. "When I'm not in my illusionary form, my magic is at full strength."

"What are you doing?"

"Showing you my true powers. After I blow the doors in, charge inside and take out the guards."

"What?" Kade grabbed her robes. "Don't—"

Beldroth yanked her robes from his grasp. "Be ready." She moved to the corner, just far enough where she could see the door. Pulling a small platinum ball from a pouch within her robes, Beldroth mumbled a barely audible phrase. She placed the small, rare metal ball in the palm of her left hand.

"Stein nim tsak srot."

A light pulsed from within the ball.

"Stein nim tsak srot."

The valuable metal ball vanished from her hand. The stone corridor walls cracked as if being pushed aside by some invisible force. The force stood still for a moment.

Beldroth's eyes focused on the Great Hall's elaborate double doors, ignoring the guards in front of it. "Stein nim tsak srot."

As if following Beldroth's gaze, the force cracking both sides of the corridor accelerated towards the double doors.

Realizing their fate, the guards turned and pounded on the doors.

The force flattened all six guards as it slammed into the heavy oak double doors.

"Stein nim tsak srot."

The guard's remains fell to the floor as if the force pulled back from the door.

"Stein nim tsak srot!"

In a split-second, the bodies were picked up and thrown into the Great Hall as the doors imploded.

"Follow me!" Kade yelled as he charged through the rubble.

Sword drawn, Kade emerged from the smoke into the Great Hall. The smell of charred wood pierced his nostrils. His right foot slipped on the slick floor. Kade looked down to see that he was standing in a pool of blood. Bloody pieces of armor were thrown about, with the soldiers still inside them.

Beldroth clung to his side, and the ten Dark Elf knights split up to cover both sides of the Great Hall.

Kade stepped forward, studying every body, trying to determine who was still alive. Then he saw them, the couple that stood in his way. Galin and Nina were thrown to the floor in front of their thrones amongst their unconscious advisers. "What happened?"

"When the door broke apart, the concussion from the blast stunned everyone behind it for fifty yards," Beldroth replied. "They'll come to in a minute."

As if on cue, Galin and Nina began to stir.

Kade motioned to the Dark Elf knights. "Quickly, secure them."

Two knights yanked Galin and Nina to their feet, dragging them in front of Kade.

"What about the others?" Beldroth asked, pointing at the advisers.

"Kill them. They'll just be a problem later if we don't," Kade replied.

The remaining eight knights moved from body to body, decapitating their victims.

Galin's groggy eyes cracked open. "Kade, stop this."

Nina opened her eyes. Staring directly at Beldroth's true form, she screamed.

"Easy, Nina," Galin said. He turned back towards Kade. "Please, we're family, Kade. Don't do this."

Kade stared at his brother, unable to speak.

Beldroth rubbed her ring and it began to glow. Her mouth was moving, but no words could be heard.

Galin stared at Beldroth. "What are—?"

"Where's my nephew, brother?" Kade asked.

"*She* did it. Kade, Beldroth is controlling you. You can resist, you must resist. Please, resist that evil thing!"

"I—" Kade stared at Beldroth. "I—"

Beldroth rubbed her ring again.

"I'll kill Nina if you don't tell me," Kade said as he raised his sword.

"Galin, don't tell him," Nina begged. "They'll kill him!"

Sweat poured down Galin's face. "I can't."

"Wrong answer." Kade slammed his sword into Nina's chest, piercing her heart.

Galin's eyes widened as he watched his queen's lifeless body fall to the ground. "I hate you."

Kade kicked Galin's right knee, breaking it in two.

Collapsing in pain, Galin reached for his beloved. "Nina," he sobbed. "I'm so sorry."

Taking some pleasure from Galin's torment, Kade stepped on his broken knee. The more pressure he put on it, the louder Galin screamed, and the bigger his smile got.

"Kade, she's controlling you. For the love of the gods, please stop!" Galin said.

"Last chance," Kade said.

Galin bit his lip. "Never." He looked over to see Beldroth's ring was glowing even brighter.

"Suit yourself." Kade thrust his sword into Galin's stomach.

Galin's eyes closed as he rolled over.

Kade directed his attention towards the ten knights. "I want you to search the rooms behind the Great Hall for the baby."

"Yes, sir," said one of the knights. The Dark Elf knights disappeared into the door behind the thrones.

"He's not dead," Beldroth said.

Kade smiled. "Brother, let's try this again."

With her sword drawn, Thea entered the kitchen. No smells of fresh bread or recently cooked meat or even giggles from the servant wenches; there was nothing. A fire still blazed in the hearth across the long rectangular room on the far side of the solid oak island. A large block filled with knives sat on the end of the island's countertop. Just because she didn't hear anything, didn't mean she was alone. Placing her feet softly on the ground, Thea moved across the room, examining under every table and bench that lined the walls. Pausing, she listened. With Robert gone and Brock protecting the baby, she was alone in the war against the Darkstriders.

Metal crashed to the floor.

Maybe a fork? Thea thought. Her heart thumped faster and faster. Her ears became filled with her own heartbeat. *Come on, where are you? Utensils don't just jump off the counter.* She moved close to the end of the counter and stopped. Peering over the countertop, Thea grabbed the chef's knife from the knife block. The springs in her feet were poised and her sword arm was itching to strike with each step around the island. Between the island and the counter along the wall, someone could be hiding under the island. Was she just being paranoid? True, sometimes things just fall down, especially at the wrong times.

She took another step.

As soon as I clear the island, I'm just going to thrust my sword under the counter, Thea thought.

Another step.

Stab so blindly? That's not me. What if it's a child underneath?

Another step.

What if it's not? Could the Dark Elf be baiting me to second guess myself?

Another step.

No more time now. May the gods help me.

In a single motion, Thea dropped in front of the island with her legs split and threw the chef's knife into the darkness. With both hands, she swung her sword under the island, hitting nothing but wood.

Thea sighed. *Nothing. Nothing but my nerves.*

"R zersh," a voice in the hall said.

What to do? She was too far from the door for an ambush. Thea had no bow to hit them across the knife block. She pulled the knife block underneath the island with her. In those close quarters, her sword would be almost useless, but not the knives.

"Noi ro, alsh r lm f r him."

Whoever is saying that is obviously the leader of—how many? What language is that? Dark Elf? Thea carefully put her sword down and grasped two knives. She closed her eyes, listening only. The soft steps of two elves made themselves known, each going around opposite sides of the island. The one on the other side of the island wouldn't see her until he came completely around it, but the other could see her much sooner.

The footsteps behind her sounded closer.

They're not as careful as I was earlier. Overconfident? Wouldn't I be if it were three against one?

The elf moving between the island and the wall came closer to her hidden position.

Thea peered through the darkness. A muscular, dark-blue-skinned elf with razor-like tipped ears and sword in hand was scanning everywhere for his prey.

If he sees me first, I'm dead. If I strike too soon, I'm still dead.

Both elves slowly moved in closer.

My only chance is to get them both at once. Thea looked for at least one target. If she hit the elf on this side of the island, the other would be thrown off balance, right?

"You can't hide, Thea," the voice said.

Thea? They know me. That means— almost Thea threw the chef's knife at the elf on her side of the island, knocking him down, dead. She rolled from underneath the island to around the corner, staring up at her opponent. With a powerful upward thrust, she stabbed the elf on the inside of a thigh, severing his main artery.

Clanging feet from the armored elf rushing towards her rang through her ears.

Thea recoiled back underneath the island, knocking over the knife block. She grabbed a meat cleaver in her right hand and her sword in her left.

Clang. Clang.

Which way is he coming from? Thea closed her eyes for a millisecond.

Clang. Clang.

Only one shot at this. Spinning around, she flung herself against the wall. Thea smiled at the surprised elf. The cleaver sailed through the air like a bullet, embedding itself into his stomach.

The shear force knocked the elf back, disarming him as he hit the ground.

Thea leaped over the island, on top of her enemy, and raised her sword to finish him off.

"You're too late," he said.

What did he mean? Is the king dead? The queen? The prince? Am I doing this in vain? Thea stopped her sword from impaling his chest.

"Did you hear that explosion in the halls?" he asked.

"Yes," Thea replied.

A triumphant smile crawled across the elf's face. "That's my lady Beldroth killing your king and his family."

"You won't live to see the spoils of your war," Thea said as she slammed her sword through his heart. She yanked the sword from his lifeless body. Blood poured out of the new orifice. "Now for the king," Thea said as she ran out of the kitchen.

Thea found little resistance using the servant corridors leading to the Great Hall. The corridor walls leading towards the doorway were cracked, as if some force pushed against them.

"I want you to search the rooms behind the Great Hall for the baby," a voice said.

Was that Kade? Thea asked herself.

"Yes, sir," another said.

Thea peered around the door to see ten Dark Elf knights running through the small door behind the thrones. There was just Kade and Beldroth left, no security at all. Since Beldroth was an illusion the whole time, did she see all of her powers? Probably not.

"He's not dead," Beldroth said.

Who's that on the floor next to the king? Thea thought. *It's—Queen Nina!*

Kade stood over the king and smiled. "Brother, let's try this again."

Thea looked down at a soldier's crushed corpse. *An ax. I've got to go now!* She grabbed the ax with her left hand and her sword was in her right.

Kade raised his sword over his brother. "Just so you know, our father didn't die of natural causes."

Galin's eyes flashed over at Thea and stared directly into Kade's eyes. "Did you . . . ?"

"Yes." Kade thrust his sword towards Galin.

Thea threw the ax at Kade.

Sensing danger, Kade turned his head. The ax nicked his hand, causing him to drop the sword.

Fear overtook Beldroth's eyes. She touched Kade's wounded arm. "Treherkis Lit. Treherkis Lit."

Thea charged at Beldroth with her sword out in front.

"Treherkis Lit!"

The bastard sword skewered Beldroth. Thea glanced over at Kade.

A light came over Kade, blinding everyone around him.

Thea blinked, and he was gone. Her face reddened as she twisted the sword inside Beldroth. "Where is he?"

Blood spewed out of Beldroth's mouth. "Safe from you." She reached for her ring while silently moving her lips.

"No, you don't." Thea pulled her sword from Beldroth's gullet and raised it above her victim. Her eyes focused on the ring hand. With one hard slash, Thea sliced off Beldroth's hand, making the magic ring useless.

Recoiling in pain, Beldroth clutched her severed limb.

"Where is he?"

Beldroth only smiled. "Sa—saf—safe from—" She took her last breath, then she was gone.

"Thea—" a voice behind her gasped.

"Sire." Thea spun around towards Galin. "I must get you to a healer."

Galin shook his head. "No, it's too late for me. This wound is fatal."

She looked down at the dark blood spilling from his abdomen. "I see."

He grasped her arm. "My son, save—you've got to save my son, please, Thea."

"Where are they? I sent—"

"They're in the king's antechamber. Kade and I used to play in the secret passages throughout the castle all the time, so he knows most of them, but not these."

"Why not?"

"The royal escape passages were not told to us until Nina and I actually took the throne. You've—"

"Yes?"

"Got to get them out. Save my son. Fulfill your vow to me, please. I—I—" Galin's eyes went dark as he gasped his last breath.

Thea closed his eyes. "I won't fail you." She bolted through the small door behind the thrones.

CHAPTER 11

The Prince

THE CLANGING OF SWORDS AND SCREAMS FROM SKEWERED soldiers echoed through the corridors. Holding her sword at the ready, Thea quietly and swiftly moved down the hall.

Almost there, Thea thought.

Her eyes bore down on the intersection ahead. Slowing down, Thea's steps were as quiet as a feather hitting the ground. With her back pressed against the wall and watching the opening on the opposite side, Thea took another step.

Come on, you bastards!

Metal striking metal became louder.

Thea's ears perked up. *Where are you?*

The clanging became faster, as if another sword joined the melee.

A human scream pierced her soul. *It's—it's behind me!* Raising her sword, Thea leaped around the corner.

99

Two Dark Elves just smiled at her. One pulled his sword out of the dead soldier's stomach. The other raised her sword and charged.

Thea braced. Her eyes bounced from the female elf to the male elf and back.

With his sword at the ready, the second Dark Elf charged in.

The female elf poised her sword, ready to thrust into Thea's chest.

"May the gods help me," Thea said. In one fluid motion, she dropped to the floor with her legs split.

Unable to stop their forward momentum, the two elves looked down.

Letting out a battle cry, Thea swung her bastard sword at the two elves. The female elf lost her foot as Thea's sword passed right through the elf's leg, just above the ankle.

The second elf attempted to jump back, but he merely stumbled.

Thea slashed his calf as he crashed to the ground. She jumped to her feet. They're not taking prisoners, why should she? Thea raised her sword above her head. The shiny blade sailed through the air until it severed the male Dark Elf's head from his body.

"Please, please don't," cried the female Dark Elf. "I'll give you anything you want. Please, spare me!"

Thea grinned at the elf. "I already have everything I want." She slammed her sword into the elf's chest. Thea stared into her eyes until her life was gone.

A young woman's scream bellowed down the hall.

"Sally!" Thea ran around the last corner towards the king's Antechamber.

Clanging swords and Sally's desperate screams flowed through the wooden door, piercing Thea's soul. She bit her lip. She kicked the door in, knocking it off its hinges.

As the door crashed to the ground, three Dark Elves wrenched their heads towards Thea.

Seeing an opportunity, Brock thrust his sword into his opponent's chest.

Only for a second, she looked over at Sally with the baby in her arms. They had no obvious injuries. Thea charged into the room, getting between Sally and the elves.

One elf attacked Brock while the other lunged at Thea.

Brock parried then sidestepped.

Thea blocked the thrust.

The elf recoiled.

She faked a slash towards his head.

Her opponent moved to block.

Thea circled her blade underneath his sword and slashed his stomach open.

Surprised, the elf grasped his innards as he collapsed to the ground.

Brock parried another blow. Seeing Thea's opponent drop down, Brock sidestepped again.

The Dark Elf raised his sword.

Seeing the danger, Brock raised his blade to block the onslaught.

The Dark Elf's sword crashed into Brock's blade.

Brock dropped his sword. He collapsed to the ground in a vain attempt to avoid the elf's blade.

Sally screamed.

The baby cried.

The elf raised his sword to pierce Brock's heart.

Thea swung her sword, knocking his head from his body.

As the headless elf crashed to the ground, Sally ran over to Brock. "Are you all right?"

Brock nodded. "Thank you," he said to Thea.

Thea extended her hand. "You'd have done the same for me." She moved closer to the baby in Sally's arms. For the first time, she looked directly into his blue eyes. "He's so —helpless."

Brock pulled the two women to the side, away from the open doorway. "We've got to get the prince out."

Thea nodded. "Sally, the king said you knew a secret way out, one that even Kade doesn't know."

"Yes, I do. Unlike the other escape tunnels, this one comes out on the southern end of the castle walls," Sally said.

"How do we get to it?"

"The queen's antechamber. It's—"

Thea clamped her hand over Sally's mouth. "Keep it to yourself until we get there, in case one of us doesn't make it."

Sally nodded. "Okay."

"Let's go." Thea led the small group out of the room.

With her sword at the ready, Thea moved towards the queen's antechamber. Her eyes peered ahead at the intersection, straining to detect danger. Thea's steps became lighter the closer she got to the intersection. Hugging the wall, she looked around the corner. "Clear."

"Wait," Brock said. "Do you hear that?"

Thea closed her eyes. No sounds of clashing swords or screams from slain soldiers and elves; there was . . . *nothing*. "Did the fight move elsewhere?"

"Or we lost."

Sally tugged Thea's arm. "We've got to hurry."

"What's the fastest way to get there from here?" Thea asked.

"Take a right, then the second hallway on the left. At the end, there is a secret door behind the tapestry," Sally replied.

Thea saw Sally holding back her tears. Soon, they would all train the prince to retake his throne, but they had to get him out of the castle first. Remembering her oath to the king, Thea's eyes twinkled at the little prince. She would make sure he was safe, no matter the cost. "Come on."

When they reached the intersection, Thea led the trio silently down to the right corridor. Her steps were light and her eyes were sharp. Nothing was going to surprise them. As the catlike trio approached their left turn, Thea held up a fist.

Brock froze in place.

Sally clamped her hand over the baby's mouth. Her feet remained planted as she hardly took a breath.

Thea closed her eyes and concentrated on hearing what was around the corner.

"Beb noi zu rim?" an elven voice asked.

"Fo, om beb'r," another replied.

At least two, Thea thought.

"Ozan, limo noil vaos," said the first elven voice.

Unable to understand them, Thea concentrated on their footsteps. She looked back towards Brock, motioning around the corner. Once he nodded, she knew he understood. The prince had to escape unnoticed. Otherwise, they would be hunted down like wild animals. That could only happen if no *living* Dark Elf saw them escape.

"Nu, zel," a third elven voice said.

Thea listened to the clanging of feet on the stone floor. A single pair of footsteps seemed to be going the other direction while two more were heading right towards them. The elves no longer hid, nor walked stealthily down the halls.

If we're too noisy taking them down, more will come, Thea thought.

Clang. Clang.

Do we grab them before we kill them? Thea's heart raced.

Clang. Clang.

Too late. "Screw it." With her sword horizontal at chest level, Thea charged around the corner, with Brock close behind.

The two Dark Elves fumbled to pull their swords from their sheaths.

Thea drove her sword through the stomach of the elf on the left.

Brock slashed the other elf's throat as he came to Thea's side.

The Dark Elf grabbed Thea's sword as he fell to the ground. "Sev, vsoa zomoo sv iz!" he screamed. "Vsoa sev iz!"

"Shut him up," Brock demanded.

Thea yanked her sword from his gullet, spilling his entrails onto the floor.

"Look out!" Sally yelled.

Thea looked up.

A Dark Elf was standing at the end of the hallway. His eyes bounced from Thea to Brock and to the baby in Sally's arms. "Ep foi ro valso!" he screamed.

Thea grabbed a knife from her belt.

He turned and started to run.

She threw her knife. It hit its mark, the middle of the Dark Elf's back. Thea watched him fall the floor, scrambling to pull the knife out. She walked up behind the terrified elf. Thea pulled the knife out, grabbed him by his hair, and slit his throat. Did she silence him in time?

"Come on, Thea," Brock urged. "We've got to go!"

Thea wiped her knife off on the elf's cloak. "Coming." She moved towards Brock and Sally, who were standing in front of the tapestry. *What was that?* She turned. More Dark Elves were coming towards them. Her mind raced from the prince to her oath to the king to the sounds of more enemy fighters heading their way. What should she do? How important was honor to *her*?

"Thea, come on!" Brock said as Sally opened the secret door. "We've got to go, now!"

If they all ran, would they be found? Yes. Kade would send every fighter he had to chase them down. The prince—the prince was all important now. His survival and training *must* happen. "Brock, make me a promise."

"What? Come on already!"

"Promise me you will raise the prince to avenge his parents and retake the throne."

"We'll do that together. Thea, we've got to go!"

Thea shook her head. "You and Sally go, I'm staying."

"What's she saying?" Sally asked.

"None of us will make it if we all go. Kade will send everything he has to chase us down." Thea grabbed Brock's hand. "You know I'm right."

Brock bit his lip. "All right. After you get out, let's meet at—"

Thea shook her head. "No, I don't want to know where you're going or how you're even getting out. Just in case."

Sally gasped in horror. "You're not going to make it, are you?"

Thea looked away.

Brock put his arm around Sally. "Let's go."

"But—"

He gave her a slight push. "We've got to go, now."

I'm not going to make it. Thea watched them disappear behind the tapestry. She needed to create a diversion. Something big enough to keep the Dark Elf fighters in the castle long enough to give Brock and Sally enough time to escape. *Time to kill Kade,* Thea thought. But, how? Kade would be on the throne, his life-long ambition, surrounded by Dark Elf knights. In the Great

Hall, there was a catwalk from where she could shoot the traitor; its entrance was in the next room, not in the hall itself. She would certainly be trapped, with no chance of escape, but the prince would be safe. With Kade's pyromancer dead, all she would need is a bow. Thea headed towards the armory.

CHAPTER 12

Bittersweet

THEA CREPT DOWN THE HALLWAY. SHE HAD TO STAY HIDDEN
and not fight every Dark Elf she saw. Her only chance to kill
Kade and maybe get out alive was to take him by complete
surprise. Her ears perked up as she froze in place. Voices,
coming her way. If she fought now, it would have all been for
nothing. Quickly, she looked for a place to hide. Behind the
tapestry in the corner? No, too easily seen. The garderobe?
She hated using it, let alone hiding in it.

The voices grew louder.

No choice now. Thea snuck through the door. As she
closed the door behind her, the smell of feces and urine in
the chamber pots assaulted her senses. The light . . . she
needed to get rid of the light. Quietly, she moved across the
room and grabbed the torch from the wall.

The elven voices were closer, nearly outside the door.

Thea doused the torch in a full chamber pot. She started

moving through the darkness back towards the door. Her leg brushed against an empty brass chamber pot. It crashed to the floor.

The elven voices went silent.

Her heart stopped. She hid in the corner, just a few feet from the door.

Creaking from the door cracking open echoed through the garderobe. Torchlight from the hallway pierced the darkness.

Thea stopped breathing. Her hand grasped the hilt of her sword.

"Zen," a female Dark Elf said.

"Fo," another replied.

"Iesz sso robler zez Sezo him."

The door closed and the elven voices moved on. "Thank Odella," Thea said to herself. She put her ear to the door and listened. Once she was sure the elves were gone, she went back into the hallway.

Nearly there, Thea thought to herself. Moving like a cat hunting its prey, she quickly moved down the corridor.

The iron armory door at the end of the corridor stood between Thea and the bow she needed for her plan. Normally, the guards maintained the keys. She half-expected the Dark Elves to place a guard here to prevent the human soldiers from getting more weapons, but they hadn't. Her plan revolved around the idea that the Dark Elves would have seized the armories first to reduce human resistance within the castle, *but that required an elven guard with the keys to be standing outside the door.*

She tried pulling on it, just in case. Locked, of course. *What now?* Thea asked herself.

Three sets of footsteps were turning the corner, coming towards the armory.

Thea drew her sword. There was no hallway to the left or

right, and the door behind her was locked; she had nowhere to run.

They came closer.

I'll make my stand here, she thought.

Closer.

Thea was at the ready, poised like a lioness ready to pounce on her prey.

Three of them came around the corner and smiled at her.

"Robert!" Thea sheathed her sword and hugged her fellow knight. "I thought they killed you!"

"They nearly did. A healer took care of me before they killed her. There's nothing like magic healing," Robert replied. He looked down at his blood-soaked breastplate. "We've been busy."

"Me too. Who are they?" Thea asked, pointing at the two soldiers with him.

"Thea, meet Karl and Ivan. We sort of bumped into each other."

Thea stepped back. "Why are you here, Robert? The armory, I mean."

Robert blinked. "We needed—a few bows. Kade is somewhere in the castle and we have to take him out. Did you see what they did to the king and queen?"

Thea lowered her eyes. "Yes, I did."

"We came earlier but couldn't get in. So we captured an elf and tortured him until he told us where the keys were kept, or rather who had them. So—"

"You've got the keys?"

Robert smiled as he pulled a key ring from his pocket. "Aye." He walked over to the iron door and slipped the key into the keyhole. He opened the door, revealing the rows upon rows of swords, bows, quivers, and other tools of war.

Thea smiled as she entered the armory. "We may actually survive this yet." She picked up a bow and a full quiver.

"What's the plan?" Robert asked.

"We kill Kade and escape through one of the tunnels."

"No, Thea, we have to save the prince first. He is far more important than killing Kade."

"He's safe."

"How? Where?"

"Just trust me."

Robert looked back at his two companions, who nodded back at him. "All right, let's get some." The three men picked up bows and quivers as they headed out of the armory.

Thea grinned. "Follow me." She led them towards the Great Hall.

We may actually survive, Thea thought.

The entrance to the catwalk was next to the door behind the thrones in the Great Hall. If it were only her, the catwalk would be her best chance to kill him. The only downside was she would've been trapped, with no chance to escape. But with four of them, and the elves searching for the remaining humans, their chances greatly increased. They could kill him and escape if they did it from the floor level.

Every turn and room where there were no Dark Elves, the more nervous Thea became. Where did they go? Why are they not guarding the very room where Kade would demand to control the attack from? Would he? Of course, his lust for that stone throne was his driving force; it always has been.

At last, they arrived at the two doors. The door on the right led to the catwalk, and the other was the Great Hall entrance behind the throne. Thea looked back at Robert.

He gave her a nod.

Thea reached for the left door.

Robert and the two soldiers poised, ready to rush inside.

She threw the door open.

Robert and the two guards charged in before the door slammed the wall.

Sword drawn, Thea rushed inside. Expecting to find at least a squad of fighters, adrenaline rushed through her veins.

"What the—? Kill them!" Kade screamed.

Two human soldiers stepped in front of Kade with axes in hand.

Robert and his two companions drew their bows, aiming at the humans' hearts. "Don't even think about it."

The human guards looked at each other and dropped their axes.

"Move against the wall," Robert commanded.

They bolted for the door.

Three arrows chased the human guards. Two hit one in the back and the third sailed through the other's neck. Both dropped to the ground, dead.

The three aimed their bows at Kade.

"You deserve much worse than this for murdering your own family for the throne," Thea said.

Kade slid back down into the throne. "If you kill me, who will take the throne? *You?*"

"No, the rightful heir. Galin the V of Ravenward."

"It's true," Robert said. "She saved the child."

Kade laughed. "You actually believe that? Tell me, Thea, where are they then?"

"I don't know."

"How then could you know that they're still alive?"

Thea looked at Robert. "I don't know where they are right now, but I can try to get word to them. I don't know the details because I—I thought I was going to die." Her eyes focused like a laser on Kade. "Let's finish this and get out of here." Thea raised her sword.

Kade held his arms up in an attempt to block the blade.

Thea slashed her sword down towards him.

An arrow pierced her right shoulder, forcing Thea to drop her sword.

What? Thea thought. She turned her head to see Robert's other companion with his bow aimed right at her.

Another arrow embedded itself behind her left knee.

Thea toppled over, clenching her wounds. "Robert, help!"

"What's going on?" Kade demanded.

Pain shot up through Thea's leg and shoulder. Her heart raced. Sweat began to flow from her pores. Tears of pain poured out from her eyes. "Robert, please!"

Robert just smiled at her. "Robert died many years ago."

Thea's eyes widened as he began to transform. His medium-length blond hair turned into short black hair. Robert's blue eyes flashed; as the flash faded, they became a resolute brown. Worst of all, his tanned skin turned a deep blue. "No!" Robert was a Dark Elf.

He moved in closer.

"Tanyl, is that you?" Kade asked.

"Be quiet, fool! You nearly blew the whole thing," Tanyl replied.

"Tanyl? Is—is that your name?" Thea asked.

"Where's the child? How were you going to meet up with them?"

"I wasn't. I expected to die here." Thea turned her head away from Tanyl.

"I see." Tanyl drew his sword and thrust it into her leg. "Where?"

Thea squeezed her eyes shut. *It hurts. I must resist, I must.* "I don't know."

Tanyl twisted the blade, opening the wound even more.

The pain begged her to say something. But what? She really didn't know anything, except what side they were going to come out of the castle. She couldn't. She wouldn't.

Her leg begged for the pain to stop. "Please stop. I don't know where they are."

"Your methods are crude and ineffective, Tanyl," Kade said. "Give my people a few days with her and we'll get anything we need." Kade stepped up to Tanyl. "I need this more than you."

Tanyl glared at him. In one swift motion, Tanyl back-handed Kade, sending him flying back into the throne. "This is not about you or your petty rivalry. Be careful, Kade. Your usefulness is nearing its end."

Kade's mouth dropped. "But—"

"If you want to be king, you need to do exactly what you're told, when you're told to do it. Got it? Or you'll be joining your brother."

Kade's face fell into his hands. "What have I done?"

Thea's eyes began to close.

"Oh no, not yet." Tanyl kicked the knee that had the arrow embedded in it. "Tell me!"

Pain, the pain was overtaking her. "I—so—nor—north side. The tunnel they used comes out the northern wall. We made no plans to regroup."

Tanyl yanked his sword from her leg; blood poured out of the wound. "Was that so hard?" He motioned the other two out of the room. "We'll have them soon."

Blackness. Spots. Cold. "How'd you find me?"

"Our mages found you almost immediately, but we needed you to lead us to the child. We can't see him. He seems to have some magic ability in him."

Thea coughed. "Not...possible. Human males can't do...magic." Blood began to form a pool around her.

"The Prophecy of Axain is why we're here. Our seers, more than three centuries ago, warned us of a human king that would unite humans, dwarfs, and gnomes alike. He would be able to use magic to enhance his warrior skills. He would even convince the Vulwin Elves to turn on their brothers."

"You think that's the prince?"

"Yes, that's the only reason we helped this pathetic creature," Tanyl said, pointing at Kade. He drew his sword. "Even though we're enemies, Thea, I respect you. May you die in honor."

"The prince will kill you and retake the throne from the usurper. Even after I'm dead, I'll still win." Thea closed her eyes.

Tanyl's sword slashed towards Thea's neck, separating her head from her body. "Good-bye, Thea."

A few hours later, Tanyl was pacing in the Great Hall. "Why haven't they reported in?"

"Maybe Brock killed them," Kade said.

"Perhaps."

A Dark Elf rushed into the Great Hall and knelt in front of them. "Lord Tanyl."

Tanyl whirled around. "Find them?"

"I—I—No, my lord. There was no sign of them."

"What?!" Tanyl whipped a knife from his belt and flung it across the room.

The small throwing knife lodged itself in the elf's eye socket. His body crashed to the floor.

"Was that really necessary?" Kade demanded.

Tanyl's face tightened and his eyes narrowed. "I—we were outsmarted by a *female* knight."

"But—"

Tanyl held up his hand, silencing Kade. "We're going to tell the people that the prince is dead too, killed by the Vulwin Elves."

"You mean we're going to let them go?"

"No, we're going to hunt them down in secret."

"Why?"

"If more human armies arrive while we're searching the countryside for the child, our lie will be exposed and they will hang you." Tanyl started to pace around the dais. "No, we must have complete control before we tear this wretched kingdom apart looking for him."

"So, you *are* letting them go."

"For now."

Kade looked down at Thea. "What if he *is* the one?"

Tanyl smiled. "Then he'll come looking for us. Kade, with Beldroth gone, I'm your new consular." Tanyl extended his hand.

Still shaking, Kade shook Tanyl's hand. "Aye, this is just the beginning."

～

Brock pushed through the thick underbrush beyond the southern castle wall. They moved quickly and quietly across the pasture. Smoke from the castle burned his nostrils. *Just a little further*, he thought. They needed a place to hide until morning. But, where? As they moved past a cow and her calf, a three-sided structure became visible. "Over there."

Sally nodded.

Inside the structure were stacks of baled hay. Brock smiled. "Perfect." He shifted the square bales around to make a fourth wall with a peephole looking towards the castle. "Sally, in here."

Sally followed her fiancé inside the makeshift shelter. She sat down against a wall, rocking the baby back and forth.

"This is our boy now," Brock said. "Will you still marry me, Sally?"

She smiled. "Of course I will." Sally passed the prince to Brock. "What do we do now?"

Brock held the young prince close to his heart. "We go into hiding, far from here." As he stared into Galin's blue eyes, Brock smiled. "Galin the fifth of Ravenward, I promise that we're going to raise you and train you to retake your throne from the usurper and his allies. I swear that someday, you will be the ruler of Axain and avenge the death of your family." Brock looked up at Staerdale Castle in flames. "Someday . . . someday soon."

PROPHECY OF AXAIN

PROPHECY OF AXAIN, BOOK ONE

THERE COMES A TIME IN EVERY MAN'S LIFE WHEN HE MUST PUT aside childish dreams to do his duty, and this was one of those times.

Spring's morning sunshine warmed Seth Faren's face as he walked down the compact dirt road towards the center of Crey Village. Today was his birthday, and everything was perfect. He smiled at Sally, his adoptive mother. "Are we almost there yet? What are you getting me?" His blue eyes twinkled and his light-brown hair rustled in the breeze.

Her blond hair was tied up in a bun. "I promised you something suitable for your thirteenth birthday."

The aroma of baking bread, cookies, and cake invaded his nostrils. The small shops in the center of town huddled around the docks. His eyes diverted to a small fishing vessel just coming into town with a full load. Seth smiled. Someday he would be a fisherman and—

"Hey, Seth," a young girl's voice said.

Seth turned around to see a young girl with long blond hair waving at him. "Jena!"

Holding Jena's hand was a 28-year-old woman with shoulder-length blond hair and brown eyes. "Sally, sorry we're late," Keya said.

"It's okay." Sally led the group past the fishmonger.

"What do you want for your birthday?" Jena asked.

What did he want? He'd given his adoptive parents ideas every day for months, but which one did he want? "I—a new fishing pole," Seth blurted out.

Jena rolled her eyes. "Really?" She pointed over at the fishing boats. "If you do that, you'll stink, and I won't have anything to do with you."

Seth frowned.

She couldn't hold back her smile.

He hated being teased. Who didn't? Jena was different. She—

"Make way!" a man yelled in the crowded square.

"What are *they* doing here?" Sally asked as she turned around.

Seth looked up. Sally's faced had turned white. He grabbed her clammy hand. "Who are they?"

"They're—they're dragging someone," Sally said.

Six knights in dark armor pulled a man by his collar towards the lone tree next to the docks. There was a symbol on their shields and their right shoulders. It was a tan circle with a sword in the middle above an olive branch, surrounded by a red crescent moon and a yellow lightning bolt. "Who are they, Mother?"

"Dark—Darkstriders," Sally said. "How—why are they here?"

The largest of the six stepped in front of the crowd. "People of Crey Village, it has come to the attention of King Kade Ravenward that there are traitors in this village!" He pointed at the pummeled man. "This traitor once served the House of Ravenward, before King Galin died. Now, he betrayed the royal family and you." He nodded at the other knights.

"What are they going to do?" Seth asked.

Sally and Keya just stared at each other.

"Mother?" Jena asked.

Seth stretched his neck to see over the heads of the ever-increasing crowd. The knights tied a noose around the man's neck. They tossed the rope over a branch, and hoisted the man up. Seth turned his head, but his ears caught every gasp for air.

"We've got to go, *now*," Keya said. She grabbed Jena's hand.

Sally pushed her way through the crowd. "We've got to tell Brock." After they had passed the ring of people, she put Seth down and moved out. With each step, their pace picked up.

With the crowd to his back, Seth tried to keep up. Home, they were heading home. He glanced up at Sally. Why was she so afraid? Sure, those knights hung the traitor, but isn't that what you do with traitors? Two more turns then they'd be close to home. "Mom, can we slow down?"

Sally's eyes were big. "No. Keep up." She turned right, just past the magic component shop.

Seth was nearly at a run. One more turn, then they were home free. Another thirty feet. *Come on, legs, keep up.*

Two dark-clad knights with the Darkstrider symbol on their shoulders jumped out. "Where are you going?"

They skidded to a halt.

"Nowhere," Sally said as she took a step back.

Seth stepped in front of Sally. "Keep away from my mother."

They drew their swords. "A hero? Erik, what shall we do?" the smaller man said.

Erik's long, brown hair was up in a braid. He stepped

forward and grabbed Sally's hair. He put it up to his nose and smelled it. "Our orders are to make an example for the locals. Why not start with these?"

"Go about your business and leave them alone." A fit woman wearing leather armor carrying two short swords moved in front of Seth. Her blond hair was bundled into a ponytail.

The men blinked. "What are you—?"

She leaped forward, knocking Erik to the ground, and slit the smaller man's throat. After the smaller man had fallen to the ground, she mounted Erik. Holding her crossed swords above his throat, she grinned.

His face went white. "But—"

Then it was over. She got off the dying man and turned towards Sally. "Are you all right?"

"Yes, thank you," Sally said.

"I'm Alya," the woman said. "We need to get off the street."

Seth couldn't take his eyes off the pool of blood forming around Erik's body. Breakfast began to make its way up his throat. He covered his mouth.

Alya stared right into Seth's eyes. "It's all right."

"Let's go, Seth," Sally said. "We've got to get home."

Jena's eyes seemed to fog over.

"Would you like to come with us? We can at least offer you lunch for what you did," Sally said.

Alya grinned at Seth. "I'd love to."

Twenty minutes later, Seth followed Sally and the others inside the humble home. The living room was in the center of the house, with a fireplace big enough that a man could stand straight up inside it. Across the dirt floor was a wobbly wooden table surrounded by mismatched chairs.

"Seth, please start a fire," Sally said.

"Sure, Mother," Seth said.

Jena smiled at him. "I'll help you."

"Okay." Seth and Jena started placing logs into the fireplace.

Sally motioned Alya over to the table. "Please, come and sit down."

"Thank you." Alya leaned her sword up against the wall as she took a seat.

Keya looked over at Jena and Seth. "You could have saved them today. If you didn't come along—I—I could have—"

Alya shook her head. "I'm no hero. I'm just trying to do the right thing."

Sally frowned. "None of that here. You're our hero. Those two knights could have killed us, or worse." She shivered. "The world is no longer safe for the children."

"Do you have any ale?" Alya asked.

Seth looked up. Ale? His adoptive father drank a lot, but never before dinner.

Sally swallowed. "Sure. One moment."

"Are you married?" Alya asked Keya.

"I was before—but—he was—he died a long time ago." She looked over at Jena. "She's all I have left. If I lose her, what's the point of living?"

Alya frowned. "You humans always—"

"What?"

"I mean, humans always talk like that, but—" Alya's face fell as tears escaped from behind Keya's eyes. "I'm sorry." She looked away. "Sometimes, I forget that I'm not the only one who lost—family."

Sally handed Keya a handkerchief.

"It's okay," Keya said. She took the hanky and wiped her eyes.

Sally handed Alya a mug of ale. "Haven't seen you around here before. Traveling through?"

Alya took a swig. "I guess you could say that. I'm—well, I shouldn't."

"Shouldn't what?"

Sweat glistened on Alya's face. "I guess you're not one of *them*. I have been fighting the Darkstriders whenever I can." She looked away. "It's what my father would have wanted. He used to be a knight at Staerdale Castle."

Sally leaned closer. "Who?"

Alya blinked. "Paul the Bold. Why?"

"Before the world went insane, I worked at the castle. As the—in the kitchen," Sally said.

"Were you there when the castle fell? When Kade killed Galin the IV?"

Sally shook her head. "No, I was visiting my mother in Shapus. They have a beautiful little place on the River of Souls."

Alya nodded. "I see." She took another swig. "After they murdered my father and my brother, I swore to avenge them. So, I've been killing Darkstriders ever since."

Sally frowned. "The humans are not Darkstriders. They may have sided with them, but they're not one of them."

"How do you know that?"

Seth stood up and walked behind Alya.

"Brock was a blacksmith and friends with Thea the Loyal," Sally said. As soon as those words escaped her mouth, her face went white.

Alya's eyes focused on Sally. "I see."

"Where'd you learn to fight like that?" Seth asked.

"My father, of course. Isn't your father teaching you?" Alya asked.

Seth grimaced. "He is, but I don't want to be a knight or hurt anyone. I just want to be a fisherman and live in peace."

She put her hand on his shoulder. "Seth, everyone needs to learn to defend themselves. There's nothing wrong with that. Those two men today, what would have happened if my father didn't teach me?"

Seth lowered his eyes. Maybe, Father was right? Maybe? "We'd probably be dead."

"Seth, come back and play jacks with me," Jena said.

Sally laughed. "Go and play with her already."

"Come on!" Jena said.

"Okay," Seth said as he plopped down next to Jena.

"You said something about lunch?" Alya asked.

Sally jumped up. "Sorry, you're right." She rushed over to the counter and pulled out a loaf of boule bread.

"Are you in town long?" Keya asked.

"Hopefully not too long. If I'm in a spot for too long, things get tricky," Alya said. She looked down at the two children playing jacks. "It'll all be worth it if our kids can live in freedom."

Sally handed Alya a chunk of bread. "I'm sorry, but it's all we have."

Alya smiled. "It's wonderful." She tore a piece off and tossed it in her mouth.

Keya put a chunk of bread in her mouth too. "I am so happy…"

Seth rolled his eyes. How is it that their parents are happy to talk about nothing?

"Are you going to toss them?" Jena asked. Her eyes grew as she looked at him.

"Yeah," he said as he tossed the jacks from the small leather pouch.

Jena frowned. "You lucky—"

"Come and say good-bye to Ms. Alya, kids," Sally said as she stood up.

Seth jumped up. Alya's blue eyes and long blond hair was what all the women he dreamed about had in common. "Good-bye."

Jena shook Alya's hand. "Will we see you again?"

Alya looked right at Seth. "I think so." She grabbed her sword as she headed towards the door. "May I call on you again if I'm still in town?"

Sally nodded. "Sure."

"Until next time then." Alya closed the door behind her as she left the house.

Seth went up to Sally. "Mom, why did you lie to her?"

"What?"

"Why'd you lie? You never worked in the kitchen. You and father—"

Sally clamped her hand over his mouth. "Never say that in front of strangers or anyone your father hasn't cleared."

His heart skipped a beat as the fear poured out of her eyes. "But—"

"Never, understand?"

Keya pulled Sally back. "Easy, he didn't mean anything by it."

Her stern face collapsed as she looked at him. "I'm sorry." Tears broke through the dam behind her eyes. "I'm so sorry." She grabbed him and held on tight.

Barely able to breathe, Seth said, "It's okay, Mom. I love you."

She looked right into his eyes. "Your father and I will do anything to protect you. I promise."

Seth blinked. "Protect me from what?"

Sally just stared at him with an ashen face. "Just, go to your room."

"But—"

"Now."

He rolled his eyes. "Fine." Seth lumbered past the couch and through the small door. *Why won't they tell me?*

CHAPTER 2

T HE EARLY MORNING SUN CREPT THROUGH S ETH'S WINDOW. He pulled the wool sheet over his face, blotting out the light. Banging dishes from the next room rang through his ears. The rooster crowed just outside the window. Seth's eyes opened up. Yup, it was time to get up.

"Seth, you up yet?" Sally yelled from the other room.

He rolled his eyes. "I'm up. Be right there." He threw his bedding on the floor and grabbed a shirt from the basket in the corner of his room. Tossing his small pack over his shoulder, he left his bedroom.

"About time you got out here," Sally said. "Your father is already at the blacksmith shop. He's fitting you for a new sword." She put a small bowl of oatmeal on the table. "Eat up before it gets cold."

Seth sighed. "This sucks. I want to be a fishermen, not a blacksmith." He plopped down in his usual chair at the table. "Can we have something else besides oatmeal?"

Sally frowned. "Someday, you'll—" She bit her lip.

"What? What now?"

She turned back to her dishes. "Just eat your breakfast."

He scooped the grainy oatmeal and shoved it in his mouth. He loved his adoptive parents, but they could be such a pain. Sure, they kept things from him all the time. Whenever he asked Sally about his parents, she would quickly change the subject and tell him to go clean his room. "I'm going to meet Jena and Ellis at the market. Can I go to the shop after lunch?"

"I—I suppose so. You're not working today, only being fitted with a sword." She grinned. "Bring back a chicken, okay?"

"Sure." He rose from the table and grabbed his sack.

Sally watched him moved towards the door. "I love you."

As if he didn't hear her, Seth bolted out the door.

A fresh breeze blew his light-brown hair out of place as he walked down the dirt road towards the center of town. He had to make one stop first, to pick up Jena. They'd been friends as long as he could remember. His eyes twinkled. Maybe, they—nah, no way.

As he turned left around the corner, Jena's modest house came into view. Symbols and doves representing Odella, the goddess of Light, littered the exterior walls. On the door, there were three converging stars with an eye in the middle.

Seth knocked on the door. He couldn't help but smile when Jena opened the door. "Want to come to the market with me? I'm going to hang out with Ellis for a bit."

Jena looked back and frowned. "Mother's healing a fisherman who lost his hand to a baby sea dragon."

He blinked. "Lost? You mean bit off? I thought being a fisherman would be safe!"

"Everything we do in life has risks," Jena said.

"Jena, who is it?" Keya called from inside.

"It's Seth, Mother. Can I go with him to the market?" Jena asked. "Unless you need me still."

"Do you want to be a healer, like me?" Keya asked as she stepped behind Jena.

Jena turned toward her mother. "Yes, Mother, of course. I want to please Odella and help those in need."

"Then you need to stop finding excuses not to study," Keya said.

"It's my fault," Seth said. "I asked her to come because—" He stared into Jena's blue eyes. "I have to get a chicken from the market and—and I would like the company."

Jena smiled at Seth.

Keya grinned at the two of them. "Jena, be back by lunch. Okay?"

"Yes, Mother," Jena said.

"Bye, ma'am," Seth said as they headed toward the market, chatting as they went.

The salt air invaded Seth's nostrils. The half-mile walk seemed shorter than it normally did. Whenever he was with Jena, time and the rest of the world appeared to vanish, and today was no different.

"Did your parents ever tell you what they're protecting you from?" Jena asked.

Seth looked away. "They're not my parents and no, they wouldn't tell me. It's not like I'm twelve or something."

Jena giggled. "No, you're thirteen."

"Let's not talk about it. Okay?" Seth asked. He closed his eyes as the aroma of baking boule bread overtook him. "Let's look for Ellis. He should be here already."

"Sure," Jena said.

People were bustling around the market square near the docks. Merchant booths selling everything from clothes to fish to baked goods to fruit to magical components to live-stock circled the market square. They walked towards the animal vendor. The small booth had cages filled with plump, live roosters.

"My mom wants me to grab a chicken for dinner," Seth said.

"Who's going to harvest it?" Jena asked.

He sniffed. "Who do you think? They never do anything for me. Even my birthday got ruined yesterday."

"Come on, Seth, we were attacked yesterday!"

"I suppose." His eyes caught sight of something. Another Darkstrider patrol, but—they weren't human. They were as tall as a human, but their skin was blue, a dark blue. Each of them had pointed ears and dark, soulless eyes. They all carried a sword and shield, save one. She wore red flowing robes with a leather satchel over her shoulder. "What—?"

Jena shook her head. "I don't know."

As the patrol entered the square, the people moved, eager to get out of their way. Seth could almost smell the fear emanating from the crowd. He tapped a man standing next to him. "What—who are they?"

"Darkstriders, the real ones," the man said.

"But—what are they?"

The man frowned. "They're Dark Elves from Setan, west of Staerdale Castle and across the Fadyhl Waters. Ten years ago, they helped Kade Ravenward overthrow King Galin the IV of Ravenward."

Jena pulled Seth away. "What do we do? Why are they here?"

"I don't know." Seth watched the patrol leave the market square. He shrugged. "Let's get a chicken."

She grimaced. "Sure."

Seth walked up to the vendor. "How much for a rooster? My mom needs one for dinner."

"How many in the family?" the old man asked.

"Three."

"One moment." He turned and pulled down a cage with

an average-sized rooster inside. "Two silver pieces. For three, I can have my boy deliver it to your house."

Deliver? Yeah, then he wouldn't have to worry about leaving Jena too early. For an extra silver piece, he could… "Sure." Seth tossed the old man three silver pieces. "Please bring it to Brock Feran's house on Sycamore Street. My mother, Sally Feran, is home."

"Boy!" the old man yelled as he turned around.

"Yes, Father?" a young man said.

The old man handed the caged rooster to his son. "Deliver this to the blacksmith's house."

"Yes, Father." The old man's son disappeared into the crowd.

"Thanks," Seth said. He looked into her eyes. "How about—"

"Hey guys, where've you been?" a young man's voice said.

Seth looked over towards the docks. A stout thirteen-year-old boy with short black hair and hazel eyes was waving at them. "Ellis, about time you got here!"

Ellis blinked. "I've been here, fool! What do you want to do?"

What did he want to do? Spend time with Jena, of course. But, he couldn't say that to his best friend. "Walk along the docks? Listen to sea stories? I don't know."

Ellis licked his lips. "I'm hungry. Want an apple or something?"

Jena smirked. "He spent his last silver piece to get a chicken delivered."

"Please tell me that you didn't pay for a chicken," Ellis said.

"Yes," Seth began, "I don't steal stuff. It's wrong."

Ellis rolled his eyes. "You're just a wimp. Are you hungry or not?"

"I guess, but—"

Jena glared at Ellis. "Don't you dare."

He grinned at Seth. "I'm grabbing a few apples, want one?"

Seth's stomach growled. Yeah, that lumpy oatmeal didn't hit the spot. Was it stealing if he didn't take it? No, Ellis would be the thief, not him, right? Jena would be pissed until she bit into that red, delicious apple. "Sure—"

"Seth, you can't," Jena said. "I—I can't believe you would go along with that!"

"Look, just distract the vendor while I sneak behind him and grab some apples. Okay? It's simple. She's an old woman who can barely see," Ellis said.

Stealing from an old lady? Could he stoop any lower? It was like taking food right out of Grandma's mouth. But— what would losing a few apples really do? Would she really be hurt over that?

"Are you in or out?" Ellis asked.

"Seth, don't," Jena said.

His eyes were ensnared by Jena's glowing face. "I—I don't know. Maybe we shouldn't."

Ellis rolled his eyes. "Just go talk to the old bag." He disappeared into the crowd.

His friend and his stomach were counting on him. Seth walked up to the vendor.

"Can I help you, young man?" the old woman asked.

"I—" he looked back at Jena, who turned her back towards him. "How much for the apples?"

"A copper piece for one and four for five," she said.

Seth saw Ellis creeping up behind the old woman. "How about two?"

"That would be two copper pieces," she said.

Ellis reached for the apples on the very edge of the display.

Seth pointed to a yellow apple, away from Ellis. "How about that one?"

"The same price," she said. "Are you going to buy or—" The old woman saw Ellis reach for the apples and smacked his hand away.

Ellis ran.

The old woman glared right into Seth's eyes. "Did you really think I didn't know who you are? I'm going to tell Brock that you tried to steal from me!"

Seth's face turned white. "No, please don't. I'll—I'll do anything."

"No, stealing from an old woman is inexcusable," she said. "Now get out of here."

It was supposed to be easy and fun, but it wasn't. Jena was mad at him, just as he was making progress with her, and now he was going to get his butt whipped by his adoptive father. If he hadn't been lazy about bringing the chicken home, he could have paid for the apples and everyone would have been happy. But no, he had to show off to Jena. He walked over to Jena. "I'm sorry."

"For what? Getting caught?" Jena asked. "I have to get back to my studies." She stormed out of the square, heading back towards her house.

"Boy, you really pissed her off," Ellis said. "Want to get some bread?"

Seth glared at him.

"Not stealing, from my dad's bakery."

"No thanks, I have to get to the shop." Seth turned his back on Ellis as he pushed his way through the crowd.

Ellis shrugged. "I'm sorry."

"Whatever." Seth trudged down the street.

~

He's going to kill me, Seth thought. He followed the wet dirt road east along the water. The family's blacksmith shop was not far from the market square. All his life, his adoptive Father had told him what he was going to do when he grew up. But, he never actually told Seth why. It was almost as if he was the family secret; more likely the family joke. Hell, this was supposed to be his day off. Live and let live. Why can't his parents just let him be? What the hell do they know? They're—they're old. Twenty-eight years old is ancient. Nothing is dorkier than spouting off about honor, duty, and courage. Who needs that crap?

The shop was a small building with the overhead cover extending away from the water. Smoke rose from the chimney and stung his nostrils. Banging from the dirty, muscular man hitting the steel on an anvil rang through his ears. Seth's stomach dropped. He swallowed. There was no chance his adoptive father knew… yet. If it came from him, he'd be in a lot less trouble. His will to yell and scream to be left alone escaped him.

Weapons racks filled with swords and axes stood proudly facing the street. On the far end of the overhead cover stood a display filled with chains, hooks, and pieces of armor. Seth stepped between the two displays, underneath the roof. Brock Feran was dabbing his face with a towel. He tossed it onto a nail next to the forge. His hazel eyes glistened as he looked up. "About time you got here."

Seth couldn't look at Brock. "I—I've got something to tell you."

Brock tightened his ponytail. "What is it?"

"You know the old woman who sells fruit at the market?" It was done. No delays or excuses or lies could cover it up now. Seth straightened up. Yes, this was the right thing to do. He wasn't Ellis, who would sell his sister for a gold piece.

The long-brown-haired man nodded. "Sure, Mrs. Williams. Her husband died at sea last year. What about her?"

"I—we—Ellis—"

"What is it?"

"We tried to steal some apples from her and got caught." Seth closed his eyes, waiting for the slap to cross his face. Maybe if Brock hit him hard enough, the guilt would turn into anger. Maybe the days of slave labor would—

Brock sighed. "Why? Why, son?"

Seth shook his head. "Just being stupid. I'm sorry." He braced himself for the smack across the face. "I'm sorry."

"I—"

Here it comes.

"I'm disappointed in you. That's the most dishonorable thing you have ever done," Brock said. He opened the door to the small building and slammed it shut behind him.

That's it? His words stung like a dagger through the heart, far worse than any slap to the face or punch to the gut. Dishonorable? How could he go *that* far? Seth charged inside. "I said I was sorry." His cheeks reddened, but his eyes welled up. Was he angry or sad? Or both? Or neither?

Brock took a seat at the small wooden table in the middle of the small one-room building. He motioned towards the chair next to him. "Seth, sit down." There was no hatred or anger in Brock's eyes, only disappointment.

Shaking, Seth sat down. "I'll make it up to her. I promise."

Brock shook his head. "First off, don't make promises you have no intention of keeping."

"But I will."

Brock glared at him. "No, you won't. As soon as that little thief comes along, you'll forget your promise. Just like before."

It was true. Whenever Ellis showed up, Seth followed him

like a puppy. He was so relaxed and carefree and he never got in trouble at home. "You're right."

"I treat you like a man because you are one. Not later, but now. You're taught about honor and duty because… because…"

"Because why, Father? I'm nothing special." Seth pointed towards the forge. "I don't want this life. You wanted that life, not me." All the anger, that frustration finally broke free from his silence.

Brock's face fell. "You don't understand."

"How can I understand when you and Mother don't tell me?" Seth asked. "If you need me to understand, you have to tell me. Why are you teaching me to be like a knight?"

"It's because of your parents. I promised to raise you to be…" Brock got up and closed the door. "To be like them."

Seth leaned forward. "What was my father like? My mother?"

"What I am about to tell you, you can never repeat. Understand?"

Seth nodded.

"Your father was a great man. He fought against Kade the Usurper and the Darkstriders. Honor, duty, loyalty, and righting wrongs describe him quite well. He was a knight, and I was his blacksmith," Brock said. "I was a knight for a time, but… it didn't work out."

"Are you nobility?"

Brock shook his head. "No, but true nobility is earned, not something you're born with."

Images of a great knight appeared in Seth's mind's eye. Battles, swords, magic, dragons, and… and death. "What happened to him?"

Brock got up and grabbed the pitcher of water off the shelf and poured it into two cups. "He was killed when the Darkstriders conquered Axain."

Seth took a cup of water. "My mother?"

"She was beautiful and kind. Sally knew her very well. Actually, she worked for your mother."

"I don't understand."

Brock took a sip. "What?"

"Why couldn't you tell me that before?" Seth asked. "What's the problem?"

"I—well—I wasn't ready to tell you," Brock said.

"Can't I tell Jena? She wouldn't tell anyone. It's not every day that you find out that your father was a knight."

Brock shook his head. "You can't. It's too dangerous. If you tell her, or if they think she knows anything, you'd put her in danger. Is that what you want?"

Seth leaned forward. "Danger from what?"

"I—I've told you too much." Brock grabbed a measuring stick off the shelf. "Come over here."

Obediently, Seth stood up. "Aren't you putting me in more danger by *not* telling me?"

"Stand up straight." Brock extended the measuring stick until it was over Seth's head. "Five foot, two inches. You've grown some."

"What does that have to do with fitting me with a sword?"

"The ideal blade length for you is based on your height. For example, you need a sword with a twenty-eight-inch blade," Brock said.

Seth frowned. "You're ignoring my question."

He sighed. "All right. The meetings I have at the house, you know, the ones where you go and play with Jena."

"Sure."

"We're having another one soon, but I want you to stay and listen," Brock said. "We have a duty to Axain, the Raven-ward family, and the people."

Seth looked away. "You're not going to tell me, are you?"

"No, not yet." Brock put his arm around Seth. "Let's just

say that you have some wrongs to right and I'm going to teach you how to do it."

"Soon?"

Brock shook his head. "Ten years or more, probably."

"Do I have a choice?" Seth asked.

"I'm sorry, son, it's your duty. Now go home and tell your mom I'll be home soon." Brock started putting his tools away.

"See you at home," Seth said as bolted out the door. Halfway down the street, Seth looked back at the blacksmith shop. *What wrongs?*

CHAPTER 3

WITH THE SUN CREEPING THROUGH HIS BEDROOM WINDOW, Seth threw on a soiled brown shirt and wool pants. Today was different. Yesterday, he wanted to be a fisherman, with no desire to follow his adoptive parents. Now he wasn't so sure. How many boys find out their father was a knight—and a hero at that? Could it be that Brock was exaggerating? Sure, but why would he? Telling him anything at all was more than he had ever been told before. While tempted to bring it up at dinner last night, Seth didn't. He walked through his bedroom door.

Sally was making oatmeal, again! Seth could smell the rancid, if not diabolical, meal cooking over the fire. "Morning."

"Morning. I'm making extra oatmeal this morning. Your father asked me to bring by some oatmeal when I had a chance this morning," Sally said.

Seth slid into his seat at the table. "Why did he leave so early?"

"Something about fitting a rich man's bodyguards with

new armor. The job should really help us out." She grinned. "Maybe we can have something else besides this nasty oatmeal for breakfast."

Seth blinked. "You don't like it either?"

Sally grimaced. "No, who does? But, it's all we can afford right now. We have to get your sword and armor paid for and that's very expensive."

Seth's chest tightened. Why? All because of a promise they had made before he was born? Or just after he was born? "Can't that wait? So we can get better food? At least no more oatmeal?"

Sally stirred the pot. "Well, I—" She shook her head. "No, we have to do this. It's for your own protection."

Seth frowned. "The sword, sure, but the armor? I'm not going into battle or anything. Why must we suffer for something that won't happen for a really long time?" *If ever*, he thought.

She stopped stirring the pot in mid-stroke. "What did your father tell you?"

"Didn't he tell you? We talked after I said that I was caught stealing apples from Mrs. Williams."

Sally's face reddened. "You did what?" She closed her eyes as if trying to restrain herself. "What did your father say?"

Seth frowned. This wasn't going well. No, not at all. "Father already punished me. But, he did tell me about my parents, my *real* parents."

Sally bit her lip. "I see. Oatmeal is done." She scooped out a heaping helping into two small bowls, placing both of them on the table. Pulling a chair next to Seth, Sally sat next to her adopted son. "What did he tell you about them?"

Seth shrugged. "My dad was a knight and you worked for my mom and that they were honorable people."

She nodded. "Yes, that's all true."

He cocked his head. "He told me they died in some battle before Kade the Usurper took the throne. My mother, too. Can you tell me about her?"

Her hands shook. "I need to talk to your father first." Sally's face soured as she took a bite of oatmeal. "This is nasty."

Seth giggled. "I've been telling you that." He straightened up. "The last thing Dad said was that I had to right some wrongs."

Sally swallowed.

His shoulders relaxed. "What wrongs? What was he talking about? He wouldn't tell me."

She turned away. "There's a real reason why we haven't told you. I'm… surprised he told you that much."

"What reason? Mom, if I'm in danger, I need to know everything. Please," Seth said.

Sally grabbed a bowl from the cupboard and scooped some oatmeal from the pot. "Come with me to drop his breakfast off and I'll talk to him about it, okay?"

"You promise you'll talk to him?"

Her lips trembled. "I promise. Let's go." She covered the bowl with a small towel.

Maybe I'll find out the whole story, Seth thought as he followed her out the door.

To get to the family blacksmith shop, they had to go through the market square. Seth couldn't help but smile as they walked towards the dock. It was like a lifelong mystery was about to be solved. He came down here lots of times this early in the morning, and it was always like this. Near the docks, vendors were setting up their booths and pulling out their wares. Fishing boat captains were calling for their crews. Even in the early morning, the square was bustling. He looked over at the fishmonger, next to the docks. "Mom, isn't that Alya at the fishmonger?"

Sally gazed at the young woman warrior. "I think it is. But we're not going to stop and chat. We've got to see your father." She pushed through the crowd, towards the blacksmith shop.

Seth gulped. Up ahead along the road was a group of dark-clad knights, no—Dark Elves in Darkstrider armor. They were drinking wine and laughing and pointing at the village folk and laughing some more.

Sally stopped short. Her grip on Seth's hand tightened. "When did they get here?"

"I saw them yesterday at the market. A man told me they were—"

Sally clamped her hand over his mouth. "Act like you don't see them or care. Got it?"

Seth nodded.

She released her iron grip. "Come on." Her knees shook as they approached the group. Her palms were sweating.

Seth bit his lip. He resisted the urge to look at them. He forced his head forward, fighting every fiber of his being that wanted a closer look at the Dark Elves. His stride lengthened. Smoke; he smelled the smoke of Brock's forge. Just around the corner, then they were home free.

"Stop, you there, stop," a Dark elf said.

His heart stopped.

Sally froze in mid-stride.

Seth looked up at Sally. Her mouth dropped and her face went white. It was as if fear stole her voice.

"Elmar, leave them alone," the Dark Elf with long black hair pulled back into a ponytail said. He wiped the sweat from his forehead with his muscled forearm. "We're not here to play with the humans."

"No, Malon, there's something—" The large Dark Elf grabbed Sally's shoulder and whipped her around. His deeply recessed brown eyes studied her. Sweat formed on his bald, dark-blue head. "I—do I know you?" he asked.

Her legs began to shake. "No—I—I don't think so," Sally said.

Elmar looked down at Seth. "Who's the boy?" the well-built Dark Elf asked.

Was this a wrong he needed to right? Was this what his adoptive father meant? His stomach twisted. *Here we go.* Seth stepped between Elmar and Sally. "I'm Seth, her son." He threw the elf's hand off Sally's shoulder. "What do you want?"

"Get away, boy, before you get yourself hurt," Elmar said. "Were you at Staerdale Castle a few years back?" he asked Sally.

Seth saw Alya watching from the docks. Why wasn't she helping? Was she afraid of Dark Elves?

"No, never been there," Sally said.

Elmar looked down at the bowl she was carrying. "What's this?"

She pulled it close to her bosom. "Oatmeal for my husband. He's the local blacksmith." Sally stepped back. "Please, let us go."

"I'll take that." The elf snatched the bowl from her grasp.

"That's my father's!" Seth said. "Give it back."

Elmar backhanded Seth, knocking him to the ground. "Someone needs to teach you some manners, *boy.*"

Sally dragged Seth back. "Leave us alone."

He dipped his finger in the oatmeal and stuck it in his mouth. Elmar spit it out. "This is worse than orc grub." After he gave Seth a taunting smile, he smashed the bowl on the ground. "I did your father a favor."

Seth broke free from Sally's grasp and kicked Elmar's shin.

Elmar drew his sword. "Next time, I'll roast you over a fire." He leaned forward, staring right into Seth's eyes. "Got it?" he snarled.

Sally yanked Seth backward. Tears ran down her face. "We got it. Can we please go now?"

Elmar slapped Sally, hard, knocking her back. A red handprint was embedded on her right cheek, rippled with welts. He grabbed Seth's shirt and stared into his eyes. "I'm gonna draw and quarter your hide if you don't show me some damn respect." Elmar tossed Seth towards Sally.

Seth's face twisted.

Sally slapped Seth in the back of his head. "Do what you're told!"

"Sorry." Seth couldn't take his eyes off Sally's new decoration.

Elmar laughed. "Now that's what I'm talking about." He waved them off. "Get out of here."

With one hand on his shirt, Sally dragged him to the blacksmith shop.

As soon as they got close, Brock came running out. His face fell as he saw the welts on Sally's cheek. "The Dark Elves, they're here."

Brock grimaced. "Come on."

Seth and Sally followed Brock inside.

Sally's hands shook. "I… saw them and it all came, all of it. I… Thea, the castle, my lady." Tears flowed from her eyes like a mountain river.

Brock took her into his arms. "It's okay, love. They don't know that."

Seth looked up at Sally. "What are you talking about?"

Ignoring him, she looked right into Brock's eyes. "One of them recognized me from the castle."

"Mother?" Seth asked.

"What about the boy?" Brock asked.

Seth took a cup off the shelf and threw it against the wall. "I'm right here! Stop talking about me like I am some wall ornament. What's going on?"

Brock's eyes softened. "They are the ones who killed your father. Probably not those Dark Elves, but it was the Dark Elves with Kade."

Sally wiped her eyes. "You asked why we didn't tell you everything. What danger are you in?" She pointed back towards town. "We are protecting you from *them*."

Seth straightened up. "What are we going to do?"

Brock shook his head. "Nothing. We don't want to draw attention to you."

"Nothing? You saw what they did! Aren't you angry?"

"I'm furious." Brock closed his eyes, only for a moment. "But if we rush in, we'll all die. Boy, you've got fire, but no experience. Go home. I'll be there shortly."

Seth looked at the handprint on Sally's face. *I'm going to make them pay.*

~

Later that afternoon, Seth was picking tomatoes from their small garden behind their house.

"I only need three," Sally said through the kitchen window.

He looked up at Sally. "Okay," Seth said. He tore his eyes away from his injured adoptive mother. Every time he looked at her, his nostrils flared. That face… that face twisted his soul. Those… things hurt the only mother he had ever known.

He picked a plump red tomato and placed it into the small basket. Those bastards needed to pay, but Brock wasn't going to do anything. If anything hit Jena like that, he'd skin them alive and roll them in salt and do it again. Yeah, maybe he should do it? Why not?

Seth picked another tomato and put it in the basket. He was with her when they smacked her and stood between them. But he was tossed aside like a used incense. He could have stopped them if he'd tried harder. Yeah, he'd find them and give them matching handprints on their sick blue skin. He rolled his eyes. Who was he kidding? He was only thirteen and didn't really know how to fight. Sure, Brock tried to teach him, but he only went through the motions. Yeah, he needed to learn. "When's Father coming home?" Seth asked as he tossed the last tomato into the basket. He headed inside.

Sally was slicing lettuce on the counter. "Soon. He should have been here already."

Seth put the basket next to the cutting board. "When is the meeting tonight?"

She smiled. "Looking forward to seeing Jena?"

He grabbed a knife from the block and started slicing a tomato. "No, father said I need to start attending his meetings."

Sally frowned. "Why don't you want to play with Jena? Do you want to go to the meeting tonight?"

Seth opened his mouth but said nothing. Did he really want to hang around with Brock and the other old men over playing with Jena? He straightened up. "Father said it was my duty to go."

"Do you even know what it's about?"

He shook his head. "No, he didn't tell me. But, I need to go." He put the tomato slices into the salad bowl and started cutting another one. "Will we have time to spar tonight? I—I need to learn."

Blood drained from her face. "You've got lots of time for that. Be a boy while you can."

Seth frowned. "I'm not a boy anymore." He stared at the welts on her cheek. "I won't let that happen again."

She touched her cheek and shook her head. "No, you can't—" She sighed. "I guess you have to start sometime." Her eyes welled up. "Sure, I'll make him help you before the meeting. Go get the practice swords."

A smile erupted on his face. "Be right back." Seth raced to the small, weathered shed in the backyard. He flung the door open. Amongst the cobwebs and dusty yard tools were two wooden longswords. Brock had given them to Seth for a birthday present a few years ago and they'd sat there ever since. Whenever Brock asked about learning to fight, Seth always had something else to do that was more important.

He batted the cobwebs away from his face as he walked inside. A beam of light shined through the cracks in the walls, reflecting off the glossy finish. Maybe Brock gave them to him too early? Or perhaps, he just needed a good reason to care enough. Yeah, that was it. Now, he had a goal. To make those elves who hurt his adoptive mother pay the price. His friends would see him less, sure. But, they'd understand. Seth smiled. They may even help him punish them.

"Seth! Your Mother said you wanted to see me," Brock called from the yard.

Seth snatched up the practice swords and bolted out of the shed. Brock's face was worn from the day's work. "Yes, Father. I need to learn."

Brock licked his lips. "Yes, you do. Toss me a sword."

Seth took one sword in his right hand and gave the other to Brock. "I'm ready."

"Show more your stance," Brock said.

Holding the hilt with both hands, Seth held the sword out in front of him. His feet were a little more than shoulder width apart and he stood straight up. "Like this?"

Brock sighed. "We've got some work to do." He stuck the

wooden sword in the ground and walked over next to Seth. "Let me show you."

Seth smiled. "Yes, Father."

Two hours later, Sally finished the finger foods and placed them on the table. She walked back over to the window. "Brock, they'll be here any minute."

Sweat poured down Seth's back. He dropped his sword to the ground. "I can barely lift my arms. Is it always like this?"

Brock shook his head and smiled. "No, it gets easier." He picked up Seth's practice sword. "Go inside and wash up. They'll be here soon."

"Who? Who comes to your meetings?" Seth asked.

Brock put the swords back into the shed. "Old knights and others who want to see the kingdom restored. Seth, I want you to listen tonight," Brock said.

Listen? To how Brock's friends could help him avenge his adoptive mother. He smiled. "I will."

Twenty minutes later, Seth lit another candle and placed it on the table. Brock's friends had started showing up about ten minutes ago. They were eight in all. Seth noticed the most significant similarity amongst all of them; they were all ancient, at least thirty! A few were still in good shape like Brock, but most of the men looked more pregnant than gallant. Yeah, they're past it. Whatever *it* was. He'd be more apt to beat down those Dark Elves if they were still training. Tired or not, Seth knew they had to pay. What could these people possibly show him?

Brock motioned Seth towards the couch. "Seth, come sit next to me."

"Yes, Father," Seth said.

Brock shifted in his seat. "Before we eat, I want to thank everyone for coming. I—"

"Why are we still doing this?" a fit graying man said. "We've been doing this ever since you and Sally arrived at Crey Village."

He glared at the man. "Larry, we're trying to figure a way to return the rightful king to the throne."

"Nearly thirteen years you've been and we've had these meetings," Larry said. "My family was always loyal to King Galin, but he's gone. Too much time has passed to continue to pretend that we are kicking the Darkstriders from Axain, or Crey Village for that matter."

Seth looked right at Brock as he lowered his eyes.

The others murmured in agreement.

Brock sighed.

Why is he not saying anything? He knew everything but remained silent. Seth bit his lip. Should he say something? Anything?

A plump man with gray hair weaved into his black topknot spoke. "He's right, Brock," Paul Lyons said. "What have we accomplished besides putting targets on our back?"

Seth watched Brock's face twist. "Father?"

"We had to wait until the rightful king was at the proper age," Brock said.

Larry frowned. "Is he?"

Brock nodded. "Yes, he just had a birthday."

Seth blinked. Birthday? Was the king the same age as him? Did he know him? Ellis, maybe? As a descendant of a great knight, he was expected to take up the fight.

"Have you even seen him?" Paul asked.

Brock smiled. "Yes."

"Where is he?" Larry demanded. "We need to see him.

Even if we do get him on the throne, how do we know he won't be worse than Kade and Dark Elves?"

Brock shook his head. "No, for his safety you can't know who it is."

Larry stood up. "I'm done. Thirteen years is long enough." He headed towards the door.

"Me too," Paul said as he followed Larry.

Brock's face went white. "Stop. Please come back."

"I'm not endangering my family anymore, especially when nothing will ever come of it," Larry said.

Seth stood up. "How do you know?"

Larry blinked. "Know what?"

"That nothing will come of it?" Seth asked. "Is it my Father's fault for bringing everyone together to try and figure something out, or is it your fault for not even trying?"

Brock put his hand on Seth's shoulder. "Son, stop this."

Seth pulled away. "What kind of cowards are you? When my father asked me to start sitting in on these meetings to figure out how to free the people of Axain from the Dark Elves, I expected to see the bravest men around. I was wrong."

Paul's face turned blood-red. "How dare you!"

Brock stepped between Paul and Seth.

"Thirteen years. You said you waited for thirteen years, right?" Seth asked.

Larry nodded. "Yes."

"Would it be so painful to wait for just one more?" Seth swallowed. Where was this coming from? He never talked like this, ever. His adoptive father's training? Or maybe his real father was coming out in him? "If nothing happens, then quit."

Larry's mouth dropped. "Did your father tell you to tell us that?"

Brock shook his head. "No, I don't talk like that." He smiled to himself. "But, my son is right. What do you say?"

Paul and the others looked at Larry.

Larry grinned. "What's one more year?" He sat down and the others followed suit.

"The Dark Elves are in the village," Brock said.

Larry shrugged. "So? They can't hide with that blue skin of theirs."

Brock put his hand up. "Let me finish. As we know, they typically only send their human knights this far out—"

Paul rubbed his chin. "So they must want something that's here."

"Or that they *think* is here," Seth said.

Brock smiled. "The boy's right."

"What are we going to do?" Larry asked.

Seth stared at Larry. What was his game? His speech wasn't that inspiring. One minute he was ready to run for the sea and the next he wanted to take the fight to the Dark-striders.

Brock leaned in. "Find out where their camp is and what they're after. It could be one of us, or someone else, or something magical. Who knows? That's why we need to find out."

Maybe this was his chance? Seth smiled. "I'm helping, too."

Brock shook his head. "No."

"The boy would draw less attention," Paul said. "He can do it."

"It's just—" Brock looked away. "Too dangerous, especially for him. He's not ready yet."

Seth glared at him. "Father! I can spy on those *bastards* who hit Mother."

All eyes stared at Seth. "What happened to Sally?" Larry asked.

His eyes welled up. "They hit her and pulled their sword

on me," Seth said. "I can't fight them, but I can spy on them." He jerked his head right at Brock. "Please let me, Father. Let me be the man you think I am."

Brock bit his lip. He nodded. "Okay, from a distance... a far distance. Got it?" Brock asked.

Sally dropped a bowl in the kitchen.

"Yes, I promise." Seth stared at the door. *Those bastards are going to pay.*

CHAPTER 4

THE MORNING SUN PEAKED OVER KYHR DEEP AS SETH'S FEET dangled in the water. He sat on the small dock, just outside the blacksmith shop. He gripped his fishing pole tightly and tossed the line in front of the dock.

Last night, he dreamed the same image over and over again. He was on top of that Dark Elf, slamming his head into a rock. The more the elf begged, the harder Seth hit him. He raised the rock over his head to deliver the killing blow. White lights shot from the dark elf's fingers right into Seth's chest. The rock fell from his hands. Seth clutched at his heart as he fell over. He couldn't breathe. The Dark Elf slapped him, like he did Sally, and smiled. Seth's world went dark.

The cool breeze whisked Seth's hair. As he stared at the cork bobber riding the current, last night's dream tried to break into his mind. Seth shook his head. All he wanted was revenge and it was consuming him.

"Catch anything yet?" Brock asked as he sat down next to Seth. A faint smile climbed onto his face. He looked deep into Seth's eyes. "Couldn't sleep?"

Seth shook his head. "Not really."

"You said some great stuff last night. You showed *real* leadership. I'm so proud of you." Brock's eyes twinkled. "For a moment, I thought you sounded like your father."

"Thanks."

Brock got up. "Come on, we've got a few things to do before we check the traps."

Seth smiled. "Sure." He followed Brock into the shop.

Brock tossed a few logs in the iron forge just outside the overhead cover. "Seth, could you set up the two displays?"

Seth headed inside the small building. "Yes, Father." Towards the back of the one-room building was a large locked wooden closet. He fumbled with the key ring. "The diamond-shaped one?"

"That's it," Brock replied.

He put the key into the lock and turned it. Seth opened the closet. There were supposed to be baskets of chains, armor pieces, iron hooks, etc., but there wasn't. There was a small table in the center, covered with red velvet. His eyes widened. The sunlight glinted off the polished blade. A little dragon was etched on the blade just above the hilt. Tight leather strips covered the longsword's handle. He reached out for the precious treasure.

Brock put his hand on Seth's shoulder. "What do you think?"

Seth gulped. "Um—you've made some customer happy. It's-it's gorgeous."

Brock handed the sword to Seth. "I hope so."

His hands were trembling as he took the sword. "For me?"

"Yes, you deserve it." Brock reached inside the closet and grabbed the scabbard. "You'll need this, too."

"I—" Seth's eyes couldn't leave the beautiful blade. "Thank you, Father." He slid the sword into the scabbard and secured it to his hip. "I don't know what to say."

Brock smiled. "You said it last night. Your speech was just like your real father. I now know that Thea's sacrifice wasn't in vain."

Seth looked down at his new sword. "Who was she? Mom mentioned her, too."

"Thea the Loyal," Brock said as he settled back into a wooden chair. "She was the first and only woman knight in the Kingdom of Axain."

Seth blinked. "A woman?"

"Yes, and she was a great warrior and fierce tactician." Brock looked right into Seth's eyes. "Thea was the bravest knight I've ever known. She had saved your father's life before you were born. Thea led the charge, attacking the Feral Orcs at Nightfall Meadows." He laughed to himself. "She humiliated Kade on the battlefield."

"Kade Ravenward? The king?" Seth asked.

Brock nodded. "Yeah, she won all the honor that day."

Seth shrugged. "What does that have to do with me?"

He leaned in close to Seth. "She saved us all. Thea sacrificed herself to save you and me and your mother. I promised her that I would do everything I could to put the rightful king back on the throne and free the people of Axain." Brock leaned back into his chair. "That's why we have those meetings."

"Did the Dark Elves kill her, too? Like my father?" Seth asked.

"I think so. The last time I saw her was inside Staerdale Castle heading towards the armory. She forced us into the tunnel." Brock bit his lip as if deciding how much he should say. "Sally was holding you in her arms and I was charged by Thea the Loyal to protect and raise you to—for your father's sake."

Seth rubbed his chin. "Last night, you said you knew the boy king."

Brock nodded. "I do."

"You also said he just had a birthday, is that right?"

"I—yes, it's true." Brock stood up and walked over to the window.

Seth leaned forward. "Is he my age?"

Brock nodded.

"Who is it? Do I know him?"

Brock headed outside. "Customer."

Seth chased after his adoptive father.

Brock slipped on his apron as he walked just outside his shop.

At Brock's side, Seth looked at the oncoming horse. It was as black as the night and its coat was as shiny as the moon. The rider was wearing worn chain mail underneath a purple cloak. Her fiery red hair flowed in the breeze. "Do you know her?"

Brock's mouth opened wide. "No, I don't." His eyes couldn't leave the apparition.

"Good morning," the *mature* woman said as she dismounted the horse. She tied it to the hitching post.

Brock smiled. "Good morning. How can I help you?"

"I'm Alicia." She looked down at Seth. Her lips curled. "Who are you?"

Seth squinted. He couldn't focus on her. Her entire body was almost shimmering. Not fuzzy, it was barely noticeable, but it was there. "Seth. The blacksmith is my father."

"I'm the blacksmith. Brock Feran."

Alicia nodded. "I know—I mean, nice to meet you."

Brock frowned. "What do you need?"

"I need two steel daggers and a short sword." She stared right a Seth. "How much?"

Brock stepped in front of Seth. "Four gold pieces. I'll need half now to start the work."

Alicia nodded. "Of course." She reached into a pouch and handed Brock two gold coins. "When can I pick them up?"

"I need a week, okay?" Brock said.

"See you then." She got back on her horse and headed back to town.

Seth stared at Alicia, still unable to focus on her. Did he imagine her? He could focus on everything else, but not her. "Was that normal?"

Brock shook his head. "Not one bit." He started back inside. "After I put these away, let's check the traps and then you can go."

Alicia's black stallion galloped down the dirt road towards town. Along the water, just before the market square, was the Red Scale Tavern. The outside was worn by the salt air and years of harsh winds off Kyhr Deep. She pushed her way inside.

A long bar along the left wall was surrounded by empty seats. Wooden planks creaked as her boots hit the floor. On the far side was the staircase heading up to the rooms for rent.

"Can I get you anything, dear?" an old beer wench asked.

Alicia never turned her head. "No, I'm going to my room."

The old woman blinked. "I see."

She turned left at the top of the stairs. Alicia entered the third room to the left.

"What took you so long?" the bald, blue-skinned elf asked. His pointed ears twitched. "I have to get back to the castle."

Alicia threw her chain mail down on the bed. "Ryul, I had to be sure." She clasped her hands together and closed her eyes. Her mouth moved as if speaking, but no audible words came out. Her red hair grew another three inches as it change from red to black. Her chest expanded. Alicia's beautiful skin morphed into a dark blue. Her ears grew and became pointed. Her green eyes sank and turned brown. She was a Dark Elf. "That's better."

Ryul grinned. "Nice to have you back, Shania." His smile vanished. "What did you find out? Are they the ones?"

Shania walked over to the window and shut the drapes. "I'm not sure. But—there was something strange about the boy."

Ryul raised an eyebrow. "Yes?"

She stared right at him. "When do human females get their magic ability? Puberty, right?"

He shrugged. "I suppose, why?"

She sat down on the corner of the bed. "He had an… aura around him. I can't explain it."

He rolled his eyes. "Not possible. Human males cannot use magic. It has never happened and never will. I don't care what that stupid ancient prophecy says."

She cocked her head. "Why don't you believe in the prophecy?"

Ryul sniffed. "Give me a war mage or a pyromancer and I am all for magic. I saw the fire come from the sky and vanquish our enemies. I saw Beldroth put huge holes in castle walls. That I believe in, not some ancient scribblings in a language that's hardly spoken."

She motioned him to sit down. "What if it's true?"

"A human king that can wield magic *and* unite the remaining humans, dwarfs and gnomes to the north to wipe out the Darkstriders?" He laughed. "You must be joking."

Shania grabbed him by his tunic, staring into his soul. "Answer my question!"

Ryul pushed her onto the floor. "I've got three battalions of Feral Orcs to the north at Iron Fist Keep. I can kill everything in this miserable town in a matter of hours."

Shania shook her head. "No, we have to be sure, and we

don't want to make martyrs. That would only fuel a rebellion." She rubbed her chin. "If the prophecy is true, then—then the boy would be Galin the V of Ravenward and—"

"If it's *not* true, we know that Brock and Sally Feran escaped with the child." Ryul's thin lips twisted like a pretzel. "Brilliant."

"I'm already close to the family. I'll send some orders to the squad you sent me," Shania said. "I may have to kill a few Dark Elves to prove myself to them."

Ryul grinned. "Don't worry, I only sent you warriors from the peasant class. If you get into trouble or need help, just send word to the orc commanders at Iron Fist Keep."

Shania nodded. "Okay."

"One more thing, Tanyl's patience has run out. His seers are certain the boy is here. If you fail or take too long, I'll send the orcs to kill everyone." Ryul's eyes focused on Shania. "Including those who fail me."

She swallowed. "I—but—"

Ryul pushed his way past her towards the door. "No excuses. You've had thirteen years and that's long enough." He slammed the door shut.

She sat down on the bed. Shania was of noble blood, dating back to when the dark elves were second-class citizens in the Vulwin Elf kingdom, nearly six centuries ago. Her father was killed by the humans at Port Eldham and her brother was murdered by Thea the Loyal in Staerdale Castle. She rubbed her eyes. Shania was the last in her family line and there was no way she would dishonor it. She had to find the boy king and kill him.

~

Brock was silent during the walk out to Sarun Grove. Seth's new sword was dangling from his right hip as he stepped over a fallen tree. The long grass was nearly waist-high. Ahead, the pasture turned into a dark wood. Pine trees encircled Sarun Grove. "I'm going to ask Ellis and Jena to help me."

Brock looked down at Seth. "With what?"

"Finding out what the Dark Elves want. You know, what I said at the meeting." Seth grabbed a long piece of grass and stuck it in between his teeth. "What do you think?"

"Dangerous."

"How suspicious would three kids playing around the marketplace be?" Seth asked.

Brock nodded. "That's a good idea, but it's still dangerous."

"But—"

He glared at Seth. "We'll see."

Seth forced his eyes back at the woods. Yes, Ellis would be perfect. His rogue talents could help a lot. Jena was striving to become a priestess for Odella and a healer. She had as little experience as he did. So, so what? All Seth promised he would do is to spy on the Dark Elves. Yeah, they could do that. He looked up at Brock. Did he really need to know? No, he'd tell Brock *after* they found out the dark elf's goals in Crey Village.

Brock pushed the underbrush aside as he stepped into the woods. "There, about fifty feet or so."

Seth nodded. "Yes, Father." The circle of pine trees gave way to oak and birch trees. Dried leaves crunched under his feet.

Brock froze.

Seth did the same. His ears perked as he heard the leaves

rustling beyond the underbrush. He heard a trap snap shut and a man screamed. Seth looked up at Brock.

"Damn it," a man's voice said.

"Someone tripped one of our traps." Brock got up and pushed through the underbrush. "You hurt?"

Seth followed Brock into the clearing and saw three men. A strong man with short brown hair was wrestling with the bear trap. Blood oozed down his right ankle. "I'll help you." Seth rushed over and knelt down next to the moaning man. He clicked the lever on the bottom of the trap, releasing the spring.

The man snatched his foot out of the trap's jaws. "Thank you. I'm Dane the Devoted or used to be."

"Can you walk?" Brock asked.

Seth perked up. "Are you knights?"

A smaller man helped Dane up. "We used to be, under Galin the IV. I'm Jacob." He pointed to the third man. "And this is William."

Dane put some weight on his foot and collapsed. He shook his head. "I can't."

Brock leaned over and grabbed Dane's left shoulder. "Let's bring him to my house. We'll get a healer."

Dane nodded.

"Seth, run ahead and get Jena's mother," Brock said.

"Yes, Father," Seth replied.

Brock waved him off. "Go, hurry up."

Seth bolted out of Sarun Grove and headed straight for Jena's house.

TEN MINUTES LATER, SETH WAS NEARLY THERE. HE TURNED left down a dirt village road. Jena's modest house was decorated with symbols of Odella. He banged on the oak door. "Ms. Keya, my father needs help!"

Jena opened the door. "My mother is in the library. Come in."

As soon as Seth entered the small house, he was overtaken by the incense. The living room and kitchen were a large single room. Underneath a large window in the back stood an altar with a bowl of burning incense on top. Paintings of Odella and battles between the gods decorated the room. In front of the giant fireplace were two couches with a small table in front of them.

"I'll get her," Jena said as she disappeared into the back.

A moment later, Keya entered the living room. "What is it, Seth?"

Seth swallowed. "A man got stuck in one of our bear traps. He's bleeding and—and father said to get you."

"I just finished up with another patient," Keya said.

Alya stepped out of the back room and smiled at Seth. "I'll go too, maybe I can help."

Keya nodded. "Sure." She started putting incense, bandages, candles, and other magical components into a bag.

Seth frowned. Why didn't Alya help them when the Dark Elves slapped his mother?

"Where are they taking him?" Alya asked.

"My house."

Keya hoisted the bag over her shoulder. "Let's go." She rushed out the door.

It took them fifteen minutes to reach Seth's house. He opened the door and they were already there. Dane's foot was wrapped tight with a bandage, and he was sitting on the couch. William and Jacob stood back, shifting their weight from one foot to the other. "I got them," Seth said.

Sally rushed over to Keya. "What can I do?"

Keya started to clear the small table in front of the couch. "Take these," she said as she handed Sally the unwashed plates. Keya pulled out a small bowl and placed it on the table.

Seth leaned over to Jena. "What's she doing?" he asked as Keya put the little bag of incense on the table.

Jena's eyes glistened as she looked into his eyes. "She's going to cast 'Odella's Touch.' It's the healing spell she's been trying to teach me."

"Trying? What happens if you don't do it right?"

Jena looked away. "You make the wound worse. I was trying to heal a sprained ankle, but I turned it into a broken leg. Mother was not happy with me."

"Can you do it now?"

Jena shook her head. "Not yet."

Seth blinked. "I'll remember that."

Keya poured the incense into the enchanted bowl and lit it. She bowed her head and said a silent pray to Odella, the goddess of Light. Dane winced as Keya placed his foot on the table. With her eyes closed, she put her face over the burning incense. "Min touch Helbred nom," Keya muttered in a soft voice. "Min touch Helbred nom." Her left hand began to glow. "Min touch Helbred nom." She grasped Dane's ankle.

Dane arched back in pain. He screamed.

Seth's eyes opened wide. "Did she fail?"

Jena smiled in pride. "Nope."

As Dane's bone healed and his flesh regenerated, Keya screamed. Her right ankle began to bleed. The cracking of bone echoed through the house.

Sally rushed over to her friend.

"No!" Jena yelled as she pushed Sally away.

Keya screamed again.

"Get out of the way," Brock said as he pushed Jena aside. "She's hurt."

The pain was visible in Keya's eyes as she shook her head. She bowed and silently prayed to Odella. After a moment, her right ankle glowed and Keya collapsed.

Seth walked behind Keya and looked at her ankle. "It's healed."

Jena nodded. "Yes, this spell causes the healer to take on the wound, removing it from the patient. Afterward, a prayer will heal the faithful priestess." Her eyes glowed. "Isn't it beautiful?"

"You want to do this the rest of your life?"

"Yes."

Seth grimaced. "You're nuts."

Sally moved next to Keya, helping her up. "I'll bring her to the bedroom to rest."

Brock nodded. "Okay."

Dane struggled to his feet. A smile latched onto his face as he started to jump up and down. "Amazing. I haven't seen anything like that since—" He sank into the couch. "Since the

Battle of Staerdale Castle. She's a real priestess of Odella, isn't she?" he asked.

Jena grinned. "Yes, and she's my mother. She's teaching me to be a healer, too." Her eyes wandered over towards Seth and her smile grew bigger.

"Jena!" Sally called from the bedroom. "Your mother needs you."

She frowned. "Coming!" Jena ran into the back.

Seth's eyes grew big. "Were you at the Battle of Staerdale Castle?" Seth asked.

Dane's eyes grew tired. "I fought at Port Eldham. The attack ended up being a ruse. We lost a lot of good men. The king was so confident that Port Eldham was the Darkstriders' main attack that he left a woman in charge of defending the castle."

Brock's face reddened. He clenched his fists. "She was a better knight than most."

Dane sniffed. "She didn't do such a good job, did she? The castle fell."

Brock started to rise when William moved between them. "No more. Reliving past mistakes will not lead us to overthrowing Kade and putting the rightful king on the throne. We've been down this road too many times with too many people."

"Dane," Jacob said. "We should stop this ridiculous quest. The prince is most likely dead or sold as a slave… or worse."

Seth swallowed. "What could be worse?"

Jacob looked down at Seth. "Nothing you need to worry about now. Let us talk with your father."

"No," Brock said. "The boy stays. If you want him to leave, then I suggest you lead by example."

Dane glared at Jacob. "He's okay. He's the one who freed me from the trap, not either one of you."

Brock settled back into the soft couch. "Why are you here? Crey Village is out of the way and quiet."

Sweat began to glisten on Dane's forehead. "We're—" He glanced up at Jacob. After he had nodded, Dane continued. "We're trying to join the rebels so we can end this nightmare that has befallen the kingdom. There's something that scares the Darkstriders more than one hundred legions of war wizards. It's insane, but they believe it. They're sending their defense forces out to search for him while leaving the beer wenches to guard the castle."

Brock frowned. "They may not be beer wenches."

Dane raised an eyebrow. "What do you mean?"

He leaned forward. "Dark Elves can change their form to appear to be any humanoid creature, but they had to be in contact with that person first. I don't know if a male elf can turn into a human female, but I wouldn't put it past them. They would never leave Staerdale Castle and Port Eldham undefended. It sounds more like a trap for overambitious knights to me."

Alya sat down next to Brock. "Would it hurt to find out if it's true?"

Seth smiled at Alya. She may not have helped them when the Dark Elves attacked, but she did save them from the Darkstriders in the market. She was brave, no question there. Yeah, she was the real thing.

Brock grunted. "How do you propose we do that? Staerdale Castle is a two-week journey from here."

She lowered her eyes.

Seth stood up. "How about we question the Dark Elves that are here?"

Dane frowned. "We'd have to kill them. The moment they got back, they'd wipe out everyone in Crey Village. Leave this to the adults, *boy*."

Brock glared at him. "I think you may have outstayed your welcome here. That's my son you're talking to."

Dane bucked up on Brock. "You're pathetic."

Alya whistled. Both men froze and stared right at her. "The boy is right. Maybe not interrogate them, but at least follow them. If it's their army, they'll have their regular equipment and complement of mages. Then we can grab one to confirm the story or not. At the very least, we could get them to tell us what they're afraid of. Maybe we could use it to our advantage."

Brock and Dane sat back down. "I can agree to that," Brock said.

Seth turned towards Alya. "Tell me what I need to look for."

She smiled. "I think your father is better for that than me."

Brock nodded. "Thank you. We're having a meeting tomorrow night. Please, come and join us. We'll decide then whether or not to bring you in."

Dane looked over at Jacob and William. "Yeah, we'll be there."

Brock looked back at Alya. "You want to come?"

Alya grinned. "I'd love to."

Seth stared at Alya. Her lips were fuzzy for just a second, then it was clear. He rubbed his eyes. *I must be getting tired.*

~

The next morning, Seth and Jena were walking along the dirt road towards the market square. When he looked into her eyes, she smiled. "What do you think Ellis will say? Think he'll help?"

Jena laughed. "We'll have to hold him back." She moved in closer to Seth.

His gut twisted. Sure, she liked him, but… maybe he was a coward. Seth smiled as he took her hand. Relief crashed over him as she pulled him closer. "I like this," he said quietly.

She blushed. "Me too."

Seth's stomach growled as the aroma of baking bread from Messer Bakery overwhelmed him. "Think Ellis is there?"

Jena giggled. "His father probably has him chained to a mixing bowl."

"Yeah, I can see that," Seth said as he entered the bakery.

Seth's mouth began to water. The front half of the shop had shelves filled with bread, fruit pies, and cakes. In the center of the room were two tables littered with a variety of baked goods. Past the displays behind a long counter sat a slender man with black hair. "How can you *not* get fat working here?"

Jena squeezed his hand. "I couldn't."

"Can I—oh, it's you two," Jim Messer said. He continued to scribble in his log. "Ellis can't come out and play. He's still in trouble for stealing."

"Who's here, Father?" Ellis called from the back.

Seth giggled as Ellis emerged, covered in flour. "You're supposed to get it in the bowl, not on your head."

Ellis frowned. "Not funny."

Jena couldn't hold back anymore. She burst out laughing.

Ellis rolled his eyes. "Father, I'm going out for a bit."

Jim glared at his son. "No, you'll end up in the stocks."

"For what?"

"For whatever you three are up to," Jim said.

"I won't steal anything," Ellis said as he crossed his fingers behind his back. "I promise."

Jim went back to his log. "Be back by supper." Jim waved them out of his bakery. "Get out, you're scaring away the customers."

Ellis followed Seth and Jena outside. "What are we doing?" he asked as he dusted off the flour. "Another try at the apples?"

"No," Jena said, "something better. You'll love it."

"What?"

Seth grinned. "Spying on Dark Elves. They should be in the square."

"Sounds like fun." Ellis followed Seth and Jena down the street.

When they arrived at the market square, Seth stopped in the middle of the street and looked around.

"What's the plan?" Ellis asked.

Seth turned towards Jena. "Is there a prayer or something you can do to help us find them?"

Jena shrugged. "Maybe, but if there is, I don't know it."

Ellis sniffed. "What kind of acolyte are you? That would have been the first thing I would have learned." A grin crawled across his face until he broke out in a giggle.

Seth punched Ellis in the shoulder. "Leave her alone."

"Who are you looking for?" a voice behind them said.

They whirled around. In front of Seth stood a tall man with curly black hair. Seth swallowed. "Have you seen the Dark Elves?"

The man blinked. "The Darkstriders?"

"Yeah," Ellis said.

Jena blinked. "Who are you? Are you new here?"

He smiled. "I'm Zeffer. I'm here with a merchant from Port Grurg, just south of Methos Lake."

"Have you seen them?" Seth asked.

Zeffer shook his head. "No, not today." He stared right into Seth's eyes. "You should leave them alone and go play."

Seth frowned. Should he have asked just anyone? What if Zeffer was a sympathizer? "We just wanted to ask what it was like being a Darkstrider, that's all."

A smile cracked Zeffer's face. "Still, best to leave them alone."

Seth watched Zeffer walk over to the herb merchant near the docks. "Should we spread out and wait?"

Jena shook her head. "Let's stay together." She reached for Seth's hand.

Ellis rolled his eyes. "Please, knock that crap off."

"She's right," Seth said as he took her hand. "Let's wait." They wandered around the square until they found a spot under a tree along the water and sat down. "They'll be here soon, I know it."

Six hours later, Ellis was drawing in the sand for the millionth time. "This is stupid. They're not coming."

Jena's eyes were dull. "Maybe he's right."

Seth sighed. "Whoever thought to do something this exciting would be so boring." He shrugged. "Try again later?"

They nodded.

"Let's go."

Zeffer looked on as the trio left the square. As soon as they were out of sight, he bolted into the Red Scale Tavern. Straight up the stairs, then he entered the third room on the left.

Malon was sitting in a chair reading a leather-bound book.

"They're gone," Zeffer said as his human form melted into a Dark Elf.

Malon looked up. "Elmar, what do we tell Shania?"

"That this boy may be with Brock and Sally Feran, but he might not be the one." Elmar peeked out of the window. "I don't understand why Tanyl fears a boy king. These humans could not overwhelm our forces, even if they raised an army. Don't you agree?"

"Not sure," Malon said as he shook his head. "I just don't know."

Just before dinner, Seth was sparring with Brock behind the house. When the sunlight began to fade away, Brock tossed his practice sword to Seth. "Put them away."

Seth watched Brock head back into the house. He smiled at his reflection in his sword's blade. Brock may not be his real father, but he *was* his father. Yeah, whenever he needed something, Brock and Sally were there for him, no one else. Seth grimaced. How would they react when they find out he failed to find the Dark Elves? Brock promised to raise him as his real father, the knight, would have. Would he take that as a failure? Seth was so sure that his little party would find them that it never occurred to him that he could fail. His stomach twisted as he entered the house.

"Seth, come out for dinner!" Sally yelled from the kitchen.

Seth was sitting on the edge of his bed. "I'll be right there!" The gleaming sword that Brock made for him stood in the corner. Whenever he was alone, its beauty commanded him to admire it. Someday he would be worthy of that great gift and avenge the family he never knew. Maybe perhaps even avenge the woman who saved his life. But first he had to get past tonight and tell the others that he had failed.

As Seth sat down, his mouth began to water when Sally placed the pork pie in front of him. "Thank you," he said as he heaved a forkful into his mouth.

Brock grinned. "He's getting better, Sally. He really is."

"I know, but, Brock, is it too soon?" she asked.

Seth looked up from his plate. "Too soon for what?"

"We're easing into it, Sally," Brock began. "Trust me."

"Easing into what?" Seth demanded. "Father, I love you, but sometimes you talk about me like I'm not even here."

Sally bit her lip.

Brock sighed. "You're already involved. The meetings, learning to fight, your volunteering to find the Dark Elves and finding out what they're up to are all part of it. I've told you about your father being a knight, but—there's more."

Sally shot Brock a fearful glance.

"I—it has to wait, son. I promise you will know soon enough." Brock's eyes softened. "You have to trust me, Seth."

"Do I have a choice?" Seth asked.

Brock shook his head. "No, you don't. I—"

Knock. Knock. Knock.

"Are they here already?" Sally asked as she got up to answer the door.

Seth smiled as Alya, wearing a red cloak, walked through the door.

Alya saw that the family was eating dinner. "Am I too early?"

Brock smiled. "It's okay."

"Would you like some? It's pork pie," Sally said as she motioned Alya to the table.

"You'll like it," Seth said.

"Why not?" Alya said as she sat down next to Seth. "Thank you for inviting me to the meeting," she said to Brock.

"No problem." Brock straightened up. "Seth is really doing great with a sword now."

Alya winked at Seth. "I had no idea."

Brock let out a small chuckle. "Let me tell you what happened today. You, see…"

Seth rolled his eyes as Brock told Alya how he disarmed his father. It was evident that Brock was proud of him, but —*but will he still be after I tell them I failed?* He took another bite of pork pie.

Thirty minutes later, Paul, Larry, Dane, William, and Jacob were drinking ale around the fireplace. Seth stared out the window, waiting for his special guest. His eyes lit up as Keya and Jena came around the corner.

"They're here," Sally said as she opened the door.

"Sorry we're late," Keya said. "Recovering from healing a broken hand. It took longer than I thought."

Brock put his ale down on the table. "Now that everyone's here, let's get started."

Seth stood next to Jena and reached for her hand, hoping that she'd take it. He wanted her to be unafraid to show the world that they cared for one another. The blood rushed to his face as he felt Jena's warm touch. He looked into her eyes and touched her soul. For a moment, he felt they were one.

Alya, Larry, William, and Dane sat in the remaining chairs around the kitchen table. Keya, Sally, Jacob, and Paul sat on the couch, facing them. All eyes were focused on Brock as if he was the leader of this small band.

"I first want to introduce Dane the Devoted and his companions, Jacob and William," Brock said.

Larry swallowed hard. "How do you know them?"

"We found them injured in the Sarun Grove," Brock replied. "Turns out they were knights under King Galin."

Paul frowned. "How do you know? Were they with you at Staerdale Castle?"

"No."

Paul leaned forward. "Did they tell you? Was that it?"

Dane looked uncomfortable. "If this is a problem, we'll move along."

Brock glared at Paul. "Are you purposely trying to make things harder than they already are?"

"Just answer the question," Paul demanded.

"Yes," Brock began, "they told us after we pulled Dane out of my bear trap." He glared right into Paul's eyes. "Do you trust me?"

"With my life."

"Then trust me now." Brock watched Paul ease back into his seat. He looked over at Seth.

His gaze brought forth the realization that he had to report his failure to the group. After his glorious speech at the last meeting, he was expected to come back with results, not a failure. It was hard enough that the other men did not respect him as a man, not yet. His telling on himself would only reinforce their doubt in his abilities to join the fight, to be like his father.

"Seth, you ready?" Brock asked.

Seth gasped for air. The time was now, where he'd tell his adoptive father that his faith in him was misplaced. His stomach twirled like cotton candy. "Yes, Father." He shot Jena a pleading glance, who merely smiled back at him. *How could she take this so lightly? She knew we failed and—*

"Seth?"

"Sorry, Father," Seth said. "My team went to the market all day, looking for the Dark Elves, and they never came into town." There, he'd said it. His muscles tensed, waiting for the verbal spears to be skewered through his heart. "We pretended to be playing by the water. No one noticed us, but we were vigilant."

Paul laughed. "I knew the boy was full of it."

Larry glared at Paul. "Really? What did you find out?"

"Nothing, but I didn't promise anything, either," Paul said.

"We were all supposed to go looking, not just the boy," Brock said. "I didn't see any either but—" He shot a questioning glance at Sally. After she had nodded, he continued, "Even though you didn't see them, they could have been there."

Alya blinked. "What do you mean?"

"Father, how can that be?" Seth asked. Was Brock trying to cover up for his failure? Could it not be his fault? Maybe he wasn't a complete failure after all.

"Sally and I served at Staerdale Castle under King Galin," Brock said.

"Kade's brother?" Alya asked.

Brock nodded. "Yes. Sally was the queen's handmaiden and I was the king's blacksmith. At one time, I trained to be a knight."

Dane scoffed at him. "You? A commoner?"

"Galin's father didn't care about bloodlines, only character. It wasn't until I defeated Kade in a match that there was pressure put on him to remove the commoner from among the knights. As my duty was to the Kingdom of Axain, I stepped down. He didn't force me," Brock said.

"I don't understand," Jacob said.

Brock straightened out. "There's more. We were friends with Thea the Loyal."

Only for a second, Alya's face twisted.

"One night at the Rusted Feathers Tavern, Sally was waiting for a friend to plan our wedding. She sat in a back booth along the wall. When Kade and Beldroth came in, she hid her face. After about ten minutes or so, her head hurt to the point where she had to close her eyes. When she opened them, the room was filled with dark elves."

Alya's face went white. "What?"

"Yes," Sally said. "Dark Elves can appear human. Beldroth cast a spell so Kade could meet their leader, but not know which human form he took. I happened to be in range."

Alya frowned. "That's ridiculous."

"What are you saying, Father?" Seth asked.

"They could have been right in front of you and you wouldn't have known," Sally said. "The Dark Elves infiltrated the king's court, the knighthood, and just about everything else."

Brock nodded. "That's right, we had no idea."

I'm not a failure, Seth thought. "How can we see them?"

Alya rolled her eyes. "This is silly. They cannot do that. Can we focus on real life?"

Brock ignored her. "I don't know. But we still have to find out what they are looking for."

"What's the plan?" Larry asked.

"Larry, you and Paul head up to Arrowhead Pond and watch it for a couple days," Brock said. "Tell the others about this... development, too. We're going to need all the help we can get."

"Sure," Paul said.

"Others?" Dane asked. "What others?"

"Just friends, that's all," Brock said.

Alya rubbed her chin. "I can keep an eye out in the market square."

"Sounds good," Brock said. "Dane, could you and your

party look for signs of a campsite on the west side of the Bahr River?"

Dane nodded. "I can do that."

"What about me, Father?" Seth asked.

"Sarun Grove, you know that area best," Brock said.

Seth nodded and said, "Yes, Father." He looked into Jena's eyes. "Will you help me?"

Her smile filled Seth's heart with warmth. "Of course I will."

Alya got up from the table. "I have to go. When do we meet again?"

"A week," Brock replied. "Here, after dinner."

Alya waved as she walked out the door.

For the next hour, the serious conversations turned into laughter as they drank more ale. Keya and Jena left, leaving Seth with the loud adults. Dane pulled out a cigar. "I'm going to smoke this outside. Be back in a minute."

Seth stared out the window onto the moonlit street, hoping to see Jena running back. That dream would not happen and he knew it. The cherry of Dane's cigar lit up. His eyes were drawn towards Dane as he walked across the street. A hooded figure stepped out of the shadows.

Who's that? Seth thought. Was Dane betraying them or just trying to get some companionship after he left? No, there was no hugging or advancing on the dark figure. He stayed back like he—he talks to Jacob.

As soon as Dane turned around, Seth jumped away from the window. Should he say anything? Yes—no, of course not. He was just jumping to conclusions, right? Yes—no, his head began to hurt from the war being waged inside. Was he the man his father wanted him to be? No, not if he didn't do anything. But, he's only a boy. He should stay out of it, or maybe tell Brock. Yes, that's it. Seth shook his head. *No, I am the man my father wants me to be.*

As soon as Dane came back into the house, Seth grabbed his shirt sleeve. "Who was that?"

"Mind your business. You're not too young to not get hurt," Dane said as he pushed Seth away.

"What's going on?" Brock demanded.

"I saw him talking to someone across the street in a hooded cloak," Seth said. "I just asked him who it was."

Brock glared at Dane. "Well?"

Dane frowned. "A merchant asking for directions to the market square. How should I know?"

"Seth, did you hear anything?"

Seth shook his head.

Brock sighed. "I think we've all had too much ale," he said as he motioned everyone to the door.

Seth watched the last man leave the house when Brock put his hand on his shoulder. "Seth, I know you meant well. But, leave the accusations to the adults," Brock said.

"I did the right thing. I'm trying to be the man you want me to be," Seth said.

"I know," Brock said, "I know. Now go to bed."

His soft words were like a dagger piercing his soul. They echoed not with pride, but disappointment. After closing his bedroom door, Seth stared out his window onto the street to see Dane and his men stumble into the darkness. *I don't trust him.*

~

Elmar and Malon paced around their room in the Red Scale Tavern. "Where is she?" Malon demanded.

Shania quietly stepped into their room in the Red Scale Tavern, laying her red cloak down on the bed. Elmar and

Malon were pacing around the room, appearing anxious. "Has the squad from Iron Fist Keep arrived yet?"

Elmar nodded. "Today, and I gave them your instructions."

Malon rolled his eyes. "Shania, this is completely unnecessary. Just kill the boy and get it over with."

Shania glared at him. "No, not yet."

"Why not?" Elmar asked. "We know the blacksmith and his wife smuggled Prince Galin out of the castle."

"That doesn't mean that Seth is the prince," Shania said. "Look, we have to be sure."

Elmar cocked his head. "Why do you care about him? Humans are no different than the pigs they slaughter for food."

Ignoring Elmar, she turned towards Malon. "What did the squad leader say? Do they have a war mage with them?"

Malon nodded. "Yes, but he's an apprentice, not a full wizard. Maybe this is not as important to Tanyl as you thought. Elmar has a point; just kill them and get it over with."

Shania looked away. Sure, Malon had a point, but… why was she hesitating? She had to avenge her family. What if—

"It would be easier, but then we would leave Crey Village without certainty that the prince is dead. No, we have to make sure first. That is the only way."

Elmar sniffed. "You're weak."

She kicked Elmar in the groin. "Enough of this insolence or I'll report you to Tanyl and his mages will punish you," Shania said. "Now get out."

Malon helped Elmar to his feet. "Make sure the reason you're delaying is for the benefit of the Darkstriders, not yourself." He dragged Elmar out of Shania's room.

Shania stared out the window at the full moon. "Prince Galin, where are you?"

CHAPTER 7

SETH AND JENA WERE SITTING ON THE SMALL ROCK WALL behind her house. He picked a yellow flower with a red center. It almost looked like the plant was bleeding. "Thanks for inviting me over."

She blushed.

"Lunch!" Keya called from the front room.

"Coming!" Jena yelled back as she jumped to her feet.

Seth and Jena sat at the kitchen table. He saw Jena's eyes get big when Keya put a slice of mushroom tart in front of her. "Is that your favorite?"

Jena inhaled the aroma from the slice of pie. "Yes."

Seth took a bite. "Whoever thought anyone could make the mushroom pie taste good?"

Keya gave Seth a stern look. "Was that an insult or a compliment? Hard to tell with you sometimes."

He smiled. "Definitely a compliment."

Knock. Knock. Knock.

"That must be Ellis," Jena said as she jumped from the table and opened the door.

Ellis' face lit up. "Got any more?"

Keya smiled. "Of course, I've got plenty of mushrooms growing on the manure pile out back."

Seth gagged and spit out a mouthful. "I'm full."

"Yeah—um, I'll pass," Ellis said.

"You sure?" Keya asked. "It's Jena's favorite."

Ellis' complexion turned a slight green. "I'm sure. We ready to go?"

Seth nodded. "Yes."

Keya's face fell as she saw Jena follow the boys to the door. "How long are you going to be?"

Seth shrugged. "Not long. We should be back by supper."

Keya grabbed Seth's shoulder and looked directly into his eyes. "Take care of my daughter. She's all I have left."

Fear, there was genuine fear on Keya's face. Alya would most likely find them in the market square, not in some random location in the woods. No, this was most likely to be another failure for the son of a great knight. "We'll be fine." He pushed his way out the door.

"Oh, Jena, pick up some valerian root!" Keya called after them.

Jena looked over her shoulder back towards her house. "I will, Mother."

They stopped by the herb vendor on the way out of the village. Seth watched Jena slip the valerian roots into her satchel. "What does it do?" he asked.

Jena waved at the old woman. "Thanks for the herb." She looked at Seth. "This is for a spell that puts a patient to sleep."

Ellis glared at Jena. "And I thought you just enjoyed hurting people as you cured them. What kind of sadist are you?" Unable to hold back any longer, he burst out laughing.

Jena's face reddened.

Seth covered his mouth, trying to smother his giggles. "Come on, let's go." He led them towards Sarun Grove.

What do I do if we find them? Seth thought as he entered the grove. His hand rested on the hilt of his sword. Every step was careful and silent. His eyes looked behind every bush and tree and stump. He looked back at Jena and Ellis; they were just as quiet as he was. How long could they keep this up?

After ten minutes, Seth felt a rock hit him in the back. He spun around, sword drawn, ready to draw Dark Elf blood.

"This sucks!" Ellis yelled. "Talk about boring."

"Ellis, stop it," Jena said. "This is important to Seth."

Seth glared at Ellis. "You don't have to stay if you're going to be an orc's ass."

"An orc's ass?" Ellis broke out laughing. "Really?"

Jena giggled.

Seth's nostrils flared. "Can you take it seriously or not?"

"Sure, but can't we walk normal and be quiet if we hear or see something?" Ellis asked.

Seth nodded. "Yeah, I—you're right."

"How long will it take to find them out here? I have to get home by supper," Jena said.

Seth looked around at the thick woods. "Not long. If they're here, we'll find them by then."

"How can you say that?" Ellis asked.

Seth smiled. "Trust me. No more than a few hours."

They followed Seth deeper into the grove.

Eight hours later, Jena plopped down next to a tree. "I'm tired."

"I guess they're not here," Ellis said. He looked right at Seth. "You said if we don't find them by now, they're obviously not here. So, let's head back."

Seth leaned against a tree. "But we haven't found anything yet." If they headed back now, would Brock think of him as a failure? How could he face the group again when he runs away because his stomach growls? No, he couldn't. How could he live up to his real father's memory by not going on? His palms began to sweat.

"Yeah," Ellis began, "so, let's go home."

Jena yawned. "I need to get home too."

They were about to leave him. "You're right. I said that we could find them quickly and I said the same thing before about finding them in the market square."

Ellis nodded. "Yup, you did."

"I was wrong both times," Seth said.

"What do you mean?" Ellis said as he pointed to the setting sun. "It's getting dark. We have to get home. I'm hungry."

Seth stood up. "If we go back, they'll never trust us again. Why should they?"

"Why should I care?" Ellis said.

"Because they think we're just kids that can't do anything real. My father, my *real* Father, was a knight."

"How do you know?" Jena asked.

Ellis burst out laughing. "You've been sucking down too many mushrooms."

Seth looked into Jena's eyes. "My adoptive Father, Brock, told me. He fought with him until the fall of Staerdale Castle. You know those meetings the adults have been going to for years?"

Both Ellis and Jena nodded.

"They're trying to help put the rightful king on the throne and I'm going to help them. I want to be like both my fathers," Seth said. "But I can't do it alone. I need your help."

"What about my mother? She told me to be home by dinner," Jena said.

"Does she go to those meetings too?"

Jena nodded.

"When we left, did she act like we were going out to play or to go on our mission? When someone puts a time limit of suppertime on how long you have to help the cause, is she taking you seriously? She was there when the group assigned us the grove." Seth pointed into the dark grove. "If we leave only because it's suppertime, they will never trust us again. My father's heart would be crushed. The idea that I am ready to learn to be like my real father will be whisked away in the wind."

Jena and Ellis leaned forward.

Seth held Jena's hand. "Please stay with me. I can't do this alone. I need your help. "

Jena blushed. "Okay."

They both looked at Ellis.

He shrugged. "My father won't even notice that I'm gone." He put his hand on top of Seth's and Jena's. "I'm in."

Seth smiled. "Let's find them." He led them further into Sarun Grove.

The moonlight broke through the treetops. Rain began to sprinkle on Seth's party. Droplets of water on the leaves sparkled as Seth walked through the underbrush. "How far to Bahr River?" Seth whispered.

Jena shrugged.

"Well," Ellis said, "we're heading north and we haven't hit it yet, nor have we run into Arrowhead Pond."

"I know that," Seth grumbled.

"Does it matter how far it is? Really?" Ellis asked.

"Can we rest for a minute?" Jena asked.

"Sure," Seth said. His butt became soaked as he sat on the wet leaves.

Ellis and Jena plopped down next to a large tree.

Jena yawned. "Rest for just a few minutes."

Ellis pulled a small blanket from his pack. "Good idea. Just 10 minutes or so."

"I didn't mean sleep." Seth stretched his arms and let out a yawn. He looked up at the moon directly above his head. "Yeah, fifteen minutes would do us some good." He settled back against the tree and his eyes slammed shut.

Fog rolled across the beach, covering Seth like a blanket. He sat up to see an Elf, not one with blue skin, rather a tanned complexion with long, silky blond hair. She was dressed in animal skins and carried a longbow across her back. Her green eyes were cold.

"Who are you?" Seth asked.

She knelt down next to him and her lips curled up. "Does it matter? You're in over your head, little boy." She pushed him back down. "Now go home before you get yourself killed or worse, captured." The elf turned and started to walk away.

"I've never seen an elf like you. How could I be dreaming this?"

She stopped. "Elf? You think I'm an elf?" The elf turned and glared at him.

"Aren't you?" Seth asked.

"I'm a *Vulwin* Elf," she said. She yanked him up by his tunic. "Nothing is as it seems."

Seth's face whitened as the Vulwin Elf screamed. Her hair turned black and her skin melted away and became a dark blue. Her ears grew and became more pointed at the end. "What? What are you?"

She threw him to the ground and kicked him in the side. "Nothing is as it seems." She drew her bow and notched an arrow. "Are you Galin the V or Galin the Orc's Ass?"

Sweat poured down his face and his stomach twisted. "Please—please don't."

"Just what I thought, Galin the Orc's Ass." She loosed the arrow.

"No!" Pain shot through his body as he looked down at the wooden arrow lodged in his chest. "No!"

S eth jumped up and his tunic was drenched. It was dark, really dark. The moon was gone behind the Wailing Mountains. It was right above them when fell asleep, so—it had not been minutes, but hours.

Off in the distance, a firelight cracked the darkness. Seth closed his eyes and listened. He heard laughter, talking, and crying. Could it be the Dark Elves? Maybe, maybe not. His legs began to shake and his shoulders tightened. If they left now, he could tell Brock they didn't find any Dark Elves in Sarun Grove. How would he know different? No one would know, and Jena and Ellis wouldn't blame him, right? Who would know if they all lied to Brock and ran back to his house? Only one person would know, *him*. All his speeches would be in vain and he would have shown Jena and Ellis how to be a *real orc's ass*. What if he—what if he went out to see what was out by the firelight?

A scream.

Was someone in trouble? It was a woman's voice. What if it was Sally? Would he just sit back and let her be violated or murdered? No, he wouldn't. He would charge in without hesitation, blazing a trail for others to follow. Yes, nothing could stop him from severing the head of the thing that hurt his adoptive Mother. Should he let that happen to someone else's mother? No, he wouldn't.

Seth moved over to Jena. Her soft face glistened from the sprinkling rain. He shook her. "Jena, wake up."

Her eyes cracked open. "What? What is it?"

"Found something," Seth whispered.

She shot up. "What? Here?"

Seth nodded. "Yeah." He reached over to Ellis and shook him.

"Leave me alone," Ellis said as he rolled over.

"Get up," Seth said as he jabbed Ellis in the ribs. "We found something."

Ellis sat up. "What are you waiting for then?"

Seth slipped his pack over shoulder. "Follow me."

The small party crept through the underbrush. Seth held his breath as he stepped over a fallen log. His eyes were fixated on the firelight ahead of them. The screams seemed to quiet down. Pits formed in Seth's stomach, weakening his heart. What happened to the woman? Did she give in or was she killed? He took another step and stopped. He closed his eyes and listened. The leaves rustled in the breeze. Nothing, nothing at all. Seth motioned Ellis and Jena forward as he took another step towards the light.

As they got closer, everyone was silent. Their pace slowed down to a crawl. Seth's eyes darted from tree to tree, from stump to stump, looking for anything, keeping watch. There was nothing but his own fear. Less than 100 yards from the campfire, he searched for a place to get a better look. Ahead to his right was a large fallen tree; it must have been at least six feet in diameter. Yes, it was big enough for all of them. He waved them to follow and they did.

Seth never took his eyes off the group around the campfire as he hid behind the tree. With Ellis and Jena behind him, he focused on the blue-skinned humanoids surrounding the fire. A naked body of a human female with her throat slashed was tossed on the ground like a piece of trash. His heart sank. Was he too slow to save her? Could three *children* take out fifteen Dark Elf knights? No, no they couldn't. If he charged in, they'd all be like that poor woman lying on the ground. What would they have done to Jena? Seth shuddered. He couldn't bear to . . . no, he wouldn't even give them the chance. Maybe—maybe, he needed to wait. They could take out one or two, but not fifteen. Yes, that was it. They had to search the camp and come back with—something. Seth leaned over to Jena. "That spell you put your patients to sleep with?"

Jena nodded.

"Can you do more than one?" Seth asked.

"No," she whispered, "and I have to touch the person."

"Will it work on Dark Elves?"

She nodded.

"We'll wait until they go to sleep and take out their sentry."

Both Ellis and Jena agreed.

Seth turned back towards the camp. *Come on, go to sleep before I lose my nerve.*

An hour later, Seth readjusted his seat behind the tree. *Do elves ever sleep?* His eyelids grew heavy. The glow of the rising sun was inching over the horizon. One of the Dark Elves stood up and began barking at the others in Elfish tongue. Seth could hear what was being said, but he couldn't understand it. He could be hearing something crucial; or was the leader just telling the others to hunt for breakfast?

Seth's right knee began to feel numb. He looked back at Jena and Ellis; both were in a quiet slumber. Should he wake them? No, not yet. Not until they—

Seth leaned forward as the Dark Elves arose, grabbing

their swords and bows. Something was happening. Without understanding the orders, how could he know what was being said? He nudged Jena and Ellis, pointing towards the camp. All three peered around the tree and almost immediately retreated behind it.

"What are they doing?" Ellis asked.

Seth shook his head. "I don't know, but we may be able to get into the camp."

Jena looked over at the horizon. "The sun's coming up. My mother is going to kill me."

"She may have to take her place in line," Seth said as he peered around the tree again. "They are—they're leaving one Dark Elf behind."

"So, so what? If he screams, they'll come running back and capture all of us," Ellis said. "If they catch us, they wouldn't just put us in the stocks for a day or two. They—they'd kill us."

Seth frowned. "Coward. What did you think you were going to do when we got here?"

Ellis looked away. "I knew I could do it before, but . . . now I'm not so sure."

Jena grabbed Seth's hand. "I'm with you."

"I know." His eyes softened as he gazed into her eyes. Those swirling pools within her eyes entrapped his soul. Seth couldn't help but smile. His grasped tightened.

Ellis rolled his eyes. "Please, stop it. Fine, I'll go. If it's only to get away from you two." He pulled out his daggers.

"Where'd you get those?" Seth asked.

"Your father."

Seth blinked. "He made those for you?"

Ellis frowned. "Of course not. I *borrowed* them from the shop."

Jena glared at Ellis. "You're such an imp."

"Quiet," Seth whispered. "Jena, can you put him to sleep?"

"If I can get close enough." Jena pulled the valerian root out of her pouch.

"Asleep? Please, let's just gut the bastard," Ellis said. "If we don't, that thing will just tell the others what happened."

Seth shook his head. "No, not yet." He leaned towards Ellis. "Can you help grab him so she can put him out? Please."

Ellis slid his daggers back in their sheaths. "I was just kidding. Let's go, I'm getting hungry."

Jena lowered her head in a silent prayer to Odella. In a moment, she raised her eyes and grasped the root in her left hand. "I'm ready."

Seth drew his sword and left the protection of the downed tree. The Dark Elf was sitting next to the campfire with his back towards Seth. Without taking his eyes off the foul creature, Seth moved left while Ellis slithered towards the right. He looked back and Jena was holding the roots and her lips never stopped moving. Confident that Jena was ready, Seth moved forward. His breath shortened and his heart beat faster and faster. Seth's eyes glared at his target. Maybe he was one of the Dark Elves who hit Sally? Maybe? Yeah, he must have been one of them, right? Who cares? All those bastards must pay. Seth glanced over at Ellis with his daggers poised to slay the Dark Elf. Seth knelt behind a tree, a mere twenty feet behind him.

Ellis crept towards the Dark Elf from the far side. He raised his daggers.

What is he doing? We should be doing this together. Seth's stomach twisted. Was it too late to turn back?

Ellis dashed towards their victim.

The Dark Elf's head jerked towards Ellis. He snatched up his sword and charged at Ellis.

Seth jumped up and raised his sword.

Ellis' face went white as he tripped over a root and dropped a dagger.

Seth's heart sank as the Dark Elf swung his sword at Ellis. "No!" Seth screamed.

He missed. The Dark Elf kicked Ellis in the gut, knocking the wind out of him. He turned towards Seth and smiled. "Come here, little boy. I haven't fed my dog yet," the Dark Elf said.

Seth swung at the Dark Elf. Their blades connected. The sword was knocked out of Seth's hand. He collapsed on the ground, backing away from the Dark Elf's blade.

His blue lips curled and his eyes narrowed. "And we're worried about you?" The Dark Elf burst out laughing.

Jena leaped up and grabbed the Dark Elf's neck. "Kan Odella frijori tene dinar. Garin pa vale!"

The Dark Elf crumbled to the ground.

Jena's eyes rolled back as she fainted.

"Jena!" Seth cried as he stopped her from hitting the ground. "Is she all right?"

Both Jena and the Dark Elf began to snore.

Ellis laughed.

Seth rolled his eyes. He shook Jena until her eyes opened. "What happened?"

"Did I forget to tell you that I would fall asleep too?" Jena asked.

He grinned. "Yeah, you left that part out."

"Help me search the camp," Seth said.

"Sure," Ellis said.

Twenty minutes later, Ellis was rummaging through a small unlocked chest. "Hey, I found something." He passed a letter to Seth.

Seth opened the parchment and began to read it.

. . .

K olvar,

I hope your journey from Iron Fist Keep was without incident. We have located the blacksmith and the queen's handmaiden that escaped Staerdale Castle with the prince. They are here in Crey Village with a thirteen-year-old boy, but I'm not sure he's the one. He lacks certain qualities that are usually found in royalty. However, if he is not the one, I'm sure we can follow Brock and Sally Feran to the real prince.

I have infiltrated into a local resistance group that is obsessed with removing Kade from the throne. Foolish humans, don't even realize that Kade is Tanyl's puppet.

Tanyl is convinced that the prince could be the one that the prophecy is about. I have not seen any human male child that has magic ability in Crey Village. I will keep looking.

We have to move in soon. I'll contact you.

S hania

"W hy is it in common?" Jena asked.

Seth shook his head. "No, idea." He looked down at the sleeping Dark Elf. "What about him?"

"Leave him," Jena said. "We've got to get home. I'm tired."

Ellis gathered up a few purses from the chest. "I'm ready."

Seth smiled at Ellis. "Let's go home."

. . .

The sun was up and Seth's stomach twisted as he approached his house. But how upset could they really be after he succeeded in his mission? A smile stretched across his face. Yeah, he did well. Brock would be so proud of him. Why was he nervous? There was no reason to be nervous. Visions of Sally hugging him and saying how much she loved him flooded his mind. He opened the door.

"Where have you been!?" Brock demanded as he leaped towards Seth. He slammed the door shut, throwing Seth onto the couch. "We thought—we—we were worried sick!"

"But, Father I need to show—"

Brock slapped him. "Sally was crying all night because of you. Go to your room."

Seth grabbed his pack and closed the door behind him as he plopped on his bed. The sting on his right cheek shattered his dream of a hero's homecoming. He pulled out the letter and read it again and again. The same question repeated in his mind. *Who is Shania?*

CHAPTER 8

SETH CHOKED DOWN ANOTHER SPOONFUL OF GRUEL. IT WAS AS cold as the absence of conversation at the breakfast table. He sat next to Brock; his adoptive Father couldn't even look at him. Tears ran down Sally's cheeks into her lumpy meal. He tore his eyes away from her and bore them into his wooden bowl. "I'm sorry. I'm sorry I stayed out all night."

"It's okay," Sally said before bursting out into another round of tears. Unable to control herself, she rushed to the master bedroom.

Brock cocked an eye at Seth. "I believe that you're sorry, but that doesn't cover it." He leaned towards Seth. "We sacrificed everything for you, even our own lives, and you nearly pissed it all away."

"But . . . I . . ." Seth's heart hit the floor. Brock was right, kind of. When he saw their camp, all he could think about was accomplishing his mission and coming back a hero. Was it smart for three teenagers to take on several Darkstrider knights? No, no way. Pride; his pride nearly got Ellis and Jena killed. Maybe he wasn't ready for this yet.

Brock glared at Seth. "Well? Spit it out already."

Seth tried to look at him, but he couldn't. "Don't you at least want to hear what happened?" He glanced down at the pocket that held the letter Seth had liberated the night before. As if it gave him a burst of courage, he looked right into Brock's eyes. "Don't you want to know why we were out so late?"

Brock stared at the welts on Seth's right cheek. "Do I?"

The indifference ran through Seth's soul like a spear. Did Brock even care that his adopted son found the enemy, subdued one, and stole a copy of their orders? Did Brock even care that his adopted son had proof that his petty little group was already infiltrated by the Darkstriders? Seth's face reddened. Yeah, Brock should care, if he was a *true* leader and not some wannabe knight, unlike his *real* father. If his real father were here, Seth would have been greeted with pats on the back, not a slap in the face. His eyes wandered over towards the master bedroom door. What about Sally? She was always there for him and—he needed Brock to find those bastards who hurt her.

"Well?" Brock asked.

Seth swallowed. "We found them."

"Who?"

"The Darkstriders' camp."

Brock's eyes narrowed. "You what?" Veins started to pop out on his forehead.

Sweat rolled down Seth's back. "We found their camp. There were a lot of Dark Elf knights there."

"Why didn't you come back and tell us?" Brock demanded. "We could have done something about it."

"We hid and waited until there was only one left," Seth said. "We knocked him out and looked around the camp."

Brock's jaw tightened.

"After that, we left," Seth said.

"What about the Dark Elf? What did you do to him?" Brock asked.

Seth shook his head. "Nothing. We left him there. I—"

Brock punched Seth square in the jaw, knocking him to the ground. "How could you? Now, all of them know exactly what and who to look for!"

Seth shook off the buzzing in his head. "What? I thought you would be proud of me!"

"For what? Endangering your family? Jena and Ellis? For nothing!" Brock leaped from the chair and headed towards the door. "I was wrong. You're not like your father, not at all." He slammed the door behind him.

Seth looked down at the letter in his pocket. "No, not for nothing."

As suppertime approached, Seth was helping Sally cooking the pork chops. Even the pleasant smell of his favorite food couldn't fill the gaping hole in his soul where Brock skewered it. Seth looked over at Sally preparing the carrots and his heart fell. The only mother he ever knew barely spoke to him all day. In the midst of his loving family, he never felt so alone. His eyes darted towards the door as it opened. His jaw ached as Brock entered the small home.

Brock didn't even look at Seth. Instead, he went right up to Sally and hugged her. He whispered something into her ear.

Seth's veins burned as he turned back towards the fire. *Hate, all he's showing me is hate,* Seth thought. He did every-thing his real father would have done and what did he get for it? A slap in the face. Yeah, if Seth's wife were threatened by those Dark Elves, he'd be the first one in line to slit their throats. But Brock didn't seem to care about how they treated Sally. Seth looked back at Sally talking to Brock. At least one man in the house was going to protect her, even if it was not her husband. The fire under his skin raged on as he flipped the pork chops.

"Okay, I will," Brock said.

Seth forced himself not to look back. *I will, I will what?* He felt a hand gently grasp his shoulder. Instinct or courtesy wanted him to turn around and look at Brock, but he willed himself not to.

"Seth," Brock began, "I'm sorry."

Seth's jaw tightened. *Sorry? Like hell he was.* "For what?"

Brock sighed. "You know what for."

Seth spun around and his eyes bore a hole through Brock. "You mean she made you apologize."

Brock bit his lip. "No, she didn't."

She gave Brock a pleading glance.

"I'm sorry for hitting you, isn't that enough?" Brock grabbed both of Seth's shoulders and his eyes softened.

He really is sorry, Seth thought. His frown began to crack.

"Please forgive me, son."

Seth's eyes narrowed. "Your son? I'm not your son. My real father would have been proud of me for finding them as I promised. Don't you remember that you were the one who assigned me to the Grove?"

Brock recoiled. "I remember. I also remember sending you there because I thought they wouldn't be there. I can't afford to send you on a real mission. I—" Brock's face went white as he slammed his mouth shut.

Seth's heart crashed to the floor. "You never expected me to succeed?" His eyes withered as he slid onto the couch. "You never trusted me. I—"

Sally rushed up behind Seth and hugged him. "That's not what he meant. You're a very special little boy and . . . unique."

"How?" Seth glared at Brock. "You lied to me."

Brock shook his head. "No, I didn't. I . . . the Sarun Grove needed to be checked, but . . . yes I didn't think you'd find anything. I swore to keep you safe and I—I love you as if you were my own son." He looked up at Sally and sighed. "You're the only one to come up with anything and I'm sorry for not listening before. I—I'll listen before I cast judgment on you again, I promise. Please forgive me?"

A great smile stretched across Seth's face as he nodded. "I forgive you." He latched his arms around Brock's neck. "I'm sorry too, Father. Sometimes I forget that you are the only father I ever really knew."

Sally smiled.

The front door slammed opened, knocking a picture off the wall.

Seth jumped up.

Brock moved in between Seth and the door.

"Help," Alya said as she dragged Larry into the little home, with Dane in tow.

Blood was pouring out of Larry's right arm. "I'm sorry, so sorry."

Brock grabbed Larry. "Sally, get some blankets."

He laid Larry down on the floor. "We're going to patch you up."

Larry's eyes wavered. "They—they got Paul and the others."

"Never mind that now," Sally said as she put the blankets on the floor next to him.

Brock looked up at Alya. "Help me shift him on the blankets."

She nodded.

"One, two, and up." They heaved the large man onto the blankets.

"Alya, what happened?" Brock asked.

"The Darkstriders knew where the camp was and killed them," Dane said. He sat down on the couch.

Brock blinked. "What are you doing? Get over here and help him."

"What do you expect me to do?" Dane asked.

Brock's fiery eyes glared at Dane. "How about putting pressure on the wound?"

Dane sighed. "Really? For him? He's a commoner."

"I wasn't asking! Now get over here and do it or I'll run you through myself. Got it?" Brock demanded.

Dane swallowed. "Okay, okay. Don't have a cow over it." He moved over next to Larry and pressed on the slash across his bicep.

"Father, what can I do?" Seth asked.

"Get Keya and tell her we need her help," Brock said.

"On my way," Seth said as he dashed out the door.

Fifteen minutes later, Seth rushed inside with Keya and Jena, with a sack over her shoulder. He looked down at Larry, wrapped in a blood-soaked blanket. His stomach lurched as he moved closer and the smell hit him.

Jena covered her nose with her hand and rushed to the door.

Keya's nose twitched as she knelt down next to Larry. She caressed his profusely sweating forehead. "Shhh," she said. "Larry, it's going to be okay. Let me help you relax some." Keya looked up at her puking daughter in the doorway. "Jena, snap out of it and get over here."

Jena wiped the corner of her mouth. "Yes, Mother."

"Sally, we need some towels, towels that you can throw away," Keya said.

"Sure," Sally said as she ran into her bedroom.

"Mother, what can I do?" Jena asked.

"Do we have valerian root in the bag?" Keya asked.

Jena dug deep into the sack. "Yes, we have enough."

Keya's hands shook and her face went white. "Okay, use it and make him comfortable."

Brock pulled Keya to her feet and glared right into her eyes. "Comfortable? Don't make him comfortable, heal him. I didn't send my boy so you could put him to sleep."

Tears flowed down Keya's cheeks. "I—I—I can't save him."

"He's asleep, Mother," Jena said.

"I've got the towels," Sally said as she entered the living room. Her mouth dropped as her eyes focused on Larry's unconscious body. "Is he . . ."

Keya burst into tears.

Brock pulled her in close. "Keya can't help him."

Keya wiped a tear from her eye. "He lost too much blood. I—I'd die if I healed him. When I heal someone, I take their injury until Odella removes it from me. If I—I can't. I'm so sorry." She buried her head into Brock's immense chest.

"It's okay. Will he suffer?" Brock asked.

Keya shook her head. "No, not now. He'll be asleep until he passes or heals on his own."

"How many patients have you seen heal on their own from something like this?" Brock asked.

"None," Keya said before bursting into another round of tears.

"Dane, let's move into the other room," Brock said.

"Okay," Dane replied.

Brock and Dane grabbed Larry and moved him into the master bedroom.

The ten minutes it took for Sally to brew a pot of tea was an eternity. Seth couldn't take his eyes off the blood stains on the floor. Was that the work of the infiltrator the letter he lifted from the Dark Elf camp spoke about? He looked over at Dane; he was silent and heartless. Seth's blood raged through his veins. How could someone care so little about anyone just because he was a commoner? Were all knights like that? His father? No, not his real father. Brock was a commoner and spoke so highly about Seth's real father. It was not possible that his father was like that. Why else would someone act like that?

Sally brought in a tray of simple cups filled with tea. "Maybe this will break the silence." She attempted to smile but failed.

Seth held Jena's hand and squeezed. He looked into her eyes and there was a faint twinkle when they made contact. Yeah, even among all this evil or the possibility that the betrayer was in the room with them, he knew everything would be okay because she was with him. She smiled at him and his heart softened. He looked at Dane. "What happened?"

Dane sipped his tea. "Well, Jacob and I were at the camp with Larry, Paul, and the others. They were in charge of security and . . . well . . . they failed. Paul was the perimeter and never saw them coming." He rolled his eyes. "You can't trust commoners to do *important* work. Brock, you should know that by now."

Brock glared at him. "That's it?"

Could the infiltrator be Dane? Seth thought. He tightened his grip on Jena's hand. "Did they take anything?" Seth's eyes bore into Dane.

As if Dane felt Seth's scrutiny, he blinked. "No, they took nothing from *me* and Jacob."

"Does that qualify something as *important*?" Brock asked. "You're a real ass."

"Hey, leave him alone," Alya said. "It wasn't his fault the Darkstriders attacked the camp."

"Were you there?" Seth asked.

Alya swallowed. "No, I saw them coming out of the woods."

"So you don't know what happened," Brock said.

Dane threw his cup across the room. "What are you saying, commoner? How dare you imply that—"

Brock jumped up from his chair. "You bastard!"

Alya wedged herself in between the two large men, pushing them apart. "Knock it off, you two."

"Brock, please," Sally said.

Seth stared right at Dane. His muscles tensed as his adoptive father was threatened.

Brock backed off and shook his head. "Yeah, she's right. We've got the Darkstriders to fight, not each other."

Dane shook Alya's hand off him. "If you would let me be with the other knights you are hiding in exile, instead of with this—"

"Why should I?" Brock asked.

"Because I—"

Alya clamped her hand over Dane's mouth. "Who else could be as arrogant as a nobleman knight?"

Brock smiled. "You've got a point."

Dane tore Alya's hand away from his mouth. "How dare you!" He lunged towards Brock, but Alya knocked him to the floor.

"He certainly talks like Kade," Brock said.

"Who?" Alya asked.

Seth stared at her. Who's Kade? Kade the Usurper was the King of Axain. Why did she not know that?

"Do not put my name in the same sentence with that— that traitor," Dane said as he climbed to his feet.

"Calm down," Brock said. "They're at Arrow Lake. Behind the waterfall there's a cave." He smiled at Alya. "You both can go."

Alya shook her head. "I prefer to stay in town, but I'll escort Dane there so he doesn't get himself hurt."

Dane's face flared up but he remained silent.

"I'll come by the shop tomorrow afternoon," Alya said. "Night." She led Dane out the door.

Seth closed the door behind them. "Father, I—I don't think you should have done that."

Brock yawned. "Done what?"

"Sending Dane to the knights in hiding," Seth said. "I don't trust him."

"None of that tonight. Go to bed, Seth," Brock said.

Should he show Brock the letter now? Before it was too late? No, in the morning he'd show him the spoils of his attack on the Dark Elves. "Goodnight, Father," he said as he headed into his bedroom.

CHAPTER 9

SETH STARED OUT HIS BEDROOM WINDOW INTO THE MOONLIT night sky. Should he have shown the letter to Brock? Yeah, well, maybe. Was it his fault that his adoptive father didn't even want to hear about what they'd found when they first got back? No, it wasn't. If the letter was true, could Dane be the traitor? Yes, well, he did want to know where the other knights were that Brock was hiding. Dane hated commoners, no doubt there. His complete disregard for them and lack of caring for the deaths made that clear. Was it because he was a stuck-up noble who missed his privilege, or something else? When Seth told Brock about his suspicion, he was dropped down a few notches.

Seth blinked. What if he misread the letter? He pulled the letter out from the pair of pants lying on the floor. He crept up to the window and opened the letter in the moonlight.

. . .

K olvar,

I hope your journey from Iron Fist Keep was without incident. We have located the blacksmith and the queen's handmaiden that escaped Staerdale Castle with the prince. They are here in Crey Village with a thirteen-year-old boy, but I'm not sure he's the one. He lacks certain qualities that are usually found in royalty. However, if he is not the one, I'm sure we can follow Brock and Sally Feran to the real prince.

I have infiltrated into a local resistance group that is obsessed with removing Kade from the throne. Foolish humans, don't even realize that Kade is Tanyl's puppet.

Tanyl is convinced that the prince could be the one that the prophecy is about. I have not seen any human male child that has magic ability in Crey Village. I will keep looking.

We have to move in soon. I'll contact you.

S hania

W hat would Brock and Sally say when he showed them? Would they be mad? No, he would be told how much he was like his father by Brock. Sally would . . . she would just say how proud she was of him for saving the family. What then? It was obvious, wasn't it? Seth and Brock would find the traitor and make him die a traitor's death. What if they were upset because he didn't show them earlier? They wouldn't be. It wasn't because he didn't want to; no, it just wasn't the right time.

A smile crept across Seth's face. They would both be proud of him. Yeah, he would be their hero. Seth climbed back into bed and sank into sleep.

Hours later, and just before the sun came up, Seth went into the living room. Brock was sitting at the table eating a bowl of gruel. He felt the letter in his pocket, reluctant to pull it out.

Brock looked over at him. "What are you doing up?"

Seth swallowed. Should he just blurt it out or hand him the letter or . . . or was this a mistake? "Are you going to the shop this morning?"

Brock frowned. "You know I am. Did you want something? I wasn't expecting you up for a while."

Seth swallowed, hard. "I—well, yes, I wanted to show you something." There was no turning back now. Why was he afraid? Brock would tell him that he was just like his father the knight. He moved closer to Brock and pulled the letter from his pocket. "Me, Jena, and Ellis found this," Seth said as he handed it to Brock.

"What is it?" Brock asked. Without waiting for an answer, his eyes dove into the letter.

A knot began to form in Seth's stomach as he waited with a tiny smile on his face for Brock to tell him how proud he was of him. His smile began to fade as Brock's face reddened. "Father?"

It was almost like fire was coming out of his eyes when Brock glared at Seth. "Where did you get this?"

Seth's heart sank as his naive dreams were shattered once

again. "I—I—we got it from the Dark Elf camp a few nights ago. I tried to tell—"

"Why didn't you show me this before?" Brock demanded. "You put the whole family in danger!"

Seth backed away from him. "You wouldn't let me tell you! Every time I tried, you either ignored me or told me to go to my room or—please, Father, I did try to tell you."

"What's all the yelling about?" Sally asked from the bedroom door.

Brock handed her the letter. "Read this."

Seth's pleading eyes begged Sally to comfort him. Her beautiful face turned white and her mouth opened wide. What had he done?

"Brock, I can't go through that again," she said. "I can't bear to lose any more family or friends for—" She slammed her mouth shut as her eyes looked over at Seth.

"What?" Seth asked.

"We won't," Brock said. He looked right into Seth's eyes. "You mentioned something about Dane last night. You said that you didn't trust him. Was that because of the letter?" Brock asked.

Seth nodded. "He came into town recently, and after the Dark Elves hit Mother. He also wanted to be with the other knights you have hidden at Arrowhead Lake."

"What about Alya?" Brock asked. "Why don't you suspect her?"

Seth shrugged. "She arrived before this all started happening."

"He's right," Sally said. Her fearful face looked right into Brock's eyes. "What do we do?"

Seth moved towards Brock. "We question Dane and find out the truth. He either tells us what he knows or clears his name."

Brock smiled. "I wish. No, we're leaving."

"What? You can't do that. I have a life here and I won't give it up," Seth said.

Brock grabbed Seth by the shirt and slammed him against the wall. "Don't you dare tell us about sacrifice. We gave up everything for you! My sister was tortured and killed to protect you." His face hardened. "Many people died to save your lousy goblin ass."

Sally pulled Brock's arm back. "Stop it. It's not his fault."

He dropped Seth. "I—I'm sorry."

Tears tried to burst through, but he held them back. "What's not my fault? Damn it, you have to tell me! I'm not some magical component or a side of beef. I'm your adopted son. Talk to me!"

Sally glanced at Brock.

"No," Brock said. "You proved you're not ready. Your father would've shown this letter regardless of whether I wanted to see it or not."

The dam cracked and tears rolled down Seth's face. "I'm not leaving."

"Are you willing to watch them torture and kill Jena and Ellis because of you?" Brock demanded. "How far are you willing to go?"

Seth's tears began to turn into fire. He moved closer to Brock and his face hardened. "At least I'm willing to do something about it."

Brock slapped Seth, knocking him to the ground. "Mind your place, boy. Pack up your things today, we're leaving in a few days."

Seth rubbed the handprint on his right cheek. "I hate you!" He ran out, slamming the door behind him.

〜

Seth's heart raced as he bolted down the street towards Jena's house. He never should have shown Brock the letter. If he didn't, he wouldn't be leaving, right? He clenched his jaw. Yeah, it was because he had to be the hero. Seth was so anxious for praise that it never occurred to him that Brock could be angry. A slap in the face or punch in the gut he could handle, but not moving away. Everything was perfect until those damned Dark Elves showed up. They destroyed his life and hurt his adoptive Mother while Brock did nothing, like a coward.

The sun cast long shadows on the road. Another few turns and he would be at Jena's house. Seth picked up the pace. What would he tell her? His stomach twisted. Would he tell her why he really doesn't want to leave? Should he? Maybe he'd just make it worse. Yeah, that's it. Seth swallowed as her house came into view.

Seth felt the tears pressing from behind his eyes as he knocked on the door. What if she's not up yet or maybe . . . maybe her mother sent her to get some herbs. His mouth dried up. Maybe this was a bad idea. No, he had to tell her, right? Seth turned around and started walking. Maybe later.

"Where are you going?" Jena asked.

Seth turned and smiled at Jena standing in the doorway. "I—I thought it might be too early for you to be up." He felt the tears trying to free themselves, but he beat them back.

"We're always up before dawn. You know—what's wrong?" Jena asked.

He hugged her. "I—can we talk?"

Jena nodded. "Sure."

Seth followed her inside.

Alya and Keya were chatting on the couch, drinking tea.

Freshly cooked bacon invaded Seth's nostrils. Normally, he'd be charging at the breakfast plate, but not today.

"You're here pretty early. Everything all right at home?" Keya asked.

Jena glared at her mother. "He wants to talk."

Alya's face dropped as she put her tea down. "Are your parents all right? They weren't—"

Seth shook his head. "No, nothing like that. I just need to talk to Jena."

"Talk about what?" Keya asked.

Jena pushed past them. "We'll be out back where it's private."

Seth looked back at Alya before he went out the back door, just for a second. Her hair was fuzzy, as if he needed spectacles. He blinked and it was gone. *I'm going nuts.*

Jena sat down at a small wooden table with benches on either side. "Have a seat."

Seth swallowed as he sat down across from her. What if he gave her the wrong idea? That this was not bad news? Should he tell her the *whole* truth? He reached across the table.

Jena grabbed his hands and smiled. Her gaze broke down all the walls Seth built up during his short walk here. "What is it?"

"Do you remember the letter we found at the Dark Elf camp?" Seth asked.

She nodded. "Yeah, what—"

Seth leaned in. "I showed my adoptive father the letter."

"What did he say?"

A single tear broke free and rolled down his right cheek. "He got angry with me. I thought he would've praised me for finding it. I even told him that I thought Dane could be the one described in the letter."

Jena blinked. "The letter talks about a woman."

He nodded. "I know."

"What's he going to do?" Jena asked.

He pulled her hands close to his heart. "He's making us move." His eyes softened as he stared into hers. "I don't want to go. I want to stay with you." Seth swallowed. Should he tell her? Did she already know? If so, there was no need to tell her, right?

Jena's face blushed. "I—I don't know what to say. I don't think my mother would have a problem if your parents are fine with it."

Seth shook his head. "There's more. Brock said that they'd kill everyone here to get at us if we stayed."

"Why?" Jena asked.

Seth blinked. "I'm not sure. It has something to do with me, but I don't know what. They won't tell me."

"Why not?"

"I—I don't know." Tears rolled down his cheeks.

Jena got up and pulled Seth into her arms. "I'm here."

Her touch soothed his heart like magic. He pulled her in tightly. "I can't let anything happen to you. I couldn't—I couldn't bear it."

"Nothing's going to happen to me," Jena said.

Seth looked right into her eyes. "There's something I have to tell you." *No backing out now.*

"What is it?"

His stomach twisted and his throat became dry. "I—I—I love you." There, he'd said it. Seth braced for a forcible rejection.

Jena's eyes glistened. Her smile stretched across her face. "I love you too. I always have." She kissed him.

"I can't stay here. But, you can come with us? Maybe?" Seth asked with pleading eyes. "We love each other and—well, maybe we can get married someday."

Jena stepped back. "I can't go. Why can't you stay?"

"What if they torture you to get to me? I couldn't have that on my conscience," Seth said.

"They won't," Jena said as she moved away from him. "I can't go because my mother needs me. I'm not the one who has dreams about being something that I am not. I want to be a healer like my mother. I need to learn from her," Jena said.

Her words were like a sword through Seth's heart. "But, I love you. You said you love me, too."

"I do love you, Seth, but not enough to leave my home." Tears flowed down her cheeks. "I'm going to miss you so much."

Seth hugged her with all his heart. "I—I can't let anything happen to you."

Jena's puffy eyes looked into his soul. "I know. I—"

"What's going on?" Alya asked. She had put on her leather armor and her swords were at her side. "You heard me."

"How long were you standing there?" Seth asked.

"Long enough," Alya said. "Where are you going, Seth? What letter?"

Could he trust her? Alya? Yes, she had been there for him and Sally, since the summer. "We're moving. Father says it is too dangerous here. I—I don't know why."

"The letter?"

"We found that at a Dark Elf camp in Sarun Grove," Jena said. "He showed it to his father before—"

Seth elbowed her in the side. "Jena, stop."

Alya smiled. "It's okay. Your secret's safe with me."

"What's going on out here?" Keya asked.

"It seems that Seth and Jena are in love," Alya said.

Keya smiled. "How sweet."

Seth rolled his eyes. "Please." He gave Jena a kiss on the cheek. "I've got to get back. I'll see you later. I promise."

"I'm sorry I can't go with you," Jena said. "I love you."

He looked over at Alya. Was it a mistake to tell her? "Bye," Seth said as he left the house.

CHAPTER 10

After an hour of wandering the streets of Crey Village, Seth returned home. Brock and Sally were embracing each other and both had wet cheeks. "I'm back." He looked right into Brock's eyes. "I'm sorry."

Brock put his hand on Seth's shoulder. "I know you don't want to go. Sometimes, to protect those we love we have to make sacrifices. I'd do anything for her and you."

"I still don't want to go. I want to stay with Jena," Seth said. "But, if you're right, and they kill her because of me, I don't know what I'd do."

"We can come back to see her in a month or two," Brock said. "I know how important she is to you."

Seth blinked. "How?"

Sally smiled. "We have eyes, you know."

"You look at her the way I looked at Sally when we were dating," Brock said. He tossed Seth two sacks. "Pack up your stuff and help pack up the shop afterward. Okay?"

Seth nodded. "I'll do it."

. . .

Three hours later, Brock and Seth arrived at the blacksmith shop. Seth was collapsing the displays and tossing them into the cart. "Father, where are we going to go? I mean, where will we be safe?"

Brock came out of the little building carrying a full sack. "The letter said that there are more Darkstriders at Iron Fist Keep."

"Where's that?"

Brock put the sack into the cart. "North and just west of Drusas."

Seth took another sack out of the cart and started loading up Brock's tools. "So, where do we go?"

Brock sighed. "The best place would be in the middle of nowhere, but we couldn't make a living there. We have to be close enough to civilization to live, but far enough away not to be noticed. I thought we should go west, cross the Wailing Mountains, and try Nia Village. It is surrounded by farmland and traders visit there from time to time."

"How do you know that?" Seth asked.

Brock ran his fingers through his hair. "Well, it used to be that way, about ten years ago. I'm sure it hasn't changed that much."

Seth put the sack in the cart. "What about the prince? Who's going to take care of him when you're gone?"

Brock rubbed the back of his neck. "I—well—he's coming with us."

Seth grinned. "I get to meet him? When? When do we pick him up?"

"Um—we don't." Brock shook his head. "I can't do this anymore."

"Do what?" Seth asked.

"Let's go inside," Brock said as he headed towards the door of the small building.

"Sure," Seth followed him inside.

Brock and Seth sat down at the small table, which was the only piece of furniture left inside. Brock swallowed. "Where do I start?"

Seth blinked. "What?"

"Okay, you know how I told you that your father was a knight of the Kingdom of Axain?" Brock asked.

"Yes."

"He was more than that. Your father was Kade's brother." Brock paused as if he was having an argument inside his head. "The king is your uncle."

Seth's mouth opened, but no words came out. What did this mean? Was he the brother of the prince? A cousin maybe? Could he *be* the prince? Seth shook his head. No, he couldn't be. He can't overthrow the Darkstriders and Kade the Usurper. No, it wasn't possible. If he were, he would just let down his adoptive parents. "What do you mean? Am I related to the prince?"

Brock stared directly into Seth's eyes. "Your last name is Ravenward. You're Galin the V of Ravenward, the rightful heir to the throne. Your duty is to overthrow Kade and take back your kingdom. It'll be a long quest, but you have to do it."

"Prince?" Seth walked over to the window. "All of this is because of me? The meetings and all that talk about going against the king."

Brock nodded. "Yes."

"What about the man last summer who was hanged in the market square?"

"He was a former knight of Axain and he was helping us. Instead of giving us up, he sacrificed his life for you," Brock said.

Sacrificed? *That man sacrificed his life for—me?* Seth thought. "Was he the first to die because of me?"

"Why do you ask such a thing?" Brock demanded.

"I need to know."

"I—"

"Please, tell me," Seth said.

"No, he wasn't, and he won't be the last." Brock grabbed Seth's shoulder. "No one can know who you really are or they will kill everyone you care about."

He nodded. "I'm still your Seth." Seth stared out the window into the midday sun. *Was this an honor or a curse?*

~

Sally was in her kitchen putting the last pot into the sack. Hard to believe they were moving again. Was it going to be like when they first escaped Staerdale Castle? Since the Darkstriders found them, why wouldn't it be? Never staying in one place for more than a few weeks . . . Beads of sweat formed on her back as her stomach twisted. At least Seth was safe. That made it all worth it, right?

"Where are you going?"

Sally whirled around. Her face became white as she saw three Dark Elves enter her home. "What—what do you want? I've done nothing wrong."

The woman Dark Elf had long dark hair which accented her deep blue skin. "Yes, you did," Shania said.

The bald one frowned. "Shania, we've got to make this quick," Elmar said.

"We've got plenty of time to have some fun," Malon said. His fingers raked through his short dark hair. "Do we have to kill her right away? We should have some fun with her first. Look at her; she likes me."

Sally stepped back as they moved towards her. "What do you want?"

The corners of Shania's mouth curled up and her eyes narrowed. "You were at Staerdale Castle."

Sally shook her head. "No, not me."

"You were the handmaiden for the queen."

"No."

"You were friends with Thea the Loyal who killed my brother!" Shania lunged at Sally, knocking her to the floor.

Tears flowed from Sally's eyes. "Please, no!"

Shania took a dagger from her belt. "You want to live? Tell me about Seth."

She couldn't take her eyes off Shania's blade. "What about him? He's thirteen and my son," Sally said.

Shania shook her head. "No, he's not your son. He makes it no secret that you are his adoptive parents." She jabbed the dagger close to Sally's breast. "My father was killed in the battle of Port Eldham. Maybe I should cut off a limb for every family member I've lost because of you!"

She felt the tip of the dagger poke her breast. "How is that my fault," Sally asked. "Please, leave me alone!"

Shania licked her lips. "Tell me about the boy or I'll give you to them," she said, pointing at Elmar and Malon. "They're not known to be nice to their human lovers."

Sally took a deep breath. What should she do? If she told them everything, would they leave her alone? No, they'd kill her anyway. What if she lied? "We're going to Port Grurg on Methos Lake. We were going to catch a boat and go into exile."

Shania frowned. "Really?"

The fire erupted in Sally's eyes. "I told you what you wanted."

Shania leaned in close. "I don't believe you."

Elmar grabbed Sally's shoulder. "We've got to hurry."

"Are you sure there's nothing else you want to tell me?" Shania asked.

I'm going to die, Sally thought. "No."

"Well?" Malon asked.

Shania grinned at Sally. "Take her in the bedroom and . . . make it hurt."

Sally's face went white as her will dissolved. "No!"

Elmar dragged the screaming woman into the bedroom, with Malon in tow. "Come on, wench."

Sally clawed at the huge Dark Elf. "Stop, please, don't!"

Malon backhanded Sally. "Shut your mouth."

Elmar grabbed her hair and flung Sally on the bed.

"Have fun," Shania said as she closed the door.

The ride back in the horse-drawn cart was a quiet one. Even as they rode through the market square, Seth was silent. As Brock turned the cart, Seth gazed upon the fishmonger near the dock. How many people died because of him? Did he put the fishmonger in danger simply by being here? Seth sighed. Was Jena in danger because of him too? Yes, of course, she was.

As they approached the bakery, the sweet smell of baking bread overpowered Seth's senses. "Father, I think I understand," Seth said.

"Understand what?" Brock asked.

"Why we have to leave." Seth looked at the Ellis' father's bakery. "All my friends are in danger because of me, especially Jena."

Brock's eyes dropped. "I—I know how you feel. When we get on the road, things will get better."

"When can I see Jena again?" Seth asked.

Brock shook his head. "I don't know. Soon, maybe."

Their house finally came into view. The door was flung

open. Packed sacks were tossed about and one was dumped onto the ground. "Something's wrong," Seth said.

"No!" Brock said as he cracked the reins.

As soon as the cart stopped, Seth leaped down. His heart pounded in his chest. Seth's jaw tightened as he entered the small house. The couch was overturned. His head swung left and right, searching for his adoptive mother. Nothing.

"Sally?" Brock yelled as he ran into the house. His face went white. He swallowed. "Check your bedroom."

Seth nodded and sprinted into his tiny bedroom. Nothing. It was just as he'd left it that morning.

"No!" Brock yelled from the other room.

Seth's heart skipped a beat. "Mother!" He bolted out into the living room. Not there. *Their bedroom.*

As he entered the bedroom, his breath left him. The only mother he ever knew was naked on the bloody bed. Her once beautiful hair was torn from her skull and tossed on the floor. Those fingers that caressed him when he was feeling down were severed and tossed about on the bed. Sally's chest was torn open and—he couldn't look anymore. "Mother! Was this because of me?" Unable to stop himself, tears flowed down his cheeks.

Brock was holding what was left of his wife, crying. "No, it's all my fault. I'm so, so sorry. Please, Sally, forgive me."

Seth knelt down next to Brock. He put his arm around his father. "I'm sorry."

Brock shook his head. "No, I—"

"Sally? Brock? You all right?" a female voice said in the living room.

Seth looked back towards the living room.

"Oh—Sally!" Alya gasped as she entered the room.

Tears rolled down Seth's cheeks. "Alya, they killed her! They killed my mother!" He looked back at Brock, who wouldn't even look at him. Seth latched his arms around Alya. "Help us."

Alya gave him a big hug. "I will." She put her hand on Brock's shoulder. "How can I help?"

Brock's teary eyes looked up. "Help me bury her."

Alya smiled. "Sure."

Seth looked down at the only mother he had ever known. "The Dark Elves did this, didn't they?"

"Probably," Alya said as she escorted Brock into the living room.

Something caught Seth's eye on the bed. He reached down and picked up several black hairs. Sally was blond, so —these must have come from whoever killed her. Dark Elves have black hair, but so did Dane, right? He must work for them, right? A collaborator. *They're all going to pay*, Seth thought.

CHAPTER 11

TEN MINUTES LATER, SETH SAT ON THE COUCH WITH BROCK, waiting for Alya to return. He looked up at his father. Tears flowed like a mountain river down his cheeks. There was a strong man crying like a babe in the woods. Seth blinked. Why wasn't he crying? Sure, he did earlier, but why did he stop? Was he really that strong or did he desire something else?

Alya rushed through the door. "Keya and her acolytes are on their way to dispose of—I mean, to take care of Sally." She turned away, just for a second.

Did she smile? Seth thought.

Brock nodded.

Seth looked towards the closed bedroom door. He would find Dane and those . . . those Dark Elves and . . . skin them . . . no, roast them alive. Yeah . . . no . . . well, maybe. Sally getting slapped in the market square was nothing compared to this. *Surely, Father will get past his grief and do what is right, avenge his wife.* This boy prince had been turned into a vengeful one. But, he was still young and inexperienced. He couldn't do it alone, right? *Father will be at my side, surely.* What about Jena and Ellis and Keya? Who could say no?

"Can I get you something?" Alya asked Seth.

"Tea, please," Seth replied.

"Sure." Alya threw a log in the fireplace.

Keya, Jena, and four acolytes dressed in light-blue robes with yellow borders rushed into the house. Keya knelt down next to the sobbing blacksmith. "Brock, I'm so sorry."

Brock's soaked, red eyes looked up. "Thank you."

"Where's the deceased?" an acolyte asked.

Alya pointed to the bedroom door. "In there."

"Thank you." The acolytes went into the bedroom and closed the door.

Jena, already crying, sat down next to Seth. "I—I'm so sorry." She reached for his hand.

Seth put his arm around her and pulled her in tight. "Thank you. I—" What was he doing? Sitting on the couch grieving when he should he finding those creatures who slew the only mother he ever knew. He looked into her eyes. "Will you help me set this right?"

Jena blinked. "Set this right? What . . . I . . . sure, of course I will."

Seth couldn't help but notice the confused look on her face. Did she know what he meant? Did he care? After all, she already promised to help him, right? Sure, he'd fill her in later on the details. He looked towards the bedroom door when he heard it open. His heart sank as the acolytes carried Sally's body out of the house on a wooden stretcher and covered by a blue wool blanket. As they passed by him, a tear broke through the dam behind his eyes. All that hatred and rage fell apart as her fingerless hand fell from underneath the blanket. He pulled his eyes away as they left the house. "Why did they do that to her?"

"To question her, probably," Dane said as he entered the house.

Seth's face reddened and his eyes narrowed. "You! What are you doing here?"

"I came to offer my condolences," he replied.

Brock put his hand on Seth's shoulder. "Easy, don't take this out on him."

Seth nodded. He couldn't take his eyes off Dane's black hair.

"What are you doing here, Dane?" Brock asked. "You're not the type to give condolences to *commoners*."

"I—well, you're right," Dane said. "I have to know that the prince is all right."

"I'll have to check on him," Brock said. "I haven't seen him in a few days."

Dane couldn't look directly at Brock, as if shame was taking over. "Look, I know I've not been . . . pleasant, and that I owe you a lot." He sighed. "The truth is, I'm not a nobleman anymore either. I'm a washed-up knight from a previous kingdom whose lands were stripped as soon as Kade took the throne."

Seth glared at Dane. What was he doing? That was not the Dane he knew. Humble? Really? Surely, he was up to something.

"I appreciate that," Brock said. "But why do you want to know about the prince?"

"If he dies, I lose the only purpose I have left," Dane said.

Brock looked over at Seth. "I know he's okay. I'll be checking on him in a few days, maybe next week. I need to collect myself first."

Alya smiled. "That's a good idea."

Keya sat down next to Brock, holding his hand. "We're here for you."

"Next week then? Can I go with you?" Dane asked.

Brock nodded. "Sure."

"Can you leave now?" Seth asked.

"You should go, Dane. You're upsetting them," Keya said.

Dane frowned. "Fine." He stormed out of the small house.

What is he up to? Seth thought.

~

Later, Keya and Alya unpacked some of the kitchen pots and were cooking supper on the fireplace. They were cooking Seth's favorite, fresh rabbit. But, it might as well have been gruel. The images of his slain adoptive Mother kept flashing in his mind. Every time he saw it, his face grew redder.

Jena rubbed his hand. "Can I get you anything?"

Seth shook his head. "No, I—I'm fine."

"Liar," Jena whispered. "You're not. How could you be?"

"Seth," Brock began, "we need to talk. Let's go to your room." He wiped the tears from his cheeks. "I need to talk to my son. We'll be out in a few minutes."

Keya nodded. "Take your time."

Brock followed Seth into his bedroom.

Seth sat down on the edge of his bed and Brock closed the door behind him.

"Seth, we've got to change our plans," Brock said as he sat down.

"Yes, we've got to find whoever did this and kill them. Sounds good to me," Seth said.

Brock sighed. "Not what I meant."

Was his adoptive Father afraid? Were all those words about duty and courage real, or just words coming out of a coward's mouth? "That's what I meant," Seth said.

"Seth, look—"

"No, you listen to me. I want to avenge the only mother I ever knew. When she was slapped by those Dark Elves in the market square, you did nothing."

"But—"

Seth's eyes narrowed. "Now that she's gone, you're still going to do nothing about it?"

Brock shook his head. "I won't do this with you. Seth, we have to—"

Seth jumped up. "No, we *will* do this! I won't stand by and let her killers get away with it."

Brock advanced on Seth. "You don't even know who did it."

"Dane had something to do with it," Seth said. "Remember the letter? The Dark Elves would need someone to get close to us."

"Why's that?" Brock asked.

"Because we would spot them. It's kind of hard to miss their blue skin."

"Did you forget?" Brock shook his head. "No, the Dark Elves could be anyone. Keya, Alya, or even Jena."

Seth blinked. "You're crazy."

"Everything all right in there?" Alya asked through the door.

"We're fine. We'll be a few more minutes." Brock sat back down and motioned Seth to do the same. "Seth, please sit."

Seth obediently sat back down. "What?"

"Dark Elves can change into human form, like . . . like a chameleon. Sally saw them do it when were at Staerdale Castle. The castle was already heavily infiltrated long before they attacked," Brock said. "We can't trust anyone."

"Dane I can see, but not Jena."

Brock sighed. "Maybe, I just don't know."

"Is it magic?" Seth asked. He stared into Brock's soft eyes, looking for the knight he'd heard so much about. "This is even more of a reason to find them."

"No, you don't understand. I have to protect you. If I go after them, they'll surely find out who you are."

Seth's mouth dropped. "Don't you dare lay your cowardliness at my feet."

"I'm no coward! I'm a father," Brock said. "We're not leaving yet. We'll tell them we changed our minds and we want to be close to our friends at this time."

Seth shook his head.

Brock's eyes hardened. "You will play along until we get you to safety. Got it?"

"No, I can't believe it."

"What?"

"You're really a coward. Is the real reason you didn't try to overthrow the Darkstriders before because you were waiting for me to grow up or were you just afraid?" Seth demanded.

"Seth—"

Seth stood up. "No, I will not play along. I will find my mother's killers and make them suffer."

"I forbid it."

Seth glared at him. "Nothing you can do about it."

Brock slapped Seth, knocking him to the ground. "You will obey me."

Seth rubbed the handprint on his left cheek. "So, you're brave against a boy, but not your wife's murderers. Coward."

Brock grabbed Seth by the shirt and threw him on the bed. "I'll not let Sally die in vain. You will do as I say, period."

"No."

Brock punched Seth in the jaw.

"Brock, no!" Keya said as she pulled him back. "He's just a boy!"

Jena pulled Seth off the bed. "You okay?"

Seth rubbed his chin. "I'm going to find my mother's killers."

"No," Brock said. "You can't."

Seth grabbed his sword from the corner and stared right through Brock. "I'm no coward." He stormed out.

CHAPTER 12

SETH HURRIED DOWN THE STREET TOWARDS THE MARKET square. He'd show them; he'd show them all. Anyone who had anything to do with Sally's death would suffer far worse. Yeah, he'd make sure of that. But, where should he start? Could he do it by himself? Did he have a choice? No, not really. He would die if anything happened to Jena. What about Ellis? Maybe.

"Seth, hold on," Jena said from behind him.

Don't look back, Seth thought. "I want to be alone." He picked up his pace.

Jena grabbed his shoulder. "Stop being an ass already, and you don't want to be alone." She reached for his hand.

His will shattered as her pleading eyes invaded his heart. "I—I—sure," Seth said as he took her hand. "I'll talk—a little."

Jena nodded. "Okay."

Her warmth brought a smile to his face. "Let's sit by the docks."

"Sure." Jena's grip grew tighter. "Are you okay? You're not going to go nuts, are you?"

Seth glared at her. "My mother was just killed."

"I—I know, but—"

"But what?"

She turned her eyes away from him. "I need to know that I made the right choice."

Seth slowed his pace towards the docks. "What choice?"

Jena swallowed. "Well, I—I just know how I would've felt if that was my mother, plus I couldn't let you go alone."

Seth blinked. "Your Mother approved this?"

She shook her head. "No, but I told her that I didn't care."

"Maybe I didn't want you to come. I'd have no reason to live if that happened to you," Seth said. Tears welled up in his eyes. "I love you, and I want you to be my wife."

She blinked. "I think we're a little young."

Seth laughed. "Yeah, a little young for going after my mother's murderers, too."

Jena grinned. "Maybe. It's nice to see you smile."

With the rage expelled from his body, the sweet smell of salt air invaded his nostrils. The market square was lit by the fire in the center and all the booths were empty. Merry laughter and singing poured out of the Red Tail Tavern's windows from across the square. Seth sat down on the dock with Jena next to him. "Umm—how do we do this?" Seth asked.

Jena leaned into his shoulder. "I've got no idea."

"How to do what?" a male voice asked.

Seth smiled as Ellis came into the light. "Ellis, what are you doing here?"

Ellis' face was solemn, maybe for the first time in his life. "I heard what happened." He put his hand on Seth's shoulder. "I'm sorry. Anything I can do?"

Seth stood up. Should he ask him? Sure, Ellis would be a great help. What did he have to lose? "Help me find those bastards who did that to her."

Ellis stepped back and rubbed his chin. "Hmmm, stay here and get up in the middle of the night to knead dough or kick ass. What to do?" A smile stretched from ear to ear. "Of course I'll come with you. I can't let you take all the glory. Besides, maybe I'll find a few coins along the way."

Seth shook his hand "Great." He helped Jena up. "The three of us then? We'll do this together."

"I'll always be with you," Jena said.

Ellis grinned. "Anything's better than working at that stupid bakery. Sure, I'm with you."

"Where to?" Jena asked.

"Father sent Dane to the knight's camp around Arrowhead Lake," Seth said. "We probably need some supplies and —I can't go back."

"Me either," Jena said.

Ellis rubbed his hands together. "No worries, meet me here in 30 minutes. Okay?"

"What are you doing?" Seth demanded.

Ellis giggled. "Trust me," he said as he disappeared into the shadows.

M alon was looking through the second-story window of the Red Tail Tavern down at Seth and Jena. The inn room was dark and disheveled. Elmar was sitting at the small desk scribbling on a parchment.

The door flung open and Shania tossed her two swords onto the bed. "Well?" she asked.

"You were right," Malon said. "The boy and his two friends were down there and it appears they're getting ready to do something. I couldn't hear what they were saying."

Shania grinned. "He's going after you and Elmar."

Elmar laughed. "I'm not afraid of that."

Malon sat down on the bed. "Any word from Tanyl?"

Shania shook her head. "No, nothing. We have the squad in Sarun Grove, but we don't have a verified target for them yet."

"How can you say that?" Elmar demanded. "We've got the queen's handmaiden and the king's blacksmith. The boy is the right age. He must be the prince. Let's just kill him and get it over with."

"No, we don't know," Shania said. "Yes, we got Brock and Sally Feran, but we didn't confirm the boy. We have to be right when we deliver him to Tanyl."

Malon glared at Shania. "What do you mean, deliver? Let's lop his head off and be done with it!"

A wiry smile clawed its way onto Shania's face. "Nothing would make me happier nor avenge my family better than having his head on a stick in front of Brock before I gouged his eyes out."

"So, why fight it?" Elmar said.

Shania frowned. "It has something to do with the prophecy. I'm not sure. I'm not a seer," she said. "We just have to bring him to Iron Fist Keep. The seers there will do—"

"Do what?" Malon demanded.

"No idea," Shania said. "But, we get to kill him afterward."

Malon pointed down at Seth and Jena. "Why not just pick them up now?"

Shania pushed Malon back down on the bed. "Because Brock is always saying that the prince is elsewhere."

Malon shoved her on the floor. "So? You know he's just protecting the boy. Why are you insisting we play this game?" He glared into her eyes. "Tell me."

"If we just grab him and he's the wrong one," Shania said as she got up, "we'll lose the real prince. What do you think Tanyl would do to us for failing so close to victory? Simply because we were impatient." She sat down next to Malon. "No, we continue as planned and let him go after Sally's killer."

Elmar rolled his eyes. "Why? How does this help us?"

"The prince in the prophecy will have courage and magic," Shania said. "He probably doesn't even know who he really is yet."

"What if Brock or Sally told him?" Malon asked.

Shania smiled. "It doesn't matter. All that would do is encourage him to act even sooner. Once we confirm that he is the one, we grab him." She walked over to the window and looked down at her prey. "You two can have Ellis and Jena. I want Galin the V of Ravenward. Once the seers are done with him, I'll give him a slash for every friend I lost in the Battle of Staerdale Castle and cut a limb off for every family member I lost." She smiled out the window at Seth and Jena. "Soon, very soon."

Thirty minutes later, Ellis came strolling back towards the dock with two packs slung over his shoulder. Seth shook his head. He hated the stealing, but they needed the supplies, right? If Seth didn't actually do the stealing, was it really that bad?

"How does he do it?" Jena asked as she stood up.

"Not sure I want to know," Seth replied. Seth and Jena moved towards the center of the market square near the fire to meet Ellis.

Ellis had a grin on him that stretched across his face. "Told you I'd take care of it," he said as he tossed a pack to Seth.

Jena frowned. "Where's mine?"

"Umm, I only found two," Ellis said. "Besides, you don't want to carry a pack all night, do you?"

"Where am I going to keep my spell components? You may need to be healed, you know," she said.

Seth rolled his eyes. "Stop it already. Jena, you can store your stuff in mine."

"Okay," she said as she passed a small pouch of incense to Seth.

"Any idea where on Arrowhead Lake the camp is?" Ellis asked.

Seth shook his head. "Not really."

Jena's loving eyes blinked. "How do we find them?"

Seth's stomach twisted. How indeed? Arrowhead Lake was huge and fed Bahr River, not to mention that half of the lake was in the Ithsein province. The Bahr River was wide and deep enough where you had to use a bridge to cross it. Since the knights, whom Seth had never met, had to stay out of sight, they probably would avoid using it, right? Sure . . . well, maybe. Why would anyone recognize them? It was not like they wore armor with the Ravenward family crest on their shields. The only bridge was closer to Crey Village. Would that be too dangerous for them?

"Well?" Ellis asked.

"I think they would be on this side of Arrowhead Lake," Seth said. "When we get there, we look for any signs of a camp and that's probably it."

Jena sighed. "There's probably more camps than just them."

"When we get closer to them, we'll figure it out, Jena," Ellis said. He smiled at Seth. "What are we waiting for?"

Seth slung his pack on his back. "Let's go."

. . .

Shania watched the trio disappear into the darkness. She flung the torn curtains closed and turned around. She smiled at Elmar sitting on the bed.

"They're gone?" Elmar asked.

"Yes," Shania said.

Elmar smiled. "Looks like Malon left just in time."

A twisted smile crept across Shania's face. "Indeed."

Seth paused as they approached the outskirts of Sarun Grove. The moonlight illuminated the woods in front of them. Before him stood his point of no return. He could turn back, but his mother's killer would get away. That bastard Dane deserved to die, right? If they turned back, he could make amends with Brock and they could just disappear. Who would know the difference? His stomach twisted into knots.

Jena bit her lip. "I . . . are we sure about this?"

"Lost your nerve?" Ellis asked. He sniffed. "Typical."

Seth took her hand. "We can do it together. I think we need to head northeast."

Ellis adjusted his pack. "Let's go then."

"Follow me." Seth pushed his way through the underbrush with Jena and Ellis in tow. The thorns tore at Seth's legs, but he didn't care. The three walked silently deep into Sarun Grove.

Hours later, they came to a small hill on the edge of the grove. Seth's ears perked up as he heard faint laughter. He pressed his finger over his lips. After Jena and Ellis had nodded, they got down and moved up the hill.

The closer Seth got to the top, the more the campfire smoke stung his nose. Were they on the other side of the hill?

Were they closer to the water than he thought? Were they lost? Seth stopped, closing his eyes. He stretched out his ears to listen. Nothing. He pushed forward.

Seth's eyes narrowed on a clump of trees with saplings growing from its base. The broadleaf saplings were perfect. He crawled up to the clump of trees and pushed aside a few saplings, just enough to see the other side.

Nine men surrounded a blazing campfire. They were leaning on their packs with pots thrown about. The horses were tied off on the outskirts of the firelight. Empty plates were in a pile near the fire, right next to a beer keg.

The largest man tossed another one his mug. "Dane, get me another one."

Is that him? Seth thought. His eyes focused through the saplings on the man filling the mug. That hair, that walk—it was him.

Dane passed the large muscular man his mug. "Here, John."

Why was Dane taking this treatment from them? Wasn't he the one always talking about how great of a knight he was and how being a noble meant he had privileges? Seth blinked. Yes, it was him. He stared at Dane's face. It wasn't hard or proud or—no, it was fearful.

A medium-built man with long black hair pulled back into a ponytail took a swig of his beer. "Are you really going to take that crap from him, Dane? Don't be an ass."

Dane grimaced as John growled at him.

John burst out laughing. "And you were a knight? Ha, you don't hold a candle to that woman knight."

"I was a great and fearless knight. I fought with them at Nightfall Meadows as we crushed the Feral Orc Army," Dane said. He sipped his beer.

"Really?" John said. He pointed at the medium-built

knight. "We fought there too, as well as Port Eldham. Do you remember him at Nightfall Meadows, Jason?"

The medium-built man shook his head. "Can't say that I do. Unless—" Jason couldn't stop giggling.

"What?" Dane asked. "Why are you laughing?"

Jason swallowed. "Unless you were a servant or a manure boy." The rest of the knights burst out into laughter.

Dane's face reddened. "How dare you!" He lunged toward Jason. "My honor is at stake."

John smiled. "Well, if you didn't have any in the first place, you can't lose it, can you?"

Jason laughed so hard he fell over.

"Sit down, Dane, and stop pretending to be a knight. We know better," another said.

Dane stared right at him. "Peter, I'll kill you."

John stumbled to his feet. "No, you won't."

Peter jumped to his feet. "Dane, sit down before you get yourself hurt. The only reason you're here is because Brock insisted on it." He spat on the ground. "If you were a *real* knight, where was your manor? How come we never saw you in court?"

"I—I didn't like going to court," Dane replied.

Peter sniffed. "Sure, is that the same reason we never saw you in formations, or battle, or in the tournaments that Galin held?" He sat back down. "Those are things knights had no choice but to attend. I don't believe you."

"I am a knight!" Dane said. "I…"

Seth's mouth dropped to the ground. Dane was a fake! He was no knight. Seth heard leaves crunching behind him and turned his head.

Ellis tapped Seth on the shoulder as he pulled himself next to him. "Well?" he whispered.

Seth pointed at Dane. "He's here, and he has a lot more to answer for than I thought."

"Like what?" Jena asked as she moved alongside Seth.

"He may not even be a knight," Seth said.

"...**H**ow dare you even imply that I—I'm not a real knight!" Dane shouted. He drew his sword, pointing it directly at John's heart. "I challenge you to a duel to restore my honor."

John laughed so hard that he fell over too.

Dane's face grew a fiery red.

"You can't be serious," Peter said. "He'll kill you."

"Stand up and fight me," Dane demanded.

After John had regained control of his laughter, he smiled. "Sit down before I skewer you like that goblin this afternoon. I'll use your hair for a mop." He took another swig.

Dane poked John in the side with his sword. "Get up."

The laughter fled from John's face as his massive body stood up. Instead of his sword, John grabbed a two-handed battle ax. The corners of his mouth curled as Dane's face went white.

Ellis elbowed Seth. "What do we do? If he kills Dane, are we done?"

Seth shook his head. "No, we still need to get the Dark Elves."

. . .

Dane lunged.

John side-stepped and hit Dane in the butt with the flat side of his ax, knocking Dane down.

The others burst out laughing.

Dane's eyes narrowed as he focused on his opponent. He slashed and lunged at John, who easily knocked away Dane's blows. "Damn you!" Dane charged at John.

John struck Dane's head with the ax's hilt, knocking him to the ground. He kicked Dane's sword away and raised his ax. "Give me one reason not to kill you."

Dane curled into the fetal position, covering his head with his hands. "Please—please don't."

"You're no knight," John said as he kicked Dane in the face. "In Ramir's name, I'll bet you were never even trained with a sword." He kicked him again.

"Come on, John, be nice to him," Jason said. "Brock wanted us to look after him."

John kicked Dane again. "I don't take orders from black-smiths." He looked down at Dane. "I heard that during the raid, you were on watch when the Dark Elves killed every-one. Instead of fighting or even warning them, you just ran off." He grabbed Dane by the collar and looked right into his eyes. "I heard you were a useless coward." He looked back at the other knights. "We should kill him."

Dane shook his head. "No—please no."

"Just let him go," Peter said. "He's a liar and a coward, but he's no threat. We'll be gone before he can tell anyone where we are, anyway."

John tossed Dane against a tree. He threw Dane's sword into the ground, right between Dane's legs. "Get out of here before I change my mind. If I see you again, I'll feed you to the goblins. Got it?"

Dane nodded.

John lunged at Dane. "Boo!"

Dane leaped to his feet and ran into the darkness.

The others burst into laughter.

John frowned. "What a coward."

Seth looked up. "Time to go."

Ellis and Jena followed Seth down the hill.

SETH NEVER TOOK HIS EYES OFF HIS PREY. AS DANE WEAVED IN and out of the underbrush along the river, Seth's little band followed suit. Swiftly and silently, the small party moved through the woods like a swan on a lake.

Dane looked back as he heard something.

Seth froze. Did he hear them? They were silent, but—maybe he sensed them. Yes—no—maybe? Dane was heading southwest from Arrowhead Lake along the river. But, where was he going? Back to Crey Village? No, that couldn't be so. Why would he go there? Once word got back from the knights about Dane's lack of credentials, he'd be finished, right? Seth glanced back at Jena and Ellis. They'd be with him forever, especially Jena. Would she be his queen?

Ellis tapped Seth's shoulder and pointed at Dane.

Seth swallowed.

Dane was on the move. He broke out from the woods to move along the riverbank.

Seth moved up behind a great oak tree as Dane stopped. He pushed a sapling aside as he tried to get a closer look. Dane was looking across the river at—what? He couldn't see.

Dane looked along the river towards the bridge, then back across the river. What did he see? Seth leaned over to Jena. "Can you see anything?"

Jena shook her head. "No."

"Want me to get closer?" Ellis asked.

"I—I'm not sure," Seth said.

Dane bolted along the riverbank.

Seth jumped to his feet. "Come on."

Ellis grinned. "This is where the fun begins."

Jena rolled her eyes. "Please."

Seth sprinted toward the riverbank and stopped just inside the wood line. As if doing a left face, he pivoted towards the southwest, following Dane.

Dane kept looking across the river as he sped up as if something was chasing him.

Seth stopped and looked across the river. Something caught his eye, but what? What got Dane so scared that he was running like the cowards he always claimed others to be. Yeah, Dane's yellow spots were showing through his false demeanor.

Ellis pointed at a small figure running along the other side of the river. "Look."

Seth's eyes focused on the short sprinting soul barreling down the far riverbank. He was strong, with long, brown hair pulled back into a ponytail. The short man was carrying an ax and—he was not human. Seth blinked. What was he?

Ellis pulled on Seth's arm. "He's getting away."

Dane! Seth broke into a sprint. He lost sight of the murderer, but where could he go?

"He can't be far," Jena said as she pushed through the underbrush.

Seth broke out into the clearing right next to the bridge. The moonlight illuminated the road and the bridge. Where was he? Seth scanned both sides of the road and looked towards Crey Village. Nothing. Seth stomped his foot onto the hard-packed dirt road. "Damn it!"

"Take it easy," Jena said. "We'll get him next time."

"Did he know we were following him?" Seth asked.

Jena shook her head. "I don't know."

Panting, Ellis swallowed his breath. "I don't think he cared. He was more afraid of the dwarf across the river."

"Dwarf?" Seth asked.

"Yeah, didn't you see him?"

Seth nodded. "Yeah, but—I never saw one before." He looked over the bridge. "What's over there?"

Jena squinted her eyes as if she saw through the darkness "Never been there."

"Across Bahr River is the Long-Tail Forest," Ellis said. "Father used to talk about selling bread in Qrento."

"Where's that?" Jena asked.

"About 15 miles up the road," Ellis said. "Unless he's planning on scaling the Wailing Mountains, there's nowhere else to go."

Jena frowned. "I'd just go back to Crey Village."

Seth shook his head. "He can't. Once word gets back that he's a fake, they'll string him up." He grinned. "Wouldn't mind seeing that, though."

Jena hit Seth in the shoulder. "Stop it."

"Where to?" Ellis asked.

Seth looked across the bridge. Once they crossed that bridge, there was no turning back and they would've chosen their destiny. They could always go back to their parents, right? Sure, it would be so much easier than—no, he had to go on. Brock was a coward at heart, no better than Dane, right? Seth shook his head. No, if his adoptive Mother was to be avenged, he had to do it. There was no one else. His mouth dried up as he stepped towards the bridge. "Let's find him at Qrento. It shouldn't be that hard once we get there."

"What about the dwarf?" Jena asked.

Ellis laughed. "Are you afraid of some short, fat guy who needs a step to look over the bar? Please." He pulled out his daggers. "I'd skewer him without a second thought." He grinned. "I'd use his bones to pick my teeth."

Seth smacked Ellis in the back of the head. "Shut up." He moved towards the bridge. "Let's go."

Jena sighed as she took one last look towards Crey Village. "Are you sure, Seth?"

Seth nodded. "Yeah, there's no other way."

Ellis dragged Jena by her cloak. "Come on already."

Jena pulled away from Ellis. "Okay, I hope you know what you're doing."

Seth smiled. "Me too."

The hard-packed dirt road stung Seth's feet every time his foot hit the ground. Hours, it'd been hours since they'd left the bridge. His normally vibrant step was replaced by lumbering as they moved towards Qrento. His sword—his sword seemed to gain weight the further they went. How far had they gone? At least ten miles, he hoped. Yeah, could he take another five miles? No, no way.

"Can we stop please?" Ellis said as he dropped his pack on the side of the road. "I hate this crap." He pulled off his soft leather shoe and began rubbing his foot. "Maybe we should stay here."

"Why?" Jena asked as she moved next to Seth.

"Because I'm tired," Ellis snapped. "We can get there in the morning. He'll still be there."

Seth looked around. "I suppose, but—shouldn't we get off the road?"

A small limping figure emerged from the darkness, trudging along the road towards them.

Seth straightened out. "Who's that?"

Ellis blinked. "The dwarf? Yeah, that must be the one Dane was running from."

Jena tugged on her sack. "He's hurt. I can help him." Determined, she headed towards the dark-haired dwarf.

"Jena, hold up!" Seth said. As soon as he figured out that she wasn't stopping, he ran up next to her. "What are you doing?"

She sniffed. "My duty as a healer."

Ellis ran up beside them. "It's probably a trap."

Jena shook her head. "How could someone like that hurt anyone?"

"I don't know," Seth said. "Jena, are you sure about this? Ellis may be right."

Jena laughed.

Ellis frowned.

"Just be careful." As the dwarf collapsed to the ground, Seth sprinted towards him. Jena may be the healer, but he wouldn't let anything happen to her. His stomach wrenched in anxiety, not for him, but for her. Yeah, he had to get there first. If it were a trap, the short bastard would spring it on him, rather than his future bride. He knelt down next to the dwarf.

The dwarf wore leather armor with two axes by his side. His long brown beard was knotted and he stunk like sour ale. Was he drunk? A dwarf that can't get enough ale? Maybe he wasn't hurt at all, just passing out?

Jena shook him as she knelt over the dwarf. "I'm here to help you." Her nose wrinkled as he exhaled in her face.

Ellis waved his hand in front of his nose. "This guy stinks. Jena, how can you stand being that close to him?"

Jena coughed. "It's not easy."

Seth never took his eyes off the dwarf. No groaning. No fidgeting when Jena was caressing his shoulder. Nothing.

Crack. Crunch.

"What's that?" Ellis asked.

Seth drew his sword and stepped over the dwarf towards the edge of the road. "We're not alone."

"What about him?" Jena asked.

"Come on, let's go," Seth said.

"What about him? We can't just leave him here," Jena said.

Crunch. Snap.

The noise from the woods was very close. They had no torches and the moonlight didn't pierce the shadows just inside the woods. No, but the moon illuminated them, so whoever was in the woods could see them. Seth backed up. "Come on, he's one of them."

Jena shook her head. "No, he can't be."

The dwarf's eyes shot open. He grabbed Jena by the upper arms, throwing her to the ground. "Got you!"

Seth whirled around. "No!" He raised his sword.

"Look out!" Ellis whipped out his daggers and side-stepped as four dwarves bolted out of the woods.

A dwarf knocked Seth to the ground.

Ellis threw a dagger.

The dwarf on top of Seth reeled back in pain.

Jena screamed.

One dwarf charged at Ellis, knocking the other dagger from his hand.

The last two tackled Seth, tossing his sword aside. One held down his arms while the other raised his ax.

Seth glanced over at Jena as the dwarf tore off her tunic. What did he do? He got them killed—no, worse, he got Jena raped by a dwarf. Some knight he would be, Seth the Pathetic. He would not die. He would not die and let those—things—have their way with Jena. A tiny tingle tickled his heart. As his face grew redder, the more the tickle spread throughout his body. He felt tiny shocks—no, pinpricks—all over his skin. Seth's strength returned to him, tenfold.

The dwarf's eyes flew open. "What are you doing?"

"Leave us alone!" Seth's hand's glowed a fiery red. He grabbed the dwarf holding his arms.

The dwarf screamed as his arm melted into nothingness.

Seth's fiery-red eyes stared right at the other dwarf with the ax.

The dark dwarven face went white. "He's possessed. Run!" He grabbed the one-armed dwarf and sprinted into the woods.

Seth grabbed his sword. As his hand touched his weapon, it began to glow.

Ellis pushed the dwarf off him and stared at Seth. "What's happening?"

Seth kicked the last dwarf off Jena.

The dwarf curled up into the fetal position. "Please, spare me. I won't do it again."

Seth licked his lips. He wanted this creature to pay for what he did to Jena. His sword glowed brighter, then its glow receded.

"Stupid humans," the dwarf said as he pulled out a short sword from underneath his cloak. "I'll kill you and then she's mine."

Lightning jumped all over Seth's sword. "No!" A bolt of lightning shot from the tip of Seth's sword into the dwarf's chest. In half a second the dwarf flashed, then he was gone. All that remained was a small pile of ash. The fire in Seth's eyes dwindled and tiny bolts of electricity along his sword and his skin vanished. What happened? Was he a demon like the dwarf said? Or possessed by demons? Seth knelt down next to Jena. "Are you all right?"

Jena backed away. "That was—magic. Human boys can't wield magic. What are you?"

Ellis got between Seth and Jena. "Yeah, you'd better tell us what's going on. How'd you do that?"

How did I do it? Seth wondered. He shook his head. "I—I—I don't know." He stared at his sword. "I didn't even swing at him."

Ellis looked down at the pile of ash and smiled. "Just don't get mad at me."

Seth grinned. "I won't." He reached for Jena.

She backed away.

"Jena?"

She shook her head.

Ellis cocked an eye at her. "What's wrong with you? He saved us."

"I—it's not possible," Jena said. "Boys can't use magic."

"Are you saying that I'm not human?" Seth asked. His eyes softened. "I love you. I couldn't let anything happen to you." He reached for her again. "Please." Tears nearly broke free from behind his eyes.

A smile cracked Jena's face. "I'm sorry. I—I just didn't know."

"Me either," Seth said.

Ellis grinned. "Let's go before we get attacked by the midget squad again."

Seth nodded. "Okay." They continued down the road towards Qrento.

An hour later, the trio was still on the road toward Qrento. Seth's eyes were heavy. Firelight from the town up ahead could be seen in the distance. "Is that it?" Seth asked.

Ellis sighed. "I hope so."

Crunch. Crunch. Crunch.

Seth's head jerked toward the woods along the road. "Not again."

Ellis pulled out his daggers. "I'm ready this time."

"What's that?" Jena asked, pointing to a faint haze.

Seth tried to focus. The haze was pink. As it got darker, the heavier his eyes became.

"What's going—?" Ellis collapsed to the ground, snoring.

Jena sank to her knees. "Sleep, it's—" She rolled onto her side.

Seth blinked, fighting off the pink haze. His world became blurry. Three green creatures emerged from the woods. They were just a bit smaller than him, wearing chain mail armor. He blinked.

"This one is still awake," one said in a gruff voice. He was the biggest amongst them.

"Not possible," another said. "Only magic-wielding creatures can resist my sleep spell."

The large goblin grinned. "I've got a sleep spell for him." He hit Seth with the hilt of his sword.

Seth's world went black.

CHAPTER 14

SETH WAS LAYING IN HIS BED BACK HOME. HIS EYES CRACKED open. *Where am I?* He sat up, looking at his window. Something was different. His eyes couldn't focus. As if Seth's energy was sapped from his body, he laid back down.

His door opened and a figure wearing a red hooded robe entered his room. The hood covered the person's face.

Seth tried to get up, but couldn't. "Who are you?"

She pulled her hood back as she knelt next to the bed. It was Sally. "Easy."

Seth shook his head. "Not possible."

Sally put her finger in front of her lips. "Shhh, never mind that. Someday, you'll learn how special you really are. Brock has no idea about your potential."

"What are you talking about?"

"I love you." Sally beamed at him. "I am so proud of what you will do."

"But—"

She grabbed him by the shoulders. "You must wake up." Sally shook him. "Wake up, Seth. Wake up!"

Seth jumped up, only to yanked back down by the rope that tied him to the oak tree. His clothes were damp with the early morning dew. He blinked. The small camp was on a river. Had to be the Bahr River, right? There were no other big rivers this side of the Wailing Mountains. They were deep in the woods, not near any road or regularly used path.

Jena and Ellis were tied to the same tree and both were still asleep. Seth smiled; at least they were all right.

Smoke from the campfire stung his nostrils as the wind blew the smoke into his face. Around the fire sat four green creatures. They were short, and all were bald. One was noticeably larger than the others. Was he in charge?

"Taz, do we have any tea left?" the larger said.

The smallest out of the four looked up. "Yes, Dez, we do."

Dez grinned. "Well?" The others began to laugh as Taz got up to do Dez's bidding. "He'll have courage, someday."

"I have courage," Taz snapped.

Dez's face grew dark. "Fix my tea already."

Taz's hand began to shake. "O—okay."

The others burst out laughing, again. The goblin wearing the gray tunic looked up at Dez. "When do we get paid?" He pointed at Seth. "The longer we have to hold onto them, the riskier this venture becomes."

Seth blinked. *What was he talking about?*

Dez grinned. "Take it easy, Mor. Soon, we'll be a thousand crowns richer."

"I know," Mor said, "and I don't want to lose it. You saw the dwarves."

Dez looked over at Seth. "I did, and I saw what the boy did, too. That's how I know he's the right one. There's been a bounty on his head for over ten years and I got him."

Mor cleared his throat. "*We* got him."

"Yes, of course," Dez said. "Sorry."

Taz handed Dez a crude porcelain cup. "Here's your tea."

"Good, now sit down," Dez said.

"What's next?" Mor asked. "When do we get our money?"

Dez sipped his tea. "We'll contact Shania and let her know that we have her prophesied boy king."

Mor shook his head. "She won't believe you. How do we prove it?"

"Just tell her what he did to the dwarves," Dez said. "Pretty simple, I think."

"I guess," Mor replied. "What do you think?"

Seth nudged Jena and Ellis. "Wake up, we're in trouble."

Jena's eyes popped open, frantically looking around. "Where—what happened?"

"There's a bounty on us," Seth said.

Ellis yawned. "Really? Finally, someone realized how important I really am."

Seth frowned. "It's not a good thing."

Jena looked over at the four goblins. "What are they going to do with us?"

Seth swallowed. "Seems like they are going to turn us over for a thousand crowns."

Ellis' eyes flew open. "A thousand crowns? I'd turn you in for that."

Jena glared at Ellis.

"Sorry," Ellis said as he looked away.

"What do we do?" Jena asked.

"Can you use your—stuff—to get us out of this?" Ellis asked Seth.

Seth shrugged. "I don't know. I don't know how I did it before." Seth felt a clawed hand slap him on the back of his head. He stared into Dez's deep red eyes.

"No magic, boy, or they die," Dez said. He pointed at Ellis. "Starting with him."

Ellis' face went white. "Me? Not me. Why not her?"

Seth glared at Dez. If he backed away in fear, all hope would be lost. If he came off too brazen, they wouldn't get their chance to escape. Seth took a deep breath. "Why are we here?"

Mor looked up. "Don't tell them anything."

Ellis smiled at Mor. "You don't sound as stupid as you look. How'd you manage that?"

Mor jumped up with his dagger in hand. "I'll slit your throat. We don't need you."

"Well, if you don't need us, just let us down and we'll be on our way. We don't want to inconvenience you any more," Ellis said as he winked at Seth.

Dez started to laugh as Mor's face reddened.

Mor punched Ellis in the stomach. "Can I eat this one?" He smiled. "Alive."

"Later, after I have *my* crowns," Dez said.

Mor smacked Dez in the shoulder. "*Our* crowns."

"Of course." Dez grinned at Jena. "Then you can eat them both."

Seth glared at Dez. "Are you afraid to tell me? I'm going to be turned over and they're going to be lunch. What do you have to lose?"

Dez looked over at Mor, who shrugged his shoulders. "They're dinner. My mother always said to have a light lunch."

"Well?" Seth asked.

"Why not?" Dez sat down next to the fire. "The Dark-striders put a ransom on your head since the fall of Staerdale Castle. It started at 50 crowns. They publicly said it was for the handmaiden and the blacksmith, but privately they told our tribe the real target, you."

"Why me?" Seth asked.

Dez shrugged. "I dunno. But, they said they are looking for a prophesied boy king who wields magic and will unite the world against them."

The other goblins laughed.

"Dark Elves get a little dramatic," Dez said. "But, we saw what you did to our competition."

"Competition?" Jena asked.

"Yeah, a few months ago they told everyone that your friend here was somewhere east of the Wailing Mountains." Dez grinned. "They were right."

"So—the dwarves were after us too? For the—reward?" Seth asked.

Dez nodded. "By you killing them, you saved us the trouble."

"Can we get something to eat?" Ellis asked.

"No." Dez started to giggle as the others burst out laughing.

Seth tugged on his ropes. They had to escape, *soon*.

Seth stared at the goblins over the next few hours. It didn't take long for them to get bored with the trio. They returned to verbally torturing Taz. The more ale the goblins drank, the louder they got. One by one, they fell asleep. Taz was put on the first watch, maybe the only watch. Who knew?

Jena shivered. "I'm getting cold."

Ellis moved his head around the tree so he could see Taz. "Hey, toad face, can we eat something?"

Taz grumbled next to the fire as he poked it with a stick.

Ellis' face went red. "I'm talking to you."

Seth kicked him in the shin. "Shut your mouth."

"I'm hungry."

"We'll be dead if you wake up the others," Seth said. "We need to be smart."

"He didn't mean it, Taz," Jena said. "He's always mean to everyone." She glared at Ellis. "Even those who care about him."

Taz shook his head. "I've got nothing to give you. Even if I did, I wouldn't give it to you. Dez would throw me out of the raiding party."

Was this an opportunity? Seth thought. "Why do you want to be with them anyway, Taz? They treat you like crap. You must have a family."

Taz snorted. "I do, and he's right over there." He pointed at Mor. "He cares more about impressing Dez and doesn't care about me at all. I'm not a rogue, as they are."

"Can't you go home? To your parents?" Jena asked.

"No, they sent me on this trip to become brave like Mor," Taz said. "I…"

Seth closed his eyes. *How did I do that magic before? I need it now!* He desperately tried to remember every detail about their encounter with the Dwarves. What did he do? A word? A thought? A feeling? Was it so simple? What was he feeling? He looked over at Jena. Her, it was her. Jena was in danger and he—no, he wouldn't lose her like he lost his mother. A tingling began in his chest.

"…I wish we didn't have to take him back," Taz said, "but, the Darkstriders will kill our kin if we don't."

Ellis gulped. "What about Jena and me?"

Taz shrugged. "Rations are running low." He pointed at Jena. "Dez says she has other uses, so we'll eat her last."

Electric tickles ran up and down Seth's skin. His eyes began to glow in the darkness.

Jena pulled away from Seth.

Ellis did the same. "So—where is home, exactly?"

Taz blinked. "What's wrong with his eyes?"

The rope touching Seth's skin began to smolder. He blinked as the smoke entered his eyes.

Ellis shook his head. "Not sure. Head cold? Don't you get allergies?" He shot a worried glance at Jena, who reciprocated the gesture. "If you give him some water from the river, he'll be all right. I promise."

"No," Taz said as he stood up. "I have to tell the others."

Small arcs of electricity jumped from Seth's skin, burning not only the rope but the tree they were tied to.

Ellis shook his head. "No, we just need water. Now, go and get some."

Taz's green face went white as the rope fell away from Seth's wrists. He kicked Mor. "They got out."

Mor shot up. "What?"

Taz ran into the woods.

"What's going on?" Dez said.

The fourth goblin just snored louder.

Ellis and Jena tossed the rope aside, looking at Seth. "Weapons?"

As if he didn't hear him, Seth moved towards the camp with his hands glowing like the lightning from the sky.

Mor grabbed a dagger and charged at Seth.

Seth sidestepped and grabbed Mor's shoulders.

Mor began to convulse, dropping the dagger as his eyes popped out of his head.

Seth dropped him to the ground and stared right at Dez. "You're next."

"No!" Dez said as he stared at Mor. "No, that's not possible. Even the—even the pyromancers can't do that." He backed away, tripping over the fourth goblin. "Get up, Lil."

As soon as Lil saw Seth glowing in the darkness, he bolted into the woods.

Dez grabbed his short sword.

Seth saw their weapons near the fire. He tossed Ellis his daggers as he picked up his sword. As soon as he touched the weapon, it began to glow.

Dez dropped his sword. "I'm sorry. I—I'm sorry."

Seth raised his weapon.

Dez fell to his knees. "Please, spare me."

Rage. Hate. Love. Friend. Foe. Enemy. Seth blinked. He kicked Dez over.

Tears ran down Dez's eyes. "I'm sorry. I won't tell Shania anything. I promise."

Sparks jumped from Seth's eyes. "Who is Shania? I must know."

Dez backed away. "Shania is a Dark Elf, a Darkstrider assassin. She blames you for the death of her brother and father." He gulped. "Please, let me go."

Seth shook his head. "You were going to eat my friend and the woman I love." Would a true knight kill an unarmed foe, begging for his life? What would his real father, Galin the IV of Ravenward, do? But, it would be so easy to kill him. No one would know, except for Jena and Ellis. Why would they care? He'd saved them, right? As if the power within his body was trying to take the reins, Seth's thoughts were all about the good reasons to kill Dez.

"Seth, don't do it. Let him go," Jena said.

Jena? Why would she object? He loved her. He was doing this for her. Seth blinked. What if she was right? Yes, she was. Seth's glowing eyes glared at Dez. "Run."

Dez jumped to his feet, but he hesitated.

"Run, before I can't stop it from killing you," Seth said. The power, the rage, he had to expend it. Focus his anger and hatred on—something else.

Dez bolted into the woods.

"Can I help you?" Jena asked.

"Get away!" It was as if the power he now possessed wanted to control him. He had to expend it or dispel it, but how?

Ellis dragged Jena away. "You're starting to scare me."

Seth glared at Ellis. Was he jealous of the power Seth now possessed? Was he after Jena? That bastard, he always wanted to marry Jena, didn't he? No, where did that come from? He does. No, he doesn't. He does. No. Yes. No. Seth dropped to his knees. "I can't control it. Back away."

"No," Jena said as she lunged towards Seth.

Ellis grabbed Jena and dragged her into the woods.

Seth had to expend it. But, how? He summoned all his rage and hatred, focusing on the campfire. His skin glowed brighter.

"I hope he never gets this pissed at me," Ellis said.

Jena gulped.

Seth raised his sword above the fire. He hated that fire. Those embers were the cause of all his troubles, right? Yes, those embers killed his parents and wanted to kill his future wife. Seth closed his eyes. "You bastard!" He slammed the sword into the center of the fire. The fire and all the ground within five feet vanished. Seth fell into the hole. The voices and the tingling left him. His skin no longer glowed.

Jena ran up to him. "Are you all right?"

Was he? The voice was gone and those evil feelings were gone, for now. "I couldn't control it. I—It wanted me to kill all of you." Tears flowed down Seth's cheeks. "I'm so sorry."

Jena hugged him as if her life depended on it.

Ellis stared at Seth. "We need to go. They'll get some courage and try again."

"Where to?" Jena asked.

"Home," Ellis said. "I'm not sure I can continue on like this."

"But, Ellis," Seth began.

Ellis frowned. "No, after what just happened there's no way. I—I need to think."

"What about Dane?' Seth asked.

"He can wait," Jena said. "We need to figure this—thing —out."

Seth sighed. "Fine, let's go home." He picked up some rations from Dez's pack. *What would've happened if I couldn't focus the energy into the campfire?* Seth led the trio out of the camp towards Crey Village.

CHAPTER 15

Seth's stomach grumbled, yearning for lunch, or at least a snack. Pain shot through his feet with every step on the hard dirt road heading into Crey Village. Jena's hand occasionally took his. She had not been the same since he almost lost control of his new *power*. Did he blame her? Was anyone more scared than him? The hatred and rage took over, merely hiding the terror that engulfed his heart. Maybe that's what it was like on the battlefield.

Ellis twirled his daggers and dropped them into their sheaths. "All this walking, damn. If I'd known, you'd have gone by yourself." He tried to hide his smile.

Jena squeezed Seth's hand. "We'll be home soon."

"Yeah, I guess," Seth said.

Jena's deep blue eyes softened as she looked up at Seth. "He'll understand."

"No, he won't. I stormed out, and my last thought about him was hatred," Seth said. "I can't forgive him for not trying to avenge my mother's death."

"She's not your real mother," Ellis said.

Seth glared at him. "She was the only mother I ever knew.

I may not be her son by blood, but I will always be her loving son."

Ellis backed away from Seth. "Sorry."

Jena's hand shook as she hugged Seth. "You can come home with me if you like."

Seth drew back. "Jena, you're shaking. Why are you still shaking?"

"I—" Jena turned away. "I'm still not—I don't know."

Seth pulled her in close to his heart. "Do I scare you?" he asked softly.

Jena tightened her embrace. "Some, but I know you'd never hurt us. I—I just never saw a boy do that before."

"I had a birthday, you know," Seth said. "I'm no longer a boy."

Jena opened her mouth.

Seth put one finger over her mouth, motioning her to be still. "I love you. I don't know what this is either. I think Father knows." He continued down the road.

Ellis blinked. "You want to tell people?"

Seth shook his head. "No, that could make us more of a target. I—I just don't know what to do. I wish that dwarf was Dane." His eyes narrowed. "I want him so bad, I can smell it."

Ellis pointed down the road at the small collection of simple buildings. "Crey Village."

"Are you coming with me?" Jena asked Seth.

Seth sighed. "No, I have to talk to Father about this. Meet me later?"

"Sure," Ellis said as he started to run towards the village.

"I thought he hated it here," Seth said.

"Only when he has to work at the bakery." Jena kissed him. "After dinner?"

Seth beamed at her. "I'd love to." Hand in hand, the couple walked into the village.

About ten minutes later, Seth and Jena stopped in front of his home. He sighed.

She embraced him. "I can come in with you. Maybe it won't be so bad if I'm there too."

Seth sighed. "No, I have to do this alone." He kissed her forehead. "I'll see you later. Okay?"

Jena nodded. "Yes. Remember, I love you." She kissed him.

Seth watched Jena stroll towards her house. Yeah, he was alone. He stared at the door. Brock was either not home or didn't see him outside. Once he opened that door, there was no going back. He took a step. His throat began to dry up. Seth picked up his pace towards the door. Maybe the faster he got it over with, the easier it would be, right? His jaw clenched tightly as he pushed the door open.

Seth closed his eyes as he entered the door, as if that would soften Brock's screams. He stepped inside. Nothing. He opened his eyes and saw a once proud man sobbing on the couch.

Brock looked up. His cheeks were red and wet as if he'd been crying all night. "Where have you been?"

"We went after Dane," Seth said as he sat down next to Brock. "We didn't get him."

Brock's face tightened, but cracked as soon as more tears flowed down his cheeks. "My Sally will have died for—for nothing if you get yourself killed before you take back the throne." He put his hand on Seth's shoulder. "I know she wasn't your real mother, but did you love her?"

Brock's tenderness pierced Seth's heart. His fear and anger for Brock melted away. "I loved her so much." Seth hugged Brock.

Brock looked right into Seth's eyes. "I—I know you did what you thought was right. I don't blame you. I wanted to kill him too, it's just that, I have to protect you."

"Have you eaten?" Seth asked. "I've been gone for more than a day and the house looks just like I left it."

Brock laughed. "I don't remember when I ate last."

Seth walked over to the cupboard near the window. He found a loaf of boule bread inside. "Split it?"

Brock wiped the tears from his cheeks. "Sure." He joined Seth at the table.

Seth broke the bread in two and handed a half to Brock. "Are you really not mad at me?"

Brock's tired eyes surrendered. "I'm furious, but—you're home now." He munched on some bread. "What happened?"

"Me, Jena, and Ellis went out, not too long after I left here." Seth studied Brock. Should he hide what happened until he's stronger? No, that would only make things worse. Was he strong enough for the news that his adopted son can wield magic? What choice did he have? "We found Dane with the other knights."

"Which knights?"

"The ones you're hiding. They all thought he was lying about being a knight," Seth said. "Something about—damn it. I don't remember exactly. But, they chased him off."

Brock frowned. "Really?"

"We followed him to the bridge. The funny thing was that he seemed to be running from a dwarf," Seth said. He nibbled on his bread.

"Dwarves? This far south?" Brock rubbed his chin. "They'd have to cross the River of Souls and the Wailing Mountains to get here. Dwarves come from Shumnar."

"Where's that?" Seth asked.

"North of Nightfall Meadows and Tarc. About a 4-week ride from here," Brock said.

Seth swallowed. "We lost Dane and decided to catch up with him at Qrento."

Brock sighed. "That's a real rough town."

"I know. After we crossed the bridge, the dwarves attacked us and—that's when it happened." Seth's stomach danced, sapping his strength to continue.

Brock put the bread down. "Did Jena and Ellis survive?"

Seth nodded. "Both times."

"Both times?"

Seth frowned. "Please, Father, let me finish."

"Sorry." Brock tossed a piece of bread in his mouth.

Seth swallowed. There was no turning back now. "When the dwarf attacked Jena, I—I got so angry. That's when I felt it."

"Felt what?"

"A tingle, in my chest, and then—small lights, like the lightning from the sky, covered my body." Seth's eyes dropped as Brock sighed. "I'm telling the truth."

Brock leaned forward. "Human males cannot use magic. It is a well-known fact."

Seth glared at Brock. "Then how do you explain the dwarf turning into dust when the lights went through my sword and hit him in the chest?"

"What?"

"You heard me. That wasn't the only time. A group of goblins did something to make us fall asleep. When we escaped, I grabbed one by the shoulders and he—died. His eyes popped out of his head." Seth's eyes welled up. "I—I—I had to expend the—whatever it was on the campfire not to hurt anyone else. I can't explain it."

Brock hugged Seth. "I'm sorry for doubting you. What did the goblins want with you?"

"They mentioned the same name in the letter, Shania. They said there was a bounty for me," Seth said. "One thousand crowns."

Brock blinked. "Wow."

"This—power scared Jena and Ellis, but not as much as it

scared me," Seth said. He tossed a piece of bread in his mouth. "Do you have any idea what's wrong with me?"

Brock started to pace around the room. "Not too long after Staerdale Castle fell, me and your mother were in Iprand."

"Where's that?"

"It's just south of the main bridge crossing the River of Souls, near Port Shapus. Anyway, we heard a rumor of a boy who would unite the world against the Darkstriders and destroy them. The boy is human, and the only male that can wield magic." Brock sniffed. "We always thought it was a nice story to give the people hope. It never occurred to me that—"

Seth leaned forward. "Is it me?"

"Probably not, but they might think you are. That puts you in even greater danger." Brock sat back down.

"Greater?"

"Yes, now instead of looking for King Galin the IV's heir, they're looking for the prophesied king who'll destroy them. It doesn't matter what I believe or if it is even true, as long they believe it." Brock's face went white. "We can't stay here. We have to leave."

Seth blinked. "If we pack to leave, why wouldn't they come after us, like they did before?"

Brock sighed. "They will, of course."

Seth's eyes widened. "What if they think we're going to stay? Then they'll think they have all the time in the world."

Brock beamed at him. "Brilliant."

"Father, if they attack us, should I use my power?" Seth asked.

Brock grimaced. "Only as a last resort."

Seth looked out the window at the afternoon sun. *Where will we go?*

CHAPTER 16

THE NEXT MORNING, SETH FELT GOOD. THE SUN POURED through his bedroom window. He truly bonded with Brock for the first time last night. He was so engrossed with his newfound friendship with his adoptive Father, Seth forgot to meet Ellis and Jena at the market square. Today was going to be a good day. He tossed on a tunic and pants, getting ready for the long day ahead.

Brock as sitting at the table eating a bowl of gruel. "Morning."

Seth couldn't hold back his smile. "Morning. I hate that stuff." He sat down as Brock slid him a bowl.

"It's good for you," Brock said.

"I've taken up the quest. I will be king," Seth said. "I was thinking—"

The door flew open. "Anyone home?" Alya said as she raced inside. Her face relaxed. "You're here. I heard that Seth disappeared." She moved behind Brock and rubbed his shoulders. "I came as soon as I heard the kids ran off. I'm here for you, Brock."

He looked up at Alya. "We've decided to stay."

Alya's face dropped. "Why?"

"Where are we supposed to go?" Brock asked. "The Darkstriders rule everywhere that we could go. What's the point? They can only kill you once." He rolled his eyes. "Why are you here?"

Seth studied Alya. He couldn't focus on her face, it was as if the outlines of her face were—blurry. He shook his head. "Alya, will you help us set up the shop?"

"Alya, why did you come?" Brock asked.

"I came to make sure you were all right. I heard that Seth was gone so—I thought you could use the company," Alya said. She tore her eyes away. "I care about you."

Brock's face reddened. "My wife is barely dead and you tell me that?"

"I didn't mean it the way it sounded," Alya said. She moved in closer. "I—you're just—I'm here for you. I know how close this family was."

Seth jumped up. "Is. How close this family is."

Alya backed away from Seth. "Sorry." She rubbed a small signet ring and it glowed.

Brock blinked. "Of course she knows that, son." His soul took in her deep blue eyes. "Of course she does."

Seth blinked. Was she trying to take Sally's place at Brock's side, already? *Grown-ups are weird!* "Father, don't we have to set the shop back up?"

Brock simply stared into Alya's eyes.

Seth punched Brock in the arm. "Father, we've got stuff to do."

As if snapped from a dream, Brock jumped back from Alya. "Yeah—I—let's go, son."

Seth glared at Alya as he pushed his way past her.

"I'm coming," Alya said as she followed Brock out the door.

The cool morning breeze tickled Seth's nose as they

headed toward the market square. It was as if he was alone. Brock and Alya were talking like they were courting. Seth shook his head. Well, at least Brock wouldn't be alone. Alya was more heroic than most men Seth knew; she'd keep him safe. Why did he care so much anyway? Brock would leave him alone now, right?

Clop. Clop. Clop.

Seth turned around. Seven dark-clad knights wearing the Crest of the Darkstriders on their shoulders trotted toward them. The knights were human, not Dark Elves. Why were they here? Did they find out? Dez. Dez must have told them about his powers. They must—no, they are coming for him. Seth focused on the lead knight. He was confident, with short brown hair and a scar on his right cheek. He looked young—only a few years older than Seth, perhaps.

Brock yanked Seth off the street, just before Seth was knocked over by the lead knight. Brock looked at him. "No, it can't be."

Alya came up by his side. "What?"

Brock blinked. "It's Sir Robert. We were friends, but—he hasn't aged."

"He's on their side now," Seth said.

"Maybe—or—maybe he's..." Brock started off after the knights. "Go home, Seth. I have to find out the truth."

"I'm coming with you," Seth said.

Alya grabbed him by his arm. "No, do as he says. Your Father told me who you are."

Seth's shoulder's tightened.

"It's okay, I'm on your side," Alya said. She looked right into Seth's eyes. "I'll take good care of him."

Seth looked at Brock running towards the market square. "Are you sure?"

Alya smiled. "I promise." She turned and ran after Brock.

"I hope I did the right thing," Seth said as he turned towards home.

~

Seth paced around the couch. The past hour seemed like days. What was Brock thinking? Was he captured? Alya, too? His palms began to sweat. He looked out the door. Alya said to go home, but—how long should he wait? It'd been an hour already. Surely, that was long enough. Seth circled the couch again.

He walked to the back door. Seth smiled. He practiced in the backyard with the new sword Brock made for him. Seth could almost see Sally smiling in the window when he beat Brock in a sparring match. He sighed. *Where are they?*

Knock. Knock. Knock.

Seth bolted for the door. Brock would never knock, something must be wrong. He yanked the door open to see Jena and Ellis jump back.

"Easy, killer," Ellis said as he pushed his way inside.

Jena kissed Seth. "Feeling better? I missed you last night."

Her lips warmed his heart. "Sorry about that, but—for the first time—we actually talked, like men."

Ellis grinned. "Where's your new playmate now?"

Seth frowned. "He chased after some Darkstrider knights. He seemed to know one of them." He cocked an eye at Ellis. "Why are you here? You never came here before. I always had to meet you somewhere."

Ellis wandered over to the table and plucked the last apple from the small basket in the center of the table. "I saw Dane." He crunched into the apple.

Seth blinked. "You did? Where?"

Ellis smiled. "At the Red Scale Tavern. He had an ale with

a few locals. No, actually, I've never seen them before. They were merchants or travelers or something."

"What if Brock comes back?" Seth asked.

The smile dropped off Ellis' face. "What if he doesn't? He may be captured, or worse—"

Jena punched Ellis in the arm. "Knock it off and leave him alone."

Seth put his hand on Jena's shoulder and looked into her eyes. "It's okay. He's right. I'll go crazy if I stay here too much longer." He pointed to the door. "After you."

"Try to keep up," Ellis said as he hurried out the door.

The trio slowed down as they approached the market square. The air was filled with the scent of fresh blueberry muffins and banana bread from the bakery. As usual, the merchants had their stands lined along the market square, and the fishmonger held her spot right next to the docks. The Red Scale Tavern was on the left, just behind a row of merchants. Small tables surrounded by simple chairs were outside the front door. Seth looked through the bustling crowd, looking for Dane. "Do we go inside?"

Ellis grinned. "How else are we going to find him?"

"Come on," Jena said as she weaved her way through the crowded market square.

As Seth got closer to the tavern, a group of Darkstrider knights sat down at the outside tables. They casually forced the locals that were there to find another seat. "Stop, come back!" Seth said as she disappeared into the crowd.

"What?" Ellis asked.

Jena grabbed Ellis' tunic. "Come on." She dragged him back into the crowd.

Seth stared at the knights. Their faces seemed—fuzzy. Just a little, but fuzzy, all the same.

Ellis sighed. "Dane will get away. I'm beginning to think you're afraid of him."

Seth shook his head. "No, I'm not." He pointed at the knights sitting at the outside tables. "See them?"

"Yeah," Jena said.

"That's who my father and Alya went after," Seth said. "Where are they? They're more important than Dane."

Ellis looked around. "I—good point. I'll look around."

"We should all go," Jena said.

"No." Ellis frowned. "I can sneak around better when I'm alone. Give me a few minutes and I'll let you know if they are in the tavern."

"Don't get caught," Seth said.

Ellis smiled. "Trust me." He disappeared into the crowd.

Jena strained her eyes looking for Ellis. "How does he do that? He's not magical too, is he?"

"No," Seth replied. "He's just a good thief."

Jena held Seth's hand. "You know, if they leave, we'll need a horse to follow them."

Seth gulped. "We don't have horses."

"I've got an idea." Jena ran towards the stables.

"Jena, wait—come back!" Seth sighed. "Damn it." He couldn't stand in the middle of the street, right? He moved over near the fishmonger, where he was hidden by the crowd but could still see the knights. What if they left before Ellis and Jena came back? Brock should have been home long ago, and the only link he had was those knights. He had to find the last living member of his family and save him. What exactly did Brock see that spooked him so badly? It was almost like he saw a ghost. Was that all of them? Seth started counting the knights at the table. There were only six knights sitting at the table. Where was the one Brock recognized?

Seth moved in a little closer for a better look. No, the one Brock recognized was not there. Maybe the knights left that one with Brock and Alya? A hand grabbed his shoulder. Seth whirled around.

Jena was glowing. "I did it."

Seth closed his eyes, only for a moment. "You scared me." He breathed. "What did you do?"

"The stable master's wife and daughter came with the black sickness last winter. My mother cured them, but it nearly killed her," Jena said. "He didn't have any crowns to donate."

Seth frowned. "Jena, you didn't."

"I told him we needed some horses—only to borrow. But, he insisted that I just take them, saddles and all," Jena said.

"You got us horses?" Ellis asked as he reemerged from the crowded market square. "You're the best. I couldn't pull that off."

Seth glared at Ellis. "Did you find them?"

"They're not inside," Ellis replied. He pointed at the knights. "They may go to them. I'm not sure what else to do."

Seth nodded. "I was thinking the same thing. We need to follow them."

Jena pointed at the knights. "Look, they're getting up."

"Let's get to the horses," Seth said.

"Come on." Jena led them through the crowd towards the stables. The plain pole barn was surrounded by hitching posts. "There they are." Jena moved towards the last hitching post where three mares were tied off.

"Where's my stallion?" Ellis demanded. "Really, Jena?"

Seth slapped Ellis on the back. "Be thankful you're not walking."

"The stable master said that the knights' horses are at the other end. All we have to do is wait here," Jena said.

Seth stared at the painted brown and white horse. The horse's black mane highlighted her beauty. It's brown eyes were soft and gazed upon him. She lowered her head as if she knew something. "I'll take this one." He reached out and patted the horse's head. "I'll call her Thea, after the knight my father always talks about."

Jena jumped on the brown horse with one patch of white around her left eye. "This one's mine. I'll call her Tyra."

Ellis looked at the last horse. She was the smallest and a good three hands smaller than Tyra. Her tan body was riddled with black spots as if she had some kind of disease. Her mane was black. "Seriously? I get the runt?" He climbed on her back. He patted the horse. "Yeah, your name is 'Runt.' Be thankful you even get one."

Jena glared at him. "Ellis! How could you?"

"What did I do?" Ellis demanded.

"Hey, stop it. Look." Seth pointed at the knights climbing on their horses. "They're going."

Jena grasped Seth's hand. "After we get back and everyone is safe—"

Seth blinked. "What are you talking about?"

Her blue eyes invited him into her soul. "Yes. Let's do it. If we wait, it may never happen. We could be captured, or worse."

Seth smiled.

"What are you talking about? They're getting away!" Ellis said.

Seth leaned over and kissed Jena. "I'm supposed to ask you."

Ellis' face turned red. "What is going on?"

"We're getting married," Jena said.

"Good, great even," Ellis said. "Can we go after the knights now?"

Seth kissed Jena's hand. "You'll be my queen."

"What?" Jena asked.

Seth grinned. "Come on." They followed the knights out of the market square.

. . .

Sir Robert stared out the inn room window above the Red Scale Tavern. "This had better work, Shania."

Shania was sitting on the bed, staring at him. "You're the one who insisted on proof that the boy is or isn't the one in the prophecy. I say we just kill him and get it over with."

Robert spun around. His medium-length blond hair turned into short black hair. Robert's blue eyes flashed; as the flash faded, they became a resolute brown. Worst of all, his tanned skin turned a deep blue. "Watch your tongue."

Shania frowned. "Why are you here, Tanyl? In person."

Tanyl leaned over Shania. His eyes narrowed and his jaw tightened. "Because you don't understand the predicament you're in."

Fear came over Shania's face. "I—I—"

Tanyl slapped her, knocking her off the bed. "I should give you to the seers for questioning." His narrow lips curled. "They can make your blood boil while still in your veins. The screams are so satisfying to listen to."

"I'm loyal and you know that," Shania said. She stood up. "I'd be done with this mission long ago if you didn't insist on waiting for sign about that stupid—"

Tanyl slapped her again. "I was there when they escaped! Our mages spotted every human in Staerdale Castle save one, the baby. The only way to avoid detection was if the baby had magical powers. *Natural magical power.*"

Shania sniffed. "No infant can wield magic."

"It was either that or Ramir, the god of Justice, played a hand in their escape. If he uses magic in front of you, bring his head to me," Tanyl said. "You have three weeks, no more."

"If he doesn't use magic in front of us?"

Tanyl glared at her. "Then bring him alive."

"No, I demand justice. That brat is responsible for my brother and father. The war never would have happened if it wasn't for that damned prophecy. I'll bring him to you in pieces," Shania said.

"Only if he uses magic in front of you," Tanyl reminded her. "I have reports that a goblin raiding party saw him use magic. Not fire or ice, but lightning."

Shania's mouth dropped. "How did you know that? I just got—"

Tanyl leaned in close. "Because I am loyal to the Dark-striders, not to my own vengeance! If I don't have the boy in three weeks, I'll take you in his place." Tanyl transformed back into Sir Robert. "Use that fool blacksmith to entice the boy to use his magic. You've had over ten years, Shania, that's long enough." Tanyl walked towards the door. "You know the price of failure."

Shania nodded. "I do."

"You'd be better off to die trying to get them than come to me in failure." Tanyl grinned. "Have a nice day."

Shania sat down on the bed as Tanyl slammed the door shut. Her blue face reddened. "That bastard."

CHAPTER 17

SETH LED THE TRIO DOWN THE DIRT ROAD FROM CREY Village. The cool afternoon breeze blew his light-brown hair off his shoulders. The knights were barely in sight. The road went right through Sarun Grove as if a mage bore a path through the forest. This road led to only one place, the bridge. Seth wiped the sweat from his eyes. Would they lead him to Brock? Or did he leave Brock behind at the Red Scale Tavern? Seth nudged Thea's ribs and she sped up.

Ellis rode up next to Seth. "Hey, don't get too close. They'll see us."

Jena rolled her eyes. "We're the only other ones on the road, of course they see us."

"As long as we don't act suspicious, we'll be fine," Seth said. "You of all people should know that." He moved ahead and his eyes never left the group of knights. Was he on the way to becoming a real knight for good? Was he acting as his true father would? Seth sighed. King, he would be king someday. He looked back at Ellis. His friend was more loyal than the fishmonger's dog. If he really succeeded in fulfilling his father's dream, what would he do? Seth knew nothing about leading—or ruling a kingdom, for that matter. Maybe he needs to do one thing at a time. Seth glanced over at Jena.

Yeah, marry Jena, as soon as they got back. His heart knew it was the right thing to do, but Seth's mind had doubts. If they got married, Jena would have a baby. How could any sane person raise a baby in this world? Maybe once he was on the throne, or perhaps Jena was a high priestess, someday. What if—?

Jena moved closer to Seth. "What are you thinking?"

"About us," Seth said.

Ellis made a gagging sound. "Please, you make me sick."

Jena's smile stretched across her face. "No, he's wonderful. Thinking about our wedding? Our future family?" Her eyes glistened.

Seth swallowed. "Yeah, sure."

Ellis pointed at the knights. "They're turning."

Seth cracked the reins. "Let's go."

Ellis grabbed Jena's hand. "Go easy on him. At least wait until we actually get back. Okay?"

Jena nodded. "You're right."

"Come on, let's go," Seth said as he brought Thea to a gallop. The knights crossed over the bridge. He was sure of that, but where did they turn off? Just north of the river is where they'd escaped from the goblins. Where these knights allies with them? Or the dwarves, perhaps? Maybe that's who had Brock. As soon as Seth crossed the bridge, he dismounted Thea.

Ellis crossed too and jumped off Runt. "Looking for tracks?"

"Yeah, I was never good at that. Father always had to correct my tracking when we used to go hunting," Seth said.

"You never talked about him like that before," Jena said as she got down off her horse. "You miss him, don't you?"

Seth nodded. "I do. I really do. I—I'm not sure that I'll find where the stupid knights went to."

Ellis slapped Seth's shoulder. "No worries, Seth, I can actually hunt without my father's help." He laughed.

Seth frowned.

Jena laughed.

"Can you find their tracks?" Seth said.

Ellis handed Runt to Jena as he scanned the ground along the road. "I've got them, come on."

Jena and Seth climbed back on their horses. Ellis led Runt along the road as he followed the tracks on foot.

"Can't you do that on horseback?" Seth asked.

"Can you track them? If we depended on you, we'd probably starve," Ellis said.

Seth glared at him.

"No, I can't." Ellis knelt down and felt the tracks along the side of the road. "They entered the woods here. No doubt." He looked up.

Seth jumped down. "We have to be quiet. If they spot us before we have them, they could kill my father." His heart sank to his feet. If he lost the last member of his family, it would be worse than the underworld. Jena's beauty caught his eye. No, even if he lost Brock, he'd still have her.

Jena dismounted. "What do we do with the horses?"

Ellis' mouth opened, but nothing came out.

"I—well, we—we find a spot to tie them off and—go back for them after we're done," Seth said.

She cocked an eye at him. "What if someone else finds them?" Jena said.

Seth swallowed. "I—well—"

Ellis rolled his eyes. "What if a giant ogre ate the world? Please, Jena, knock it off. He's right and that's that."

Jena laughed. "I suppose."

Seth stepped into the woods, passing through the

underbrush. Occasionally, he'd look back at Ellis, who'd point where to go. He grimaced. How many times had his father told him to pay attention? How many lessons did he fail to learn what he needed to know now because his mind was elsewhere? His father might die because Seth was daydreaming when Brock was trying to teach him something important. Why? Why didn't he pay attention?

Crack. Voices.

Seth stopped, raising his hand in a closed fist.

Ellis and Jena froze.

Seth motioned away from the voices.

Ellis and Jena stared at him blankly.

Seth frowned. He quietly walked his horse over to where he was pointing and tied Thea to a tree.

Jena and Ellis tied off their mounts and joined Seth next to a large oak tree. "What now?" Jena whispered.

Seth put his finger over his lips, quieting Jena. "Follow me."

The sun started to descend behind the trees. A breeze passed through the leaves. Seth softly lowered each step to the ground, heel to toe. He listened.

Nothing.

He closed his eyes as if that would enhance his senses. Smoke. He smelled smoke. Fire. It must have been a campfire, like when they found Dane along the river. Yeah, they were really close, but where? He opened his eyes.

Trees and more trees and more trees laid in front of them. Bushes, saplings, and every other green obstacle known to the human race stood between him and the Darkstrider knights. He blinked. How stupid was he being?

Seth pushed forward, one step at a time. When he stepped on a stick, he knelt down and remained silent. There were six knights and only three of them. Well, two and a half if you count Ellis. Anyway, they had to surprise them if they were going to save Brock.

He crept forward. Seth knelt next to an oak tree and behind a bunch of lilies. The ground dropped off in front of them. A path to their right entered the small clearing. The smoke smell was stronger than ever as the wind blew it in their direction from the campfire in the center.

Ellis covered his nose as he crawled next to Seth.

Jena moved up next to Seth, staring at the six knights below.

The humans were removing their armor and packing it on their horse, which were tied off on the trees away from the fire. They were saying something, but Seth was too far away to make it out.

"I don't see him," Jena said.

Seth focused. He had to find Brock. He must be here. Must be—right? Behind the knights were the trees the horses were tied off on with little underbrush. To the left of the camp were trees surround by thick vegetation and the right side was no different. No, he wasn't there.

"What do we do?" Ellis whispered. "We can't stay here long." His eyes watered as he held back a sneeze. "I can't stay here long."

"Maybe we can find Alya back in town. She may have an idea," Jena said.

Seth bit his lip. What if they caught him and made him talk? Torture him, like they did to Sally. Yeah, why not? He shook his head. Then he'd be no different, just a lowlife murderer after revenge, nothing more. "You're right. Let's—"

"Achoo!" Ellis sneezed.

"Up there! You four, bring them back here," one of the knights said.

"Yes, sir." Four knights jumped on their horses, heading to the trail out of the clearing.

Seth smacked Ellis. "You stupid troll."

Wide-eyed, Jena grabbed both Seth and Ellis. "Come on, now!"

They bolted for the horses.

The two knights still by the campfire watched the trio disappear from sight. Their human forms dissolved into their true Dark Elf features. They became Elmar and Malon.

"Are you sure about this?" Malon asked.

Elmar grinned. "Shania has a plan, give it a chance."

Malon laughed. "If those humans only knew."

Seth jumped over a stump, pushing a sapling out of his way. Sweat rolled down his cheeks. He looked back.

Jena dodged an oak tree.

Ellis ducked under a vine.

The four knights emerged from the bowl. One of the knights pointed directly at Seth. "Over there!" He cracked the reins.

Seth jumped on Thea. "Come on!"

Jena leaped on Tyra's back. "Let's go, Ellis."

"Quickly, they're going to get away!" said one of the knights as he got caught up in the underbrush.

Ellis mounted Runt. "What are you two waiting for?" He cracked his reins and Runt bolted through the brush towards the road.

"Jena, go!" Seth said as he slapped Tyra's butt. He watched Jena bolt after Ellis.

"We got one," a knight said as he entered the small clearing.

Seth drew his sword.

"Don't go after him alone," another called out.

The knight charged Seth.

Seth turned Thea and kicked her ribs. Thea jumped, galloping down the path.

"No you don't!" the knight yelled. His kicked his horse's ribs, making him go faster.

Seth called out to Thea, "Yah! Yah!" Thea picked up speed. He ducked under a low branch.

"Damn it," the knight yelled as the branch hit him. "I'll kill you!"

Almost to the road, Seth thought. As soon as they got to the road, it would be a race—to where?

"Wait for us, Allen!" a distant voice yelled. "You're gonna get yourself killed!"

"I almost have him!" the knight said. He ducked under a vine hanging from an oak tree.

Seth's eyes opened wide. The small path began to open up. The road—he'd reached it. "Come on, Thea, we've got to —" As soon as he came out onto the road, he saw Jena holding something in her hand, saying—something.

"Get out of the way, fool!" Ellis yelled.

Seth moved the reins, guiding Thea to go left.

"Lia fol penia," Jena said, staring down the path where Seth just came from.

Allen emerged from the wood with his sword drawn. As if he knew something, the knight reared his horse, trying to move out of Jena's line of sight.

"Lia fol penia." A flash almost as bright as the sun came out of Jena's eyes in the shape of a cone.

Allen fell to the ground, clutching his eyes.

Jena fell to her knees, rubbing her eyes.

"I'm blind!" Allen said. "What have you done to me?"

Seth jumped off Thea, running to Jena's side. "Are you all right?"

She nodded. "Give me a second. The pain will pass."

"We don't have a second," Ellis said. "We've got to go now."

"Can you see?" Seth asked.

"Yeah, I'm—I'm good," Jena said as she got back on Tyra.

Seth jumped on Thea. "Let's go."

"Where?" Ellis asked. "Back to Crey Village?"

"There they are, get them!" The three were almost to the road.

Seth looked west at the Wailing Mountains. "There." He cracked his reins. Thea crossed the road and darted into the woods. He looked back. Jena and Ellis were close behind. He ducked, weaved, and jumped over the natural obstacles in Long-Tail Forest. Seth urged Thea forward. Thea moved faster and deeper into the forest.

The trees and underbrush gave way to rocks and small bushes. A clearing at the base of the mountains. Seth scanned the red rock face. Where could they hide? Were they ready to fight?

Ellis pointed at a small opening, barely visible through the shrubbery. "There!" He galloped towards the hole in the rocks.

Seth looked back. Nothing. He and Jena charged after Ellis. As soon as they went over the rise, the saw that the small hole was really a cave opening big enough for a tall man to stand up.

Ellis was already inside. "Come on."

Seth and Jena led their horses inside the cave. They moved into the shadows. Seth closed his eyes, listening for their pursuers.

Wind. Drips of water behind them. More wind. No voices

or horses crashing through the brush. Nothing. "We lost them," Seth said.

Ellis looked around. "Where are we? I never heard of this place."

Seth turned towards the sound of dripping water. "We need to stay here a while before we try to find them again."

"Again?" Ellis said.

Seth glared at him. "Yes, I must find my father." He looked into the shadows, trying to see where the dripping water was coming from. "We can stay here a bit. Sounds like there's fresh water here."

Jena pulled out a small piece of quartz. "Wen opel gia. Wen opel gia. Wen opel gia." The piece of quartz began to glow. It illuminated a ten-yard radius around Jena.

"How'd you do that?" Ellis asked.

Jena smiled. "I am a priestess in training. We can fight too, you know."

Seth tied Thea off onto a rock sticking out of the ground. "Let's leave the horses here." He pulled the feed bag out of his pack and put it around Thea's head. The horse began munching on the sweet feed. After Ellis and Jena had tied off and fed Tyra and Runt, he looked into the darkness beyond the light. "Let's find some water."

"Are you sure about this?" Ellis asked.

Jena giggled. "Afraid? Don't worry, I'll protect you."

"No, it's just—"

"I'm sure. Let's go." Seth, with Jena at his side, headed deeper into the cave.

CHAPTER 18

THE CAVE WALLS HAD A GREEN TINT TO THEM. SETH'S FEET sank into the soft, wet sand. With his hand on the hilt of his sword, he pushed forward. He felt that there was a downward slope, but he couldn't be sure. After all, he was not a dwarf.

Ellis swallowed. "Looks like a turn ahead. If we take it, we won't be able to see the cave mouth. We'll have to rely on that." He pointed to the piece of quartz in Jena's hand. "No offense."

Jena grinned. "I've never seen you so nervous."

Ellis stepped back from her. "Nervous? Me? I—I don't think so. I'm thinking of—you. That's it. I was thinking about you."

"Come on." Seth led the trio around the corner. Bumps grew on his skin as the air temperature began to drop. The farther they went in, the colder it got. The passage was getting narrower. "Wait a minute." He closed his eyes and listened.

"What?" Ellis asked.

"Shhh." Seth concentrated. Listening.

Drip. Drip. Drip.

"Okay, let's go." Seth headed toward the sound of dripping water.

After another twenty feet, the passage emptied out into an opening. The walls were not rough rock, but polished granite. The floor was no longer dirt, but decorative marble. It was a square room with an archway at the far end. On the walls were old, moldy paintings.

"Where are we?" Ellis asked.

Seth moved close to one of the paintings. It was a battle. Humans fought side-by-side with elves. Not elves with blue skin, but elves with fair skin. They were fighting Dark Elves and orcs. There was a human, a king maybe, standing out in front, charging into battle. It was almost as if the painting recorded an event long ago.

"What is this place?" Jena asked.

Seth looked around. "I don't hear the water anymore." He knelt down, feeling the marble floor. "Where are we?"

"This is Porp Hollows," a female voice said.

Jena flashed the light towards the archway.

Ellis drew his daggers.

Seth jumped to his feet, in between Jena and the woman.

The gray-haired woman's wrinkled face smiled. "I hope I didn't scare you."

"Who are you?" Seth asked.

"I am Sumia." Her grin emphasized the scar under her left eye. "I'm the last one."

"What is Porp Hollows?" Jena asked.

Ellis put his daggers away as his face softened.

Seth frowned. Could they trust an old woman who lives in an underground—whatever?

"It's a—rather, it used to be a stronghold for the Vulwin Elves. Long ago." She walked over to the painting that Jena was looking at and pointed to the human leading the charge. "That is King Galin the II of Ravenward during the first war against the Darkstriders." Her voice softened. "It took place on Etrana, when we took the fight to them and won. The alliance between humans and the Vulwin Elves was unbreakable—until Kade." She swallowed. "No sense crying over the past." Her mouth spoke inaudible words and she clapped her hands. The chamber brightly illuminated. "I have some food and drink. You're welcome to join me."

Ellis' stomach grumbled. "Sounds great."

Jena looked over at Seth.

"Why should we trust you?" Seth asked, taking his hand off the hilt.

The old woman's teeth were exceptionally white and glistened as she smiled at him. "My boy, if I wanted to harm you, you'd already be dead. I'm not as frail and helpless as I may look." She smiled. "Follow me."

Seth, Jena, and Ellis followed Sumia down the corridor. The granite walls were covered with elaborate tapestries illustrating battles, love, and treasure. After a few turns, they entered a simple room with a lit fireplace. Inside the fireplace hung a cast-iron kettle filled to the top. Surrounding a small table were four stools. The aroma of potato soup tickled Seth's nose.

Sumia started to stir the potato soup.

"Smells great," Ellis said as he sat down.

Jena whispered into Seth's ear. "I can tell if it is poisoned or not."

"It's not," Sumia said, "I assure you." She gave a bowl to Jena. "There's really no point trying to whisper around me."

Jena looked away. "I'm sorry."

Sumia put a bowl in front of Ellis. "No, don't be. I'd be suspicious too."

"Thanks," Ellis said.

She brought over two more bowls of soup before sitting down. Sumia slid one over to Seth. "Eat up."

Seth's stomach growled as he looked at the tempting soup. "Thank you." He picked up a spoon and tasted it. The creamy liquid passed over his tongue and his stomach wanted more. "This is good."

She smiled. "Thank you. I learned that recipe from a human—I mean, my mother."

Seth frowned. "Human? Why'd you say that?"

Sumia shook her head. "I've lived around elves my whole life. I'm sorry. Sometimes, I forget that I'm human."

"Where is everyone?" Seth asked.

"Yeah, what happened here?" Jena asked as she popped another spoonful of soup into her mouth.

"Do you know why the Darkstriders attacked Axain?" Seth asked. "I think my father knows, but he never told me." He looked into his soup. "I never got close to him, until—until it was too late."

Sumia sat back on her stool. "It depends on who you ask. The trade route between the Etrana and Ceyceuna continents was limited to that small area. The Fadyhl Waters are far too rough for ocean voyage except in that one spot. The Vulwin Elves controlled the ports on Etrana, and the Kingdom of Axain controlled them on Ceyceuna. Anyone who wanted to travel or trade had to pay fees to cross."

"Are you saying it was about money?" Ellis asked.

Sumia shook her head. "Some folks do. Because now the Darkstriders control both sides. Not only did they take over human lands, but the Vulwin Elves fell to them as well. Most were killed, but some went into hiding."

"Is that what this place was? A place to hide?" Jena asked.

Sumia nodded. "Yes, at first. Warriors did raids on the Darkstriders while waiting for the prince to emerge. The

Darkstriders fear the prince more than two legions of Vulwin Elf warriors."

"Why's that?" Seth asked.

She smiled. "Are you sure you want to hear this?"

"We don't have anywhere to go," Jena said.

"Okay. Almost two thousand years ago, the Darkstriders' seers had a collective vision. A human king would unite the humans, dwarves, and gnomes from the north, as well as the snow and mountain elves against them. This king would be nearly invincible in battle because he was a war mage and a knight. His spells would not need components nor incantations, it would be natural to him," Sumia said. The firelight glistened on her forehead. "It's believed that there was a series of events foretelling the arrival of the prophesied king."

Ellis swallowed. "What were the signs?"

She shook her head. "I don't know. But, they waited until fifteen years ago to make a move. They believed it was about to happen. That was why they sent Beldroth to ensnare Kade. They infiltrated the kingdom and it was over in a single night. That is, once they'd given up the frontal assault."

"You know a lot," Seth said.

"I am an old woman who lived through all of it," Sumia said. She leaned toward Seth. "The prince just became a man. As with the females, he will gain his magic abilities during this time."

Seth swallowed.

"Yes, Seth," Sumia continued. "Your powers are the same as in the prophecy."

Seth's mouth dropped, but no words came out.

"How'd you know he has power?" Jena asked.

Sumia smiled. "An old war mage can recognize another magical child. Even your power is just beginning to form, but

—him. He requires nothing but his will. Even if he is not the prophesied king, they believe he is."

"I—I can't control it," Seth said.

"I know." Sumia got some more soup. "I can help you with that. Seth, you need my help. If you don't learn to control it, you put your friends in danger." Her lips curled. "Didn't that already happen? When you fought the goblins?"

Seth blinked. "How'd you know that?"

"It doesn't matter how I know, I just do," Sumia said. "Ever meet a war mage before?"

Seth shook his head.

"I'm on your side. I am here alone because the last of the Vulwin Elves chased after you. They thought you were dead." Sumia sat back down. "Do you want to get Brock back, Galin the V of Ravenward?"

Seth's heart nearly stopped. Was he so transparent? Could she read his mind?

"What are you talking about?" Ellis demanded. "Seth, tell her she's nuts."

"What do you want in exchange?" Seth asked.

She smiled. "I want to kill Dark Elves."

"Okay," Seth said. "When do we start?"

She smiled. "In the morning."

"We can't stay here," Jena said. "We have to get back."

Seth shook his head. "No, not yet. Those knights could still be looking for us."

Ellis threw his feet up on the table. "Let's stay here a few days and relax while Seth works his butt off."

"Please, Jena, I have to learn to control this," Seth said.

Jena nodded. "Okay."

"I'll be ready," Seth said.

Sumia's lips curled. "Very well."

~

The next morning, Seth sat in a corner in the small ante-chamber with polished granite walls and a sleek marble floor. It was a short distance from the chamber where they ate dinner, but it seemed so far from his friends. A small piece of quartz was inside a small clear crystal ball suspended from the ceiling by a golden chain. Unlike the rest of Porp Hollows, there were no tapestries or paintings or furniture of any kind here.

Sumia told him to be on time, no matter what. 'Be there at 6:00 a.m.,' she said. Seth tapped his fingers on the cold floor. Where was she? It was nearly seven. Did she have second thoughts? Did he lead his friends into *another* trap? His face collapsed in his hands.

"Good morning," Sumia said as she entered the chamber. Her red robes touched the floor. They were outlined with golden thread. She was carrying a small basket. Sumia sat down next to Seth. "May I call you Galin?"

Seth frowned. "No, my father said I have to keep that secret."

"I see." Sumia crossed her legs, putting her hands on her knees. "I need to know the truth. Did you use any magical components or incantations? I must make sure I am instructing you correctly," Sumia said.

Seth shook his head. "No."

She nodded. "I did some research last night in my library," Sumia began. "The only creatures that can wield magic without incantations or spell components are dragons. Not the cute thirty-foot-long pets on Etrana, but the big ones near the Mountain Elves."

"How does that help me?" Seth asked.

"Patience." Sumia's eyes softened. "I'm going to teach you what I can, but it's not much."

Seth swallowed. "What exactly are you going to show me?"

She leaned back. "First, how to control your powers from hurting people that you don't intend to attack. I found a single defensive and one offensive spell." Sumia looked away. "I know how magic works, but I never cast these spells before because I need to use components and incantations."

Seth's eyes dropped to the floor. Could she really help him? Sumia even said that she never did this before. Did he have a choice? He counted to ten, mustering the will to step into a new world. "What do I need to do?"

"The tome says that dragons control their magic through their emotions, specifically rage. If someone does something to you or someone you love, your power will surface. However, you can shut it down," Sumia said.

"Why would I do that?" Seth asked.

Sumia's eyes softened. "Because you want to conceal that you are the prophesied king until you are ready to take command of your forces and retake the kingdom. Once the Dark Elves find out who you really are, they'll destroy everything and everyone to get at you. Do you understand?"

Seth nodded.

She opened the basket and pulled out a one-week-old brown puppy and a scorpion.

Seth's eyes locked onto the scorpion. "What are you doing with those?"

Sumia didn't even look at him. "An exercise in control. You're to kill the scorpion and save the puppy without harming the dog." She placed both creatures directly in front of him and backed away.

"What do I do?"

"Focus your rage and hatred on the scorpion. See it turn to dust in your mind. Remember, the dog is to be unharmed," she said.

Seth stared at the scorpion.

It paused, staring at the puppy, its tail poised.

The dog began to sniff, looking into its eyes. It dropped to the floor and barked.

The scorpion backed off a few steps.

Seth liked the cute puppy, not the scorpion. His heart darkened as his eyes narrowed, focusing on the scorpion. Tiny electrical arcs raced along his skin.

Sumia's eyes widened and her face went white.

Seth's tiny arcs got bigger and bigger. He grinned. Arcs jumped across his lips. The tingle became hot and began to burn. Hate, all he had for the scorpion was hate. He wanted to scream. Seth reached towards the scorpion. A bolt of electricity lashed out from his finger. The scorpion vaporized. But something was wrong. The electrical arcs were dancing on across his body. They were getting bigger and brighter.

Sumia backed towards the door. "Stop it. You'll kill us both!"

"I—I can't stop it." Seth stood up. Arcs from his legs danced all around him on the floor. Each passing moment, they got brighter and grew even more.

The puppy ran to Sumia.

Hatred. Hatred filled Seth's mind and soul. There was nothing else.

"Anger and emotion brought you this far, Seth." Sumia shook as she sat down. "Let's meditate and be calm."

Seth backed into the corner and slid to the floor. He crossed his legs with his hands on his knees. Electricity was dancing all around him. He closed his eyes.

"Think—happy—yes, happy thoughts," Sumia said.

Seth receded into himself. Flowers and flying rice and— and Jena. She was older, much older, wearing a white dress with a veil. The high priestess of Odella stood before them holding the golden cord of life. The burning became tingling.

The arcs shrank until they were gone. Seth opened his eyes. "Is it over?"

There was a warm puddle surrounding Sumia. Her face was white and her eyes wide. "I—I—I can't believe it." She got up and her wet gown stuck to her legs.

Seth pointed at Sumia's pants. "What happened?"

Sumia was visibly shaking. "Nothing, it was—no, nothing."

Seth looked around. No arcs or scorpion—what about the —he smiled as the tiny dog rushed back into the room. He picked up the dog and it licked his face. "You can stop now."

Sumia never took her eyes off him as she backed away. "I —I don't—I can't train you. My arrogance—it's all my fault. I thought I could just read a tome and know how your magic works." She took a deep breath. "I'm sorry. I hope I didn't give you false hope." Sumia knelt down. "I am at your service, Galin the V of Ravenward."

Seth gulped. "Get up, I'm no king."

"Very well," Sumia said as she rose to her feet.

"What now?"

"You learned how to control your power and how to nullify it," Sumia said. "With practice, you should master it quickly."

"Is there anyone that can help me learn to use my power?" Seth asked.

Sumia rubbed her wrinkled chin. "I—let me look around. There may be, but—I'll let you know."

He handed her the dog. "I think we'll head back to Crey Village. Maybe my father is back or there's some word."

Sumia smiled. "Good idea."

. . .

Two hours later, Sumia was watching Seth, Jean, and Ellis disappear into the cavern, leaving Porp Hollows. "I never thought it was true," Sumia said.

A tall humanoid with light skin and pointed elf ears emerged from the ante-chamber behind Sumia. "My lady."

Sumia's old human features dissolved into a fair skinned Vulwin Elf with a long golden ponytail and deep blue eyes. Her wrinkled skin tightened. "It's true." She turned her head towards the Vulwin Elf. "We need to get word to King Faeler. The prophecy is coming true."

He bowed. "Yes, my lady." He disappeared into the darkness.

Sumia looked back at the cavern. "Anything you need, anything. I'm here."

CHAPTER 19

Some time later, Seth, Jena, and Ellis rode across the bridge over the Bahr River towards Crey Village. The late afternoon breeze brushed against Seth's face as Thea trotted along the dirt road.

"Are you going to tell us yet?" Ellis asked as he moved Runt up next to Seth.

Seth just glared at him.

Jena frowned. "Ellis, leave him alone."

"Come on, she wanted us to stay for a few days, but after one session with him, we're shown the door. What don't you want us to know?" Ellis asked.

She looked at Seth. "He'll tell us when he's ready."

Seth cocked an eye at Jena. Was that a hint? Father always complained mother would ask him things without ever really saying it, then get angry when he couldn't read her mind. Was that what he meant? Did his friends have a right to know that he could have killed Sumia and everyone else because he completely lacks control of his new powers? Was it a gift or a curse? Only time would tell. Maybe, they should—

Ellis snapped his fingers. "Seth, you in there?"

Seth shook his head. "Yeah, I'm here." He smiled at Jena. "I'm ready."

"Good, about damn time," Ellis said.

"I scared her. My magic is more like the dragon magic than human or elf magic. She showed me how to increase the potency of my attacks and how to stop it without killing anything," Seth said.

Jena's eyes lit up. "How'd you stop it?"

"I thought of the happiest thing I could think of. Our marriage." Seth nudged Thea next to Jena and blew her a kiss.

She blushed.

Ellis stuck his finger down his throat and gagged himself. "Please. You two make me sick." He moved Runt ahead of the trio. "What's the plan when we get back?"

Seth rubbed his chin. "We see if my father or Alya got back or if there is any word on them. I think, we'll go to Jena's house."

Jena nodded. "Yeah, Alya spends a lot of time with my mother."

"Well—crap, I'll have to stop by the bakery and see the old man," Ellis said. "He'll force me to make bread or something while he's lecturing me about responsibility to the family business."

Seth smiled. "I bet he does that all the time."

Ellis laughed. "You know it."

The simple buildings of Crey Village emerged around the corner from behind the trees. Seth slowed Thea down. "Remember, they may be in town looking for us."

"Damn, Seth, you worry too much. If you act natural, we'll be fine. Don't get so uptight," Ellis said.

Seth looked at his house as they rode past it. "It looks like it's okay."

Ellis shrugged his shoulders. "The inside might be torn up."

Jena glared at him. "Ellis!"

Ellis' mouth dropped. "What? It's true."

Seth punched Ellis in the shoulder. "I hate you."

Ellis giggled. "Find me later, okay?"

Seth nodded. "Sure."

Ellis nudged Runt in the ribs and galloped towards his father's bakery.

Jena's house was straight ahead. "Well, we're back," Jena said.

Seth smiled. "Think your mother's home?"

After Jena and Seth had tied off their horses, Jena threw herself into Seth's arms. "Did you hear me? We're back from going after those knights."

Seth blinked. What? His face lit up. "Let's tell your mother we're getting married."

Jena nodded as she led the two of them inside.

Keya was crying on the worn couch near the fireplace. The firelight danced across her wet cheeks. She looked up as Jena entered the small home. "Where have you been?" Keya leaped to her feet, embracing Jena with all of her heart. "I've been so worried. I—I thought they got you." She hugged Jena even tighter.

"I'm okay, Mother." Jena pointed at Seth. "He took good care of me."

With tears still running down Keya's face, she hugged Seth. "Thank you for taking care of my little girl."

"I want to take care of her," Seth said.

Keya sat back down on the couch. "Please, sit. You must be tired."

Seth sat close to Jena and held her hand. Should he really go through with it? Sure, he made a promise to Jena, but— her mother was crying—and it was killing the mood. He looked up at Jena's smile. Her whole face was glowing as if she had been waiting for this moment all her life, too. He promised. Wasn't that what he wanted, too? "We spent a lot of time together."

Jena looked into Keya's eyes. "How old were you when you married father?"

Keya blinked. "That's an odd question. Twelve, why?"

Seth swallowed.

Jena smiled. "Seth has something to tell you."

Keya glared at Seth as if she knew what he was going to say. "I—I want to marry your daughter."

Keya frowned. "She's too young."

"Mother, I'm older than you were when you got married," Jena said as she leaned into Seth's chest. "You just said so."

Keya nodded and started crying again. "I'm losing my little girl." She hugged Jena. "Congratulations." She wiped the joyful tears from her eyes and hugged Seth again. "Welcome to the family."

"Thank you," Seth said. "Have you heard anything about my father?"

Keya looked away. "Yes, they captured him. The human Darkstrider knights. Alya followed them as long as she could, but they got away."

"How?"

"They were on horseback. She wasn't. I'm so sorry, Seth. I don't know what to say," Keya said.

Seth frowned. "Do you know where she is now?"

"Yes, the Red Scale Tavern. She has a room on the second floor. The third room on the left." Keya held Jena's hand. "Now, we've got a wedding to plan."

Seth rose. "I'm going to find her. If I need—"

Keya shook her head. "No, Jena is staying right here until the wedding is planned."

Seth smiled at his future bride. "It's okay. I'll be back soon." He kissed her.

Jena held him close. "I love you."

"I love you, too." He kissed her one last time before he headed out the door.

~

Seth's heart raced as he entered the market square. Neither the sweet smell of baking bread nor the pungent stink from the fishmonger entered his consciousness. Brock's tormented face appeared in his mind. Seth's vivid imagination contrived every possible method of torture and horrible death possible. Every image, every scenario had the same catalyst. He had failed to free the only father he ever knew.

He saw the Red Scale Tavern around the corner. Any minute, those outside tables would come into view. What if those knights were sitting there? Seth grimaced. It didn't matter, especially with Alya inside. She must know something, and he needed help. With Jena staying back with her mother, Seth needed Alya to come. Why wouldn't she? It was clear that she wanted to be *very* close to Brock. When he chased after the knights, she followed.

Seth made his way through the crowded market square. He held his breath. The outside tables were empty. He breathed as he went inside.

It was still the work day, later afternoon at that, and the place was crammed with knights, fishermen, adventurers, mercenaries, and who knows what else. The mahogany bar was on the left wall and every stool was taken. The center of the room was littered with high tables and surrounded by tall chairs. Not a single seat was vacant and there were many people, human and Dark Elf alike, standing along the walls drinking and being merry.

A young beer wench was heading back to the bar with a tray full of empty mugs until she saw Seth. She hurried to intercept him before he got into the tavern. "Can I help you?"

Seth forced a smile. "Yes, I'm meeting a friend in her room. It's on the second floor."

"Who's your friend?"

"Alya. I—I don't know her last name," Seth said.

She pointed to the stairs along the wall. "Over there. Have fun," the beer wench said as she headed towards the bar.

Seth walked up the stairs.

The second floor was clean. The hallway was covered by a long multicolored rug. The stained oak walls were broken up by several doors opposing each other like two fighters sizing each other up. *The third one on the left*, Seth thought.

Sounds of lovemaking came from the first door as Seth moved past it. He smirked. Will he do that after he's married? Just like Brock and Sally used to do. A tear tried to burst free as an image of his adoptive parents kissing on the couch flashed in his mind. Sure, at the time he found it disgusting. Who wouldn't? Who wanted to watch their parents kiss—or worse? One time, he even told them that he didn't want to be corrupted. Seth swallowed. How he missed watching them make out on the couch while his stomach turned.

The third door on the left opened and Alya stepped into the hallway. Her face softened and her eyes lit up. "Seth, you're okay." She rushed over and hugged him. "I was so worried. Let me look at you." She put him at arm's length, scanning his torso. "You don't look hurt."

Seth frowned. "I'm fine, but my father is not. Can we talk?"

Alya nodded. "Of course. Let's go inside." She lowered her voice. "The walls have ears in this place."

Seth followed her inside.

The inn room was simple. A large bed, with its sheet disheveled, was in the center of the room. A small desk was in the corner, and there was a window overlooking the market square. There was a chair by the window with a green pillow on its seat. Seth sniffed. A smell—a smell like—sweat or—it was like Brock's and Sally's bedroom in the morning. He looked right at her. "Are you alone?"

Alya swallowed. "I—yes, I am now. I had—" she pulled her eyes away from his gaze. "Company. I needed some companionship."

Seth turned the chair to face Alya and sat down. There was no way he'd sit down on *that* bed, now. "Where's my father?"

Alya sat on the corner of the bed. "I don't know."

Seth focused on her face. Alya's eyes were going left and right, occasionally looking at him, as if—as if something was wrong or she was hiding something. "Well, can you tell me what happened?"

Alya sighed. "After we saw him chase after those knights, I followed them to the square. After I got closer, I recognized the one he called 'Sir Robert.' He used to be a knight under King Galin the IV and the years were kind to him."

"If he was a knight under King Galin, why was he with the Darkstriders?" Seth asked. How many other knights defected after the fall of Staerdale Castle? Where was their true loyalty?

"Well, I don't know." Her eyes welled up. "Once he caught up with Sir Robert, they got into a fight. Brock yelled the name Thea the Loyal, and then the other knights took him down."

Seth leaned forward. "What did you do? Why didn't you free my father?"

A tear rolled down Alya's cheek. "Don't you think I

wanted to? I—I want to be with him." She grabbed the pillow and sobbed into it. "They took him. I'm so sorry."

Seth's face reddened. "Did you at least see where they took him?"

Alya nodded. "They headed north. One of them said something about returning to camp to—to question him."

Seth nodded. "I know where that is."

"What? How?"

He glared at her. "Never mind." Brock could already he dead, but he had to be sure. If he were dead, Seth would draw and quarter every Dark Elf that he finds, just like they did to Sally. What about the human knights? Traitors to their own, they deserved and would get far worse. He'd make sure of it. He was no longer a little boy who reached the age of manhood, now he was truly a man. But, he couldn't do it alone. Jena's mother wouldn't let her go and Ellis—well, he didn't know where Ellis was, and there was still a chance to save Brock's life. There was no time to look for Ellis. He stood up and reached out towards Alya. "Come with me and help me save my father."

Alya blinked. "I—no, I can't."

"I thought you liked him," Seth said.

"I—I do, but I can't go with you. You're too young. I already lost Sally and Brock. I will not lose you too." She grabbed his arm. "I won't let you go."

Seth wrenched himself away from Alya. "I'm not a child. I am my own man and I will save my father."

"You're only thirteen years old. What makes you so special that you're a man while the other thirteen-year-olds are still boys?" Alya demanded. "Why should I follow you?"

"Because I—" Seth slammed his mouth shut. Could she be trusted? Brock told him never to tell anyone that he was the prince everyone has been looking for. What if—what if she was a traitor too, like that human knight that Brock recognized? They'd take him and—they would treat Jena like they did Sally. Those sick bastards would probably make him watch, too. No, it was too much of a risk. "Because I will not lose my father too." He forced an image of Jena being killed, trying to conjure up a tear. He welled up and his eyes became puffy. "I'll go alone if I have to." He wiped his eyes as tears started to flow down his cheeks.

Alya shook her head. "I won't be part of your death. I owe that to Brock, but I won't stop you, either. I'll be here when you get back."

"If I come back." Seth ran out the door.

A lya watched him jump on Thea's back and ride out of the market square.

The door slammed open.

Alya whirled around to see a tall, dark-blue-skinned elf with a sword on his waist. "I heard everything." Elmar smiled at Alya.

CHAPTER 20

SETH CRACKED THE REINS ON THEA'S BACK. SHE GALLOPED towards the bridge, crossing Bahr River. The breeze whipped through Seth's hair, tossing it from his shoulders. His knee bumped the sword in its sheath on Thea's saddle as he leaned forward. He urged her faster, and Thea raced towards the bridge.

If Brock was still alive, Seth had to get to him quickly. Sure, Brock would never give him up, but—what if he broke? What if—what if he had no choice? No, his father would never betray him, ever. He'd lost too much. He'd never let Sally die for nothing. No, never.

Thea ran across the bridge. Seth pulled back the reins, slowing his mount. He jumped down and grabbed Thea's reins. Where was that path? *Damn it*, he thought. Why didn't he get Ellis? He kicked himself. Seth was no tracker. All the time he saved by not looking for Ellis, he'd waste trying to find the damn camp. Worse, what if he couldn't find it at all? The path was here, somewhere. It had to be.

Clop. Clop. Clop.

Seth looked up. Three horses were bearing down on him.

He cocked his head. The riders were . . . different. They were not human, and they didn't have blue skin. It was—green, a dark green at that. Seth pulled Thea off the road. Maybe they weren't after him at all. Maybe, they were just passing through.

Clop. Clop. Clop.

Seth walked Thea along the edge of the road, towards the creatures. If he ran, surely they'd chase him if just to find out why he was running from them. Yeah, he'd definitely make them suspicious. He pulled his cloak tightly around his shoulders. *Here they come.*

"Whoa," the lead rider said, stopping his horse. His smile with the two oversized canine teeth protruding from his lips was ominous.

Seth could not take his eyes off the creature's monstrous face. He had two axes strapped to the horse's saddle. The creature was bald. It looked something like the monsters in Brock's stories about the old days. What did he call them? Aha, Feral Orcs, the infantrymen of the Darkstriders. What did warriors respect? Courage. He tightened his jaw. "What do you want?"

"Is your horse lame?" the largest feral orc asked.

"Who are you?"

It sneered at him. "All you need to know is that I'm from Iron Fist Keep on patrol."

Patrol? Here? "Never seen your kind before," Seth said, trying to hide his shaking knees. He smiled. "My horse isn't lame, thank you, though. I was just taking a break from the ride."

It leaned back into its saddle. "Hmm, I see." He waved the other two over. All three jumped from their mounts and drew their axes. He felt Seth's shoulder. "How old are you, boy?"

"Thirteen, why?"

The other two licked their lips.

"Out here by yourself?" the orc asked.

Seth stepped back and drew his sword from its sheath. "What do you want?"

The large orc smiled. "Lunch." It raised its ax.

Seth sidestepped and dropped. In one motion, he rolled to the left and slashed the orc's calf.

It dropped its ax, screaming in pain.

The other two orcs charged in with an ax in each hand.

Hatred, Seth thought, *hatred. I must feel the hatred.*

The orc on the ground grabbed a boot knife and stabbed Seth in the thigh.

Pain. The pain shot through his heart. But the pain turned, it turned into anger and rage. Seth's eyes were on fire. His skinned glowed red. His sword glowed like embers in a great fire.

The other two orcs screeched to a halt. "He's a wizard!"

Seth swung his sword at the largest orc, severing his head from his body. There was no blood, the wound was cauterized. He whirled around to face his other two opponents.

They backed away, dropping their axes to the ground.

Seth's eyes turned black. His skin became brighter and brighter. The rage turned into fear.

The two orcs shielded their eyes from the glow of Seth's skin. "What magic is this!?" They ran towards their horses. "Tulak," the smaller one said, "I saw nothing."

Pain. His fire began to burn his skin. It grew brighter and brighter.

The Orcs leaped on their horses. "Let's get out of here," Tulak said as he slapped his horse's butt.

The burning reached Seth's nose. His flesh—he had to turn it off. He knelt down. Jena, he had to think of Jena and their life together. An image of Jena and Seth on their wedding day flashed through his mind. In his mind, they grew further in love with each passing day. The fire in his heart softened. The burning vanished. He opened his eyes. The pain from his left arm shot through his body. He looked down to see the back of his hand blistered, as if from a burn. "How—why? Did I do that to myself?" Seth muttered. If he could burn himself, could he—kill himself, too? Sure, why not? He had to either not use his powers at all or learn to control them. He sniffed. Seth needed help. One more encounter like this and he'd kill his enemy, but he would kill himself too. What good was that?

Seth searched through the feral orcs clothes. He pulled out a rotting mouse. "A snack for later?" he asked the corpse. Teeth, throwing knives, and a parchment. "What's this?" He unrolled the scroll.

Shania,

The clock is running out. I have an impaling stake with your name on it if you don't deliver the boy, as we agreed. I have two legions of Feral Orcs on standby at Iron Fist Keep. Once you have the boy, I'll send the orcs to kill everyone in Crey Village. Tanyl wants to blame the dwarves, so we have plenty of evidence to leave around the village. I was ordered not to do anything until I hear from you. Please hurry.

. . .

R^{yul}

Seth put the parchment in his saddlebag. He patted Thea. "Okay, girl, let's get some help." He climbed onto his mount. With a flick of the reins, he headed towards Porp Hollows.

~

Seth slowed Thea down as they approached the cave mouth. He jumped down and led Thea inside. As he stepped into the cave, Seth bumped into a small rail mounted on the wall. It was a four-foot-long piece of wood nailed to the rock. It was like—like a hitching post. Seth smiled. That was new, did Sumia—? He grinned. Yeah, she must have expected them back. He tied Thea to the hitching post and pulled her feedbag from her saddlebags. After feeding Thea, Seth pulled his sword from the saddle and placed it in the sheath on his waist. He took out the parchment and placed it in the pack on his back.

Seth pulled a dry torch from the saddlebags and knelt down along the cave wall. He couldn't start a fire from scratch, but with flint and steel? That was easy. After only a few strikes, Seth lit the torch. He patted Thea. "I'll be back soon." Seth headed into the darkness.

As Seth approached opening into Porp Hollow, the light spilled into the cave. He stepped into the square room with tapestries hanging on the wall.

Yeah, he found it all right. He placed his torch in the bronze sconce on the wall. He closed his eyes and listened. Voices. Not just Sumia, but others, too. Was she in trouble? Seth drew his sword. He followed the hallway towards the room where they ate with Sumia. His soft leather boots were silent as he moved towards the room.

Firelight danced on the corridor wall, just outside of the simple room with a fireplace. The voices were getting louder.

"My lady," a male voice said, "I don't think you understand. King Faeler wants to speak to him now. The humans can't protect him, and letting him go on with this—this game only puts the kingdom at risk."

"Learn your place," a women's voice said. "I..."

Is that Sumia? Seth thought.

"...will not do anything that may undo the prophecy. When you interfere with a prophetic event, you can change required events and conditions for the prophecy to come true," Sumia said. "That boy is our people's last—"

Seth blinked as a bright light flashed in the room.

"Come in, Galin," Sumia said.

Seth sheathed his sword and entered the small room.

Standing next to the old woman was an elf. Not a Dark Elf with blue skin, this one had fair skin, long golden hair, and pointed ears. He was wearing a light-yellow tunic and green trousers. His face—his face was ghastly white, staring directly at Seth. He was no warrior. He was a coward. "How long have you been standing there?"

Sumia waved him off. "You have my answer. Now, leave us be."

Without taking his eyes off Seth, the Vulwin Elf fled.

"Who was that?" Seth asked.

"A messenger from the Vulwin Elves," Sumia said as she sat down next to the fireplace. "Join me?"

Seth down on a pillow next to her. "Were you talking about me?"

Sumia bit her lip. She stared at him, just for a second, as if having a debate in her mind. "Yes, we were. You see, that's the bad part about prophecies; you have to let them happen. Too often people lack the patience to allow the prophecies to reach their full potential." She smiled at Seth. "Why are you here, now? I was expecting you to come back, just not yet."

He pulled out the parchment. "I ran into some orcs today and found this." He handed it over to Sumia.

Her eyes widened as she scanned the note. Her mouth dropped, but nothing came out. She swallowed. "Two legions? I'll—I'll be right back." She raced out of the room.

"Okay," Seth said.

Not even five minutes later, Sumia came back into the small room. "I had to tell the Vulwin Elves. They might be able to help."

Seth blinked. "I thought they were on the coast? We're on the opposite side of Axain from there."

Sumia nodded as she sat back down. "Yes, but they believe in the prophecy too." She put her hand on his shoulder. "There's a lot of people waiting for you to lead them to freedom."

Seth pulled away. "I don't care about that now. All I care about is getting my father back."

"Can't your friends help you?" she asked.

Seth showed Sumia the burn on his arm. "Look, this was not from the orcs. I did it."

She took his arm. "I've never seen this before." Her wrinkled face softened. "What do you need me to do?"

"I ran off angry because no one would help me. I even went after them alone, but I realize that I can't do it alone," Seth said. "I also know that I can't control my magic. So, for me not to use it, I can't do this alone."

Sumia smiled. "You want me to fight with you?"

Seth nodded. "I also want you to help me convince the others to help me, too. I can't lose both my parents. I just can't."

"I may be a little rusty, but why not?" Sumia got to her feet. "Rest tonight and we'll head out first thing in the morning." She smiled as she left the room.

Seth leaned back into a pillow near the raging fireplace.

CHAPTER 21

THE NEXT MORNING, SUMIA WAS RIDING HER GRAY MARE WITH a silver mane. She wore a dark-blue cloak with gold stitching and a small pouch hung from her belt. Both she and Seth's saddlebags were filled to the top with supplies.

Well rested, Seth nudged Thea forward. "Ever been to Crey Village before?"

Sumia grinned. "A long time ago."

The cool morning breeze blew through his hair as they crossed the bridge over Bahr River. "We'll pick up Jena and be off then?"

Sumia's eyes strained, looking far down the road. "I —maybe."

A rider on a tiny horse appeared in the distance. He stopped, just for a second, then he pressed this tiny horse at a gallop toward them.

"Who's that?" Sumia asked.

Seth smiled. "There's only one person I know who rides a runt horse that fast. Ellis." He flicked Thea's reins and she raced towards Ellis.

Sumia sighed. "Children." She raced after Seth.

Seth stopped Thea right next to Ellis. "What are you doing here?"

Ellis frowned as Sumia caught up to them. "Why is she here?"

"I need her help. Please, Ellis, trust me, okay?"

"I guess."

Seth leaned forward. "What are you doing here?"

Ellis pulled out a piece of beef jerky from his belt pouch. "Jena told me you left to go to your father."

Seth frowned.

Ellis laughed. "Come on, you can't do this without me." He pointed at Sumia. "Even if you have the old bag."

Sumia grunted. "I can handle myself quite well, young man."

"I'm glad you're here," Seth said. "Hey, Ellis, could you get Alya and Jena, have them meet at my house around three o'clock?"

"Really? Now, I'm your damned message boy?" Ellis asked as he turned Runt around. "I guess." He kicked Runt in the ribs and bolted down the road.

Seth smiled at the frowning Sumia. "Come on." He led her into the village.

Seth's house was still a mess, with small pockets of cleanliness. As soon as they entered the home, Sumia gasped and started to straighten up. She had no idea where anything went, but Seth didn't care. He just wanted to get his father back.

Knock. Knock. Knock.

Seth ran to the door and flung it open to see Keya, Alya, Ellis, and Jena. His face softened as his eyes gazed upon her. "Hi."

Jena reached for his hands. "I'm happy you're back."

"Are you sure they're not married already?" Alya asked as she pushed by them.

Keya smiled at Seth. "I'm here because I couldn't talk her out of it."

Sumia, Alya, Ellis, and Keya all sat down on the couch. Seth pulled a pair of kitchen chairs up for Jena and himself.

Alya glared at Sumia. "Who are you?" She began rubbing her ring.

Sumia grinned at her. "There's no need for that," she said as pushed Alya's hand away from the ring. "You can't control my mind with that trinket."

Seth blinked. "What are you talking about?"

"The question still stands. My young friends are more trusting than I am. I know what the Darkstriders are capable of," Alya said.

Sumia nodded. "Very well, I am Sumia. I was a war mage many years ago. Seth came to me for help to get his father back," she said as she leaned closer, "because no one else would."

Alya blinked. "How dare you!"

"It's true, isn't it?" Seth asked. "Alya, when I asked you, did you come?"

"I—I—no." She lowered her eyes. "I didn't." Alya stared at Sumia. "Why does a human war mage have an elf name?"

Sumia laughed. "Oh, you mean like Alya or Keya? Alya, is there something you wish to confess?"

Alya's face turned red. She jumped up and grabbed the hilt of her sword. "I'll give you a confession."

Ellis giggled. "Cat fight."

Seth jumped between them. "Enough of this. I need *all* your help and more."

"More?" Alya asked as she sat back down.

"The knights by Arrowhead Lake. We could run into a large amount of the Darkstriders, both human and Dark Elf," Seth said.

"Surely, we wouldn't face that many," Keya said. "They took Brock with only a handful."

Seth frowned. "I found a parchment on a dead orc addressed to Shania."

Alya straightened up. "Who?"

"Shania. It said that Tanyl was running out of patience and she was supposed to bring the 'boy' to him. They have two legions of Feral Orcs at Iron Fist Keep ready to kill everyone in the village," Seth said. "But, they won't move until the 'boy' is brought to them."

Keya shook her head. "That doesn't make any sense. If they wipe out Crey Village, the movement to overthrow Kade the Usurper would triple in size overnight. They must know that."

"Why's that?" Jena asked.

"Because the Darkstriders know about large groups of fighters in hiding, just waiting for the right moment," Alya said.

Seth shook his head. "They're going to blame it on the Dwarves."

"Is Dane with the Darkstriders?" Ellis asked.

Alya nodded. "Yes, there's no doubt. He's probably more dangerous than the Dark Elves themselves."

Jena giggled.

Ellis laughed. "Dane? He's a coward."

Alya mouth dropped. "What?"

Seth hid his smirk. "I think Ellis is right."

"What did I miss?" Keya asked.

"Let's just say that Dane's mouth was far more ferocious than his sword," Seth said.

Alya cleared her throat. "Well, anyway—what now?"

Seth stood up. "We wait until dusk then we head to Arrowhead Lake to meet up with the knights."

Alya frowned. "Who put you in charge? I'm not sure that's

the best way. I think—"

Seth glared at her. "I did! My father, my party, my rules."

"I agreed to help, but I never agreed to this," she said. "What about the rest of you."

One by one, everyone nodded, affirming their loyalty to Seth. Sumia stared right at Alya. "I follow the boy and all my power is his."

Alya smiled. "Glad to hear it." She headed towards the door. "See you tonight."

"Everyone be back here around dinnertime, ready to go," Seth said.

They nodded and left the simple home.

As the door closed, Sumia whispered into Seth's ear. "Will Alya betray us?"

Seth shook his head. "No, no way. She'd never do that." Seth disappeared into his bedroom.

Sumia was busy over the fireplace cooking a stew in a black iron pot. The aroma made Seth's stomach yearn for its contents. His few-hour nap rejuvenated him. He was ready to take on twin dragons, not just a few Dark Elves. This aura of confidence was inflated whenever Seth was around Sumia.

Jena, Ellis, and Keya entered Seth's house. They had full packs slung across their backs and weapons at their hips.

Seth's eyes widened as he saw even Keya had short swords. "I didn't know you used weapons," Seth said.

Keya smiled. "When you were still a babe, these helped your parents rid Crey Village of the last of Kade's knights."

Ellis plopped down his pack. "Dinner? Smells great." He jumped into a seat at the table. "I'm ready for it."

Sumia smiled. "Let's have one last wholesome meal before

we go. It's going to be a long night." She poured the stew into small bowls and placed them on the table.

A smile whipped across Ellis' face. "This is great. My father can't cook for crap compared to this."

Sumia smiled as she sat down. "I'll take that as a compliment, I think."

The door burst open. "Sorry I'm late," Alya said as she dropped her pack by the door. "Oh, something smells good."

Seth smiled after he gulped another spoonful. "Join us for Sumia's stew."

"Sure," Alya said as she grabbed a bowl and sat at the table.

Was this what being a leader was all about? Seth wondered. Whoever thought he could boss *adults* around?

An hour later, Seth was leading the small band through Sarun Grove, towards Arrowhead Lake where they'd found the knights. The damp night air was thick as honey, he could barely see thirty feet in front of him. Thea seemed to dislike the underbrush and its thorns more than Seth did. Not only did she insist on going around them, she utterly refused to break through any bush with long thorns. That made the group take more turns than Seth was used to and it was more difficult to keep track of where they were. But, there was always the stars; yes the stars were his guide. All he had to do was find the lake and he would be really close to finding more help against the Darkstriders.

Alya rode up next to Seth. "Are we lost? I can help. I've been up here many times."

Seth smiled. "I got it."

Alya leaned closer. "There's no harm in delegating some tasks. That's what a true leader does."

Should he? Alya had been nothing but his guardian angel the past six months. He trusted her, of course. He shook off

Sumia's warning that was still raging through his mind. "Sure, but I'll ride next to you, okay?"

Alya smiled. "Sure."

"Do you like my father?"

"I—yeah, I do." She motioned towards Keya. "I'm not the only one, either."

Seth looked around. "This seems familiar."

Alya nodded. "If you *were* here before, then you'd know that we are not too far." She swallowed. "Why did you bring a washed-up war mage with you? She may not be who you think she is."

Seth blinked. "What do you mean?"

"Well, mages are a tricky bunch. You can't really trust any magic user," Alya said. "I've known masters that were killed because they took their eyes off them."

"You can't trust anyone that uses magic?" Seth asked.

Alya shook her head. "No, and you shouldn't, either. Nothing but—" She stopped her horse.

"What is it?" Seth asked.

Alya said nothing.

Seth closed his eyes and listened. Nothing. He heard nothing, but he smelled something. Smoke that smelled like —like someone was roasting a hog. If it was a party or a large gathering, there would be laughing or yelling or even some talking. No, why would anyone roast a hog in the woods and leave it for the animals? He blinked. Unless, it wasn't a hog!

Alya's face went white as she looked at Seth.

"The camp," Seth said as he kicked Thea in the ribs, rushing over the hill.

Alya slapped her horses' butt. "Come on." She bolted after Seth.

Seth nearly slid down the finger into the camp right next to the Arrowhead Lake. It was the same camp where Dane was chased off for being a fake. The blood-soaked ground was soft. The knights' bodies were tossed into a pile, except for one, John. He was the one that gave Dane the hardest time. He was strapped to the spit above the fire. John was the roasting hog they smelled.

Keya and the others abruptly stopped once they entered the camp. "Oh my," Keya said as she covered her mouth.

Jena covered her eyes. "What kind of monsters would do that?"

Seth pulled her in close. "I—I don't know. I would've thought even the Darkstriders would have some . . . decency."

Ellis jumped off Runt. "I'm glad I'm a not a knight."

Alya glared at him. "Ellis, show some respect."

"For what?" he demanded. "If he weren't human, I'd say let's eat."

Sumia got down from her horse. "Dark Elves are known to do *this*."

Seth stepped near the fire and the roasting knight. "He gave Dane the hardest time. I bet he did it."

"Nope, no way," Ellis said from behind a few trees just outside of the circle.

"Why's that?" Seth said.

"Come here."

Seth and Alya walked over to Ellis. There was a large oak tree with a man tied to its trunk. His hands were wrapped around the trunk. His shirt was torn and his head hung low. Blood decorated his chest like a shirt. Seth lifted his head. It was Dane.

"Yup," Ellis said. "It wasn't him."

"Damn you, Elmar," Alya muttered. She slammed her mouth shut as soon as the words came out.

"Who?" Sumia asked.

Alya shook her head.

Ellis sighed. "What now?"

"Now we go after Father without any of their help," Seth said.

"Come over here," Sumia said as she sat next to the fire.

Seth, Alya, Jena, Ellis, and Keya all sat around Sumia.

"We playing bones or something?" Ellis asked.

"Shhh, quiet, Ellis," Jena said.

Sumia pulled a small pouch from underneath her cloak. Her fingers undid the bow and pulled out a goblin finger bone, claw and all. She placed it on the ground right in front of her. She closed her eyes. "Nim stor gud, hvor Brock, Nim stor gud, hvor Brock" The finger started to glow. "Nim stor gud, hvor Brock."

Pop. The finger vanished.

Seth blinked.

Jena grinned.

Ellis frowned. "That's it?" He jumped to his feet. "All that trouble to see a finger bone pop? Really?"

Sumia opened her eyes. "I know where he is."

"What spell was that?" Jena asked.

"Ramir's Sight," Sumia replied. She stood up, looking towards the lake shore.

Seth followed her eyes. A small boat was tied off to a tree. It must have belonged to the knights.

"They're across the pond in Long-Tail Forest, about five miles. They are camped, waiting for something," Sumia said.

"What?" Seth asked.

Sumia shook her head. "I don't know."

"It could be a trap," Keya said.

"How do we bring the horses across on the boat?" Ellis asked.

"We don't," Alya said. "We head downstream and find a place where we can wade across."

Jena put her soft hand on Seth's shoulder. "What do you think?"

This was it. Was Seth this Prince Galin the V of Raven-ward or was he Seth Feran who wanted to be a fishermen? Did he run or save his father? Seth grabbed Thea's reins. "We're going to get my father." He led her down to the water's edge and headed toward Bahr River.

CHAPTER 22

THEA WADED ACROSS A SHALLOW POINT IN THE RIVER AND stopped on the other side. Seth looked over his shoulder. Warriors and healers, both his age and much older, all followed him. Even Ellis on Runt was following him. Why? Why would anyone follow a freak like him? Perhaps he was truly becoming Galin the V of Ravenward. He smiled.

Runt was the one last one across the river. "How much further?" Ellis asked.

"Not sure," Seth said. He looked around. "Sumia, what do you think?"

Sumia closed her eyes. "Northeast, four miles."

Alya moved ahead of Seth. "Not far now." She kicked her horse's ribs and it bolted into the woods.

Ellis rolled his eyes. "Does that woman ever stop? Come on, Runt."

Seth raced after Alya with Jena and the rest close behind.

Racing after Alya for two more miles through the woods, ducking and weaving branches and briars, got old quickly. "Alya, slow up!" Seth said.

Alya abruptly jumped off her horse and hid behind an oak tree. She turned to Seth with her finger over her lips.

Seth clamped his lips shut. He signaled the others to stop. One by one, they all dismounted and tied their horses off to a tree.

Jena tugged Seth's arm. "What's going on?" she whispered.

"Not sure," he replied. He motioned everyone, except for Jena, to take a knee and keep out of sight. "Come on."

Jena followed Seth towards Alya.

Alya's horse laid in the bush while she was peering around an oak tree.

Seth touched her shoulder. "What is it?"

She leaned in close and whispered into Seth's ear, "Four Darkstrider knights, Dark Elves." Alya pointed towards the clearing ahead.

Seth edged up next to her. At a mere thirty feet the woods broke into a clearing. Not a road or pasture or even a hill, it was just a clearing. The smoke from the campfire stung his nose. Four Dark Elves sat around it, oblivious to anyone outside their little circle. *Is that all of them?* Seth thought. Their breastplates leaned against a few trees in the back where their mounts were tied off. Swords, where were their swords? They were not in the open or hanging, so they must have them. He looked over at Alya. *I can't use my powers, not till I'm sure.* Seth motioned Ellis to come forward.

Ellis crept up next to Seth and Alya. "What?"

Seth pointed at the Dark Elves.

Ellis nodded. "What do you want me to do?"

Seth whispered into Ellis' ear. "We need a distraction, something to draw their attention for a few seconds."

"What are you doing?" Alya demanded. "Let's just charge in and kill them. There's only four of them."

Seth glared at Alya. "Are you certain there are none on patrol or manning a listening post nearby?"

Alya frowned. "Of course not. How would I know?"

"Only a few seconds, just long enough for us to see if there are any others we have to worry about," Seth said.

Ellis smiled. "No worries. Just, don't wait too long."

"I won't." Seth smacked Ellis' shoulder. "Good luck."

Ellis sniffed. "Luck? Who needs that?" He disappeared into the underbrush.

Seth moved back to Keya and Sumia. "There's a few Dark Elves ahead of us. We're going to attack them."

Keya nodded. "I'll get my healing spell components ready."

Sumia snarled. "I'll keep my eye on her," she said, pointing at Alya. "Led us straight to them, did she?"

"Sumia, please, if she wanted to betray us, why did she stop?" Seth asked.

Sumia shrugged. "No idea," she whispered into his ear. "Do not use your power in front of her."

"I won't." Seth crawled back up front next to Jena and Alya. "Ready?"

Jena nodded.

Alya smiled. "You really got this down, don't you?"

"I think so," Seth said.

"What will Ellis do?" Alya asked.

Jena rolled her eyes. "Only Odella knows."

Alya pulled out her short bow and notched an arrow.

Seth concentrated on the four Dark Elves, completely oblivious to their presence. All Ellis had to do was get them to turn and they'd charge in the thirty feet. Thirty feet is nothing. If they weren't so involved in their own little worlds, surely they would have seen Seth and his companions. Sweat began forming on his back. He grasped the hilt of his sword. *Come on, Ellis*, he thought.

Jena grabbed her two daggers, poised at the ready.

Seth's stomach twisted. A bead of sweat rolled down his

left cheek.

"Where is he?" Alya asked.

As if on cue, a loud snap rang through the woods.

"Damn it!" Ellis yelled. "You stupid ogre brain!"

Seth's head jerked towards the far side of the clearing. "What is he doing?"

The four Dark Elves leaped to their feet with their swords drawn. They whirled towards Ellis' voice and moved towards the clearing's edge.

"I hate my damned Runt of a horse!" Ellis yelled.

Seth rose to his feet.

Alya drew back her bow.

Jena moved in right behind Seth.

Crack. The sound of a branch being broken over something echoed through the woods. "Take that you lazy goblin of a horse."

The Dark Elves looked at each other. Once the first one started to laugh, the others couldn't help themselves. They lowered their swords.

"Go!" Seth bolted towards the Dark Elves.

Alya loosed an arrow. It whistled through the trees and embedded itself into a Dark Elf's back. He collapsed to the ground. She pulled out another arrow.

The three remaining Dark Elves raised their swords and charged at Seth.

Twenty feet until glory, Seth thought. He raised his sword. "For my father!"

Jena gripped her two daggers tightly, sprinting right next to Seth.

Seth felt the tingle. *No, not now. I can't, not now.* He willed his power away and focused on his prey.

Alya loosed another arrow. The Dark Elf ducked and it flew into the woods.

Ellis emerged from behind the Dark Elves.

The lead Dark Elf swung at Seth.

Seth sidestepped, knocking the Dark Elf to the ground.

Jena pounced on him like a tigress. Her daggers flailed into his back until it was mush.

Seth swung.

Both Dark Elves skidded to a halt. One drew back into a defensive stance while the other swung at Seth's legs.

Seth leaped back.

Ellis threw a dagger into the Dark Elf's back. He staggered back. Ellis yanked him to the ground as he slit his throat.

Seth slashed the Dark Elf, catching his arm. Blood, he was bleeding. He raised his sword and brought it down towards his victim

The Dark Elf fell to the ground, using its arm to protect its face.

Seth's sword severed the elf's arm just below the elbow.

The elf screamed as it cradled its severed limb. "Mercy, please, mercy!"

Alya stepped up and drew back her bow. "What did you say?"

As he looked into Seth's eyes, blood drained from the Dark Elf's face. "Please—don't, have mercy."

Seth raised his sword. "Like you showed my mother?" he screamed as he slammed his blade into the elf's chest. His chest split open as Seth cut all the way through the creature. He yanked the sword out and walked away.

Alya knelt down to confirm with her hands what her eyes just saw. She put her fingers through the wound and felt the ground on the other side. "You cut completely through him." She rose to her feet. "How? How'd you do that? There's no way you're that strong."

Sumia rushed between Seth and Alya. "Leave him alone. He's just a boy."

Seth grimaced. "If your mother was raped and mutilated, you'd be surprised how strong you can be. I just thought of him as the one who killed her." He kicked the dead Dark Elf. "Not like he cares—anymore."

Ellis pushed Seth away from the Dark Elf and began to rummage through his pockets. "You two are way too serious. They could have some great loot."

Alya laughed. "What would they possibly have?"

Ellis smiled. "If they stole something from a rich merchant, then it's mine. Sounds fair to me."

Seth wiped his sword off on the Dark Elf's clothes. "Come on, mount up. We've got another mile to go then we free my father."

Jena beamed at Seth.

Ellis tossed two coin pouches into his pack. "Well, at least I'm not leaving empty-handed." He smiled at Jena as he mounted Runt. "Hopefully the next ones will have done more pillaging before we kill them."

Jena rolled her eyes. "Oh please."

"Come on." Seth led his party northeast.

~

Seth rode just behind Alya, who occasionally looked back at Sumia for direction. The trees grew sparser and underbrush became thicker. The sun sagged in the sky. "We're losing daylight."

Alya dismounted her horse. "We should be close." She looked at Sumia. "Are we?"

She nodded.

"Okay," Alya said as she tied her horse to a tree.

"Good idea," Seth said. "Everyone tie off your horse. We're on foot from here."

Ellis jumped off Runt. "I don't care if you run off. If you did, maybe I'd get a better horse."

Runt neighed.

Jena laughed. "She's going to kick you."

"What? A gnome is scarier," Ellis said.

"She's right, Ellis," Seth said.

Ellis put his pack on his back and slid his daggers into their sheaths. "Please."

Runt kicked him with her left rear leg, knocking him to the ground.

"Damn it," Ellis grunted as he picked himself up. He stared right into Runt's eyes. "I just might not come back for you."

Alya yanked on Ellis' shoulder. "Enough already. You're too loud." She glared at Seth. "Can we go now?"

Seth nodded. "Yeah, let's go." He led them into the darkness.

Sumia edged forward until she got right next to Seth. "They're right over the next hill."

Seth frowned. "I don't see a hill. I can't see in the dark you know."

She pointed forward and to the left. "About 400 yards, that way."

Alya put her hand on his shoulder. "Let me go first. I have more experience at this."

Was she right? Of course she was, and Seth knew it. Was he focusing on being in charge so much that he had to do everything himself, even when he wasn't the best at it? Yeah, he was guilty. "Sure."

Alya drew her short swords and crept across the forest floor.

Seth followed her closely. The cool evening breeze

rustled the leaves, giving them some cover as they crunched dry leaves beneath their feet. Every time Seth stepped on a stick, he froze and listened, just for a second. He felt the incline underneath his feet.

Seth moved up next to Alya, who was getting closer to the ground. They were almost on top of the small hill. Smoke pierced his nostrils. A campfire. The crest of the hill was a mere fifteen feet away. Seth crawled on his belly. He had to see over the top. If he could see the camp, he could see Brock, maybe. As he approached the top, a light flickered amongst the leaves. Yes, there was fire.

Alya pulled herself just at the base of an oak tree.

Seth slithered under a clump of saplings with their leaves hiding him. He pushed them aside just enough to see below. Seven humans were eating around the small campfire. They were the Darkstrider knights that chased them out of the woods before they met Sumia. He was sure of it. Barely lit by the firelight was—something. It was not a horse or a cart. No, it was a cage, a cage on wheels. It was almost like someone put prison bars on a cart. There was something else. Seth squinted. No, not something, but someone. It was Brock. He'd recognize the gentle blacksmith anywhere. He looked over at Alya.

She nodded at him.

Seth slid back down the hill to join the others.

Jena, Keya, Ellis, Sumia, and Alya all sat around Seth. "There's seven of them," he whispered. "My father is in a cage on top of the cart, behind them."

"Same as before? Want me to cause a distraction?" Ellis asked.

Seth shook his head. "No, too many of them."

Sumia pulled out her pouch that contained her spell components. "I can handle a few of them."

"We have to attack quickly and take them by surprise. We don't know if there're others on patrol or something," Alya said.

"Frontal assault?" Jena asked.

Seth grinned. "Why not?" he drew his sword as he got up. "Let's get my father back."

Seth and Jena led the small band up the hill. Alya, with her bow drawn, was off to his right. Ellis and Keya were ten yards to his left. Sumia walked fifteen paces behind them.

He was really going to do it. Seth was going to free the only father he had ever known. The other camp had no one hiding in the woods or out on patrol, why should this one? Were humans smarter than elves? The stories always said otherwise. No, this was probably it. They had to get close before they attacked, but at the first sign the knights knew they were there, they must attack, swiftly. He swallowed. *Please, Ramir, god of Justice, be with us tonight*, Seth thought.

They crept over the hill and the camp was in plain sight. Seth tread each step with care. Heel-toe, heel-toe, he focused on stealth.

The knights were laughing, taunting each other as they ate.

Seth blinked. They weren't seen, yet. His grip on his sword tightened. Between them and the camp were underbrush and saplings. The only reason they hadn't been seen yet was because those knights were staring right into a campfire. Their night vision must be compromised, had to be. Otherwise, there was no way they couldn't see them. Yeah, that had to be it.

Snap. Ellis looked down at the branch he'd just stepped on.

The knights looked up.

"Charge!" Seth yelled as he barreled through the foliage.

Alya dropped to a knee and loosed an arrow.

A knight screamed as the arrow embedded in his left shoulder. He backed away, heading towards Brock's cage.

The other knights grabbed their swords.

Keya dropped back.

Ellis threw his left dagger at the knight charging him.

The dagger pierced the knight's chest, but he kept coming.

Ellis raced directly at the knight. When he was at arm's length, Ellis dropped to the ground and kicked his feet out from underneath him.

The knight crashed to the ground.

Ellis jumped on top of him. With vicious accuracy, he slammed his dagger into the knight's throat.

Two knights raced towards Seth with swords raised.

There was a mere twenty feet between Seth and his attackers. With his sword in front of him, Seth sprinted at them.

Jena slipped behind Seth, keeping out of sight.

The first knight swung.

Seth ducked, the blade barely missing his head. He dropped to a knee and thrust his sword into the knight's gullet.

The second knight sidestepped. His sword was cutting the air as it headed towards Seth.

Seth yanked his sword, but it was stuck in the other knight's body. He raised his arm to protect himself from the blade.

The knight smiled.

"No!" Jena slammed both daggers into the knight's side. As soon as the knight fell in pain, she yanked out a dagger and slit his throat.

Alya loosed another arrow and another knight fell to the

ground. She dropped her bow and pulled out her short swords.

The last three knights stepped back, with their backs to one another.

Sumia emerged, with her eyes red and holding a lump of coal. Her mouth was moving, but the words were inaudible. Two fiery bolts shot from the lump of coal.

Two knights reeled over in pain as the bolts hit them in the chest. They glowed for a second, then they were gone.

Sumia collapsed in pain.

The last knight, the one that was shot in the shoulder, held his sword in his right hand and backed away. "Please, don't. I don't want to die."

Seth glared at him. "You have my father. Let him out, now!"

The knight trembled. "Okay, I need to get the key." He headed towards the other knights' bodies.

"I'll watch him," Ellis said.

Seth walked up to the cage. "You'll be out soon."

Brock smiled. "I'm so proud of you. Your father would have been too." He grasped Seth's hand.

"Who?" Alya asked.

"Alya, this is Prince Galin the V of Ravenward. Me, Sally, and Thea the Loyal saved him from the Battle of Staerdale Castle," Brock said.

"Really?" Alya nodded. "Thank you, Brock. Finally, you gave me exactly what I needed."

Seth blinked. "What?"

Alya whistled.

Ten Dark Elves with bows drawn surrounded them.

"Why?" Seth asked. "I trusted you."

Alya smiled. Her form became fuzzy. Her long blond hair turned black. Her deep blue eyes became a lifeless brown. Alya's ears were pointed and her tan skin became blue.

"Never trust a Dark Elf, little boy, you'll always get burnt." She pointed at the wounded human knight. "Kill that one, he's a coward."

The knight's face went white. "Please, please don't I—" Arrows slammed into his chest, knocking him to the ground.

"Was that necessary, Alya?" Brock demanded.

"My name is Shania," she said as she slammed the cage bars with her hand.

"You're the one the letter was to!" Jena said.

Shania smiled. "Elmar, where are you?"

A bald and muscular Dark Elf emerged from the woods. "I'm here."

"Put them in the cage. We'll deliver them to Tanyl in the morning," Shania said.

"Who?" Seth asked.

Shania smiled at Brock. "You know him better as Sir Robert. You know, the one who killed that bitch, Thea the Loyal."

Brock's nostrils flared. "I hate you."

Shania leaned in close. "I enjoyed making Sarah scream over and over again. She had cursed your cowardly name before she died." She smiled. "I thought you should know."

Seth lunged at Shania, only to be yanked back by Elmar. "You killed my mother!"

Her thin lips curled. "Yes, I did." She motioned to the cage. "Put them inside already."

Elmar grinned at Seth. "With pleasure."

"GET IN THERE!" ELMAR YELLED AS HE PUSHED ELLIS TOWARDS the cage.

Ellis glared at him but said nothing.

The tight circle of Dark Elves closed in. Seth swallowed. What could he do? Could they really fight ten Dark Elves with their weapons drawn? No, no way. They'd be cut down before he could say 'Staerdale Castle.' He nudged Jena towards the cage. "Let's go."

"What?" Jena demanded. "We don't know what they're going to do with us."

"He's right," Brock said. "Another time."

Sumia snarled at Shania as she passed her. "I knew we couldn't trust you."

Shania's dark-blue lips smiled. "Yes, I know." She pointed at Seth. "Maybe he should have listened to you."

Sumia and Keya climbed inside. "You'll regret this," Sumia said.

Shania slapped Sumia. "Really? I doubt that."

"Was that necessary?" Jena asked as she hopped inside.

Seth didn't move. He stared right into her soul. "I can see things now."

"What are you talking about?" Shania said.

Elmar heaved Ellis inside the cage. "I'm going to enjoy eating that one."

"I hope you choke on me," Ellis said.

Elmar slapped Ellis, knocking him towards the back of the cage. "Stupid human."

Shania waved Seth towards the cage. "Well? Go. Get inside already."

Seth just stared at her. A tingle started near his heart. His jaw tightened. "What will happen to them?"

"Examples will be made out of them," Shania said. "Maybe we'll feed them to the Feral Orcs." She leaned closer. "Or maybe we'll just eat them ourselves."

Sumia nudged Brock. "Get ready."

"For what?" Brock whispered.

Ellis grinned. "Fireworks."

Seth felt the tingle spread throughout his body. "Let them go. You have me. I'm your prize, not them." If he used his magic, could they win? He'd have to unleash it at the Dark Elves, but not too much. He had to keep it under control. Could he win?

Shania shook her head. "No, never. I lost both my brother and my father to the humans." She smiled at him. "You might say I had a personal stake in finding you. All humans are enemies of the Darkstriders."

"What about King Kade?" Seth asked.

Shania sniffed. "Kade? He's Tanyl's play thing. No, the only thing humans are good for is food for our dogs."

Seth glanced over at Jena.

"I see." Shania pulled out a pearl dagger. "I'll give her my special attention like I gave your mother!"

Ellis ducked his head. "Oh, crap."

"Duck," Sumia said.

Seth's face reddened. Tiny electrical arcs jumped across his skin.

The Dark Elves jumped back.

Shania's mouth dropped. "What's this?"

His clothes became engulfed with the tiny arcs. Seth lunged at the Dark Elves standing over their weapons.

"Shania?" Elmar yelled as he backed away.

Seth extended his arm and his sword jumped into his hand. The blade glowed white with constant cracks of the arcs jumping along the weapon. The burn, the burn raced through his body. His eyes turned white.

"It's—it's true. The prophecy is true." Shania dropped her dagger and bolted into the woods.

Seth swung his sword at a Dark Elf. As soon as the blade struck his flesh, the elf turned to ash. "Come on, fight our way out."

Two Dark Elves loosed arrows towards Seth.

He sidestepped and charged.

They both notched another arrow.

Seth leaped towards his enemies. His sword descended on one Dark Elf. It split him in two. Both halves fell to the ground like a slaughtered pig.

Jena grabbed her daggers.

Ellis grabbed his.

Sumia snatched up her spell component pouch.

Brock snatched up a Dark Elf sword.

The Dark Elf lunged at Seth.

Seth sidestepped and spun left, taking off the elf's head with one blow.

His skin grew brighter. The burn. He smelled his flesh burning.

Brock raised his sword over another Dark Elf.

He stepped back, but not far enough.

Brock's sword slammed into his head. "Seth, go after Shania. If she gets away, she'll bring the orcs to destroy the village."

"Yeah, we got this," Ellis said.

Elmar jumped towards Brock with his ax in hand.

"This is for my wife!" Brock lunged at him, thrusting his sword into Elmar's chest.

Elmar crashed to the ground.

Brock yanked out his sword. "Go, Seth, go now."

He ran after Shania.

Seth raced through the woods. The leaves burned as they brushed against Seth's skin. His sword was starting to glow red, like iron after it comes out of the forge. The burning; he felt his skin burning, but he didn't care. Nothing mattered except for Shania's head and what she did to Sally.

"Ow!" Shania yelled in the distance.

Seth ran faster. His eyes narrowed as he caught up with her. He raised his sword.

"No!" Shania scrambled to her feet.

Seth jumped on her back. The electrical arcs jumped from his body to hers.

Shania screamed. "Mercy, please have mercy!"

His face reddened. His jaw tightened. "I'll give you the same mercy you gave my mother." Seth wrapped his arms around her. The burning jumped from his skin to hers.

Shania skin began to smolder. She screamed again. Her hair ignited.

Seth jumped off her, staring at her.

"What is happening to me?" Shania's chest glowed, just for a second, then she disintegrated into a pile of ash.

"Screw you," Seth said as he kicked the ash. The arcs, they were gone. The burning stopped. He looked down at his arms, they were black. His skin was charred. How come there was no pain?

A few minutes later, Seth returned to the camp. All of the Dark Elves were in pieces on the ground. None of them survived.

Jena's mouth dropped as Seth emerged from the underbrush. "Seth!" She rushed to his side.

Seth smiled. He did it. He—he—spots, black spots appeared. His head began to swim. "I'm passing out."

"I'm coming," Keya said.

Seth's eyes began to close. A blurry face came into view, it was Brock.

"I'm proud of you," Brock said.

Seth smiled as the darkness took him.

The aroma of freshly cooked rabbit tickled Seth's nose. He opened his eyes to the bright midday sun. All the Dark Elf bodies were gone and Ellis was roasting a jackrabbit over the fire. He looked down at his arms, they were not burnt. "How?"

Jena kissed him on the forehead. "My mother healed you." She hugged him. "I love you." She stared right into his eyes. "Never do that again."

Seth smiled.

Sumia, who was sitting by the fire, turned towards Seth. "You nearly killed yourself. Your rage and hatred nearly destroyed you."

"I know." Seth blinked. "What about the Orcs? The village?"

"The Vulwin Elves are—taking precautions," Sumia said.

"What Vulwin Elves?" Brock demanded.

Sumia waved him off. "Not important." She rose to her feet. "I suggest returning to Porp Hollows to rest."

Jena beamed at Seth. "What do you think?"

Seth kissed her. "Let's go."

~

When they finally arrived at Porp Hollows, Sumia led the little band to the sitting room with the fireplace. There were long sitting pillows thrown about the floor. "Please, everyone, sit," Sumia said as she sat next to the fire.

Jena sat next to Seth. "Seth—I mean, Galin, what now?"

Seth frowned. What indeed? "I—I think we need to free the kingdom."

Ellis rolled his eyes. "How? I can't save your ass all the time."

Keya took a seat close to Brock. Her brown eyes twinkled at him. "Go home?"

Brock swallowed. "No, we need to raise an army and kick those damned Dark Elves back to their side of the Fadyhl Waters."

Sumia shook her head. "All that must wait." Her face softened as she smiled at Seth. "Claim your birth name, Galin Ravenward. There is no reason to hide it anymore. They know what you look like and they will never stop searching for you."

Seth grabbed Jena's hand. "I know."

"You must learn to use your magic; not control it, but wield it." Sumia stood up. "Remember, not all elves are evil." Her features blurred. Her gray hair turned into a golden blond. Her skin tightened and became soft.

Seth blinked.

Jena squeezed Seth's hand.

Sumia's ears became pointed and her skin was fair. She opened her green eyes.

Brock jumped up. "You're—you're a Vulwin Elf!"

Sumia nodded. "I am Princess Sumia, daughter of King

Faeler." Her sad eyes looked right at Brock. "You humans weren't the only ones to lose your home."

Brock sat back down. "I—I didn't know."

Sumia knelt down in front of Seth. "Galin, you have to go to school."

"A school?" Seth asked. "What are you talking about?"

"In the center of Methos Lake there is an island with a castle on it. This is where you need to go. Tadus School of Magic. I spoke to a friend of mine, a Snow Elf, and they can help you."

"How?"

"Magic uses components and incantations, but you don't need them." Sumia beamed at him. "You see, you wield dragon magic. Only a handful of mages have ever achieved half your power. There is only one that is alive today. A very old Snow Elf. She's over six hundred years old and she will teach you."

"What if he doesn't go?" Brock asked.

Sumia straightened up. "He'll die. His power will become uncontrollable and it will kill him—and anyone around him."

Seth stared into Jena's eyes. "Not much choice, is there?"

Jena shook her head. "Can I go with him?"

"Me too, don't forget about me," Ellis said.

"Good," Sumia said as she sat back down. She pulled a rough diamond from the small pouch on her belt and held it at eye level in her hand. "Dit onska ni jeg. Dit onska ni jeg." The diamond glowed a bright white. "Dit onska ni jeg." She threw the diamond against the wall, right next to the fireplace. A shadowy archway appeared.

Seth walked over to it. He couldn't see any light; he couldn't see anything through the magical door. "What is it?"

Sumia grinned. "Bexon's Dimensional Tunnel. Step through it and you will be at Tadus School of Magic. Step through and you're on your way to fulfilling the prophecy."

Seth looked at Brock.

He nodded.

Seth grasped Jena's sweaty hand. "Ready?"

"Maybe they can marry us there?"

Sumia frowned.

Jena swallowed. "Sorry. I'm ready."

"Oh, get out of the way already," Ellis said as he pushed through. As soon as one foot passed through the arch, Ellis disappeared.

"Father?" Seth asked Brock.

A prideful tear rolled down Brock's cheek. "Sire, it's your duty."

He nodded. "Let's go." Seth and Jena stepped through the arch together and then they were gone.

～

The story continues in Iron Fist Keep, 2nd Edition....

ABOUT THE AUTHOR

I'm Steven Atwood grew up reading fantasy books and watching science fiction whenever I could. When I was young, I played role-playing games within the fantasy genre. Close to the end of my military career, I started to write. It was something I always wanted to do but never did. I write science fiction and fantasy with a fresh perspective.

Visit my website
http://stevenatwood.net

Science Fiction

Cyber Invasion

Amari

Nano WMD

Fantasy

Prophecy of Axain Series, 2nd Edition

Prophecy of Axain

Iron Fist Keep

Full Circle

Box Sets

Prophecy of Axain Boxset